A Loyal and
Dedicated Servant

A Loyal and

JOHN GRIFFITHS

Dedicated Servant

Playboy Press

Library of Congress Cataloging in Publication Data

Griffiths, John, 1940-
    A loyal and dedicated servant.

    I. Title.
PR6057.R513L6 1981   823'.914   80-52411
ISBN 0-87223-659-5

Design by M. Franklin-Plympton

PLAYBOY PRESS
A division of PEI Books, Inc.

To Deryn, but for whose devoted nagging this book would never have been written.

PROLOGUE

August 1974

Twelve miles outside Richmond, Virginia, on the road to Williamsburg, is an estate of several hundred acres, bounded on one side by the York River and completely enclosed by a twelve-foot chainlink fence. Along the fence at regular intervals are large notices that bear, in heavy black letters, the warning: U.S. GOVERNMENT RESERVATION—NO TRESPASSING. At first glance the estate can be mistaken for a wildlife preserve, for the land immediately inside the fence is thickly wooded, and small herds of deer may sometimes be seen, drifting like ghosts among the trees. But this impression does not last; the fence is topped by triple strands of heavy-duty barbed wire, and the gatehouse at the entrance is manned by military police with carbines. Officially the place is known as Camp Peary, but those whose business takes them there call it, simply, "The Farm."

Closer inspection suggests a military base. Inside there are rifle and pistol ranges, an airstrip, football fields and tennis courts, and a patch of ground, littered with ruined masonry, whose scorched and desolate appearance suggests it has been used for testing explosives. The buildings are uncompromisingly barracks: low, wood-framed huts arranged, within their separate compounds, in orderly platoons. The people there wear military fatigues and move like soldiers, marching briskly to their destinations by the shortest possible route. Loitering, or wandering around, is evidently discouraged.

Closer inspection, for that matter, is also discouraged. Entry to the camp is by special pass only. No buildings are visible from the fence. No building, except the gymnasium, is identified by name or function, and many bear notices prohibiting entry to all but authorized personnel. There are no signposts; visitors who do not already know their way around are met at the gatehouse by military police in jeeps. Each compound is isolated, its quarantine preserved by more chain-link fences and barbed wire.

One area in particular resists curiosity. It is surrounded by a high wall of concrete blocks, and the gates are sheet metal secured with double padlocks. The windows of the huts are barred and the windowpanes covered with black paper. Here too the population wears military fatigues, but without insignia or badges of identity. If you dropped in here out of the sky—and the helicopter pad in the forecourt suggests that many do—you would find nothing (no signposts or notices, no casually discarded candy wrappers or beer cans) to indicate that you were in the United States of America, much less the state of Virginia. Officially the compound is known as Area VI, or the Debriefing Center, but those whose business takes them there call it "the grinder."

Zukovsky took a pull at his cigarette, grimaced, and stubbed it out half finished. There were already a dozen butts in the ashtray, he noticed, and lunch was still more than an hour away. Not content with threatening my sanity, he thought gloomily, they are undermining my health.

He was smoking too much, he told himself, drinking too much coffee. And the half-hour each day they permitted him in the exercise room was not enough to clear his head or clean out his lungs. What he needed was real air, a glimpse of the sky, the smell of grass and wet earth. But they would deny him that, he knew, until they were finished. They told him, of course, that it was all necessary, that this subterranean imprisonment was designed for his protection. But he knew better. They seemed to forget sometimes that he also had belonged to the profession; he knew as they did about techniques of deprivation.

"Ask him to describe Werner."

The interpreter nodded and reached over to restart the tape recorder.

"Give us please"—his German was grammatically faultless but

slightly pedantic, as if he had learned it in a language labora-
tory—"an exact description of Klaus Werner."

Zukovsky sighed. So the rest break was over. How long had it
been? he wondered. How many days had he sat here and answered
their questions? Sixty-five? . . . Seventy? He had kept track for the
first few weeks, scratching the days on his bedpost with a nail he
had pried from the window frame, but then he had started to forget
and had given it up. In any case, what did it matter? He'd been
prepared for this from the moment he made the decision. He'd
known when he walked through the gates of the Embassy in
Vienna that there would be a price for his action, and he'd understood what it would be and how it would have to be paid—how for
weeks, maybe months, the world would be compressed into this
dismal box with its darkened windows and cheap utility furniture,
how his life would attenuate and pass in a ribbon between the
spools of a tape recorder, and how the rhythm of their questions
would come at last to seem like the water torture, wearing away,
drip by drip, at his reason. And he knew also that he would survive,
not by tormenting himself with thoughts of how long it had lasted
or how long it might go on, but by concentrating simply on getting
through it—a day at a time, an hour at a time, a question at a time.

"Medium height," he said. "Slight build. Brown hair. A straw-
berry birthmark on one cheek."

"Which cheek?"

But his thoughts had wandered back to Berlin. He looked up
vacantly.

"The birthmark." The interpreter's voice was patient, almost
bored. "Which cheek was it on?"

Zukovsky hesitated. Which one had it been? More important,
what had he said last time? He couldn't remember. So was it better
to guess and risk contradicting himself, or should he fall back
once again on his faulty memory? Perhaps it would be better
to guess; it might even be good if he guessed wrong. People were
mostly unobservant, drifting through life with their eyes shut,
their recollections misty and often mistaken, so there was a danger
in too much consistency, an overexact recall of detail. Beware the
precise, coherent story—he remembered the precept from his own
training—it is probably rehearsed.

"I think it was the left cheek, but I don't really remember. I
recall it was close to the nose."

He looked around, hoping for a reaction, but there was nothing, no flicker of surprise or interest, to tell him how his answer had been received. They never did react; it was the worst thing about them. He could contradict himself if he liked, or invent outrageous details, but they would never argue or raise their voices, never smile or frown. They would simply consult their notes and move on to the next question, never dropping for an instant their mask of patience. Joke if you like, their calmness seemed to say, waste time if you like. It doesn't matter. We will simply return to this subject later, and return as many times as it takes. Time is no object. We have all the time in the world.

"Ask him the color of Werner's eyes."

That one, at least, was easy. He was vague about the birthmark, but he would never forget those eyes—or the look they had given him that cold morning in February, so many months ago, when they had brought Werner in. It was four-thirty, he remembered, and a steady drizzle was falling. There were beads of water in Werner's hair, and a thin film of it, like the sweat of a high fever, covering his face. He had stood like a child while they took the handcuffs off him, neither helping them or hindering, and when he turned, finally, to face his accusers, his eyes were dulled into terminal apathy, the look of a man who no longer owns his future. With those eyes, Zukovsky thought, a man could face anything. Werner certainly had made a good death.

"His eyes were brown."

"How was he dressed?"

"A raincoat over pajamas."

"Shoes?"

"Slippers or loafers, maybe. I don't remember."

"Why did you arrest him?"

It was what they always came back to. This, after God knows how many days, was what it reduced to. The rest—the hundreds of reels of tape on the organization, methods, operations, and personnel of his department—was just wrapping. It was good wrapping, of course, because the wrapping was always important, a tantalizing suggestion of the quality inside, but it was this, the arrest of Werner and the others, that he had really come to sell.

"He was charged with espionage and conspiring against the security of the D.D.R."

"On what evidence?"

"On information received."

Here, as always, he must be careful not to push. He was selling information, not inference, and he must let them sniff around it, like foxes around carrion, to determine for themselves if it was safe to eat.

"Received from whom?"

"From Askelov, the Resident in Berlin."

"Describe Askelov."

And then they were off again, looping another cautious circle round the subject. Height? Hair? Color of eyes? Distinguishing features? Time of meeting? Place of meeting? How many windows in Askelov's office? . . . And finally a new one: what had the weather been like that day?

"It was clear and cold, but a front brought rain towards evening."

"What did Askelov tell you?"

"He gave me a list with the names of Werner, Eberhardt, Koenig, and Krebs. He told me he had received information they were CIA agents and that when we arrested them we would find the evidence to prove it."

"What else?"

"He told me to arrest Werner first and the others eight to ten hours later."

"Did he explain why?"

"At first he just said it was instructions from Moscow. But I objected. Unless we took them all at the same time, I said, the others might take warning and escape. So then he told me that it was a matter of protecting a valuable source. It must seem as if Werner had gotten careless or unlucky, he said, and then under interrogation confessed and implicated the others."

"And the source he wished to protect was in Moscow?"

"He didn't say that." Zukovsky shook his head wearily. "He never mentioned the location of the source. All he said was the instructions came from Moscow."

But since the instructions came from Moscow—he had to resist the impulse to scream at them—wasn't it plainer than the nose on his face that Askelov had received the information from there? Or did they imagine, perhaps, that Askelov, a KGB veteran of twenty-five years' experience, was in the habit of calling Moscow for advice on the matter of protecting his sources? And though the information had obviously been sent from Moscow, were they stupid enough to think it had originated there? Did they really believe that Moscow was the place to obtain intelligence about American agents in East Berlin?

Of course they didn't. They understood perfectly the implications of what he had told them. Their problem, obviously, was bringing themselves to believe him. And there they had to contend not only with their natural suspicion of him, but with the enormous consequences of believing. It was no wonder they were still reluctant, no wonder they went on checking and double-checking, no wonder they insisted on taking him to the brink of sanity to see if he would still, even at that extreme, stand by his story.

But he had stood by it, hadn't he? In sixty-five days, or seventy, or however many, he hadn't wavered on any essential, had he? So it was more than imagination, surely, that now encouraged him to believe he was making some headway. How else to explain the sudden appearance, late yesterday, of the civilian? Why was he here, that tall angular man in the charcoal-gray suit who sat in the corner listening, making notes occasionally, fiddling sometimes with his black homburg, watching always but never speaking, unless it was because the consistency of the story had begun to erode their suspicion?

Besides, he knew who the civilian was. He was sure of it now. When the man had entered the room yesterday, unannounced, indicating with a self-deprecating, almost apologetic gesture that they should continue and pay him no attention, it had been possible to mistake him for some elderly bureaucrat indulging his curiosity in a visit to the Center. He'd seemed like a clergyman, or a college professor, his air of gentle intellectualism enhanced by the high forehead, the fine aquiline nose, and the long ironic twist of the mouth. But as the afternoon wore on, it had been impossible to ignore his eyes. Greenish-yellow and utterly devoid of expression, they had pressed on him with a steady impersonal gaze that had come to seem, to his agitated imagination, like the stare of some great cat. And he'd recalled then what Anders had said on his return from the U.S. after being exchanged for the two American agents. As his interrogation had progressed, Anders had said, he'd been questioned by an elderly man in a dark suit with the manner of a priest and the eyes of a leopard. It had been Spearman—Anders had recognized the face from a picture in a news magazine— Thomas Osgood Spearman, the CIA's Chief of Counterintelligence.

Zukovsky looked over at him; and, catching the glance, as if reading Zukovsky's thought and the appeal of his eyes, Spearman spoke. He spoke, surprisingly, in German, good colloquial German with only a trace of accent, and his voice was dry and a little raspy, like the rustle of a lizard in a pile of dead leaves.

"What do you think? I've heard what you know. I want to hear what you think."

"Think?" Zukovsky was startled.

"Yes. The instructions came from Moscow, you claim. What did that say to you?"

"It told me the source was not in Berlin. Askelov didn't need advice from Moscow on protecting his sources."

"Then was the source in Moscow?"

Zukovsky shook his head. "The information was relayed from there. But it came from somewhere else."

"Where?"

"You know where," Zukovsky said. "It could have come from two places only. You know that. Only two groups of people would have known the identities of your agents in East Berlin: the local case officers and the people to whom those officers reported. So either the information came from Berlin, or"—he paused—"it came from Langley."

"And you're telling us it didn't come from Berlin?"

"Yes," Zukovsky replied steadily. "That's exactly what I'm telling you. It's what I've been telling you for the last two months."

For almost a minute Spearman just stared at him. Then, to Zukovsky's utter astonishment, he smiled, got up, and, going over to the table, shut off the tape recorder.

"Enough," he said to the others, who seemed as astonished as Zukovsky. "He deserves a rest. And we need to digest what he's told us."

He spoke in English. But though Zukovsky understood none of his words, the tone communicated almost as clearly. It's over, he thought, hardly daring to believe it. It's over . . . and I've won.

"What do you make of *that?*"

Zukovsky had gone. So had Spearman. The translator was busy packing up the tape recorder. The senior interrogator—"debriefer," as he was officially known—was lounging back in his chair, smoking. Next to him, his assistant was doing likewise. These were the first words either had uttered since Spearman's pronouncement.

"Christ knows." The assistant shrugged.

"Seventy-three days," the interrogator pursued. "Some kind of speed record, that. Panov took fourteen months, Kyrilenko nearer two years—on and off, of course—and they never were really believed. So what makes His Majesty so certain now?"

The assistant glanced nervously at the translator. It didn't seem wise to refer to Spearman so familiarly. Unless, of course, you was sure of your company.

"Well," he ventured, "he may know something we don't. And his intuition *is* highly developed. After all, he's been in the business for more than thirty years."

"Intuition my ass." The interrogrator gave a short, mirthless laugh. "Where I come from it's called bias . . . Moles," he grunted. "He's so sure there's a mole he'll believe every piece of shit that supports the suspicion. Anything that doesn't, of course, is fabrication."

The translator left.

"I'll admit," said the assistant, emboldened by the departure, "that he does sometimes behave as if he had a direct line to God."

"Either that . . ." Instinctively, though they were now quite alone, the interrogator lowered his voice. "Either that . . . or a direct line to the Kremlin."

BOOK ONE

June 15, 1978–July 1, 1978

CHAPTER I

I

It was light now. Already the gray of the dawn sky had turned to silver and, deepening, was giving way to blue. Soon the sun would be up. It would be fine today and, by the look of the long plumes of cloud drawn out across the arc of heaven, breezy. A good day for sailing, and therefore, because the Wharf would be busy with weekend sailors needing someone to carry their tackle and help with their moorings, a good day for him.

In the meantime it was chilly, He lay in the hollow he had scooped out from the leeward slope of a sand dune, his knees drawn up to his chest and his head hunched into the turned-up collar of his jacket. Dawn was always the worst time for the cold. But the night hadn't been too bad. He'd learned how to be comfortable now: how to dig the hollow a little deeper in places for his hips and shoulders, and to fold the poncho under him because the worst cold came from the sand. Still, he wished he had one of the windproof sailing parkas with a hood attachment they sold at the shop at the Wharf. He couldn't afford one now, but perhaps at the end of summer, if things continued to go well.

He looked again at the sky. A watch was another of the things he couldn't afford, but he had a country-bred sense of the time. Another hour, maybe an hour and a half, and the Wharf would be open. He could get breakfast then: a cup of coffee, a doughnut, or perhaps, because it truly did promise to be a good day, eggs. He pulled his head deeper between his shoulders and settled down to wait.

He never minded the waiting, for there was always the sea. Last night he had let it whisper him to sleep, and he was content now to lie for a moment and listen to the crash and hiss of the breakers as they fell against the beach and were sucked back across the pebbles. It was odd, this feeling he had for the sea; odd that he, Jesus Obezo, born and, for eight of his thirteen years, raised in central Mexico, hundreds of miles from the ocean, should have developed so alien a passion. But from the time his family had moved to Baltimore, from the time he had first gone down to the port and watched the cargo vessels loading and discharging freight—vessels that appeared from over the horizon, paused briefly, and vanished, heading for Singapore or Sydney, London or Manila, names that to him were synonyms for adventure—the sea and the ships that sailed on it had seemed to offer him a life charged with mystery and promise. In time, he knew, he would be a sailor, but for now there was school, so he could serve his passion only by working at the Wharf on weekends and during vacations, hitchhiking the thirty-odd miles from Baltimore and sleeping, more often than not, on the beach.

His family grumbled but bore with him. His mother worried about the nights out, but not to the point of forbidding them. And his brothers teased him because, instead of the anatomical center-folds they pasted above their beds, his pinups were twelve-meter racing yachts: *Constellation* and *Columbia*, with their spinnakers set, running before the wind. The teasing never bothered him. He was too young for women. And truly they were right; he had a different sense of beauty. To him a boat—a real boat, a sailing boat, not one of those squat and smelly cabin cruisers—was the most beautiful thing in the world. It was not just that a sailing boat had grace. Women had that, and so did gulls—until you saw them squabbling over a piece of garbage. A sailing boat had something more: serenity and dignity. Above all, dignity.

He stretched and sat up. It offended his sense of propriety not to be up by sunrise, though here, admittedly, the difference between up and not up was largely a matter of attitude, involving no more than shaking the sand out of his poncho and running his fingers through his hair. He observed these formalities anyway, because they made him feel better, and wandered down to the water to splash a few handfuls on his face.

It was then that he noticed the sloop.

She must have rounded the headland a few minutes earlier, and she seemed to be on a course, a long diagonal beat, that would bring her to shore about where he was standing, though of course she would go about before then.

For several minutes he stood and watched her. A thirty-footer, he guessed, and with those tall sails and sleek lines, a racer. She was heeled over slightly in response to the pressure on her sails, and her progress as she dipped and rose across the swells was unforced and natural, as though the elements had agreed to grant her passage, the wind nudging her forward, the water giving way willingly on either side. It was only when she was closer that he noticed, with a touch of irritation, the slight but insistent flutter along the trailing edge of the jib. It was not trimmed properly. Then he realized that there was no one on deck to trim it. Automatic steering gear. His irritation turned to contempt. But such gadgets were permissible, he was prepared to concede, if the helmsman was single-handed. Perhaps the man had gone below for a piss. All the same, he was taking a chance. The bottom shoaled rapidly here a few yards offshore, and in a few minutes—three at most—she would run aground.

He waited a little longer, concern for the sloop warring with reluctance to see the helmsman's carelessness go unpunished. When she was a hundred and fifty yards away, he started to yell.

He was small for his age but deep-chested. Constant exercise had given him a powerful pair of lungs. The bellow he produced, he wouldn't have minded betting, could be heard without difficulty a mile away.

Nothing happened. Calmly and gracefully, without hurry, but seeming to gain momentum as the distance between them narrowed, she slid toward the shore.

He yelled again, then a third time, forcing the air from his lungs with a prolonged violence that left him gasping, the blood roaring like surf inside his ears. Still nothing. He could hear the waves slapping against her bow, the foam gurgling in her wake.

When she struck it was as if something had grabbed her from below. There was a grating bump. The bow suddenly pitched forward. The stern slued around, away from the shore. The sails, losing the wind, flapped furiously, like the wings of a bird caught in lime.

Before he knew it, he had his shirt off and was in the water. It never occurred to him to wait and see what might happen. He didn't have that kind of curiosity. For him it was enough that the vessel needed help. It was also true that, for most of the way out to her, he might have waded. He didn't think of that either. He was not a good swimmer—the sea was for sailing, not for splashing about in—but he struck out toward her anyway, arms and legs thrashing, supplying in energy what he lacked in technique.

He made for the bow because it was closer. But when he reached it, thinking constructively for the first time in minutes, he knew he wouldn't be able to board there. His arms were already tired, and the slope of the bow would afford no purchase for his feet. So he made his way around to the stern and paused there a moment to gather his breath.

It was then, when he read the gold lettering across the stern, that he realized he knew her. EXCALIBUR—ANNAPOLIS. That was Mr. Seligman's boat. She'd gone out around midday yesterday and not returned to the Wharf. He called again, but there was no answer, and by this time he no longer really expected one. Whoever was in there would be hurt or sick or . . . But he wasn't prepared to consider that alternative yet.

It took him several tries to clamber on board, his feet scrabbling against the slick surface of the hull until he was able to flop his body forward onto the deck. He rested there for a minute, panting, before he got to his feet. Then, responding either to some instinct for seamanship or to the wish to defer as long as possible the moment when he would have to go below, he went forward and winched down the mainsail, guiding it onto the deck with his free hand, careful, as he had learned, to let none of the canvas blow onto the water. He did the same with the jib. After that he went aft and dropped the stern anchor, tugging on it until he was sure it would hold, and pulling the line taut against the stern to allow the least possible play. It wouldn't keep the hull from grinding against the bottom, but it might help minimize the damage.

Then, calling out once more before he started down the hatchway, he went below.

It was dark in the aft cabin—thick curtains were drawn over the portholes—and the shaft of light entering from the hatch was barely enough to see by. Whatever he was going to find, he promised himself, he was going to find it in broad daylight, so he edged over to one set of portholes, drew the curtains, and, stepping back, let his eyes travel over the cabin.

There were bunks on both walls, which served as couches by day. They were not made up, and both were empty. Beside the far bunk was a table. It held a typewriter with a sheet of paper in the carriage, an ashtray containing half a dozen butts, a coffee cup, and a small stack of gray manila folders. He leaned down and peered under the table. There was nothing there.

A waist-high counter reaching halfway across the cabin separated the aft cabin from the galley. Cautiously he peered around it, keeping his eyes to the floor. Nothing there. He crept through the galley to the forward cabin. No one in either of the bunks. Then he thought of the head. No one. At last, though he knew it was crazy—for who would set a course for land and then curl up in a locker to wait for the inevitable?—he searched the sail lockers in the bow.

With no flashlight to help him, he had to force himself to lean in and explore the darkness with his hands. His fingers encountered canvas, neatly folded, some coils of rope, a spare anchor, and some metal objects, which from touch he could not identify. Nothing else. There was nobody on board.

And that was worse, in a way, than what he had expected to find. Someone hurt, someone sick, someone dead even: these were evil possibilities, but still natural, within the normal order of things. This emptiness was not. The *Excalibur* had become a ghost ship, and the signs of recent habitation—the cup, the dirty ashtray, the sheet of paper in the typewriter—made the emptiness all the more sinister.

Jesus Obezo was not comfortable with ghosts. He took off up the hatchway like a spooked antelope, clearing the deck in a couple of bounds and leaping into the water without breaking stride. In no time, it seemed, he was on the beach. Without pausing for breath, without even stopping for his shirt, he started to run.

II

Chief Petty Officer Richard Procter stood on the foredeck of the Coast Guard cutter *Daisy* and gazed across the fifty yards of water that separated him from the sloop.

"Tell me," he said to no one in particular, "why is it that when they run aground the fucking tide is always on the ebb?"

The *Excalibur* had settled now and was lying partly on her side.

Procter looked at his watch. Eight-sixteen. Low water would be around ten-thirty. It would be several hours after that before any attempt could be made to refloat the sloop. The cutter had powerful twin diesels, but the *Excalibur*, he estimated, must run about nine or ten tons deadweight. Trying to get her off the shoal before three would almost certainly be futile and might well damage her.

"Not much we can do for now." Procter turned to MacIntyre. "We'll have to wait for the tide. But we should row over, I guess, and make sure that everything's in order.

"You come too," he said to Jesus Obezo. "You can give us a hand with the sails."

When they boarded the sloop Procter made a quick tour through her. It was not that he expected to find anyone, he was quick to explain, conscious of an element of reproach in the way the boy looked at him as he did it, but simply that he liked to see things for himself. Then they folded the sails on the deck and stowed them away in a locker.

"You did all right," Procter said to the boy. "I'd say you have the makings of a seaman. Now tell me again exactly how it happened."

Jesus Obezo did so. Procter listened patiently, without interrupting. He was a tall man, sandy-haired, a little gray at the temples, his ruddy, weatherbeaten face creased with lines of experience and good humor. He was fond of kids, and had taken immediately to the small Mexican, admiring the boy's competence and self-possession, the way his first action on reaching the sloop had been to take down the sails and set the stern anchor. A good kid, this. A good, sensible, no-nonsense kid.

"You always sleep on the beach?" he asked when the boy had finished.

"Mostly."

"Awful cold, isn't it?"

"I'm used to it." The boy shook his head. Conscious of a certain skepticism in Procter's look, he grinned. "Well, sometimes," he conceded.

Procter thought. "There's the Coast Guard station," he said. "It's open all night. We might be able to find you a corner somewhere. It's worth a thought." He switched his attention to the sloop. "I'd say this is all pretty weird. Perhaps we'd better go below again and take another look."

It was not strictly his business, but besides his natural curiosity there was a question of the search. No one had been reported missing, but nine-ton sloops did not set their own sails and put to sea by themselves. Mr. Seligman, or whoever had been on board, had either been picked up by some other vessel or was in the Bay. If he was in the Bay and there was any chance he was still afloat, then, report or no, a search should be started. But searches were troublesome and expensive. He didn't want to start one unless he was reasonably sure there was some point to it. Possibly something below might shed some light on that question.

"Bill," he told MacIntyre, "take a look in the forward cabin—there may be a note or something. I'll start back here."

A pair of slacks and a fawn cashmere jacket hung on a hanger from a hook above the right-hand bunk. He went through the pockets. The sloop belonged to a Mr. Seligman, the boy had told him, but that didn't necessarily mean that Seligman had been on board. His search produced a pocketknife, several tissues, a scrap of paper with a telephone number on it, and a billfold. The billfold contained thirty-four dollars, several credit cards—Diner's Club, MasterCharge, and a gold American Express card—and a D.C. driver's license. The license identified the holder as Paul Arthur Seligman of 1700 Wisconsin Avenue, Washington, D.C. It was valid for all types of vehicle, including motorcycles.

He turned to the table. That probably had been the scene of Seligman's last traceable actions on board. It was there, at any rate, that the signs of his passage, the trail of garbage that litters the wake of a human existence, had started to falter. Seligman had sat down at the typewriter, apparently, smoked several cigarettes, made and consumed a cup of coffee. Perhaps the clue to what had followed lay in these actions.

The coffee cup was still half full. A gray, faintly nacreous film had formed on the surface of the liquid. It looked several hours old. So Mr. Seligman had probably parted company with his sloop sometime late last night or in the early hours of the morning. An accident? He might have gone on deck for some reason, tripped, and fallen overboard. He would not have been able to swim fast enough to catch up with his boat. Then again, he might have jumped.

Procter looked at the page in the typewriter. There were five words on it: "I have reached my conclusion"—there the sentence broke off. And though it was possible to read the words as final, Procter doubted they were meant that way. It was more likely that Seligman had expected to continue. So what had stopped him?

Then Procter noticed something that he had overlooked in his preoccupation with the message. The top right-hand corner of the page bore a number: 2. This was page two of something. But where, in that case, was page one? His glance fell on the neat stack of gray folders beside the machine.

He was about to open the top one when he heard MacIntyre.

"Dick. Come here a second. Take a look at this."

He went over. MacIntyre was standing in front of a small cubicle, opposite the galley, that contained an assortment of radio equipment. Now that he focused on it, Procter thought, it seemed like a hell of a lot of radio equipment.

"There's more in there." MacIntyre pointed to a large suitcase on the floor. "I never saw so much stuff. And did you notice all the antennae in the cockpit?"

Procter thought about it. "Even houseboats have CBs these days. This sloop is a deep-water boat. You could sail her across the Atlantic. Maybe he's into that. He'd need a good set, in that case."

"No." MacIntyre had been in Signals in Vietnam and was still a ham radio buff. "There's too much of it, and it's too sophisticated. There are things in here I've never heard of before, much less seen. But the thing in the suitcase, I do know what that is. It's a high-speed burst transmitter. You use it when you don't want anyone to listen in.

"I tell you what," he continued, "we're not on a boat at all. We're on a floating communications center. What beats me is why anyone would need all this. Who is this Seligman, anyway?"

"You tell me." Procter shrugged. "He lives on Wisconsin, belongs to the Diner's Club, and rides a motorcycle. Does that help?"

Then he remembered the folders. Beckoning MacIntyre to follow, he returned to the aft cabin and went over to the table.

"These," he said, indicating the stack, "may tell us something."

He picked up the top folder. Inside there was another, a red one covered with heavy black print. He studied it for a moment, eyes narrowed, but didn't open it.

"I think I know what he is." He shut the folder with a snap and handed it to MacIntyre. "And I think we'd better get our butts back to the cutter and radio Portsmouth. Because what that folder

tells me is, whatever we're dealing with here, it ain't an ordinary
boating accident."

MacIntyre opened the folder.

TOP SECRET, it said, U.S. EYES ONLY. THIS FILE IS THE PROPERTY
OF THE UNITED STATES GOVERNMENT—CENTRAL INTELLIGENCE
AGENCY.

It was five o'clock before they got the sloop back to the Wharf
at Lusby, and nearly seven before a more thorough search of her
was made. At eight the Coast Guard headquarters at Portsmouth
was again alerted and a full-scale search for Seligman was begun.
At this time, also, a call was put through to the Maryland police
department. A police guard was placed on the vessel, and next
morning a team of forensic technicians descended on her and
virtually tore her apart. For what the previous evening's search had
turned up, among other things, was the spent cartridge case from
a 9-mm-pistol bullet.

III

"And there's no way of telling if it's him?"

"I'm not saying that." The Chief Medical Examiner's voice was
patient. He was used to the imprecise language of laymen. "I'm
saying that medical evidence doesn't help much. You have to rely
on circumstances here. Personally, I don't doubt that it's him. I
just can't make a positive identification."

The body had shown up three days later, floating like some figment of a nightmare into the consciousness of swimmers farther
up the Bay. It had a gunshot wound in the right temple, and two
diving belts had been attached to it, one under the armpits, the
other around the waist. Their weight had evidently been sufficient
to keep it submerged until the gases produced by decomposition,
forming under the skin and bloating the carcass like a football,
had forced it to the surface. Although most of the clothing was
intact, the exposed parts of the body had been ravaged by fish.
The scalp was eaten away, the features were unrecognizable. Whoever it had been in life had dwindled, in death, to a slab of dis-
colored, evil-smelling meat.

Corporal Brady could never get used to death. He saw it often enough, but fifteen years in the Maryland police department had not been long enough to overcome his total, reflexive horror of it. To him a human body was always a person, an individual, never just an object or a statistic. For this reason corpses invariably made him want to throw up. Very often he did. His colleagues laughed at him for it. "Brady's weak stomach" was a standing joke in the department. He rejected this humor and the judgment it implied. His reaction to death was not mere, inconvenient, physical weakness; it was a gesture of rebellion against the reduction of a life to a lump of putrefaction. His "weakness" was not that at all, not an obstacle to his effectiveness as a policeman, but the expression of a concern that, to his mind, was a prerequisite for doing his job properly. But then, to him being a policeman was not a job; it was a calling.

Brady had been assigned to the *Excalibur* investigation when the original call was received from the Coast Guard. For a while he'd suspected suicide, but when the body came to light he'd changed his mind. So he'd requested help from the Homicide Division. Help had taken, in this instance, the form of Detective Sergeant Rutherford, a lanky, grizzled man whose features seemed permanently set in an expression of gloomy skepticism. To Brady he was worse than no help at all, for Rutherford shared none of his concern for Seligman. To Rutherford the body was simply a problem. Homicide was always sensitive about the size of its backlog of unsolved cases, and Rutherford obviously wished to avoid adding to the list. He seemed determined to cling to the suicide theory.

His attitude, Brady knew, was shared by the others. To Daniel, the Chief Medical Examiner, who saw more death in a month than most people did in a lifetime, and protected himself behind a wall of cheerful insensitivity, the body represented an exercise in scientific detective work. Who had died? How? And how long ago? To Dimond, on the other hand, the problem was one of public relations. The CIA got uneasy when its employees died or disappeared in mysterious circumstances. Dimond's job was to defuse the mystery. He too favored the suicide theory.

"Let's take a look at the facts." Daniel cut in on Brady's thoughts. "Identification by next of kin, the most satisfactory method, is useless here. Seligman's wife thinks it could be him, but she's not sure. The daughter is sure it's not, but she was unable to give me any coherent reasons. Her opinion may have been colored by her violent reaction to seeing the body. It does, after all"—he smiled maliciously at Brady—"make one want to throw up.

"Fingerprinting won't work either. When I tried to get a print, the skin peeled off the fingers. I've chopped off the hands and sent them to the FBI lab, but I doubt they'll do any better.

"Next," he continued, "I went to the dental records. At least I tried to. They don't exist. Seligman went to the same dentist for fifteen years, but three months ago the dentist had a fire in his office. Most of his records were destroyed. Among them, of course, were Seligman's.

"And that leaves us more or less back where we started—with a body, a boat, and a bullet. The bullet was the cause of death. It entered at the right temple, traveled slightly upward through the brain, and lodged against the left wall of the cranium. I was able to recover it, and I sent it to Ballistics. They identified it as a nine-millimeter slug, but they can't say for sure whether it belongs with the case that was found in the boat."

He paused. "The rest is really your department. But the facts are plain, and they don't seem to me to need too much sorting out. One, the sloop belonged to Seligman. Two, Seligman went out in her that night. At least he told his daughter he was going to, and there's been no indication he changed his mind. Three, Seligman is missing. And four, no one else from this area whose description remotely matches what we know of the corpse has been reported missing for the period in question. I think the inference is obvious."

"There are, however, some problems." Brady made an effort to keep the edge out of his voice. "For example, the difference in height. Seligman's passport puts him at six feet two. The estimate in your report on the corpse is five feet eleven or six feet."

"True, but not serious. People sometimes exaggerate their height—vanity, I suppose. Also, you can't measure height accurately on a corpse. A lot depends on muscle tone, the way a person carries himself. Some people actually shrink as they get older. A couple of inches isn't that significant."

"OK, weight, then. The record says Seligman weighed one eighty. The corpse was one fifty. Don't tell me thirty pounds is not significant."

"Blood," Daniel said. "The corpse had almost no blood. That's ten pounds for a start. And don't forget there was some of him missing."

"Then what about his clothes? The corpse was wearing size thirty-two pants. The slacks on the boat and the ones we found in Seligman's apartment were all thirty-fours or thirty-sixes."

"The corpse was wearing blue jeans." Rutherford answered this time. "Some shrink, some don't. And waist sizes aren't consistent. I take a thirty in some brands, thirty-two in others. I don't see how you can base anything on that."

"I'm not basing anything on a single piece of evidence," Brady persisted. "I know you have to expect errors in measurement. But when all the errors are in the same direction, I begin to get suspicious. I think the evidence here suggests that the corpse was a somewhat smaller man than Seligman's records say he was."

"Maybe." Rutherford shrugged. "But it's not enough to make me want to ignore the circumstantial evidence Dr. Daniel just referred to."

"Can't we agree on that?" Dimond broke in. "Is there any serious reason to doubt that it is Seligman?"

"I would say not." Rutherford shook his head.

"Not in my mind," Daniel agreed.

"Then the main question," Dimond pursued, "is how did it happen? Did he jump, or was he pushed?"

"I think he jumped," Rutherford replied. "I agree there are problems with that theory, but look at the alternative. We have no reason to believe he went out with anyone else that night. There were no traces of blood on the boat, and no signs of a struggle. So if we want to make a case for homicide, we have to believe that Seligman made a rendezvous with the killer after he went out, that the killer persuaded him to wear a pair of diving belts, and to stand quietly on the deck and allow himself to be shot. That doesn't make any sense."

"Neither does suicide," Brady retorted. "For one thing, suicides almost always leave a note. There was no note. At least"—he looked over at Dimond—"we were never allowed to look at the files Proctor found, but Mr. Dimond assures us there was no note."

"Correct." Dimond met his gaze steadily. "There was no note."

"And no page one to match the page two they found in the typewriter?"

"No page one."

"Then what happened to page one? It wasn't on the boat. Did he swallow it?" He paused. "Or did someone else remove it?"

Dimond said nothing.

"Then there's the cartridge case," Brady continued. "It was found in the forward cabin. If Seligman killed himself, he did it on deck. So if the case belongs with the slug that killed him, how did it get in the cabin? Did it walk?"

"Beats me." Rutherford shrugged. "But since we don't know that the case and the slug go together, we don't know if that's a problem."

"Well, try this," Brady came back at him. "The bullet wound was in the right temple. Correct? But Seligman was left-handed. His daughter says he was, and so do the golf clubs we found in his apartment. So unless you believe he shot himself like this"— he twisted his left arm around his head to point the index finger at his right temple—"you're left with these alternatives: either he didn't shoot himself, or he wasn't Seligman."

"Of course," he continued, giving full vent to his sarcasm, "it is possible that it was Seligman and he did shoot himself. He just didn't want anyone to know that he had. That would certainly explain the diving belts. And they do need explaining. Because they clearly suggest that someone was anxious to prevent us from discovering the body early enough to identify it. Now why would Seligman want to do that? It just doesn't make any sense. None of it makes any sense Nobody's even suggested a good reason why Seligman would want to kill himself in the first place."

"Depression?" Dimond offered. "He was recently divorced. He had financial problems, aggravated by substantial alimony payments."

"Hell," Brady said, "it's a hard world. Every second marriage ends in divorce. Everyone I know has financial problems. People get depressed all the time. But they don't normally sail out into the Bay and shoot themselves. And especially they don't dress up in diving belts to do it."

"Shit." Rutherford was getting bored. "Suicides aren't normal. By definition they're not. Who can say what goes on in their minds?

"Listen, we're not getting anywhere with this. The press is downstairs, and they're expecting a statement. I think it's reasonable to accept the body as Seligman. So let's tell them that. As to how he died, let's just say that we're working on an assumption of suicide, but the inquiry is not complete. I think it's safest to leave that point open."

He looked around at the others. Both Daniel and Dimond nodded emphatically. Brady didn't move.

"Brady?" Rutherford prompted.

"Make any statement you like," Brady growled. "I'm not satisfied about a thing. As far as I'm concerned, everything's open."

"Now look, Brady . . ." Rutherford had remained seated when the others rose to leave, and motioned Brady to do likewise. Now they were alone.

"No, you look, Rutherford!" Brady cut him short. "This whole thing stinks. You know it does."

"Sure it stinks." Rutherford shrugged. "But let me ask you a question."

"Go ahead. Ask."

"When was the Missing Persons report filed on Seligman?"

"I don't know." Brady thought about it. "In fact, I don't know that one ever was filed."

"Right. No report was filed."

"So what? We were notified when the Coast Guard found the cartridge case. Seligman was assumed to have been on board. The report got overlooked. That happens."

"Sometimes." Rutherford's face was expressionless. "Then tell me this. What was Mrs. Seligman's reaction to the news that her husband was missing?"

"I don't know that either. I wasn't there when she was told."

"Who told her?"

"I assume it was the Coast Guard."

"No." Rutherford shook his head. "It was the CIA. When the Coast Guard discovered the papers on the boat they notified the Security Division at Langley. That's standard procedure. The next thing that happened was that an Agency security officer named Patterson showed up, with Mrs. Seligman, at Seligman's apartment building on Wisconsin. Mrs. Seligman authorized the building superintendent to let them into Seligman's apartment. According to the superintendent, who was with them all the time, Patterson went through the papers Seligman kept there. He removed six

which he said were CIA-related and gave Mrs. Seligman a receipt
for them. Then he and Mrs. Seligman went out to the Wharf at
Lusby, where Patterson took charge of the documents found on
the boat. This time he gave Procter a receipt. And the whole time
they were there, Procter says, neither Patterson or Mrs. Seligman
expressed a word of concern about what might have happened to
Seligman."

"So?"

"Think about it. Seligman has been gone for more than twenty-
four hours. His boat shows up empty in the Bay. But when his wife
is notified, what does she do? Does she file a Missing Persons?
She does not. Does she seem at all concerned? Not so far as one
can tell."

"She's his ex-wife," Brady objected. "That makes a difference."

"It might," Rutherford conceded. "Perhaps she hated him. Perhaps she just didn't give a shit. But there's something else that might
explain it."

"What?"

"Dorothy Seligman," Rutherford said very deliberately, "also
worked for the CIA."

Brady stared at him.

"Oh, not any longer," Rutherford continued. "And she was
strictly front office. No access. No clearance . . . if you're willing
to believe Dimond, that is. But it does make you wonder, doesn't
it? At least it makes me wonder. Because the Agency never filed a
Missing Persons either. One of their employees goes missing, and
they shoot right down to retrieve any Agency property he may have
left lying around. But they don't bother to tell us. Nor does Mrs.
Seligman . . . And so I wonder whether it's because they don't give
a shit what happens to Seligman. Or whether—" he paused —"they
don't give a shit because they already know."

"Hey, wait a minute!" Brady protested. "You're way ahead of
the facts."

"Possibly." Rutherford's voice was very dry.

"They wouldn't be that stupid."

"Wouldn't they? Look at the record."

"In any case," Brady pursued, "if you're right, isn't that all the
more reason to keep digging?"

"You could look at it that way. But where would you suggest we
begin?"

"With the evidence. Isn't that the usual procedure?"

"Look." Rutherford sounded weary. "The evidence is contaminated. Half of it is missing. We'll never get to see the stuff Patterson lifted. You can forget it. It's gone."

"We could apply for a court order."

"Sure we could. But you have to show reasonable cause. And given what we know now—or what we don't know—I can't see us getting very far with that. And even suppose we managed to get the order, we'd never be sure that what the Agency gave us was the same as what it took.

"That's the trouble with this case." He shook his head. "Every which way you turn you run into the fucking Agency. And it's pretty goddamn obvious that, whatever the Agency knows, the Agency ain't telling.

"And that is why," he concluded, with a finality that was an unmistakable assertion of his authority, "you and I are going to go downstairs now and tell the assembled gentlemen of the press that we think the body is Seligman's. And we're not sure, but we think he did himself in. We may look a little like assholes in the short run, but we're used to that. In the long run, we're going to save ourselves one hell of a lot of trouble."

IV

At the age of fifteen Jacob Szymanowski, after much thought and some argument with his parents, had decided to change his name. It was not, as he was careful to explain, that he was in any way ashamed of his antecedents—a name that had been good enough for eleven recorded generations of his forebears was certainly good enough for him—but Szymanowski, being Polish, was difficult to pronounce. And a name that was difficult to pronounce was difficult to remember.

He had chosen instead the surname Horowitz. It was pronounceable yet still sufficiently Central European to clear him of any suspicion of ethnic snobbery. At the same time he'd also changed Jacob to David. That had been more difficult to justify. Jacob was a good name, he'd been forced to concede; it was just that David was . . . well, David was more euphonious.

So now he was David Horowitz, twenty-five years old and one year out of college, bringing to his encounter with the world at large a degree in journalism and a galloping ambition. The degree had landed him a job as crime reporter with the *Wilmington Gazette*; the ambition made it doubtful he would stay there. Crime reporting was OK for a start—he was intelligent enough to realize he needed the experience—but he planned eventually to find a wider theater for his talents. Political reporting for a leading daily was the next scheduled stop on his professional itinerary. The ultimate destination was national television.

The *Excalibur* incident, when he was first assigned to it, had not seemed likely to advance his cause. Another boating accident, he'd thought, possibly a suicide. It might stretch to a few hundred words, perhaps even half a column, somewhere on page three. Then he had learned of Seligman's connection with the CIA. That made it a whole different ballgame.

So he had started fishing around, casting his net much wider than usual, concentrating not on the routine of the police investigation, but on the CIA. He did not, however, waste his time going to the Agency. He was green but not stupid. You didn't go to the Agency, he knew, until you had been everywhere else, for if you went to the Agency wide-eyed and empty-handed, the Agency would see to it that you stayed that way.

He went instead to his friends. He had a lot of friends. He'd been making them assiduously, in college and afterward, and generally with an eye to the future. There was one on the editorial staff of *Foreign Affairs Quarterly*; another worked as assistant to the chairman of the Senate Select Committee on Intelligence; a third was with the Rand Corporation. He had buddies in the Brookings Institute, in the International Relations Department at Georgetown University, and at the State Department. Then there was also the girl, not smart and not pretty, but decidedly willing, who worked for a Deputy Director at the Department of Defense. "Charity fucking" was his term for that relationship. And as far as he was concerned, charity was always a two-way street.

It was a busy two days for David Horowitz. He kept up with the police investigation, lunched with his friend at Rand, spent an afternoon at the University, squeezed in some tennis with the guy from State, and rounded the whole thing off with an evening of strenuous romance. But he had what he needed. He was ready to go to the CIA. What they said to him now would almost certainly be revealing, though not, possibly, in the way they intended.

Dimond's presence at the press conference was a happy development. It was not luck—smart people, Horowitz believed, made their own luck—but it was certainly convenient. It spared him the need to go to Langley. And it confirmed, if further confirmation was needed, that he was on the right track.

There were three other reporters at the press conference: two from local papers, one from the *Washington Post*. The presence of the man from the *Post* made Horowitz uneasy. The *Post* had a highly developed nose for Washington scandal; obviously something about this situation tickled those sensitive nostrils. But the conversation he'd had with the *Post* reporter while they were waiting, a guarded exchange in which each released tidbits of information in the hope of learning how much the other knew, reassured him. The *Post* was certainly suspicious—the *Post* was always suspicious where the CIA was concerned—but the man from the *Post* was still fishing.

By tacit agreement among the reporters, the police were encouraged to tell their story first. Rutherford did all the talking, Horowitz noticed, and it was plain he was selling suicide. It was also plain from the other cop's glum, almost angry silence that he was reluctant to buy. Horowitz made a note of that. This Brady could be a man worth cultivating.

It was not until interest in the police had been exhausted that Horowitz first raised his hand.

"I have a question for Mr. Dimond."

"Yes?"

Dimond was a slim, athletic-looking man, whose straw-colored hair and deep tan suggested he spent more time on the beach than in the office. His clothes—a perfectly cut gray flannel suit, pale blue button-down shirt, sober tie, and black Italian loafers—were worn with a casualness that belied their formality. His smile was an orthodontist's dream. Dazzling and even, it seemed part of the permanent architecture of his face. He reminded Horowitz of a real estate salesman.

"The fact that Seligman was a member of the CIA"—Horowitz worded the question carefully—"is bound to raise questions as to whether his death, or disappearance, has implications for security. Can you tell us—in very general terms, of course—what he did at the Agency? I mean his status there, the extent of his access to classified information—that sort of thing?"

"Yes." Dimond's voice was easy. "I think I can tell you that. But first I should make clear, for those of you who don't already know this, that Seligman retired from the Agency in 1976. From time to time, however, he continued to do consulting work for us. He was working on one of these projects at the time of his death, and this explains the Agency documents found in his possession.

"To get back to your original question, prior to his retirement Seligman worked as an analyst of the military and economic capabilities of certain foreign powers. He had access, obviously, to the classified information necessary to his work. Otherwise his access was very limited."

"The large-scale security investigation conducted by Thomas Spearman was completed in 1976, wasn't it?"

"That's correct."

"Was there any connection between Seligman's retirement and that investigation?"

"None whatever. The timing was purely coincidental."

"How old was Seligman when he retired?"

"Mid- to late fifties. I'm not sure exactly."

"The Agency's mandatory retirement age is sixty-five, isn't it?"

"Yes."

"Then Seligman retired early?"

"Yes."

"Why?"

"His retirement was part of a general cutback in personnel made necessary by a reduction in the Agency appropriation. A review of manpower requirements indicated we were overstaffed in certain areas. Seligman's was one of them."

"So his loss will not be significant to the Agency?"

"Among those of us who knew him"—Dimond's smile acquired a tinge of melancholy—"it will, of course, be deeply felt. To the operations of the Agency as a whole, no."

"You've stated that Seligman was an analyst." Horowitz's manner, puzzled yet polite, concealed the excitement he was feeling. "I have here a report from *Time* magazine, dated June 1977, in which Agency sources are quoted as saying that the Agency lacks the capacity to analyze properly the overwhelming volume of raw intelligence data it receives. In the light of your previous statement, do you wish to comment on that?"

"Well." Dimond cleared his throat. "Even if it were true that our overall analytical capability was overstrained, that wouldn't necessarily prevent redundancies occurring in certain specific areas within the whole."

He looked around at the other reporters.

"Are there any further questions for me, while I still have the floor?"

But the others were silent. Horowitz was on to something, evidently. Dimond's replies were becoming noticeably vague and polysyllabic. He had something to hide, and he was nervous about it. That was nothing new. And there was not a reporter present who did not know what the next question should be. But they were content to let Horowitz ask it. He was young and inexperienced. If they let him talk, he would end up telling them something. He might even give them his story.

"Could you tell us, please, whose military capabilities Seligman worked on?"

Fuck! Dimond could see where this was heading. But, having denied Seligman's significance, he could hardly turn around and make a mystery of where he had worked.

"Seligman specialized primarily in the Soviet Union."

"Missiles?"

"Among other things."

"Did he have access to the K-11 satellite system?"

"The K-11 is one of our primary sources for data about the Soviet military. Seligman would have had access to the output. Yes."

"The K-11 is our major means of ensuring Soviet compliance with the terms of the proposed SALT II treaty, isn't it?"

"One of them. Yes."

"Then would you explain why the Agency was apparently willing to lose the services of an expert in the interpretation of the system just at a time when his services may be urgently needed?"

"Now hold on!" Dimond protested. "You're putting words in my mouth. I never said Seligman was an expert in interpreting the output. I said he had access to the output."

"Then he wasn't an expert in interpreting the output?"

"No."

"No?"

Afterward Horowitz realized he should have stopped there. He had the denial he needed. Anything more was baiting, just smart-ass stuff that could cost him more than it was worth. But he was having too much fun.

"No?" He sounded bewildered, an innocent at sea in the big city. "But I just got through talking with someone in the Pentagon. And this guy said"—he paused to savor the moment—"this guy said that Seligman was more than an expert. He said Seligman helped design the system."

Dimond's smile was very tight now, indistinguishable from a snarl. "You can't expect me to comment on the alleged statement of an unnamed source in another agency. You'll have to make up your own mind what to believe."

"Oh." Horowitz's return smile was openly derisive. "I don't have any problem doing that."

The other reporters were leaving. He got up too. It was time to write his story. In fact, he would write two stories. One would be what his editor expected, a neat, professional summary of the developments in the police investigation. It would fit nicely, if they bothered to print it, on page three. But he doubted they would bother to print it. For his other story, one in which the CIA and Mr. Dimond would figure very prominently, was obviously a natural for page one.

CHAPTER 2

I

It seemed to Sullivan that he was watching a movie, but one dubbed in babel and edited by a lunatic. Fragments of conversation came at him; detaching themselves from the general buzz, they enveloped him briefly and retreated—phrases in English, in the twittering birdsong of Vietnamese, in the liquid cadences of French. Images flickered and dissolved before his eyes . . . A fly tiptoed with delicate, finicky steps across a pat of butter, zigzagging to avoid the pearls of water on its surface. His eye was trapped in the patterns of the tablecloth, in the subtle textures of nap and weave . . . It moved to the delta of veins standing out on the waiter's forearm . . . It switched to the man's face, sallow and bony, the skin stretched tight across the cheekbones to form hollows underneath, the hair, black and spiky, standing up from the skull, the lips parted in a smile from which the eyes were absent . . . The face collapsed. The smile became a sneer. Lips puffed and cracked. Teeth were missing. A dribble of scarlet appeared at the corner of the mouth. But the eyes were still the same, dark and liquid; bright, it seemed to him, with hate.

The images were clear and sharp, but, like reflections in a shattered mirror, fragmented and out of sequence. In their vividness they held a kind of menace. Their strangeness filled him with dread.

Charley was talking to him, leaning forward, smiling, her elbows propped on the table. But he couldn't hear what she was saying. The lips retracted to reveal a gleam of teeth; the small, pink tongue advanced to form a labial, retreated for the vowel; the teeth closed softly on the lower lip. But the word was lost. It might have been "love." But it was lost in the hubbub.

Then the sound went. The scene became purely visual. The camera zoomed in on a doorway. The action, becoming coherent, slowed to a crawl.

The grenade must have come from the doorway, and behind it he caught a glimpse of that puffy, beaten face. But it was the grenade that held his attention. Bouncing and tumbling erratically, turning end over end in lazy, slow-motion parabolas, it rolled to a stop a few yards from their table. It lay there, squat and deadly, like a malevolent, poisonous toad.

The sound returned. There were shrieks, noises of falling bodies and breaking dishes. He found himself flying over the table, hurling Charley backward to the floor. His body covered her like a flimsy, useless shield.

He never heard the detonation, never felt the stab of the shrapnel in his calf and thigh, never realized, until later, that the blood soaking him was partly his own. All he could ever remember was the spurt of her life from the artery at her neck, the feel of it, hot and slick between his fingers, the incredible bright pools of it on the floor beside her, and how quickly the spurts had died away.

Then, as always, he awoke, clawing about him, in those dazed first moments between sleep and waking, for something to stanch the flow. And as always when his fingers encountered the cool, dry texture of the sheets, there was that flood of relief. It hadn't really happened. It had only been a dream.

But when he sat up to look at his watch on the bedside table, the bed beside him was empty. The watch told him it was 3:00 A.M., and the date was the twenty-fifth. His wedding anniversary. If Charley had lived, they would have been married eleven years. But Charley had not lived; they'd had less than a year together. It had happened. And now that the dream had receded, Morgan Sullivan, lying alone in the darkness, could not remember her face.

II

Horowitz was right about the story. His editor printed it, almost verbatim, on page one. SPY SCANDAL SHAKES CIA, the headline read. By mid-morning the wire services had picked it up, and by lunch-

time the *Post, The New York Times,* and half a dozen other leading dailies, chagrined at having let a small provincial rag leave
them at the starting gate, were sprinting to make up ground. CIA
and Pentagon telephone lines were jammed for the rest of the day.
The spokesmen for these organizations, getting home very late
that night, took their receivers off the hook, exhausted by twelve
straight hours of refusing to comment.

Horowitz had made the most of his opportunity, weaving strands
of fact and speculation into a fabric that one exasperated official,
in an unguarded moment, described as "a crazy patchwork of
half-truths and outright fiction!" Leading with a paragraph in which
the most sensational aspects of the story were mentioned, he'd
gone on to describe the discovery of the body, dwelling at length
on the problems of identification, the difficulties surrounding the
suicide theory, and the suspiciously large amount of sophisticated
radio equipment found on the sloop. He reported, without further
comment, the fact that Rutherford, apparently in charge of the
investigation, was with the Homicide Division of the Maryland
police department. He also detailed, deadpan, Dimond's assertions
of Seligman's humble status at the CIA.

Then he got out his hatchet and went after the Agency.

In fact, he asserted, quoting unnamed sources in the Pentagon,
Seligman was one of the CIA's fifty most senior officers. Seligman
was "cleared for everything." Seligman had helped plan the
SAMOS and K-11 spy satellite systems and knew them blindfolded, forward and backward. Seligman was in possession of all
the important codes for the CIA's computer system, Octopus. Indeed, Seligman, had been in a position to clean out every secret
the Agency had to its name.

He'd gone on to talk about moles. It was common knowledge,
he claimed, that two months previously, when an Agency watch
officer had been convicted of selling an Octopus manual to the
Russians, an investigation of Agency security had discovered that
several other manuals were missing, including some giving technical data on the satellite systems. This had revived suspicions,
frequently voiced in the past, that the Agency was harboring an
agent of the KGB in its upper echelons—a mole, in the current
jargon of espionage. The facts of the *Excalibur* incident, he went
on to say, lent an alarming degree of credibility to these fears.

His final paragraphs examined the wider implications:

This fall U.S. negotiators will sit down with the Russians to hammer out the final details of a proposed SALT II. Critics of that treaty, in addition to claiming that the U.S. team, in setting ceilings for the various types of strategic weapons, has already given away the store, are pointing out that the value to the U.S. of such a treaty will depend entirely upon our ability to verify that the Russians are complying with its terms. In attempting to do this the U.S. will rely very heavily on the K-11 spy satellite system.

The mysterious disappearance of Paul Seligman must therefore be ringing alarm bells throughout this nation's defense establishment. And the questions members of this establishment must be asking themselves are obvious. Is the body that turned up last Wednesday in Chesapeake Bay Seligman's? Did Seligman commit suicide? Was Seligman really Seligman at all, or was he an agent of the KGB, planted decades ago, whose withdrawal to Moscow the apparent suicide was engineered to cover?

There are as yet no answers to these questions, but one thing seems certain. If Paul Seligman shows up next spring at the May Day parade in Red Square, it will mean that the U.S., as it has done so often in the past, is playing in a poker game with the deck hopelessly stacked against it.

"This," growled the Director of Central Intelligence, "is the most irresponsible piece of reporting I've seen since I came to this town. And believe me, I've seen a bunch."

"What can you expect from the press?" Michael Eglinton's tone implied that he personally expected very little. "I must say," he added, "Dimond doesn't seem to have been at his best."

"Dimond blew it." The Director delivered the popular verdict. "But he had lots of help. Some asshole in the Pentagon did the real damage. I've told Dimond to disappear until this blows over."

The others nodded. It made sense, for both Dimond and the Agency. Getting someone to murmur soothing phrases about ill health and Dimond's crippling workload would not convince any-one—least of all anyone who had seen Dimond's film-star suntan—but it would be less embarrassing than leaving Dimond to mumble his own retractions.

"But I'm not concerned with now," the Director continued. "We can go into him later. Right now we have more serious matters to deal with.

"This morning, while you guys were probably still in bed, I was called up by the Secretary of Defense. He wanted to know our assessment of the potential damage to the satellite systems. When I told him I'd have to check back with him, he almost had a coronary. He made me feel like a sublieutenant caught sleeping on watch."

If he was expecting sympathy, he didn't get it. Eglinton exchanged glances with Roy Tyrell. Eglinton's face was expressionless; Tyrell's expressed amusement. He found it difficult to believe, he explained later, that the Director of Central Intelligence had ever felt like a sublieutenant, even when he had been one.

DCI Marshall Everett was a stocky, pugnacious-looking man with eyes the color of glacier water. He used them as a weapon of intimidation, adopting in conversation a measuring stare that seemed to suggest that the person he was talking to had something to hide. It was a trick he'd learned early in his career in the Navy, and some said he owed his meteoric rise in the service to it. For his stare gave him, whatever else he might say or do, the look of a man born to command. In fact, however, what Marshall Everett said and did was usually intelligent. He'd been smart enough, while still at Annapolis, to recognize that the future in his chosen profession would be brightest for those with training in computers and electronics, and he'd contrived, in his subsequent career, to be invariably in the right place at the right time. But his master stroke, it was generally agreed, had been to befriend at the Naval Academy a cadet whose grades and standing had given no hint of the talents that would enable him to become the fifty-first President of the United States. Everett's appointment, some years before his fiftieth birthday, to the Joint Chiefs of Staff had surprised no one—least of all himself.

He had come to the CIA a year or so previously, the latest in a series of "new broom" directors, charged with completing the Agency's post-Watergate housecleaning. It was a task more difficult than it looked, and it had blighted careers more promising than his. His start in it had not been auspicious. Within weeks of his appointment the staff of the Agency, with a unanimity surprising in a body otherwise riven by faction, had united in disliking him. Their reaction was due partly to the draconian cutbacks in personnel he'd ordered on arrival, and partly to the shock his abrupt nautical personality had delivered to the sensibilities of an organization accustomed to civilian standards of courtesy. He suffered, as Roy Tyrell had once put it, from the centurion mentality.

For his part, Everett was unrepentant. He'd come to the Agency expecting to discover a bunch of complacent, clannish incompetents, and that, in his view, was largely what he'd found. There were exceptions, of course. Eglinton, the Deputy Director–Research, was OK. A cold fish, but always on top of his job. Tyrell, too. Everett didn't like Tyrell. He disliked his playboy personality and his perpetual air of faint insolence. He disliked even more, though he would never have admitted it even to himself, the fact that Tyrell, alone among his subordinates, could hold that stare of his and return it with a look that told him as plainly as words that Roy Tyrell had outlived half a dozen Directors and would outlive him too. Still, Tyrell compelled respect. He played around outside the office, but in it he was all business. Moreover, his character was admirably suited to his role as Deputy-Director of Plans, controlling the Agency's clandestine operations. Roy Tyrell was unquestionably an operator.

Counterespionage, however, was another matter. The former chief had been forced out after a series of bitter clashes between Agency cliques in which the word "mole" had been hurled back and forth with disturbing frequency. Now Counterespionage was gun-shy, and the present incumbent, Tony Patterson, a defensive, demoralized lightweight, was largely occupied, Everett suspected, in counting the days to his retirement. He should count them carefully, Everett thought, they're fewer than he thinks.

"The Secretary's next question," he resumed, "was what the fuck had we been doing since last Saturday when that boat was discovered. It's a good question. Now suppose you guys"—he fixed his stare in turn on Eglinton and Patterson—"give me some answers."

"I've done a report on the satellite systems." If Eglinton resented Everett's manner, he didn't show it. "It's being typed now. You'll have it by lunchtime. Patterson is doing one, I believe, on the general security implications. I can summarize mine for you, if you like."

"I do like."

"Let's start with Seligman, then. It's true he had access to all the K-11 product. It's also true that in the early stages he was involved in the planning. As one of the primary users, he was very helpful in setting the design parameters. He's had a great deal of computer experience, and he knows more about the technical side of the system than most analysts."

A thought seemed to strike him, for he paused. "I seem to be using the present tense," he said. "As though he were still alive. It seems a terrible thing to say, but at this point I sincerely hope he's not.

"Anyway," he went on "the system has changed radically since he worked on it. I don't believe he'd have been able to help anyone breach it, unless he got hold of the basic technical manual."

"Is the manual secure?"

"Yes. There are only three copies. Circulation is restricted on an absolute need-to-know basis. Each copy is logged out and in, and the recipient signs for it personally. Seligman was not on the circulation list, and there's no time unaccounted for on the logs."

"Could he have gained access to a copy logged out to someone else?"

"Possible but highly unlikely. You'd have to assume connivance or a really gross lapse in security. But security is a religion with my staff. I insist on it. One slip and you're out. That's the rule, and they know it. It didn't happen. I'm sure of it."

It was a large claim, made perhaps a shade too confidently. Everyone there had extensive experience of human fallibility. Everett allowed the ensuing silence to drag on uncomfortably before he broke it.

"So the security in your division is watertight? I'm happy to know that. The Secretary will be too—if he believes it. Unfortunately, there's a matter of missing computer manuals still fresh in his memory."

"That's not Michael's responsibility," Tyrell objected. "Anyway, in the matter of leaks the Secretary has a small problem of his own. You might remind him of that."

"I already did," Everett said.

"To change the subject for a moment," Tyrell resumed, "let me ask a dumb question. Suppose, for the sake of argument, the Russians did get hold of a manual. How would it help them? As I understand it, what the system does is provide intensely detailed aerial photographs of Soviet installations. Now even if they discovered exactly how the system worked, they couldn't stop us using it, could they?"

"They could do worse than that," Eglinton told him. "They could turn it against us."

"How?"

Eglinton hesitated. Roy Tyrell was Plans. He ran agents, financed revolutions, planned assassinations, and tried—without conspicuous success, it seemed to Eglinton—to promote unrest behind the Iron Curtain. He was responsible, in fact, for the whole spectrum of activities that Eglinton, with more than a trace of condescension, was apt to characterize as "tricks." Seligman had not worked for Plans, and so far as Eglinton could see, Plans was not directly involved in this problem. He didn't understand why Tyrell was at the meeting.

He glanced fleetingly at Everett and received the briefest of nods in return.

"To understand that," he resumed, "you have to understand the basics of the system. In fact, it's not one system, but two. There's a long-shot camera and a close-up one. The long-shot satellites orbit about two hundred and seventy miles out and operate continuously, photographing the entire surface of the earth once every eight days. They function electronically, converting what they see into impulses which are transmitted to the tracking stations and converted by computer into images. The images are fairly detailed—they have a resolution of about seventy-five feet—but on their own they're not good enough to do more than alert us to areas of potential interest.

"On those areas we use the K-11. It orbits much lower—about a hundred miles up—and uses a fantastically sensitive camera which achieves, at that altitude, a resolution of less than three feet. There's a system on the drawing board now, incidentally, that promises to be able to pick up an object the size of a golf ball from the same altitude.

"Just think, Roy"—he grinned at Tyrell—"you'll have the exact specs of every golf course in the U.S.S.R. You may decide to defect."

"No way." Tyrell shook his head. "They abolished serfdom, remember. Where would I get a caddy?"

"We're wasting time." Everett was a tennis player. The game conditioned the heart and lungs, strengthened the legs, developed reflexes, and took no more than an hour to play. It was typical of the Agency, he thought, that so many of its members should forgo these benefits for the pleasures of an obsessive, time-wasting ritual.

"OK, then," Eglinton continued. "The system is probably watertight at the K-11 stage. That camera records on film—several miles of it—and the film is stored in recoverable containers. The Russians could cheat only by destroying the satellite. They could probably do that—in fact, there's some evidence that they may have taken a couple of cracks at it, using lasers—but the point is that we'd know if anything happened to one of the satellites and could pin the blame on them. Cheating is no good if you're caught, as Plans has found to its cost on more than on occasion."

He turned a bland smile upon Tyrell, who acknowledged the hit by licking his finger and marking a point on an imaginary scoreboard.

"U-2" was Tyrell's response to that.

"Would you guys cut it out." Everett turned his stare, highbeam, on Tyrell. "This is a crisis we're in here, not *Saturday Night Live*."

"Sorry." Tyrell didn't sound it. "Go on, Michael."

"It's the long-shot system that may be vulnerable. The impulses from the satellite, remember, are transmitted to tracking stations and converted into pictures by computer. If the Russians knew the conversion programs, then in theory it's possible they could learn to bypass the system."

"By teaching the camera to lie?"

"Exactly."

"And the computers that do the conversion." Everett leaned forward. "Are they part of the Octopus system?"

"They are."

"Shit!"

"It's not as bad as that, surely?" Patterson queried. "Correct me if I'm wrong, Michael, but isn't it true if the Russians wanted to doctor the pictures, they'd have to reprogram Octopus to do it? And wouldn't that mean they'd have to gain physical access to the computer?"

"They'd have to reprogram, yes. But if they knew the program code and the master entry code, they could simply make a telephone patch and call in the new program from outside. They wouldn't even have to be in the country. Hell, they could do it from Moscow."

"Then change the codes."

"We'll do that, obviously. And it will take care of the future. The problem is that it won't take care of the past. The system's been in operation for some time now. We owe to it most of our present knowledge about Russia's strategic armaments. But if the system was breached one or two years back, then what we fondly imagine to be knowledge may just be Hans Christian Andersen."

"So our SALT II team," pursued Patterson, "may have been operating on mistaken assumptions about existing Soviet strength? And the treaty, if it ever gets signed, may be entirely worthless?"

"Not worthless." Tyrell shook his head. "Worthless to us, certainly, but very useful to them. The treaty will set ceilings on the numbers of the various types of strategic weapons each side may possess. So we sign the treaty, and we abide by its terms. And so do they. Only they already have twice the number of missiles and warheads the treaty permits. If the system has been breached, they could have been stockpiling like crazy for years—and we wouldn't know a thing about it. Then what the treaty does is freeze the situation at a point where the U.S. is hopelessly behind."

"Is all this in your report?" Everett asked Eglinton.

"Yes. Except the implications for SALT. I assumed the Secretary could work those out for himself. If he can't"—he shrugged—"we're really in trouble."

"So the real question is: did Seligman, or anyone, pass the codes to the Russians? And that, I assume"—Everett turned to Patterson—"is what you're going to tell us."

Patterson's report was not particularly reassuring. Apart from some peccadilloes, Seligman's security record was spotless. His clearances had been updated regularly. He had been minutely scrutinized in the mole investigations that had resulted in the ouster of Patterson's predecessor. There were no strikes against him. His access to Octopus, however, though limited, had made him master of a body of classified information almost as extensive as Horowitz had claimed. And there were aspects of his career that, in light of the *Excalibur* incident, might be significant. From 1943 to 1945, for example, he had been employed, in a liaison capacity, in the Soviet Union. His command of Russian, particularly technical Russian, was said to be flawless. Then there were the computer courses. He'd taken them at regular intervals throughout his Agency career and arrived at a level of expertise far beyond anything required by his work. But the most troubling thing, according to Patterson, was the equipment found on the boat. It was very possible that it could have been used to communicate both with KGB stations outside the U.S. and with the computer system at the CIA. The problem was that all Patterson knew about the equipment was hearsay. No one from the Agency had inspected it.

"Why the hell not?"

Everett was finding the meeting increasingly frustrating. He liked straight answers. He liked to get them and he liked to be able to give them. And he would be called upon to give them, he knew, at a special session of the Senate Select Committee on Intelligence the next day. But instead of answers, all he had so far was a collection of disturbing imponderables.

"The equipment was removed from the sloop before we had a chance to check it," Patterson explained. "On Sunday, shortly after the police completed their check, Mrs. Seligman showed with the owner of the Wharf, took out everything, and hauled it away."

"The police didn't stop her?"

"They weren't there. Hancock, the owner of the Wharf, was in charge. Apparently he OK'd it. He even helped her."

"Well, did you ask her for a look at it?"

"Oh yes. She was very accommodating. I went down there on Monday with a guy from Communications. She showed us all there was. Or all she said there was. The guy from Communications said it was harmless—complex, of course, and way beyond what a boat of that type would normally need, but not capable of cutting into the Agency systems. Only . . . I couldn't say whether what she showed us was what she took."

"You should have taken inventory when you went with her on Saturday."

"Yes, I should have, as it turns out. But I couldn't have known, at that point, that the equipment would turn out to be important."

"You might have guessed."

"Maybe." Patterson shrugged. Then, surprisingly, he added, "But then, hindsight is always twenty-twenty, isn't it?"

III

Morgan Sullivan hated rooms like this. There was the usual wooden table, solid but graceless, standard government issue, placed in accordance with some official instinct for symmetry smack in the middle of the floor. On either side of it, facing each other, the usual wooden chairs, machines for sitting in, were straight-backed and unpadded. Directly overhead and unshaded, a single strip of fluorescent lighting emitted a faintly bluish glare. The only other light was that which issued from a small square window, set high up on the far wall and protected, pointlessly, by vertical iron bars—pointlessly because outside there would be a sheer drop of thirty or forty feet into the compound, and beyond that, twenty-five feet high and unscalable, the perimeter wall.

He wondered why he had chosen professions that seemed to put him, so often, in such rooms—rooms designed, apparently, to isolate, to intimidate, to induce in those forced to inhabit them a sense of despair. But at least in this one there were none of the normal reminders of violence. This one stank of disinfectant, not urine or stale vomit. People would not be slapped around much here—or not often. And no one probably had ever been strapped to the table, hooked up to a portable generator, and turned into a section of electrical circuit. And he would not, thank God, this time or ever again, have to drone out an endless litany of questions, each one repeated in a dozen various forms in the hope of catching the small inconsistency that might prove the crack in the dam. And that was a relief. But the place still gave him the shudders. The memories it raised, after almost ten years, still had the power to disturb him.

The door opened. A face appeared around it.

"He's here. Are you ready for him?"

"Yes. Bring him . . . show him in, please."

Bourne entered. He was thinner and paler than when Sullivan had last seen him, at the trial, but his walk still had a hint of swagger, and in his weak, sullen face the eyes glittered with defiance.

He sat down opposite Sullivan but did not speak or look up until they heard the door close and lock. Then he smiled, his lips twisting into a brief, humorless leer.

"You came up with something," he said. "You wouldn't be here otherwise. You came up with a loophole, didn't you?"

Sullivan studied him. Peter Alfred Bourne, the language of the indictment had run, construction worker of no fixed address, had, on the twenty-sixth day of June, nineteen hundred and seventy-seven, knowingly and willfully broken into the house of Alice Lothrop Faraday at 2167 Fairfax Avenue, Bethesda, Maryland, with the intent . . . But whatever the intent had been, things had gone wrong. Alice Faraday had been home that day and, reluctant to part with the thirty-eight dollars and seventy-odd cents she had in her purse, had resisted. So the intruder had hit her—a vicious side-handed chop to the base of the throat—and Alice Faraday, who was seventy-eight years old and suffered from a heart condition, had died. The indictment had called it murder, and the jury, after a bare two hours of deliberation, had found no reason to disagree. Peter Alfred Bourne had been sentenced to life imprisonment.

But he might never serve that sentence. Sullivan, who might, if things went well, be the instrument of its remission, felt a sudden revulsion at the thought. He suspected, with an intensity that bordered on conviction, that the little whey-faced punk sitting across from him had indeed struck Alice Faraday, and with no more concern for the outcome than if the old woman had been a fly.

"I've been reading the transcript," he said with some reluctance. "I believe there are grounds for an appeal."

"All right!" Bourne smacked the table with his first. "But what's the angle? What do you want me to say?"

"I don't want you to say anything. You've said far too much already. I want you to shut up and listen."

"OK, OK." Bourne was unabashed. "Just tell me the story."

"Look!" Sullivan said fiercely. "I'm your attorney. My job is to put the arguments on your side as well as I can put them. You're entitled to that. But it is not my job to sit down with you and cook up a piece of baloney in the hopes that the jury will swallow it. I don't work that way. I want you to remember that. Because if you don't, you're going to be looking for another attorney."

"Got you," Bourne said. "You're Mr. Clean. Right? Now will you please explain what's going on."

"Well, it seems to me that the officer who arrested you may have committed a *Miranda* violation. Consequently, your original statement to him may be—"

"Please." Bourne held up a hand. "I'm not a lawyer. Save that legal shit for the judge. Put it in words of one syllable."

"The *Miranda* rules are the regulations governing the police when they make arrests and take statements from suspects. They're intended, among other things, to protect you against being forced into admitting things that aren't true. Now, without your original statement, the one you made when you were arrested, I doubt the State would have been able to convict. So if the police, as I believe they did, violated the spirit of *Miranda*, you should win on appeal."

" 'Violated the spirit of *Miranda*.' " Bourne grinned. "You make it sound like rape. But if I've got it straight, you're going to tell them I was forced into making that statement and that it wasn't true."

Sullivan sighed. "No. That's not what I'm going to do. I'm going to argue that the statement was improperly obtained and should not have been admitted in evidence."

"What's the difference?" Bourne shrugged. "But if we win, what then? A new trial?"

"No. I'd have to argue that, because of the publicity surrounding your first trial, a new trial—a fair trial, that is—would be impossible. They should simply quash the conviction."

"There you go again," Bourne said. "Run that by me again, will you? Only this time in English."

"What I mean is, if the appeal were successful, you would probably have to go free."

Bourne digested this in silence. At length he said, "These *Miranda* things—why are they called that?"

"They're named after the case that brought them into being. It went right up to the Supreme Court. The defendant's name was Miranda."

"And what they mean is if a pig waves a stick in your face when he's taking down your story, you can get off on that alone? No other reason? That's really the law?"

"In this case, yes. I think so."

Bourne considered this, his expression wavering between contempt and incredulity.

"Then you know what I think?" he asked. "I think the law is perfectly fucking amazing."

Sullivan got up. "In your case," he said, "I'm inclined to agree. But don't celebrate yet. We may not win."

"Oh, we'll win," Bourne said. "They'll believe you, all right. Who wouldn't?"

He studied Sullivan for a moment. Then he grinned.

"Mr. Clean," he said. "That's you. Mr. Clean."

IV

"There will, of course," said the Director of Central Intelligence, "be an investigation. The Committee will insist on it. I hope you're aware of that?"

His tone accused them. That, and the use of the second person plural, Tyrell thought, were typical of Everett. They implied that Seligman's career, his involvement with the K-11, his interest in computers, all the tiresome uncertainties now surrounding him, had somehow been brought about by negligence on the part of the Agency regulars, and that he, Marshall Everett, the newcomer and outsider, would be left to pick up the pieces.

"Saddle up, Tony." Tyrell turned to Patterson. "The mole squad rides again."

"Shit!" Patterson said.

"Shit is right," Tyrell agreed. "About six months of it, at a guess. But that's OK. It'll pass. Afterwards, when the thunder of hooves has passed by and the dust has settled, and the casualties have been counted and tidied away, we can all get back to our jobs . . . those of us who still have jobs, that is.

"I wonder," he mused, "who the sacrificial lambs will be this time. Last time it was Spearman. And Seligman, of course." He eyed Patterson speculatively.

"It won't be as simple as that." Everett spoke with sour satisfaction. "The Committee won't let us handle this one ourselves. Not after the Spearman fuckup. They'll bring in outsiders."

"Oh Jesus. Not the FBI?" Eglinton spoke for all of them.

Everett nodded. "Either them or the DIA."

That was a good deal worse. For the Defense Intelligence Agency, or the "Siblings," as the CIA regulars somewhat condescendingly termed its employees, was the Pentagon's agency. And the Pentagon had more than one old score to settle with the CIA. The most recent dated from the last years of the Vietnam War, when the CIA's political and military reporting had consistently undercut the Pentagon's optimistic assessments. The CIA's reports had been consistently closer to the truth, but that had not helped any. In fact, it had made things worse. Nobody loves a smart-ass. The way the Pentagon felt about the Agency made Arab feelings toward Israel seem charitable.

"It's bound to be the Siblings," Eglinton said gloomily. "They're the natural choice. They're the main customer for the satellite product. They consider it their baby, and they're very protective about it. They'd love to adopt it entirely."

"That's the least of it." Patterson didn't share Eglinton's parental anxiety. "They wouldn't mind taking us over, in the bargain. The situation is tailor-made for them."

The ensuing uneasy silence was broken by Tyrell.

"We're overreacting," he said. "The Committtee's not totally naive. They know about sibling rivalry. They know letting the DIA in here is like putting Henry Ford on the board of General Motors. They won't want to do that. Not if we can give them an alternative."

"What alternative?" Everett demanded. "We need an investigation that's independent yet untainted by interservice rivalry. Who the hell fulfills those criteria? Amnesty International? The Justice Department? Ralph Nader?"

"Listen." Tyrell ignored the sarcasm. "What we have to do is get the investigation limited to Seligman. That shouldn't be hard. After all, we've had several full-scale investigations recently, and they've all come up more or less empty. You should be able to sell that, Marshall. With all your connections."

Everett frowned. Of all his subordinates, only Tyrell ever called him by his first name. He'd started to do it, entirely uninvited, within minutes of first meeting Everett. Everett didn't like it; it was bad for discipline. But he could think of no way of objecting that would not expose him to Tyrell's faint, insolent smile.

"I wouldn't describe nearly one hundred missing documents as 'coming up empty,'" he said curtly. "I might be able to sell that idea, but how, exactly, would it help?"

"If the Committee goes outside the industry for its team, the problem is security, right? Now, if they have to clear twenty or thirty bodies from scratch, we can forget it. Life's too short. So in a general security probe there's no real alternative to the FBI or the Siblings. But limit the thing to Seligman and you're talking one or two people. Three maximum. In that case, we could probably find the personnel without calling in the competition."

"Who do you have in mind?"

"Well, for a start, there's Morgan Sullivan."

"Morgan Sullivan?" Everett pondered. "I've heard that name. Who is he?"

"He's a criminal lawyer. A partner of Cooper, Cole and Trumbull. Downtown. He's respected in the profession and very well connected. His father, Austin, was a Justice of the New York Supreme Court, friend of Adlai Stevenson, big wheel in the Democratic Party. Sullivan has friends all over the Capitol. In fact, at one point he was mentioned as a possible for Attorney General."

"And he has clearances?"

"Had them, anyway. They'll be easy to update."

"How come?"

"He used to work for us."

"He did?"

"Yes. I think that was why the Attorney General idea came to nothing. Sullivan had touched pitch, the theory went, so Congress wouldn't go for him. Anyway, when he was with us he worked in Counterespionage. And he was one of the best. A natural. He had a nose for it. If he'd stayed, I think he'd have had Spearman's job. At any rate, he was headed for the top."

"Then why didn't he stay?"

"Personal reasons, mostly. He was posted to Saigon in 1967 to take charge of debriefing the more important Viet Cong defectors. Little black sheep, they used to call them, little black sheep who had gone astray. Stupid name, I always thought. Anyway, Sullivan was handling them and not liking it much. Then, one night in June he took his wife to dinner at one of the restaurants on the river. Wives weren't allowed in Saigon as a rule, but Sullivan met her there, and after they married she stayed. He insisted on it. Or rather, she did . . . Well, that was the night the Viet Cong bombed the place. They did a lot of that around then. One of the waiters, I think it was, lobbed a bunch of grenades through the doorway. Killed about twenty people, including Charley Sullivan. Morgan was hit too, but not badly.

"Charley's death finished Saigon for him. He applied for a transfer, but they turned him down. Finish out your tour, they told him, and we'll think about it.

"That did it. The next day, without a word to anyone, he just up and quit. Took the next plane to Singapore. Personnel got his letter of resignation six weeks later. He sent it ordinary mail.

"He went back to the law. He was at Harvard Law School before he joined us. So he took the Bar exams and joined Cooper, Cole and Trumbull. He's never been near us since."

Everett considered this. At length he said, "I don't know. It's a good idea, in principle. But I don't know about Sullivan. It doesn't sound as if he has reason to love us. The last thing we need is some guy with old scores to settle."

"Oh, I think he's over it. He's a feisty bastard, but he's fair. He won't carry a grudge.

"Of course," he went on, "it all depends on your ability to sell the Committee. If you can't do that, we may as well resign ourselves to the Siblings."

"I can do it all right." Everett was affronted. "All it takes is a little honey in certain congressional ears. But before I do, I'd like to know more about Sullivan."

"Check him out, then. Make a few phone calls. You'll find he's smart and tough. He has the qualifications and the clearances. And he knows the Agency, knows how we work. So he won't go rooting around where he's got no business. Really, he's ideal for the job."

"I'll do that." In fact, Everett was more than half convinced, but he had the uneasy feeling Tyrell was manipulating him. His objections were largely reflexive, mostly a matter of asserting his authority. "What makes you so sure he'll do it, anyway? I don't see anything in it for him."

"He's not like that. If it's put to him right, I think he will."

"You seem to know an awful lot about him."

"Of course I do." Tyrell might have been talking to a child. "I wouldn't recommend him otherwise. He's one of my closest friends. But I don't see," he added, "that that's necessarily a disadvantage."

"Oh, it's not." Everett looked at him for a moment. Then, almost against his will, his mouth began to twitch.

"Buddy of yours, is he?" he said softly. "I should have guessed."

The others had left, and the mood of near optimism produced
by Tyrell's suggestion had left with them. Now that he was alone
with Tyrell, Everett's antagonism was almost palpable.

"I imagine," he began, "you can guess what's on my mind."

"You're wondering about Theta."

"Yes. To be precise, I'm wondering if they turned him. I take it
you've been giving some thought to that?"

"Yes."

"And your conclusions?"

"I don't believe it."

"I envy your confidence. I wish I could share it."

"You don't have to. You weren't here when it started. If fingers
are pointed, it won't be at you."

"Believe it or not"—Everett's voice was icy—"that's not my
main concern. Although I'd naturally prefer not to preside over the
spy scandal of the decade . . . I want to know why you don't believe
it."

"His record," Tyrell offered. "Then there's the polygraph. Beyond that, it's intuition."

"What about the woman?"

"Oh, her," Tyrell said carelessly. "If we weeded out everyone
with unreliable girlfriends, there wouldn't be anyone left."

There was silence for a moment. Then Everett said, "Went to
school in England, didn't you?"

"Yes. Why?"

"I was wondering where you got your talent for understatement.
'Unreliable girlfriends,' you say. Hell, she was more than unreliable; from a security standpoint, she was murder.

"Look at the record," he continued. "Two arrests, for a start.
Drugs in L.A. in 1967, and the Chicago Convention riots a year
later. Member of the SDS. Picketed the White House over the
bombing of Cambodia."

"God bless the FBI," Tyrell murmured. "Where would we be
without them?"

"You can be sarcastic if you like, but the facts are there, and
they need an explanation."

"Youthful indiscretion. Anyway, those were impeccable liberal
credentials at the time."

"Impeccable credentials, huh? Well, how about these? Former lover a U.N. diplomat. Name of Bunin. Ivan Bunin. A Soviet citizen, and more than likely a KGB officer. Then, to cap everything, she worked for that outfit on Dupont Circle whose object is to discover and publish the names of our stationmen with diplomatic cover abroad."

"I see you've memorized the file."

"You bet I memorized it. I couldn't forget it if I tried. She was the worst kind of risk."

"Yes, she was." Tyrell smiled his infuriating smile. "That was the beauty of her."

Everett stared at him in blank amazement.

"That was the beauty of her? And you never checked her? I don't understand you guys. I don't understand you at all."

"We couldn't check her. Surely you understand that? Anyway, I think she looked more of a risk than she really was. She had convictions—not all of them silly— about how this society should be run. She was willing to act on some of them. She was willing to dissent, but I don't think she was willing to stretch it to treason."

"I take it you knew her?"

"I met her once. Casually. I liked her."

"I can imagine."

"Listen," Tyrell said, "I'm not disputing the facts. Of course she was a risk. But we weren't trusting her; we were trusting him. And the polygraph, and everything in his record, said we should trust him."

"You guarantee him then?"

"What difference does it make? The thing is done. If you're asking am I responsible, the answer is yes. It was my idea. I'm in it up to my neck . . . But if you're asking am I certain he didn't go bad, I can't help you. We're talking, in that case, about where a man lived, where his ultimate loyalties lay. You can't be sure of that. All you can do is go by the records: the interviews, the credit checks, the psych tests. They help some. They weed out the obvious ones. And the polygraph catches most of the rest. But it's not infallible. If you can lie without guilt, you can fool the machine every time. Most of us can't, of course, but some can. Who knows if Seligman was one of them?

"Look," he continued, "this is a different world. You'll come to understand that if you stay here long enough. When we talk about trust here, we don't mean the usual high-minded mixture of hope and intuition. We've been burned that way too many times. Anyone who ever knew Kim Philby—good old warmhearted, martini-swilling, never-let-a-a-friend-down Kim—can tell you that . . . No. When we talk about trust here, there's nothing intuitive about it. It's a provisional decision, based on necessity and nothing else. So ask me my intuition, and I'll tell you this: I think Paul Seligman was as loyal and dedicated a servant as the Agency ever had. But guarantee him? No way. There *are* no guarantees."

He departed then and left Everett confronting, once again, the frustrating paradox of his position. He was DCI, the overlord not only of the CIA but of every intelligence-gathering body in the nation. But he was an outsider—a fact Tyrell managed to remind him of almost every time they met. He had not worked his way up through the ranks, and the regulars disliked and distrusted him. The dislike he could handle—he was more than used to it—but the distrust was crippling. It left him Chief in name only. He could hire and fire, he had access at will to the President, he could entertain senators in his private dining room, but he was not in control. The place was too big, too compartmentalized; its past was cluttered with too many secrets. If he lived to be a hundred and spent the time reading, he would never exhaust the information in the files. And besides, he was certain that the real secrets—some of them—were not written down. So he was alone on the bridge, barking orders at his officers but never entirely sure they were being carried out, responsible in theory for everything that happened belowdecks, but never knowing exactly what was going on.

Theta was a case in point. There were no files on Theta. For obvious reasons there couldn't be. So Tyrell had had to brief him on it. And Tyrell's briefing, as Tyrell's briefings were apt to be, had been laconic. What Tyrell hadn't told him, he wouldn't have minded betting, had been greater, by several orders of magnitude, than what Tyrell had. But there was little he could do about it. For now, Tyrell was necessary, there was no one to replace him, he had to rely on him. But one day that would change . . . One day, he promised himself grimly, he was going to nail the son of a bitch.

It was something to dream about, and he let himself dream it a little. There was only one thing that took the gloss from it. If he ever did nail him, Tyrell would probably just smile.

CHAPTER 3

I

The meeting of the Senate Select Committee on Intelligence was held on the afternoon of June 28, ten days after the discovery of the body. To all appearances it was a bloodbath. The senators, particularly the Republicans, had nasty things to say about Agency security. The missing computer manuals, and the watch officer convicted of selling one to the Russians, were discussed again at considerable length. Chile was mentioned; so, at one point, was the Bay of Pigs. The relevance of these latter issues to the discussion at hand was never satisfactorily explained, but the senators were bent on enjoying themselves. Perhaps they felt that no discussion of Agency affairs could be considered complete without at least a passing mention of these subjects.

The battle was not, however, entirely one-sided. Marshall Everett also gave a good account of himself. He was properly scathing on the subject of irresponsible newspaper reporting, and his contempt included, by implication, those silly enough to take such reporting at face value. He was also eloquent on the subject of leaks. There were six congressional committees supervising various aspects of the Agency's operations, he said, and their staffers were often inadequately cleared and insufficiently discreet. Leaks had occurred, and they had done the Agency damage. Most of them, he was prepared to accept, were the result of carelessness rather than malice. But some were not. Some of them, it was his painful duty to relate—and when he did so he fixed the senators with his most arctic glare—some of them had been politically motivated.

No observers were present at the meeting; but had there been any, they might have come away thinking they had witnessed a good example of the system in action—the Legislature checking and balancing the Executive. They might therefore have been surprised to hear the comment made later that evening by Senator Scott Izakson of Wisconsin to a Republican colleague. The meeting reminded him, he said, of the all-in wrestling matches he had sometimes enjoyed watching on British television. The contestants dealt each other fearsome blows; there was a good deal of grunting and even more blood; and the pleasure of watching was by no means diminished by the knowledge that the damage inflicted was largely imaginary and that the result had been arranged before either party had climbed into the ring.

The senator was in a position to know what he was talking about. As the Republican chairman of a committee dominated by Democrats, he had not failed to notice that when the sound and fury had died away, the Democrats had quickly united behind a proposal brought forward by the Director of Central Intelligence. Being a cynical man, he was inclined to attribute this rare occurrence to a presidential breakfast held on the morning of the meeting, which several of the Democrats had attended. Had he been able to examine the White House telephone log for the day prior to the meeting, he would no doubt have considered his cynicism justified. For the log would have revealed that on no less than three occasions the President had spoken with the Director of Central Intelligence.

Shortly after the Committee reached its decision, Scott Izakson made a telephone call. He made it from a public phone booth downtown. When the other party answered, he spoke briefly and hung up. Then he went and bought himself a drink.

Fifteen minutes later he went back to the booth. Having checked to make sure that no one was hanging about, he went inside and waited, busying himself meanwhile by looking up a number.

Presently the phone rang.

"Stonemason?"

"Speaking."

"Listen. It's settled. The Committee has opted for a limited investigation. We tried to make it general, but we were outvoted."

"That's a pity." The voice at the other end of the line was flat and curiously colorless.

"Yes. Somebody got to the Democrats. No prizes for guessing who. Anyway, it's to be Seligman only, and conducted by an ex–Agency man. The name is Morgan Sullivan. He lives in Georgetown. Somewhere on K Street. He's in the phone book. He hasn't been asked yet, and he may not agree. But I thought you'd want to know."

"Certainly. It will be in the newspapers tomorrow, but it's always useful to know these things early."

"It won't be in the papers." Izakson resented any implication that minimized the value of his contributions. "Everett insisted on that. He didn't quote wish to lend credence to unfounded rumors unquote. The Committee bought that. I doubt even the Secretary will get the whole story. We can be clams when we want to be."

It was only after he hung up that the silence that greeted his last remark struck Izakson as ironic.

II

The pitch was twenty-five feet, angling up and across the face to a ledge somewhat to the left of where Sullivan was standing. The first half was easy, holds falling comfortably under the hands and feet as though nature, in carving the rock, had spared a kindly thought for climbers; but the last ten feet leaned out and would require a series of difficult moves to the left to avoid the worst of the overhang.

Sullivan, waiting to climb, was nervous. He hadn't been near a face in more than a year, and he was out of condition. Tyrell had promised him a staircase. Nothing grueling, he'd said, nothing too technical, just a gentle workout to get Sullivan back into the feel. To Tyrell it probably was; but Tyrell was an expert, at the peak of condition, and notoriously blind to the limitations of others. To Sullivan, the prospect of working around that overhang brought moist palms and tremors at the pit of his stomach.

It was therefore calming to see Tyrell moving, as always, with ease and confidence. He had paused after fifteen feet to set his protection, a chock wedged into a crack in the rock and attached by wire to a carabiner, and he was now preparing to move out around the overhang. It was the first time he had paused on the pitch, and it would probably be the last. There were two kinds of climbers, Sullivan thought: planners and improvisers. The improvisers, after a glance at the difficulties, would go at a pitch bullheaded, solving problems as they came to them, groping around for holds, stopping, reversing, considering, experimenting. Planners, on the other hand, would solve the problems before committing themselves, noting the holds, estimating the stretches, figuring out which hand or foot would go where, reducing the climb to an abstraction—a sequence of exercises in body mechanics—so that when they were committed to the rock the pitch would be taken, as nearly as possible, in a single, flowing continuum of motion. This, to Sullivan, represented the ideal of the art. Tyrell embodied it, and watching him was the chief pleasure of these expeditions. Sullivan himself would lumber along behind, sweating a lot, scaring himself a little, and letting Roy drag him over the hard places.

Tyrell was making the traverse now, moving swiftly but without strain or hurry, working out from the rock, letting his legs take the weight and using his hands mostly as anchors when he shifted his feet. There was no hesitation about his movements, no scrabbling or groping at the rock. Instead, he planted his limbs as precisely as if he were climbing a ladder.

It was still early, but the temperature was in the nineties, and the humidity rising from the marshes covered them like a fog. Tyrell, wearing Levi's to protect his legs from scrapes, had removed his shirt. Sullivan could only marvel, once again, at his condition. Tyrell was over six feet. His build was far from slight, but his ratio of strength to weight was one that Sullivan, for all his experience of college linebackers, with biceps like beer kegs and forearms like hams, had never seen equaled. There was no fat on the man. Beneath the skin, now shiny with sweat, the structure of bunching sliding muscle was perfectly defined. Sullivan, knowing the hours of labor put into that body—the thousands of push-ups, chin-ups, and sit-ups—and envying slightly the dedication involved, would sometimes tease him about it, accusing Tyrell of narcissism or overcompensation for the onset of middle age. But Tyrell only grinned. "I like," he answered simply, letting his glance rest for a second on Sullivan's surplus poundage, "to have a body that works."

He had reached the ledge and was looking around for a fissure to hold the chock that would anchor the belay.

"There's one tight bit," he called down. "It's just before you round the overhang. You'll need to change feet. Bring your right across to your left and switch so you can make the next stretch. There's not enough room for both your big feet, so if you blow it you'll be relying on your hands. There's a good place for your right, but the left is just a bump. Make sure you're locked in with the right before you try it."

"Hey!" Sullivan sounded aggrieved. "This was supposed to be a staircase, remember? It's fine for you—you weigh less than a mosquito, and you do chin-ups every night. I'm two thirty-five, and all I lift is Schlitz. I think I'm going home."

"Morgan, will you quit thinking about the beer and get on up here! It's hotter than hell on this ledge."

"OK. OK. On belay, then." Sullivan made a final check of his harness.

"On belay." Tyrell was never casual about procedures.

"Climbing."

Once he was on the rock, Sullivan's nerves left him. It was granite, rough and cool to the touch. The feel of it, solid beneath his hands, not crumbly like sandstone, or flaky like slate, reassured him. He reached the overhang without difficulty and paused there to contemplate the switch.

The toehold Tyrell had told him about was an indentation in the rock, an inch deep and maybe two inches wide, angled about thirty degrees below the horizontal. It was a good hold—if he could get his right foot into it—but to do so he would have to swing his weight across from the handholds directly above his head and two feet to the left of it. Ideally the switch would be made using the momentum of the move, so that his fingers would not have to bear the full burden of his weight for more than a fraction of a second. The problem was that the momentum, while moving him sideways, would tend to pull him out, so the force on his fingers would be as much lateral as vertical. He hoped the crack for his right hand was as solid as Tyrell claimed.

Reaching up, he explored it with his fingers. It was deep enough to accommodate two joints, and there was a slight, but heartening, lip around which his fingers would be able to form a hook. For a maestro like Tyrell, it was virtually a fortress. For himself . . . He preferred life insurance.

"You want some tension?"

"Might be as well." Sullivan's mouth was dryer than his voice.

In response Tyrell took the slack out of the rope, drawing it just tight enough to give Sullivan a stabilizing sense of its presence, but not so tight that it would interfere with his balance or impede his movement.

"OK?"

"Fine."

He swung his right foot to the hold, pulling with his arms as his body came across so the weight was taken by his shoulders. As his foot reached the hold, he slid the other out to make room for it. He felt his toe touch the lip and stick. But he was too far out, and as the full weight came down on it, it gave.

"Tension!"

Both feet were scraping at the rock. His right hand was solid, but the left, awkwardly cupped around a bump that seemed, at this moment, to have dwindled to a pimple, was starting to slip.

"Falling!"

But he wasn't. Tyrell hauled on the rope, taking the pressure off his hands, at the same moment as his foot slid back into the hold.

"Easy." Tyrell's voice was relaxed. "OK. Now you've got it. The rest is a formality."

He was grinning when Sullivan reached the ledge. "You climb like a gorilla. Effective, but terribly untidy."

The second pitch was longer, thirty-five feet to a ledge on the right. Tyrell took this one fast too, stopping after fifteen feet to fix protection, then moving upward again like a spider. Sullivan, anchored to the same belay Tyrell had used, hoped he would stop and set another chock before he reached the ledge. For by then he would be twenty feet above the last chock, and the drop, if he fell, would be all of forty feet. He would miss the ledge where Sullivan was sitting, since he was well to the right of it, but the face was not vertical, and the rock was like emery paper. He could take all his skin off bouncing down that face.

When it became clear that Tyrell had no intention of stopping, Sullivan thought of saying something. But he didn't. He was the less experienced climber, and he knew Tyrell disliked interruptions. Besides, he would pay no attention. It was his one flaw as a climber, going too far above his protection; but he did it consciously, recognizing the risk and welcoming it.

"What the hell do we climb for anyway?" he once asked when Sullivan criticized him for it. "Why don't we just stick to bouldering? The problems are the same. So are the moves. You can even try things bouldering you wouldn't dream of on a face. Because you know if you miss you'll just end up on the grass with nothing hurt but your pride.

"And right there is the difference. The degree of risk. That's what we're here for. Because here, if you make a mistake, the consequences are real. You can hurt yourself, and you can kill yourself. At the very least, you scare yourself shitless . . . Oh sure, I could set protection every five feet. But if I did that, I might just as well stick to bouldering. I'd have destroyed my reason for climbing in the first place."

It was not an argument that appealed to Sullivan. Nor, he suspected, would it persuade many climbers. There was risk enough already, even if you took the kinds of precaution Tyrell deprecated. Ropes could part, and often did. Rock could crumble. You could fall ten feet awkwardly and break your neck. People did it all the time. Even people as competent as Roy Tyrell.

He said so at the time, but it made no impression.

"Listen," Tyrell answered, "we live an average of about seventy years, right? Half that time we're either senile or babies. And what we do with the rest makes no damn difference to anyone but ourselves. To the eye of heaven it's invisible. Besides, heaven isn't watching. So we'd better make damned sure it matters to us. Oh, we can creep safely from cradle to grave. And there's no lack of people—governments, insurance companies, and the like—exhorting us to do it. But what's the point? What do we have, in that case, to prove we've ever been alive? And who gives a shit?

"But when I'm twenty-five feet above my protection and eight hundred feet off the ground, and I know that if I make a mistake or get unlucky I'm going to fall fifty to eight hundred feet and maybe all the lights will go out, when the adrenaline starts pumping and the mind hardens to a point and my body becomes a very precious part of me and not just some piece of baggage I'm forced to cart about, when all of me is focused on the business of getting me to the next ledge, then, whether I get there or not, I know, for those moments at least, I've been alive.

"And I have to know that," he concluded, smiling to take the earnestness out of his words. "I have to know it. Even if I have to kill myself for the knowledge."

"I believe I've heard Roy Tyrell's credo" was Sullivan's laughing rejoinder. "It's the ultimate variant on Descartes: 'I die, therefore I am.' "

But Tyrell would live today, he decided, watching that spiderman on the last five feet before the ledge. He was past the last real difficulty, a big stretch across to the right, and there seemed nothing but handholds between him and safety.

"Rock!"

At the sound of Tyrell's voice, Sullivan ducked. A head-sized lump hurtled past on the right, a shower of pebbles skittering after it. Automatically the fingers of his right hand clamped around the rope, his arm shuttering across his chest in the correct belay position so the friction of the rope across his back would absorb the impact of a fall.

When he looked up, Tyrell was hanging by one hand. A foothold must have given, and the jerk had torn his left hand free. Now his right arm was at full stretch, and he could no longer reach a hold with his left. He was not scrabbling at the rock with his feet, however, in the instinctive, exhausting reaction that would have been Sullivan's in the same situation. He was just hanging there calmly, his feet exploring the rock systematically for any small offer of purchase.

Sullivan could do nothing to help him. Any tension on the rope from below would only add to the strain on Tyrell's fingers. He could only brace himself and watch.

Tyrell gave up the attempt to find a foothold. The nearest one was too far above his feet. If he tried to reach it, he might jerk his hand loose. For a second he hung, gathering himself. Then, with an explosive grunt, he pulled.

His whole body shook with the effort. His bicep bunched. The muscles of his shoulder and forearm stood out in knots. Slowly, centimeter by centimeter, the angle at his elbow narrowed. But even as it did, Sullivan could see his strength ebbing, feel it draining out of him.

It seemed he must give up. His left hand, clawing, was still inches below the crack it sought. Then, suddenly it was there. His fingers, finding the hold, curled and locked into it.

The rest was easy. With both hands secure, he could pull himself up to the foothold. That done, he rested.

It was not until he was safely on the ledge that either spoke. Then it was Sullivan who did.

"Untidy," he said. "Effective, but terribly untidy."

III

Tyrell lay back in the shade of a rock, sucking thoughtfully at his beer and from time to time examining the damage to his hand.

"Hurt, does it?" Sullivan asked.

"Left some skin behind when it jerked loose from that hold. Nothing serious, but it's tender."

"Can't say I sympathize." Sullivan grinned at him. "Perhaps it'll teach you something about protection."

Tyrell shook his head.

"Morgan, for an allegedly trained legal mind you're an illogical son of a bitch."

"How come?"

"I tore my hand because I made a mistake. I'd have made the same mistake whether the protection was three feet away or thirty. So if it teaches me anything, it should be about making mistakes, not about protection."

"Well, sure. But my point was that you can make mistakes. So you should think more carefully about what's liable to happen when you do.

"You know," he continued, "I sometimes wonder why I climb with you at all. Every time I do you scare the shit out of me."

"Beats me. I think you must like it. Anyway, it's good for you."

"Good for me? The hell it is. I age visibly with every pitch . . . No. It must be the Samaritan in me. I want to be around to help pick up the pieces."

"Well, in that case, don't bother. If it came to that, I'd rather you let them rot where they lay."

"Perhaps I could put them back together. I owe you that, at least. You did it for me once, remember?"

Sullivan was suddenly serious.

It was true, not in a physical sense, but in a way just as real. It was after Charley had been killed. He had come home almost literally in pieces. One piece, his body, had continued to function; it slept, healed, fed itself, found a job, even read for the Bar exams—did all that was needed, in fact, to give a passable imitation of living. But it was an empty performance, the reflex twitching of an organism after the life has departed. The rest of him, it seemed, had decided to lie down with Charley.

He saw nobody. His family was dead, and his Agency acquaintances were simply jarring reminders of a past he had left in the ground. By day, he worked furiously, losing himself in the arid complexities of the Maryland statutes. The evenings he spent at home, playing the piano, watching the darkness fall on his garden, half listening to the Haydn quartets whose weaving melodies were like a web of sound suspended by will across a pit of silence, looking into a future that seemed unnecessarily extended.

One evening the doorbell rang. There on the doorstep, his arms full of bottles, stood Roy Tyrell.

"Morgan," he said, "I'm told you're not drinking these days. I may be wrong—I probably am—but I think you need to get drunk."

He'd known Tyrell before that, but not well. They'd joined the Agency at roughly the same time, run into each other at meetings and parties, liked each other at sight and made mental notes to see more of each other, notes that, of course, they had never acted upon. So Tyrell's appearance that evening contained an element of the miraculous. Like one of those conjuring tricks where the magician takes out of his ear a scarf he put into his pocket, it seemed a guarantee against the tyranny of the expected.

They had indeed gotten drunk that night, consuming the wine Tyrell had brought and a fifth of Glenlivet on top. And they'd talked. They'd talked about music, about football, about the relative merits of French and California wines, about the virtues of single-malt Scotch. They'd talked about the war, about the Agency, about death, about Charley. They'd talked logically at first, then lightly, and at last with the profound incoherence of the seriously intoxicated. And as they talked, Sullivan had ceased gradually to feel like an invalid. Tyrell had none of the hospital tact that Sullivan had found so debilitating. He didn't pretend that nothing had happened, but behind his acknowledgment that it had was the plain, if unspoken, assumption that Sullivan could face it and survive.

So next morning, underneath the malaise that afflicts a system half poisoned by liquor, Sullivan could sense a return of the spirit. It was not that his grief had diminished—it did later, though it never left him entirely—but simply that it had found its proper place. Living and grieving were not mutually exclusive; they were more nearly inseparable.

The pieces had started to come together.

"You're a sentimental bastard." Tyrell read his thoughts and dismissed them. "And you give me too much credit. I simply brought booze to a man who seemed to be dying of thirst . . . Speaking of which, pass the cooler, will you? I'm in serious need of a beer."

For a while they were silent, Sullivan examining the face they had climbed, Tyrell watching him thoughtfully.

"Morgan?"

"Yeah?"

"We have a problem."

"Who do you mean 'we'?"

"I mean the Agency."

Sullivan sat up.

"And it concerns me?"

"We'd like it to."

"Then you'd better tell me about it. Only I hope you don't mean what I think you mean."

Tyrell told him. Sullivan listened without interruption until he had finished.

"Why me?"

"You're right for it, primarily. Then, I'm not sure who else is available."

"So it's not a personal thing? It's something for them, not for you?"

"No. I want you to be clear about that. It's strictly official . . . Personally, of course, there's no one I'd sooner have do it. But that's neither here nor there."

"In that case . . . I'm sorry. I'm not available."

"I'm sorry too," Tyrell said evenly. "I thought perhaps you'd forgiven us by now."

"It's not that. It never was that, really. The business about the transfer was what pushed me over the edge. But I was through long before."

"Then why won't you?"

Sullivan didn't answer this directly; instead he said, "I do owe the Agency one thing. It showed me who I am."

"What the hell does that mean?"

"How can I explain . . ." Sullivan thought a bit. "It's like this. What is it they tell you at the Agency when they're trying to recruit you? What's the sales pitch?"

"I don't know." Tyrell thought about it. Then he grinned. "I seem to remember they told me I was damn lucky to be considered."

"That's what they told me too." Sullivan nodded. "Now just why were we so damn lucky?"

"The longer I'm there, the more I wonder." Tyrell made a face. "You tell me."

"I think it's this. You're lucky, the implication is, because you're one of the chosen few—one of the few smart enough, and loyal enough, and tough enough to be trusted to fight the secret war for the preservation of your country's institutions and values. There's a lot at stake in this war; the enemy is determined and unscrupulous. So we can't afford to be too finicky about the weapons we employ. Sure, there are supposed to be rules—there's the law and the Constitution—and we honor them, as far as we can. But we can't always afford to. It may be necessary to bend the rules sometimes. We may have to tap people's phones; we may have to blackmail them about their sex lives; we may have to beat the shit out of them; we may even have to kill them. We don't like to do these things, of course, but we don't have any choice. And that's why we need people like you. Because people like you have the intelligence to realize these things need to be done and the integrity not to abuse the privilege.

"There's a flattery implied in that invitation which is very dangerous. If you believe it, it corrupts you. Little by little the knowledge that you are privileged to ignore the rules for special purposes can become the belief that all your purposes are special. You stop asking: why are we doing this? is the result worth the cost? And when you do that, it's all over. Anything goes.

"I know this because I was there. I got to believing catching spies was so damn important that whatever I had to do to catch them I was damn well entitled to do. In the end I was beating the shit out of skinny little Vietnamese kids for information of marginal value in a war I had long since ceased to believe in. That's why I quit. I'd found out what I could become—if the circumstances were right. And that's why I'm not going back. Not for six months, not for six weeks. Not ever."

"You do make a production out of it, don't you?" Tyrell's voice was still calm, but his question had an edge to it that made Sullivan look up in surprise.

"Make a production out of what?"

"Guilt . . . There's a lot in what you say, of course. But I can't help feeling your confession of frailty is a little overdone. You see, I know what happened to you in Vietnam; I made a point of finding out. You didn't beat the shit out of skinny little kids at all. Just one . . . one time, in very special circumstances, when you were right at the end of your tether, you forgot yourself. So don't paint me a picture of some big Nazi bully. I know better. You're not corrupt, Morgan, you're just overreceptive to guilt."

"Perhaps." Sullivan was curt.

"And there's another thing. You wouldn't be working for us anyway. You'd be on the side of the good guys. Your mandate would run from the Committee."

"Then why doesn't the Committee do its own recruiting? Look, Roy, it's the same thing. I don't care whose name appears on the bottom of the paper. I don't want to do it. OK?"

"OK." Tyrell shrugged. "I told them you might not be willing. I guess I'll have to go back and tell them to find someone else. But before I do that, I'd like you to think about this . . ."

He paused. His voice was very quiet. He was still in the same sprawling posture he'd assumed at the outset of the conversation, but beneath his calm Sullivan could sense the gathering anger.

". . . That investigation is going to happen. Someone is going to do it, and the odds are he won't do it as fairly as you . . . There is a war going on, Morgan, and these jobs have to be done. They do need special people to do them—people like you who care about justice. But if the people like you are too damn high-minded to get their hands dirty, then we'll have to get somebody else who's not so fucking scrupulous. The problem with that is, maybe justice won't be done. Maybe somebody will get shafted. It happens all the time. And you know it does . . . But that's OK with you. You won't be involved. You'll have your integrity, and somebody else will foot the bill."

"That's not fair!" Now Sullivan was angry.

"Isn't it? Maybe you're right. In any case, I don't want to fight about it . . . But do me a favor, will you? Stop giving me that crap about corruption. Because I happen to work for the Agency myself—though it may have slipped your mind for the moment—and I manage to live with myself just fine. In fact, I think it's an honor."

"Dammit, Roy! I didn't mean it that way. You know I didn't. I was talking about me, not about anyone else."

"Weren't you? It sounded pretty general to me. Perhaps I'm being oversensitive, but I had a fairly strong sense of being included."

He got up and started to busy himself with the gear. Presently Sullivan came over and helped him. They avoided looking at each other.

"Roy." Sullivan sounded unhappy. "That was tactless of me. I didn't think you'd take it personally. I didn't mean it that way. Please believe that."

"Don't worry about it." Tyrell still didn't look at him. "We see things differently, that's all. You may be right. I don't see it. But you may be."

"Look, let me think about it. OK? I can't promise to change my mind. But I can do that at least . . . I'll call you in the morning."

"Why don't you do that," Tyrell said.

BOOK TWO

July 18, 1978–August 3, 1978

CHAPTER 4

I

"You don't have to be Einstein to guess who it is."

Sullivan said nothing. It had taken Everett most of the meal to get to the point. Now that he was there, Sullivan felt no inclination to help him. If Everett felt awkward—and his serpentine approach to the subject that preoccupied them both suggested that he did—then the cause might be worth knowing. The less Sullivan said, in that case, the more Everett's squirming might reveal. Silence, Sullivan had learned, was often the best questioner.

The invitation to lunch, on his first day at the Agency, had not surprised Sullivan. It was a ritual courtesy, he recalled, as common in government circles as it was elsewhere. Nor had the manner of it alarmed him unduly. "Welcome aboard." The note, in Everett's sprawling, confident handwriting, had awaited him on the desk in the spacious, unnecessarily luxurious office the Agency had provided. "If you're free for lunch, I'd like you to join me. One o'clock sharp. Please confirm with my secretary. Tyrell will show you where to go." The signature, Sullivan noted, occupied most of the lower third of the page.

Welcome aboard? It was not Sullivan's notion of where he now was; nor, he suspected, would it be the Committee's. But the wording was probably harmless, intended, perhaps, to remind him gently whose ship it was he was boarding, but not necessarily implying that Everett considered him a member of the crew.

What had surprised him, though, was the realization that he was to lunch alone with the Director. Having spent the morning with

Roy, being briefed on background, obtaining the ID and passes necessary for his stay at the Agency, and meeting Patterson, Brayer, Eglinton, and the rest of the officers with whom the inquiry was likely to bring him into contact, he'd assumed naturally that some of them, at least, would be present at lunch. But when the time had come, Roy had taken him up to the Director's private dining room on the seventh floor and left him at the door.

"Not invited," was his response to Sullivan's startled inquiry. "None of us were. It must be one of those occasions where three would be a crowd."

So the Director evidently had more than courtesy in mind. But what his purpose was the conversation during the first two courses—prosciutto with melon and a very lightly grilled sole— had not succeeded in making clear. It was not that the talk had been idle—Sullivan doubted the Director's talk was ever that— but it had traveled regions remote from the one Sullivan had expected to explore. Instead of getting down to business, Everett had launched, after a few offhand questions about mutual acquaintances and Sullivan's previous connection with the Agency, into a monologue on the condition of his ship.

Things were bad, he told Sullivan. The Agency's reputation had never been lower. Hardly a week went by without the publication of some new exposé of its incompetence and corruption. The whole concept of intelligence had become suspect with the American people, and the Agency's name was now virtually synonymous with dirty tricks. Morale at the Agency, in consequence, was almost nonexistent; it had become impossible to recruit personnel of the right caliber; longtime employees were resigning in droves— and most of them, it seemed, were writing books.

It was not only morale that had suffered. The revelations of Watergate had prompted the creation of a whole pack of watchdog subcommitees; now the Agency could hardly go to the bathroom without obtaining congressional clearance, and given the confiding nature of subcommittees, the news became public before the bowl had been flushed. For this reason, friendly foreign services, once a major source of product, were backing away. Liaison with the SDECE in France was at an end; the West Germans were cool and distant; and the British . . . Only last week, it appeared, they had read him a lecture on the need for greater protection of their material.

But the real question, he continued, backing away from these humbling reflections, was how the whole situation had been brought about. Watergate was obviously part of the answer; so was the Agency's unfortunate record of goofs. But the Director personally doubted that this was by any means the whole story.

"If you look at the evidence," he'd continued, "and of course we keep a record of every damn thing that's ever been written about us, you begin to suspect that there's a pattern. It's too persistent, this campaign against us, and it's too widespread. When you start checking individual stories, you find, much too often, that they originate from unnamed diplomatic sources or with anonymous phone calls. Only last week, for example"—he paused to emphasize the significance of his next words—"the *Washington Post* received an anonymous phone call. The caller said he had information about Seligman which the *Post* might find it worthwhile to check into. Seligman was alive and well, he said, and currently living in Moscow.

"Now it's easy to dismiss something like that as the work of a crank. And the *Post* won't act on it. They're not that irresponsible. But they'll file it away somewhere, and eventually someone, some cub reporter with dreams of being the next Woodward or Bernstein, will get hold of it and use it. And that suggests an explanation that's not so comforting. Maybe the call wasn't made by a crank. Maybe it was made by someone who wants to keep this story alive—just as other stories about us have been kept alive. There could be someone directing this chorus of denigration. And in that case you don't have to be Einstein to guess who it is."

He waited some moments for Sullivan to respond, resuming only when it was clear he was not going to.

"My point, of course, is that this whole episode is intensely embarrassing for the Agency. It's fresh evidence of our incompetence. It's one more nail in the coffin of our relationships with foreign intelligence services. It's another wedge driven between us and the Pentagon. And the inquiry itself will do nothing for Agency morale." He paused. "It might be as well to bear all this in mind. Seligman's death, the manner and timing of it, raise obvious questions. They're why you're here. But you shouldn't ignore the possibility that things might have been planned that way."

Sullivan considered.

"A KGB black operation?" he asked. "Seligman murdered in circumstances calculated to throw suspicion on him and the Agency? The whole thing backed by a campaign of leaks and whispers?"

Everett nodded.

"It's a possibility, I suppose. I'll certainly bear it in mind."

"Then there's something else you should consider." Everett returned to the attack. "And that's the treaty."

"The SALT treaty?"

"Yes. From that point of view, the timing is horrendous. Seligman couldn't have chosen a worse moment—if he did—to dump himself in the Bay. Look at it! Public debate on the treaty is starting to heat up. The opposition is already staking out its ground. A key issue, obviously, will be verification, our ability to ensure that the other side is not dealing off the bottom of the deck. The last thing we need, at this point, are questions about the integrity of the satellite systems . . . What I'm getting at is this: your inquiry, whether we like it or not, will be used as a stick to beat the treaty with. And the longer it drags on, the worse it's going to be."

It was Sullivan's distinct impression that the Director was inclined to blame him personally, if not for the inquiry itself, then for its continued existence. It was on the tip of his tongue to point out that this attitude was a touch premature, the inquiry being at that moment less than four hours old. Instead he said, "But the existence of the inquiry was not supposed to have been made public—or so I understood."

"Of course not." Everett looked at him pityingly. "But the Committee contains three known, and two probable, opponents of the treaty. They all placed their hands on their hearts, of course, and swore on their honor as registered Republicans never to breathe a word to anyone. But you can take it from me, as one who has reason to know, that Committee will leak like a rusty bucket.

"And that means," he went on, "that premature conclusions could be worse than none at all. I'd hate to see your findings dribble out via the Committee to the press. We've already had a taste of what those bastards can do."

"Let me see if I read you correctly." Sullivan was tired of beating about the bush. "You want this thing wrapped up in a hurry. Am I right? And in the meantime you want me to stay clear of the Committee?"

"You read me right." Everett nodded. "On both points."

"Well . . ." Sullivan considered. "As to the second, I think I can reassure you: I'll go back to the Committee when I have something concrete to report. Not before. On the other matter . . ." He hesitated. "It'll probably turn out to be a question of do you want it Tuesday, or do you want it good?"

"Both."

"I'll do my best, naturally. But if it comes to a choice, I think I can guess what the Committee's preference will be."

For a moment Everett seemed to hesitate. Then he said, "I was with the President yesterday. He specifically asked about the inquiry. He wanted to know if I could give him some kind of timetable. I told him I'd have to talk to you. My impression was, though, that as far as he's concerned, Tuesday will be barely soon enough."

There was a long silence. Everett's stare pressed heavily on Sullivan. Behind that stare, Sullivan could sense, was all the Director's impressive force of will.

He wondered once again what he was doing here. Was it a continuing sense of obligation to Roy that had brought him back? Or was it duty? Had Roy persuaded him of the existence of a debt to the Republic as yet not totally discharged? Or was it, perhaps, that there lingered in him still some remnant of the instinct that had plagued him all his life—the inability to pass a flat stone without first turning it over to see what might be lurking underneath? It was all three, probably. But if he were honest, he would have to admit that the last motive had been strongest. When he'd called Roy to announce his change of heart, he'd been depressed and apprehensive, responding, he thought, from a reluctant sense of duty. But in the days that followed, days of clearing his desk at the office, distributing his cases among his overworked but uncomplaining partners, and waiting for the update of his security clearance, he'd sensed in himself a mounting excitement. His instinct told him there was something nasty under this particular flat stone, that he would find it and bring it to the light. Beside that prospect his law practice—even the Bourne appeal, which he'd insisted on retaining—seemed humdrum. Perhaps this was why the Director's attempts to crowd him, to steer him in certain directions before he had had a chance to get his bearings, had begun to irritate him.

"You'll forgive me for saying this." He met Everett's stare with an equally forceful one of his own, the thrust of his words belying the polite formula he used to introduce them. "But there is one thing which strikes me rather forcibly—you seem very certain what it is I'm going to find."

"No." Everett's tone was definite. "That's not true at all. I have an opinion, of course. I'd be less than honest if I said I didn't. But I'd be fooling myself if I didn't admit that it's based primarily on hope. Look, no one's trying to prejudge this thing. If Seligman— or anyone—went bad, I want to know. In that case, we have a cancer, and it has to come out. And the quicker the better. All I'm saying is I don't want to spend eighteen months in exploratory surgery. That happened with Spearman's thing, and it damn near killed us.

"I guess what's bothering me a little," he continued, "is that you refused our offer of staff. I can understand your wish to preserve the appearance of being independent, but I can hardly believe you plan to do this alone. If that's the case, I imagine we can expect your report sometime in the mid-eighties—in time for SALT III, possibly, or SALT IV."

Staff, Sullivan thought. Sure. A bunch of eager little spooks looking over my shoulder and trotting off to report to you. Some independent inquiry that will be.

"I didn't refuse outright. I told Roy I didn't know what my requirements would be. I don't want to keep your people sitting on their hands until I make up my mind. When I do, I'll tell you.

"And another thing," he continued. "This inquiry takes its mandate from the Senate Committee. Not from the Agency. Not even from the President. So it won't be any whitewash. It's not just going to appear independent; it's going to be independent."

"You misunderstand me." Everett backed off a little. "I didn't mean to imply otherwise. I must have chosen my words badly . . . So I'm to tell the President you'll proceed with all convenient speed, but with no definite timetable as yet?"

"Yes. Unless what he's looking for is not a timetable but just some sort of wild, reassuring guess."

There was another long silence. When Everett next spoke, it was to change the subject.

"Have you ever been in the Oval Office?" he asked.

Sullivan shook his head.

"Odd thing," Everett continued. "I can never go in there without thinking I've stepped into a different world. It's a simple matter of a yard or two. Down the corridor you're in familiar territory: people dashing about, counting heads, planning strategy for the passage of this bill or that, trading and selling. The talk is a hybrid of Madison Avenue and the Hudson Institute: game plans, fall-back positions, polls and images . . . In there it's different. There isn't actually a placard that says 'The buck stops here'; it's not necessary. The whole room says it. It's alive with history. The ghosts are all still in there, whispering to you. 'The decisions are made here,' they say. 'They're made by the man behind the desk.' And you start thinking about those decisions, the words uttered or written there that changed the lives of millions. And it awes you. You're in the room, you suddenly realize, where the Emancipation Proclamation was signed, where the decisions to enter two world wars were taken, where the order was given for Hiroshima and Nagasaki."

Everett paused.

"It's hard to pin down the feeling that office gives you. But I guess if I had to put it in a nutshell, I'd say the difference between it and, say, the Caucus Room in the Senate would be the difference between statesmanship and politics. Politics is trading, a series of compromises between interest groups. The decisions taken in that room, many of them, affect everyone."

He pushed back his chair and got to his feet.

"I'll be speaking to the President about our talk," he said. "He's asked to be kept posted on your progress . . . And I'll expect to hear from you about staffing. In the meantime, if there's anything you need, be sure to let Roy know."

When Sullivan returned to his office Tyrell was there, lounging on the sofa, with his feet on the coffee table in front of it. He was reading the *Wall Street Journal*.

"IBM is up," he said. "Du Pont and General Motors are down. What you gain on the roundabouts you more than lose on the swings . . . How was your lunch?"

"Instructive," Sullivan grunted. "Instructive and a little de-pressing."

"Depressing?"

"Yes. He had a message for me. He didn't put it in so many words, but it came through loud and clear."

"And what was it?"

"They want a clean bill of health and they want it yesterday."

"Who's 'they'?"

"Everett and the President."

"Ah." Tyrell smiled. "Brought in the President, did he? He's fond of doing that."

"It wasn't the person so much as the office. He treated me to a history lesson. The Senate was politics, he said, referring, I imagine, to my inquiry. The Oval Office was history—"

"And the Emancipation Proclamation was signed there? Correct? And the decision to enter two world wars was made there?"

"How did you know? Do you have the place wired?"

"I've heard that speech." Tyrell shrugged. "So what did you say?"

"I didn't say anything. I was doing the listening. But I know what I wanted to say."

"Let me guess," Tyrell said. "You wanted to say what I always want to say. It was there, you wanted to say, that Lincoln signed the Proclamation. But it was also there that Nixon told Dean to go out and lie like a two-dollar watch."

"Yes." Sullivan grinned. "I think it was something like that."

II

Sullivan took the photographs and laid them side by side across the desk. They were nine-by-fifteen blowups, of varying quality, the definition, in one case, slightly blurred by the enlargement . . . Seligman at the helm of his sloop, frowning toward an indefinite horizon. An action study, Sullivan thought, and made by a photographer of some talent, conveying in the thrust of the head, the set of the mouth, the tension of sinew in the gnarled and weathered forearm, a feeling of competence and strength . . . Seligman on the deck of the *Excalibur*, a relaxed, informal portrait in which the outlines of the man semed softer, less definite. Stripped to the waist, a roll of fat spilling over the waistband of his shorts, he leaned, beer in hand, against the cabin of his boat. The prematurely white beard and the tufts of hair that sprouted from either side of his head gave him, in this shot, the air of a benevolent Neptune, running slightly to seed . . . Seligman on vacation, reclining in a deck chair. A typical holiday snap—except, perhaps, that the air of well-being seemed a trifle forced, the pose a shade too self-consciously relaxed. There were creases around the eyes,

Sullivan noticed, which could have been wrinkles of good humor—
or lines of stress . . . Seligman, finally, in close-up, the official
Agency portrait, obtained from his personnel file and taken, obviously, some time ago. A mask, this one, surface without depth;
the mouth expressionless, the eyes clouded and opaque.

Four different views of a man; yet they had qualities in common. There was intelligence, certainly, in the high forehead and
the humorous lines of the mouth. Strength, also, in the rough-cut
solidity of the features. Intolerance, too, perhaps, in the way each
feature seemed a little out of balance with the rest: the nose too
prominent, the chin too jutting, the eyes too deeply set. Above all,
there was the quality the Romans had called *gravitas*, a sense of
weight and purpose. Whatever this man had done or been, he had
chosen it deliberately, after careful consideration of the alternatives and consequences.

A line from Shakespeare intruded suddenly on Sullivan's
thoughts: "There's no art to find the mind's construction in the
face." And that was true. Faces were all masks, conveying here and
there a hint of character behind them, but leaving the real man
hidden. Actions alone revealed the man. But here the actions were
what was hidden. So he must work with what he had—words, pictures, impressions, the fragmented history of behavior—attempting to reconstruct an image of the man, and hoping to work from
what he was to what he might have done.

He turned to the personnel file. It was very thick. Seligman had
been twenty-four years with the Agency, and the file recorded, in
detail, every step of his progress from junior analyst of Soviet
military equipment to Deputy Director of the Office of Strategic
Research, a position that carried the high-powered civil service
grade of GS 17. Sullivan read it all, making notes occasionally on
the scratch pad at his elbow, and paying special attention to the
handwritten comments, many of them faded now and almost
illegible, scrawled in the margins of some of the entries. Details
like these fascinated him. It was the accumulation of them, he
knew, that would enable him, eventually, to create a portrait in
depth.

Nevertheless, when he looked over his notes after two and a
half hours of patient reading, he found they added little to the
impression he'd gained from the photographs. Intelligence and
purpose were plainly confirmed in the way Seligman had set out,

from his first moment at the Agency, to make himself master of his subject. He'd attended, it seemed, every available seminar. He'd taken courses in conversational and technical Russian, courses in computer programming, courses in statistical analysis and Marxist economics. He'd even taken a course in speed reading, presumably to enable him to keep up with the avalanche of reports that must have spilled across his desk. The efficiency reports filed annually by his superiors were a chorus of praise to his dedication and expertise.

Here and there, of course, a discordant note was sounded. "Knows it all." This ambiguous comment by a certain G. S. Travis, written in 1962 when Seligman was in line for promotion to Branch Chief within the OSR, suggested, perhaps, that with the growth of his knowledge Seligman had become a touch inflexible in his opinions. "Still not enough of a team player," the same Travis had written two years later, when Seligman had insisted on recording his objections to the departmental consensus on the proper interpretation of certain economic reports coming out of Czechoslovakia. But these comments and others like them, Sullivan thought, were perfectly consistent with the impression of intolerance, even arrogance, suggested by the photographs.

What did surprise him was the knowledge that Seligman had tended to be casual in matters of security. On seven separate occasions, it appeared, he had committed infractions of security regulations. Most of the incidents had been minor: leaving classified documents out on his desk, or forgetting to lock his combination safe when leaving the office for a moment. And most of them had occurred early in his career. But one stood out. In January 1976, the file recorded, shortly after his promotion to Deputy Director, Seligman had left the Agency for the weekend carrying in his briefcase an Octopus computer printout, classified Secret.

Beside this entry, the last infraction recorded by the file, a note was scribbled in pencil. "We spoke. Satisfactorily resolved. For details, see SF 52 107 C." The note was initialed "T.O.S." and dated March 14, 1976. That date, Sullivan noticed, was more than two months after the original infraction, and only a few days prior to Seligman's resignation from the Agency.

And this brought him to the most puzzling step in Seligman's career. The personnel file described the progress of a clever, hardworking man, a man whose promotion had been consistent, rapid, and deserved all the more because it had obviously resulted from devotion to the work for its own sake rather than from the desire for personal advancement. Yet in 1976, only a few months after his arrival at the top, and a good eight years before mandatory retirement, Seligman had apparently abandoned everything—the position, the work, and the purpose—to exist in a limbo of part-time consulting and messing about in boats. Why?

Two letters in the file recorded the decision: one from Seligman to the then Director of Central Intelligence announcing it, the other from the DCI regretfully accepting. Seligman's read:

> Dear Bill,
>
> I am writing to confirm officially what I discussed with you on Thursday—my wish to resign from the Agency. I propose to make this effective May 1. A month should be ample time in which to break in my successor, particularly since the person you have indicated will be chosen is already well acquainted with the scope and responsibilities of the position. He will do very well, I know, and all the better for not having me looking too long over his shoulder.
>
> I do not think it is necessary in this letter to set out in detail the reasons for my decision. We discussed these at considerable, perhaps unnecessary, length on Thursday. Let me simply state for the record that the concerns of the Agency and my own as a private individual no longer perfectly coincide. However, as I told you at our meeting, I shall be willing to make myself available, from time to time, for individual consulting projects in areas where the Agency feels my knowledge and experience may be useful.
>
> Yours ever,
> Paul

In response the DCI had written:

> Dear Paul,
>
> I'm sorry to learn that your decision to resign is now final. I still don't honestly believe that your method of solving this problem is in anyone's interest—yours or the Agency's. However, since you appear to have made

up your mind, I can only go along, reluctantly, with your
wishes.

With a great deal of regret, believe me
Bill

P.S. A month's notice is fine.

These, to Sullivan, were the most interesting documents on file:
in part because in Seligman's he could hear for the first time the
authentic voice of his subject, but more for the very strong sense
both gave him of having left the most important things unsaid.
"The concerns of the Agency and my own . . . no longer perfectly
coincide." What did that mean? And what problem had resignation
been a method of resolving?

Perhaps, he thought, the timing of the file entries relating to
the last security breach was a clue to the answer. Two months had
elapsed between the original error and the note by T.O.S.—whoever that was—that the matter had been "satisfactorily resolved."
What had they been doing in those two months? What had taken
them so long to resolve? And had the resolution been connected
with Seligman's decision to resign?

SF 52 107 C, Seligman's security dossier, gave a fuller account.
The absence of the Octopus printout, it recorded, had been noticed
at 8:00 P.M. on Friday, January 7, when the registry clerk, closing
up shop for the night, had checked the log. Noticing that it showed
the printout in Seligman's possession, he had called Seligman's
office and received no reply. Later it had transpired that Seligman
had taken an extra day off that weekend, departing on Thursday
night with the printout mixed in with a batch of unclassified papers
he was taking home to work on over the weekend. He had spent
Saturday and Sunday aboard his sloop and had discovered the
printout among his papers on Saturday morning. On his return to
the Agency the following Monday, he had restored the printout
to Registry and reported to the Security Division the circumstances
in which he had removed it. The printout had been in his possession, he reported, all the time it had been out of the Agency. The
only other person who could have gained access to it was a Miss
Gael Forrester, who had also spent the weekend on his sloop.
However, Miss Forrester was a longtime friend of his, and he was
satisfied that she had no idea the printout was on board. She would
have had no interest in it anyway.

A note, dated January 10, scribbled below this entry and signed

"James H. Waddell," recorded that the Agency was satisfied with this explanation and had requested Seligman to be more careful in the future.

But that, clearly, had not been the end of the matter. Subsequent entries in the dossier revealed that the Agency, once alerted to the existence of Gael Forrester, had become curious. A memo to Waddell, initialed once again by T.O.S. and dated January 13, requested him to ask the FBI for any information they might have on file about her. It had taken the FBI two weeks to respond to this request. Then the shit had hit the fan.

The next entry was dated two days after the receipt of the FBI report. It was addressed to T.O.S. and signed by the Director of Central Intelligence. Though terse, it managed to convey something of the DCI's embarrassment and dismay at the situation now beginning to develop.

"Lunched with Paul. Urged on him the unwisdom of persisting in a relationship potentially embarrassing to him and us. Paul recalcitrant. Insisted he had always maintained absolute separation between work and his private life. Recommended we do likewise. Where do we go from here?"

The remaining entries were laconic and ominous.

"We spoke. T.O.S. 2/4/76."

"Polygraph negative. Covers immediate risk, but flap potential still enormous T.O.S. 2/15/76."

"We spoke. I believe we must bite the bullet. T.O.S. 2/21/76."

Then there was a gap of ten days, and finally:

"Agreed. DCI. 3/4/76."

It was not difficult to read between the lines. Seligman 's security breach had led to an investigation of Gael Forrester. Gael Forrester's record read like a security man's nightmare—association with the SDS, arrested for drugs, arrested at a political demonstration, association with Spywatch, an affair with a U.N. diplomat suspected by the FBI of being a KGB agent. So Seligman had been asked to choose. And the choice he had made, given what Sullivan knew, or thought he knew, about Seligman's character, had not been surprising. Seligman had told them all to go jump in the ocean.

But they had not done the jumping . . . It was here that Sullivan, catching echoes of his own thinking, was struck by an irony in the way those thoughts were phrased. Jump in the ocean? It was Seligman, actually, who had done that.

Now he was going too fast. Too fast, and altogether too far.

True, Seligman had left the Agency shortly after the security investigation of his mistress, so it was tempting to assume a connection between the events. But what in that case was he to make of the entry "polygraph negative"? For that, presumably, meant that the machine had cleared Seligman. And why had the Agency continued to use him on consulting projects, when they involved giving him nearly as much access to classified material as he'd had before? These questions were troublesome enough, Sullivan cautioned himself, without stretching the chain of assumption to include a link between Seligman's resignation and his death. And indeed the assumption of death had itself to be regarded as questionable, since it rested only on certification issued in the course of what had struck Sullivan, when he read about it, as a very perfunctory police investigation.

Slow down, he told himself. Check your facts first, then theorize. Get the police evidence from the police. Get the polygraph records. Find out what Seligman did have access to as a consultant. Find out for certain why Seligman resigned. Don't start guessing this early. You'll have plenty of that to do later.

He reached for the telephone.

"Roy? Whose initials are T.O.S.?"

"Don't know offhand. Is this from a file?"

"Yes."

"Recent?"

"March '76."

"Security file?"

"Yes."

"Probably Spearman, then . . . Yes. It must be. T.O.S.—Thomas Osgood Spearman."

"Thanks."

He was about to hang up when Tyrell spoke again.

"You know who he was, don't you?"

"Wasn't he the one who handled the big security investigation back in 1975 and 1976?"

" 'Handled' wouldn't be my word for it. 'Mishandled,' possibly. Even 'fucked up' might not be going too far."

"I take it you didn't like him?"

"Like him? I liked him a lot . . . as a man, that is. He was brilliant, which is rare around here, and civilized, which is even rarer. What I didn't like was what he did to the Agency."

"What was that?"

"He made a shambles of it, that's what. He went mole crazy. He was convinced there was one here somewhere, and he was determined to find him. Even if he had to level the whole place to do it. If he hadn't been stopped when he was, there would have been nothing left standing."

"Who stopped him?"

"I think you might say he stopped himself. He made unfortunate remarks about a certain station chief in Saigon who subsequently became the last DCI but one. That put him on the shit list. And he did for himself when he went around muttering that his suspicions extended right to the very top. When our ex–station chief from Saigon heard that, he reached for the hatchet. The next thing Spearman knew, he was drawing retirement pay."

"Do you think he was wrong?"

"About the mole? I didn't say that. Although in two years of rooting around he never turned up two bits' worth of evidence. It was the way he went about it that bothered me. It was like the Reign of Terror. The whole place got the jitters; dozens of senior and valued people resigned. He couldn't have done more damage if he'd been drawing his paycheck in rubles."

"You know something, Roy?" Sullivan thought he could hear a faint echo of the conversation at lunch. "Sometimes you sound a little like Everett."

There was silence at the other end. Then:

"Morgan?"

"Yes?"

"Remarks like that will strain the bonds of friendship."

"Sorry." Sullivan chuckled. "But he did express a roughly similar idea . . . in a different context, of course."

"Marshall Everett, in the course of an average day, expresses a great many ideas—most of them fatuous. It's like the six monkeys with typewriters. Leave them alone long enough and the odds are that one of them will stumble into sense. But I refuse to be classed with that monkey merely because I utter a statement he has accidentally made."

"He's not that bad . . . Listen, Roy. Why did Seligman resign in 1976?"

This time the silence was almost tangible.

"I think . . ." Tyrell hesitated. "I'm not sure, but the grapevine had him sacrificed to Spearman's obsession."

"How? Can't you be more specific?"

"No. I wasn't in on it. I didn't need to know, you see, so I wasn't told. I heard there was some business about a security breach. A bad one. I know Spearman investigated him. Beyond that I'm guessing."

"Did you know he submitted to a polygraph test?"

"I heard."

"Do you know what about?"

"No."

"Would that have been normal?"

"They give them to people from time to time. But not generally at his level. They never gave me one—and I was on Spearman's list too . . . Look, why don't you talk to Patterson? He knows more about this than I do. His shop has the records. He should be able to tell you."

But Patterson was not able to tell him much. He did not know offhand how many of the people investigated by Spearman had been given polygraphs, and it would be a while before he could dig that information out. He did know, however, that the records of Seligman's test would not be available. They had been destroyed. This was standard procedure, he said, whenever the results were negative. The Agency did its best to respect its employees' right to privacy; since the polygraph did infringe somewhat on that right, the Agency felt the least it could do was destroy records that were irrelevant. Sullivan could see how that made sense, couldn't he?

Sullivan couldn't particularly, but he didn't say so. He had an inquiry going, and he needed those records. But if they had been destroyed, there wasn't much he could do about it. He thanked Patterson and hung up.

As he did, his glance fell on Seligman's Agency photo. After his recent frustrations, it seemed to him that perhaps, after all, the face was not expressionless. It struck him now as being slightly mocking. "Who am I?" it seemed to ask. "Go ahead, hotshot. Tell me who I am."

Don't worry, he found himself silently responding. I will. I'll get into your head. I'll crawl into your skin. I'll look at the world through your eyes. And I'll find out, believe me, who you were and where you really lived.

And it was then, as he heard himself, that he knew he was truly back.

CHAPTER 5

Patterson yawned. He put down the report, leaned back in his chair, and stretched. Then he looked at his watch. Six-thirty. Traffic on the Beltway would be starting to thin out soon. Time to think about heading for home.

It was not something he particularly wanted to think about. It was never something he particularly wanted to think about, but today it was more than usually unappealing. This evening his wife would be at home to her bridge club, a dozen women with hectoring voices and avid, unsatisfied faces, who would invade his peace, guzzle his liquor, fill his living room with cigarette smoke and the smiling malice of their postmortems. He would be forced to retreat to the den, with a shaker of martinis and a TV dinner, to resume with Kevin the long-standing battle about what they should watch— a battle he invariably lost because, when it came right down to it, a rerun of *Masterpiece Theater* was just not worth the hassle. Then, five or six martinis later, when the Yankees (or whoever) had demolished the Red Sox (or whoever), he would wander off to bed, knowing that here too there would be no rest, or none, at any rate, until his wife was finished with her hair curlers, her facial exercises, her innumerable applications of cleansing lotion and moisturing cream. And he would lie awake wondering why she still bothered. Was it the march of years she hoped to stay with these devices, or was it his advances? Either way she was wasting her time. The years would advance anyway, and he definitely would not.

There was a knock at the door. Alan Richards entered, waving a memo.

"Negative on the flutter tests," he said, coming around the desk to place the memo in front of Patterson. "Seligman's was the only one. None of the others had them. None of the biggies, that is. At least not according to their security files."

Why was it, Patterson wondered, that newcomers made such a fetish of the Agency's jargon? Was it to accelerate their acceptance by the old hands, to nourish their sense of belonging? Or did they simply want to make their own modest contribution to the impoverishment of the language?

"Spearman kept separate files." He did not look at the memo. "He might have recorded the polygraphs there. Did you check?"

"Yes. He had files on Brayer, Tyrell, Eglinton—all the seventeens. And then . . ." Richards broke off uncomfortably.

"And then what?"

"Well . . . there was one on you too."

"For God's sake, Alan." Patterson began to laugh. "Of course there was. I'd be offended if there weren't. Spearman's shit list read like a *Who's Who in the Agency.* If you weren't on it, you weren't really in the club."

Who am I trying to kid? he thought. I've never been in the club. And the little shithead knows it. He's only been here a year, but he already knows which end is up. I'm not in the club, and I never will be.

But why wasn't he? That was the question. How had he managed to spend half a lifetime in the Agency, climbing not fast but steadily, to arrive at a position of modest eminence, and never be really accepted? He was as dedicated as anyone, cleverer than most. He had worked his butt off—at least, he had until it became clear to him that it wasn't doing him any good. And yet he had always felt an outsider, excluded in some way from the real center of power.

It was difficult to put his finger on what exactly gave him this feeling. At times he was tempted to conclude that he was paranoid, that the barrier of reserve he seemed to sense between him and the real club members—Tyrell, Eglinton, and the rest—was a product of his own uneasiness, or a figment of his imagination. But that was not true. The causes might be obscure; the effects were real. It was not his imagination that Spearman—club member par excellence until he'd exhausted his credit and been asked to resign—had never really taken him into his confidence. Nor was it his imagination that, on Spearman's departure, when he might reasonably have expected to step into his shoes, the Counterintelligence Section had been deprived of its autonomy and turned into a satrapy of Security. A routine reorganization, he'd been told, made in the interest of greater efficiency. But he knew they had done it to shunt him sideways, giving him a new title but leaving him otherwise exactly as before. And that had been a mistake, he thought grimly. One day they might regret that.

He became conscious that Richards was looking at him strangely, smiling uncertainly, embarrassed somewhat, as if he'd been reading his thoughts.

"So you've checked all the files," he snapped. "And the results were negative. So call him. Or send him the memo. And let's get on with our job."

"I haven't gotten to the lower grades. That's what I wanted to ask you. There must be a hundred of them. What shall I do about them?"

"Shine them. I don't think he's asking for them. If he is, he can take his place in line. We've got enough to do around here without running errands for Sullivan."

"OK." Richards picked up the memo. He started to leave. Then, as he reached the door, he turned and came back to the desk.

"You know," he said diffidently, "I never did look in your file. The Spearman file, I mean. It didn't seem appropriate . . . or necessary."

"For God's sake!" In spite of himself Patterson was touched. "Was that intuition or delicacy?"

"I don't know." Richards flushed. "A bit of both, I think."

"Well, whatever, I appreciate it. But you can't work that way. Intuition is dangerous. Look what it did to Spearman. And delicacy—forget it. There's no place here for finer feelings. So go cover your ass. Read the file. I wasn't polygraphed, as a matter of fact. But don't take my word for it. Read the file and send the memo to Sullivan."

"OK."

Again Richards turned to leave. Patterson, watching him, felt a twinge of regret. Richards wasn't so bad. He'd been too abrupt with him. He couldn't blame him for recognizing the realities. And he really did appreciate his attempt at tact.

"Alan . . ."

Richards stopped.

"Look, why don't you bag it for today? It's going on seven as it is. Why don't we shut up shop and get us a couple of drinks someplace . . . maybe a bite to eat?"

It was almost a plea. Richards, sensing this, hesitated.

"Shit," he said. "I'd really like to. Only I half promised Christy I'd take her to the movies. She's been complaining she never sees me these days. You know how it is."

"Sure." Patterson retreated quickly. "I know how it is. It was just a thought. Another time maybe."

He did indeed know how it was. There had been a time, once, when Angie had made the same complaint: "You're never around." "Why don't you spend more time with the children?" "Who are you married to, anyway? Me, or the fucking Agency?" Now, of course, the situation was reversed. If he never went home at all, no one would notice. Somewhere along the line he had abdicated his position as husband and father. Now he was merely a breadwinner.

Whose fault had it been? His, or the Agency's? Both, probably. The Agency had taken him, chewed him, and sucked him dry, draining him of energy and ambition. But he had been, for the most part, a willing victim, knowing what it would cost, prepared to pay because the Agency had conned him into believing—as he'd very much wanted to believe—that his contribution was vital. Now, of course, he knew better. His contribution had never been more than marginal. He was a timeserver, a hack, a man whose service was to stand and wait. What cold comfort that was. But it was too late to change anything. The Agency had chewed him up. It was about to spit him out.

Sometimes, Patterson thought, he really hated the fucking Agency.

He got up. None of this gloomy self-analysis was helping to solve his immediate problem—what to do with the evening. One thing was certain, anyway. He was not going home. Not yet. He couldn't bear to in this mood. Perhaps he would cruise around and find Michael Eglinton. He was generally around at this hour. Perhaps Eglinton would feel like a drink.

He stepped out of the elevator into the lobby. Eglinton's division occupied the entire fourth floor of the main building. It had its own elevator and its own reception desk. It was, in fact, a self-contained unit within the Agency, a fortress within a fortress, with its own front office, its own registry, its own security procedures. Eglinton believed, or claimed to believe, that it was impregnable. But that was bullshit. The fortress was the symbol for an empire: Eglinton had built it, and Eglinton would defend it. It was as simple as that.

The reception desk was in the center of the room. Behind it, a single door, operated electronically from inside, led off into the labyrinth of offices, computer rooms, and corridors beyond.

Mary Channing, thumbing through the pages of *Bazaar*, glanced up at Patterson's approach. She was an elegant accessory, Patterson thought, impeccable from the soles of her Guccis to the top of her immaculately coiffed head, as much a part of the furnishings as the Calder lithos on the walls or the streamlined phone on her desk.

"Mr. Patterson." She smiled graciously, accentuating the first syllable of "mister," implying by the way she said the words that his appearance at this particular moment was an especially welcome surprise. "And what brings you here?"

"I'm looking for Michael. Has he left yet?"

"Michael Eglinton? I don't think so. Let me call Ellen for you, to make certain."

Patterson waited.

"He's there somewhere." She put down the receiver. "But he's stepped out of his office for a moment. Ellen thinks he may be in Registry. You could look for him there. Or you could go back and wait in his office."

"Thanks. I'll just go back and look around for him."

She took the log and noted in it the time of his arrival. Then she felt under the desk and pushed a button. After a few seconds the door buzzed, and Patterson passed into the fortress.

Registry was another self-contained unit. The door opened, at Patterson's ring, on an area separated from the main office by a counter. Beyond this was a large room with desks in the middle and rows of filing cabinets along the walls. On one side, a heavy circular metal door led off into a vault.

There was only one person in the room, a small, pretty brunette who looked up, frowning, as Patterson entered. Seeing him, she smiled and approached the counter.

"Hi, Mr. Patterson."

"Hi, Louise. I'm looking for Michael Eglinton. I was told he might be here."

She shook her head.

"He was, but he left. I'm afraid I don't know where he went . . . Do you happen to have the right time?"

"More or less." Patterson looked. "I've got seven-ten."

"Shit!" She made a face. "I'm going to be late. That bitch Connie. She swore she'd be back by seven."

"Got a date?"

"Yes, dammit. And my boyfriend hates it when I'm late. He never believes it's not my fault."

"That's too bad." Patterson assumed a properly sympathetic expression.

"Oh, this is always happening. Connie's got absolutely no sense of time. Still, I think she might have managed to be on time this evening. I asked her specially.

"Look . . ." She seemed suddenly struck by an idea. "I'm due to meet Charlie at seven-thirty. The ways things are going I'll be lucky to make it by eight. I knew I wouldn't have time to go home and change, so I brought my clothes here. What are you doing for the next five minutes or so?"

"Nothing much. I'm looking for Michael, but it will keep for five minutes or so. Why?"

"I was thinking I could maybe save a few minutes. The thing is . . ." She hesitated. "I'd need someone to mind the store. Do you think, maybe . . . I mean . . . It would only be five minutes."

"You want me to stay here while you go and change?"

He was about to refuse when a thought struck him.

"What the hell." He shrugged. "How can it hurt? . . . OK. But step on it. I don't want my ass in a sling."

He looked at his watch. Seven-fifteen. Take your time, he thought. Don't hurry back. This, he thought, should get them off his back.

He went over to the filing cabinets. Most of them were not locked, but the stuff inside was disappointingly low-level. Printouts mostly, and photographs. No manuals. Then he went to the vault. That was where they were, probably. But she wouldn't have left that open, would she? Surely even Louise wouldn't be that dumb?

But she had been. When he tugged at the handle, he felt it give. The heavy door, nine inches thick and solid steel, moving like silk on its hinges, swung open toward him. Stepping around it, he went inside.

At that precise moment he heard the buzzer for the outside door.

Damn! Why couldn't she have taken a couple more minutes?

He hurried across to the counter. Swinging his legs over it, he opened the outside door.

"You sure as hell took your time . . ." he began. But then his voice trailed off. For standing there, in front of him, was not Louise, but Eglinton.

Eglinton did not answer. His eyes traveled around the office. Patterson, following his gaze, saw him take in the open filing cabinets, the half-open door to the vault.

"Perhaps you wouldn't mind explaining"—Eglinton spoke softly —"just what the fuck you were doing in there."

Patterson thought quickly. Attack, he told himself. Don't let him put you on the defensive. Give it right back to him.

"It seems to me," he replied calmly, forcing himself to meet Eglinton's accusing stare, "that you should be answering that."

"What's that supposed to mean?"

"Weren't you the one who was making such large claims for the security of your division? How stringent your procedures were? How you had absolute faith in your people? Then maybe you should explain how come your Registry staff is willing to leave me in charge here, with the cabinets open and the vault not even locked."

"Louise left you in here?"

"Yes. Surrounded, as you see, by papers I'm not cleared for. She wanted to go and change, she said, because she was late for a date. She's been gone now"—he looked at his watch—"for twelve minutes."

"You shouldn't have let her." Eglinton attempted to recover some ground.

"Perhaps not. But I was interested to see how seriously she took her responsibilities. Security is part of my job, after all."

"Well . . ." Eglinton wavered. "It seems to me that you're as much implicated as she is. More, if anything, since you're senior."

"Fine," Patterson shot back. "See it that way if you want. I think my credit can stand it."

As he left he was already composing his memo. Patterson to

Eglinton. Subject: Security. Copies to: DCI, Davidson, Waddell, and—why not?—Sullivan. That should be enough to preempt Eglinton and cover his own ass. Even better, it should ruffle some feathers in the club. Indeed, he thought, that was understating it; what it would do undoubtedly was put the cat right in among the pigeons.

II

Once, at a party, Michael Eglinton's wife had said of him that he had a soul like an old boot. The remark had not offended him; it was meant affectionately, and he had taken it that way. In fact, he was secretly flattered, for the image confirmed his own view of himself—leathery, tough, serviceable, not elegant, but dependable. He was a pragmatist, he thought; he took the world as it came; he dealt in facts and the inferences that could reasonably be made from them. Beyond that, he had little curiosity. Daydreams, nostalgia, the charms of a world gone by—things his wife and her friends set so much store by—these had no appeal for him. They were distractions, obstacles to living in the present. The present, in Michael Eglinton's view, was the proper place to live.

This morning, nevertheless, as he prepared to defend the integrity of his division, Eglinton found himself revisiting the past. Not just the past in general, but a specific place, a particular occasion, a precise moment in it. The place was the stadium at Dartmouth, the year 1953, the occasion the annual game against Princeton—an afternoon late in November, the light beginning to fade, the air like smoke, and a thin drizzle, which had threatened all afternoon, beginning to fall. The moment was in the fourth quarter. Till then the game had been a slogging match, a defensive struggle in which the passing had been minimal, the gains ground out a yard or two at a time, the points coming mostly from field goals. Dartmouth had a narrow lead—three or four points, he couldn't remember which—but Princeton was threatening. Now, on third down, they were stalled on the Dartmouth ten-yard line, contained by a pair of defensive plays that had brought the entire stadium to its feet with shouts of triumph. "Dee-fense! Dee-fense!" they chanted, in a rhythm that mimicked the march of seconds to a Dartmouth victory.

The Princeton quarterback held up his hand for quiet, and the crowd—because courtesy, even to a hated rival, was still considered a virtue in those days—calmed a little. At the snap, the handoff went to the fullback, the big man—six four and two twenty—who had run his heart out all afternoon, the one Princeton supporters were calling the Wild Bull. A gap opened in the line, and he made for it like an express train, head down, legs pumping, in the all-or-nothing style that had earned him his nickname. But as he reached it, the gap closed. He collided with a wall of bodies, each as big as his own.

The impact was like the jolt of a perfectly timed punch, a jarring, bone-cracking thud that could be heard above the noise of the crowd, could be felt almost by those sitting in the stands, seventy yards away.

The wall broke, burst open, the linemen scattering like so many falling bricks. And the Wild Bull, charging through, trampled his way to the goal line, dragging, it seemed, half the Dartmouth backfield with him.

Later, in a postgame interview, the Dartmouth coach, not normally a gracious loser, had called it the greatest individual effort he'd seen in college football.

Now, twenty-five years later, that man was facing him across the desk. Eglinton studied him. The power was still there, evident in the great barrel chest, in the ridges of muscle between neck and shoulder, in the thick forearms that tapered only slightly at the wrists, and in the hands, large as soup plates, that looked as if they could tear a phone book as easily as tissue paper. The power was still there, but the years had added something—discretion, perhaps, or experience—so the impression of power was muted, and the intelligence that Eglinton guessed had always guided the power was now more apparent. He was no longer the Wild Bull, quivering with energy, electric with sheer physical exuberance. If he was like any animal now, Eglinton thought, surprising himself with the image, it was an elephant: calm, solitary, watchful, encased in a dangerous stillness.

Sullivan put down the memo and took off his reading glasses.

"I think we had better face it," he said quietly. "Your security has just sprung a leak."

Eglinton did not respond straightaway. Instead he gave Sullivan a disapproving stare, as though the remark he had just heard was beneath his comment and would shortly sink under the weight of its own inanity.

"I think you're overstating it," he said at last.

"Overstating?" Sullivan's eyebrows rose. "Do you? Why?"

"A breach of procedure occurred," Eglinton said. "Granted. And Patterson had access for approximately twelve minutes to classified papers he wasn't supposed to see. The system fucked up, and it shouldn't have. It's serious . . . but not that serious. There were no casualties. Patterson is a trusted, reliable man. He says he didn't look at anything, and I believe him. And even if he did, it wouldn't bother me. He wouldn't leak it to anyone. He doesn't have the balls."

"A breach of procedure occurred," Sullivan repeated without inflection. "There were no casualties . . . at least," he amended, "not so far as we know—not this time."

Eglinton said nothing.

"But what," Sullivan persisted gently, "about last time?"

"Last time? What makes you think there was a last time?"

"I don't necessarily. I just wonder about it, that's all. I just wonder why you think there wasn't."

"Louise said there wasn't. She said it. And I believe it. I have no reason not to. Nor, to be honest, do you."

"Patterson said he didn't look at anything," Sullivan mused. "And Louise said there wasn't a last time . . . But did she say it," he pursued, "before you fired her, or after?"

"Before, obviously. She would have been in no mood to answer questions after."

"And it doesn't occur to you, in that case, that she had a motive for lying? The desire, for example, to hang on to her job?"

"Her job," Eglinton sneered. "She cared diddly-shit about that. She's getting married next month. She can't wait to get out."

Sullivan ignored this.

"Connie Smith." He took off on a new tack. "How long has she worked for you?"

"Three years, give or take."

"And Louise?"

"About five."

"And Connie takes her dinner break at six and relieves Louise at seven. Right?"

Eglinton nodded.

"But Connie is always late, isn't she?"

"Who says so?"

"Louise says so." Sullivan took the memo and, settling his glasses on his nose, scanned it. "Here we are. 'Miss Blaine complained that Connie Smith was always late back from dinner.' "

Patterson again, Eglinton thought, vindictive little shithead. Gets his ass in a sling and starts looking for company. Well, it's not that easy, comrade, it's not that easy at all. But Patterson had finessed him neatly with the memo; there was no way he could go after him at present without adding to his own troubles.

To Sullivan he merely lifted an eyebrow and responded curtly, "So?"

Sullivan looked at him over his glasses, his gaze mingling mild incredulity and a hint of irritation. You can't be as stupid as you seem, his look said, nobody's that stupid. And you're beginning to try my patience. It was a look he used sometimes with recalcitrant witnesses.

"Let me see if I understand you," he said. "Connie was late, right? Connie was always late. And Louise had a boyfriend who didn't like to be kept waiting. So Louise asked Patterson to hold the fort for her. Just the one time, mark you. Just once in all these years. Just once in all the times Connie was late . . . Is that how you see it?"

Eglinton didn't answer.

Sullivan removed his glasses, folded them, and laid them carefully on the desk. Then he looked once again at Eglinton.

"You say there was a breach of procedure," he continued. "I've checked the procedure. And I find there was not one breach, but two. I find that visitors are to be logged in when they arrive and out when they leave. That was done. But I also find that they are to be accompanied at all times during their stay in the division— and yet Patterson was wandering around as though he owned the place. No escort in sight."

"Shit." Eglinton sounded disgusted. "Patterson is a fifteen. The escort rule is for the lower grades only. That's understood. The higher grades just have to be trusted. Brayer is in here all the time. Tyrell too. We can't follow them around like Mary's little lamb. It's demeaning. Besides, life's too short."

"To return to Patterson for a moment." Sullivan was not to be sidetracked. "You seem awfully ready to accept his explanation of what he was doing. Doesn't it strike you as odd that he permitted Louise to leave? I mean, her mere willingness to do so was infraction enough, I should have thought. Why would he want to compound it with one of his own?"

"He's a troublemaker. He always has been. He likes to stir things up. The classic counterintelligence mentality. You should understand that."

"So you think he's to be trusted?" Sullivan ignored the slur.

"He's a lightweight. Look, why are you making such a big deal of this thing? There was a security breach. They do happen, you know. Even in the tightest organizations. It's been dealt with, and it won't happen again."

"Listen." Sullivan leaned forward. "I'm here on the premise that Seligman may have been a mole, right? I'm also here because people are worried about the satellite systems. Look at it from that point of view. Seligman was in and out of the Agency all the time. He had contacts with Brayer, with you, with Tyrell, and God knows who else. Now I find that many of his contacts may have had access to the satellite systems. Because the satellite manuals were in that vault with Patterson, weren't they?"

Eglinton nodded. "But let's look," he objected, "at what you're asking me to assume. Let's assume, you're saying, that Seligman went bad. Let's assume he had an accomplice in the Agency. And let's assume that Louise was lying, that Seligman's assumed accomplice got into my vault with a Minox, and was here long enough to photograph forty-some pages of SAMOS manual. That's one hell of a lot of 'let's assume.' "

"Yes, it is," Sullivan agreed. "It's a whole nightmare of worst-case assumptions. But counterintelligence is a nightmare. It's a snake pit. An acid trip in a hall of mirrors. Normal reality means nothing. Everything is inside out: trust is lunacy, suspicion is sanity, paranoia is a healthy state of mind. It's a world where 'certain' means 'possible,' 'probably' means 'probably not,' and the assumption of innocence is a sick joke.

"Look," he continued. "In normal circumstances I'd agree with you. Probably you're right. Probably it didn't happen. But it might have. That's my point. That's the one chance in a hundred—or a thousand—I can't afford to overlook. Because Louise did leave Patterson in the registry. Connie *was* always late. And your log shows that on any number of occasions in the last couple of years, there were people wandering about unattended in your division during the minutes when Connie might have been late. And fifteen minutes is about all it would take to photograph that entire manual. All of which," he concluded, "is why I don't think it's overstating things to say your security has sprung a leak."

"Jesus Christ!" Eglinton exploded. "You're as bad as Spearman. Spies behind every bush. Yet his investigation lasted two years, and what did he turn up? Nothing. Not one goddamn thing. So I say to you what I said to him. Show me! Show me the fucking mole! Show me he had access! And when you do, then I'll start worrying about my manuals. Until then, I have better things to do.

"You say you're here on the premise that Seligman may have been a mole," he continued. "You're way off. Nobody believed that. Nobody who knew him could entertain that thought for a second."

"Then why am I here?"

"I'll tell you why. You're here because some snot-nosed reporter with mush for brains let his imagination run away with him. And because certain shit-faced politicians who make a career out of hassling the Agency couldn't bear to pass up this golden opportunity. It's a charade you've gotten yourself into, a fucking pantomime."

Sullivan looked at him for a moment without speaking. Then he smiled.

"Different singer," he said, "same old song. But you're wrong. You're all wrong. Charade is what it's meant to be. I understand that perfectly. Bu it's not the way it's going to be."

III

The man had been waiting for the taxi. As soon as it pulled up to the driveway, he stepped briskly out from behind the hedge, and was into it almost before it had stopped moving.

Automatically, as it drew away from the curb he glanced in the rear-view mirror. Nothing was moving in the street behind. No one appeared to be following. But that didn't mean anything. If they were any good—and they had that reputation—they would watch the turnoffs to River Road. Once he was into traffic the advantage would lie with them. Using three or four cars with radio-telephones, they would never need to keep any one car behind him for more than half a mile. Good surveillance, run by competent professionals, was difficult to detect. If it was very good, you might not detect it at all.

So far this tour he'd made three runs and detected nothing. That might mean, of course, that they were very good. It could also mean that there was no one there. The thought somewhat amused him. Imagine taking these elaborate precautions if no one were watching. In a way, he thought, the job was like a religion: a complex code of observances based on the postulate of an all-seeing deity. Fine if the postulate were correct; if not, he was in the absurd position of the faithful—on his knees in a deserted church, addressing his rituals to an empty heaven. But though the thought amused him, he wasn't tempted to relax. Tradecraft, like religion, was best regarded as a form of insurance. You guarded against catastrophe by observing the forms.

The office building on M Street was one of a dozen used for contacts. Each tour, three were chosen from the pool at random, just as the runners and the pay phones were chosen at random. Randomness, the avoidance of patterns, was the guiding principle of their security, for without a pattern to analyze, the opposition was virtually weaponless. They could keep on watching and hoping, of course, their computers churning, their fleet of automobiles uselessly burning gas, but the yield would be only an impotent suspicion. And suspicion, by itself, was nothing to chew on. It would simply leave them grinding their teeth.

The building's main entrance led into a lobby with a bank of elevators opposite a newsstand. He walked over to the stand, taking and paying for a magazine while keeping an eye on the entrance. Satisfied that no one had followed him in, he entered an elevator as the doors were about to close and pressed the button for the fourth floor, for the simple reason that apparently no one else was getting out there. When he reached his floor, he checked the corridor to make sure no one was around and disappeared through the fire exit. He took the stairs to the basement, congratulating himself on the luck that had given him, on this occasion, a relatively short descent, and exited at the rear of the building through the delivery entrance. Once out in the street, he hailed another cab and gave the driver an address in Georgetown.

The beauty of this procedure, he thought, was that, to anyone

watching, his behavior would seem designed to shake off surveillance. This was precisely the way it was intended to seem. If they
succeeded in following him to the building and observed his
failure to reappear, they would not find it difficult to deduce that
he had gone out at the rear. Next time, then—or even this time, if
the surveillance team had its wits about it—there would be someone waiting at the rear, congratulating himself on his powers of
deduction. Then they would follow him again through all the bars
in Georgetown and realize only when he went back home that they
had just spent half a day—say, twenty-five or thirty man-hours—
to no apparent purpose. For even if they followed him through
the stairwell—which in itself would be a breach of accepted surveillance procedure—they would be too late to find the thirteen-
cent stamp, placed one foot above the floor in the near corner of
the landing between the third and fourth floors, that indicated
Drummer was requesting a contact.

Today there had been two thirteen-cent stamps. That meant the
request was urgent.

The pay phone was at the corner of Fourteenth and K Streets.
The contact time was between 11:00 and 11:05. If the box were
occupied or out of order, he would move on to the next box and
the next time. They never used a box more than once, and the
selection of boxes was, of course, random: downtown one day,
Georgetown another, Bethesda the third. Telephones, of course,
were notoriously insecure, but there were several thousand boxes
in the Greater D.C. area. The chances of a successful tap were
negligible.

There was nobody in the first box, and the phone was working.
He waited until 10:58, checking first to make sure there was
nobody in earshot, and busied himself pretending to look up a
number. At 11:02 the phone rang.

"What will you give me on the favorite for the third at Laurel?"
It was Drummer.

"Seven to two."

"That's robbery. He'll start at fives. You guys are bandits."

The man sighed. He wished Drummer wouldn't waste time
playing around with the code words. "What do you want?"

Drummer told him.

The man listened without comment, a frown spreading over his face.

"I don't like it," he said at last.

"Nor do I." Drummer sounded quite cheerful. "But show me an alternative . . . He kept a record—that's quite evident from what we found on the boat—but it's disappeared. We'll have to find it. Because if we don't, someone else may . . . I'm sure I don't have to spell out the potential consequences of that."

"How, exactly, do you suggest we set about it?"

"Nuts and bolts." Drummer dismissed the objection. "They're your department. You can't use your own people, that's certain. You'll have to subcontract. But don't you always?" The shrug was almost audible.

"Very well." The man sighed again. "I will refer your request to the proper quarter."

"It's not a request. I want action, not advice. Convey that to the proper quarter."

"It's a big risk."

"Of course." Drummer sounded impatient. "But there are some risks you have to take. It's about time you people realized that."

There was a click, and the line went dead. Drummer had hung up. Lost in thought, the man held the receiver to his ear a few more seconds; then he too hung up.

Things were starting to come unglued, he thought. One error, one small omission, a single piece of bad luck, and you were forced into desperate measures to cover your tracks. But mistakes breed mistakes, he thought: error feeds on error. What Drummer had suggested was necessary, he would concede that, but the risks would now increase geometrically. It would begin with house-breaking—subcontracted, of course—and it would end . . . He sighed. Who could tell where it would end?

CHAPTER 6

"The police investigation is closed?"

"Not exactly." Brady shook his head. "The file's still open. It's just not going anywhere. Rutherford's washed his hands of it, and I've been assigned to other duties. Officially it's unfinished business. But if it's ever going to be finished, it'll have to finish itself."

Sullivan toyed with the remains of his salad. In one way Brady had been remarkably helpful. He'd given a summary of the police file on Seligman, a succinct yet detailed report that struck Sullivan as a model of exposition. Yet Sullivan was left with the feeling that important things remained unsaid. Brady had drawn no conclusions, he'd offered no theories, he'd leaned over backward, in fact, to avoid doing so. He was holding something back. Sullivan wondered what it was, and whether he could needle Brady into revealing it.

"You don't seem happy about that," he said.

Brady frowned.

"I think it was murder," he said. "I think there's a killer walking around out there. Free. Smiling to himself. I'm never happy about things like that."

"What are you going to do about it?"

"What can I do?" Brady sounded defensive. "Rutherford was right. The leads go nowhere. Or they go back to the Agency."

And that amounts to the same thing, he thought. But I need hardly tell you that.

"Take the diving belts," he continued. "I thought there might be a lead there. Seligman didn't go in for scuba diving, as far as I can discover, and there was no other equipment on the sloop—no tanks or flippers or what have you. So I figured if he killed himself, he must have bought the belts specially, and probably someplace locally. There aren't many stores around that sell scuba stuff, and even fewer that stock the belts we found on the corpse. So I checked."

"And you came up empty?"

"More or less. There were fifteen sales of that particular belt in the month prior to Seligman's disappearance. Ten were a bulk order from a club in Annapolis; the others were individual sales. None of the salesclerks could remember selling to Seligman. They couldn't describe the purchasers, either. The only interesting point came out by accident."

"And that was . . . ?"

"The clerk who took the bulk order worked for a big supplier in Annapolis. He sold a lot of those belts, he told me, mostly to clubs and organizations who bought in bulk at a discount. His biggest customer, he happened to mention, was the Central Intelligence Agency."

Sullivan received this information in silence.

"Which doesn't prove a damn thing, of course," Brady went on. "It doesn't even prove Seligman didn't commit suicide. He could have bought the belts earlier, or in some other part of the country. He could have borrowed them. It's even possible he did buy them at one of the stores I checked and the clerk just forgot him—though in that case, since all the sales except the bulk order were individual sales, you'd have to conclude he went to two separate stores, which doesn't make much sense . . . But, on balance, the evidence of the belts, such as it is, seems to work against suicide. What bothers me is . . ."

But here he broke off, reluctant, as usual, to venture into theory.

"Go on. What bothers you?"

"Well . . ." Brady hesitated; discretion and valor were warring in his mind. Discretion won. "Forget it. It's sheer speculation, just pie in the sky."

"Look," Sullivan urged, "I'm not the DA. We're not trying to build an indictment, for God's sake. So go ahead. Speculate. What bothers you?"

Brady thought a moment.

"When I got your call," he said, "I went to Capalletti, my lieutenant. He told me to hold off awhile. Then, half an hour later, he called back. 'OK,' he said, 'have lunch with the guy. Talk to him. Give him the facts. But,' he said, 'stick to the facts. Don't go feeding him any fancy theories.' " He paused. "Well, you've got the facts. I've even admitted I think it was murder. That's already further than Capalletti authorized me to go. I think it's far enough."

"Hell," Sullivan said, "this is all off the record. It won't get back to Capalletti . . . if that's what you're worrying about."

"It isn't, particularly." Brady seemed offended by the suggestion.

"What is it, then?"

Brady hesitated.

"Who are you working for?" he asked finally. "I mean who are you really working for? Officially, you say, it's the Senate Committee. But what about the CIA? Didn't you tell me you used to work for them once?"

"I see," Sullivan said. "Once a spook, always a spook. Is that it?"

Brady shrugged.

"That's a laugh." Sullivan didn't, however.

"Is it?"

"Yes. The Agency's flapping because they think I'm not on their team. And you're panicked because you think I am. So nobody wants to talk. It's as if I had bad breath."

"I'm not panicked," Brady said flatly. "And you still didn't answer my question. Whose team *are* you on?"

Sullivan thought before answering. No dummy, this cop. There were several answers to his question. But which one was right? Which would serve best to penetrate the barriers of his reserve?

"Whose team?" he said at last. "I don't know. I suppose you might say I'm working for Mr. and Mrs. John Q. Public, for the people who worry about mysterious disappearances, unsolved murders, and the like. You might say that; it certainly wouldn't be untrue. But it's not the whole story.

"Look." He paused. "I never wanted to get involved in this thing in the first place. I didn't like the smell of it. I still don't. But, for reasons I'm still not clear about myself, I did get involved. And since I did, I want to do it right. There's that, and something else . . . I'm getting an uncomfortable feeling people are jerking me around. I don't like it. In fact, it's pissing me off . . . Does any of that make sense?"

Brady nodded.

"And I may be wrong," Sullivan continued, "but I think you

feel the same way. You think Seligman—or somebody—was murdered. You think it had something to do with the Agency. And nothing is happening. You're not happy about this; it pisses *you* off. But you don't know what to do, because the Agency is a brick wall . . . Am I close?"

Brady nodded.

"Well, it may have been a brick wall, but it's not any longer. Because they let me in there, and whether they like it or not, I'm staying until I find out what the fuck has been going on.

"I guess what I'm saying," he went on, "is maybe we can help each other—you with your murder, me with my . . ." He searched for the right word, shrugged, and gave up. "My whatever."

"I'm off the case," Brady objected. "Capalletti won't put me back. We're overloaded as it is. And obviously he has his own orders from higher up. It's not hard to guess what they are: unhook the terminals and let the patient die."

"Forget Capalletti. He doesn't have to know, does he? I'm not asking you to get back on the case, exactly, or to drop anything else."

"Then what are you asking?"

"Ideas mostly. For a start, I'd like to hear what you were going to say before you changed your mind about it. It's speculation, you say, but what the hell else do we have at this point?"

"And what are you offering?"

"Help with leads that seem to disappear into the Agency. To the extent security permits, of course."

"Of course," Brady murmured sardonically.

"Look," Sullivan insisted, "I'm not trying to sell you a bill of goods. There may be genuine security considerations, but I won't let them make the decisions about that. I don't hold any brief for those guys. If they've done anything criminal and I find out about it, I'll help you nail them. And that's a promise."

For perhaps half a minute Brady gazed at Sullivan, eyes narrowed. Finally he shrugged.

"Shit," he said, "what do I have to lose? . . . What do I have to offer, come to that? Speculation mostly. Probably half-assed. And based on a pile of assumptions. They're all shaky, and if one of them is off, the whole thing collapses."

"What the hell. Run it by me anyway. It's something to work on."

"Well . . ." Brady took a deep breath. "My first assumption is that the body was Seligman. It's flimsy, but we have no other candidates at this point. My second is that he was murdered; I can't prove this either, but the alternatives don't make any sense to me. My third point, I think, is fact. The Agency lied to the press about Seligman's status; he was much more important than they said."

He paused and looked at Sullivan for confirmation.

"Yes," Sullivan agreed. "It is fact. They did."

"And I think they lied about the reasons for his early retirement."

"I think so too."

"The rest is pure guesswork. I think that when the boat showed up empty they already knew what had happened to Seligman. Rutherford thought so too. Or at least he wondered about it. Because they never filed a Missing Persons; they just grabbed the documents and ran. So when I find that the diving belts used to submerge the body are standard issue in the Agency, I start to wonder. And what I wonder is this: if Seligman was working for the Russians and the Agency found out about it, what would the Agency do? Would they put him on trial and let Congress and the media scream bloody murder about it? Or . . ."

He paused then and looked intently at Sullivan.

". . . Would they just quietly knock him on the head and dump the remains in the Bay?"

For several moments neither spoke. Sullivan leaned back in his chair and gazed at the ceiling; Brady lit a cigarette, but without taking his eyes off Sullivan.

"Now it's your turn," Brady said. "I don't know those guys. I have no idea, in any given circumstances, what they might or might not do. But you know. You used to be one of them."

Sullivan switched his gaze to meet Brady's; his mild blue eyes rested thoughtfully on the policeman.

"They might do that," he said. "In the circumstances they very well might. But if they were looking for a quiet life, they didn't do too well. The media screamed bloody murder as it was. And Congress appointed an investigator."

" 'The best laid plans . . .' " Brady shrugged. "It's still better than a trial. They got a trifle unlucky is all."

A thought struck him then, and at that moment the last vestiges of his reserve fell away. He gave Sullivan a grin of gleeful, almost boyish complicity.

"Perhaps more than a trifle," he added. "Considering who they're now messing with—Brady and Sullivan, the pride of the Irish. A truly formidable combination. I'd have to say they got very unlucky indeed."

"Let's hope." Sullivan grinned back.

Brady became serious again. "Of course, it's a working hypothesis only. I'm a long way from sold on it."

"It's at least a start. It may turn out to be way off. In fact, I hope it is. But it's a start, and it suggests an obvious follow-up."

"What?"

"Money. If Seligman worked for the Russians, the odds are he got paid. Did you ever look into his finances?"

"Some." Brady shrugged. "It was suggested he might have been financially strapped. I looked. He wasn't."

"Where did you look?"

"His bank statements. He kept files in his apartment. Very meticulous. I impounded them when Homicide was brought into the case."

"Do you still have them?"

"I don't know. They should have gone back to his executors. But that's not to say they did. We're Maryland's finest, but we're still a bureaucracy."

"Can you look?"

"Sure. But what for?"

"Cash payments. Periodic cash payments into the account."

"Unlikely, isn't it? I mean, if you're taking money on the side, you're not going to run the payments through the bank. Do that, you might as well just notify the IRS."

"True."

"Well." Brady got to his feet. "Capalletti will be wondering what's taking me so long. I'd better be getting back . . . If the records are still with us, I'll take a look anyway. I'm not optimistic, but it can't hurt.

"Thanks for lunch, Mr. Sullivan." He extended a hand. "I enjoyed it. I never thought I would, but I did."

"Morgan," Sullivan corrected him. "We have a partnership, remember. My partners call me Morgan."

II

The law firm of Cooper, Cole and Trumbull was housed in the ninth and tenth floors of a steel-and-glass structure on Connecticut Avenue; Sullivan's office occupied the southwest corner of the tenth floor. It was large and airy, the exterior walls being entirely glass, and filled with a variety of plants and ferns whose leaves were polished to an even gloss that made it possible, in certain lights, to mistake them for plastic. Sullivan called it "the Vinyl Greenhouse."

The furniture was Scandinavian Modern, the desk a rectangular oak box with no drawers whatever, the coffee table an oval of smoked glass balanced improbably on a free-form base of chrome, the couch and armchairs squashy leather in a color the interior designer had referred to as "cognac." Here and there, however, were incongruous touches—the set of *Blackstone's Commentaries* in the lacquer bookcase behind the desk, their somber bindings a dour protest against the surrounding chic, and the framed nineteenth-century prints, caricatures of famous British barristers, that hung on the interior walls. The designer had thrown a fit about the prints: they destroyed the unity of his conception, he said, and they must go. But on this point Sullivan had dug his heels in. It was his office, he insisted; the prints had belonged to his father, and they were staying.

Normally the office, its flaunted evidence of his senior partner's determined trendiness, embarrassed Sullivan. There was too much money in it; it lacked the sobriety, the solidity, the smell of tradition, which in his view were indispensable to the practice of law. It made him feel more like some corporate helot, enslaved to the compulsions of cost and benefit, than the servant of an armed and blindfolded goddess whose scales, at least in theory, were not to be tipped by dollars and cents. Today, however, he was grateful for it; it suited his purpose. It was this office, rather than the one provided by the Agency, he had chosen for his meeting with Gael Forrester.

He had made the choice partly for her convenience—to save her the trek out to Langley—and partly because he wanted to distance himself, in her eyes, as much as possible from the Agency. He was, to tell the truth, a little tired of the Agency; its atmosphere of watchful distrust oppressed him. And if it oppressed *him*, he guessed, it was likely to infuriate *her*, since her record described a life very largely devoted to opposing almost everything the Agency stood for. Meeting her here, well away from the campus at Langley, was a way of emphasizing his independence. Once she had recognized it, he hoped, she would be less hostile.

But this hope, he realized, was somewhat forlorn. Her manner on the phone had been chilly. She did not wish to talk to him about Paul Seligman, she'd said; she did not wish to talk to anyone on that subject. She had already told the police everything she had to tell, and unless Sullivan could give her a very good reason why she should meet him, she was afraid she must refuse. It was a pity, Sullivan reflected, that the only reason he'd been able to produce was the one least likely to thaw her: that she would meet him now voluntarily, or later under the compulsion of a subpoena. He'd said it reluctantly, knowing, as he did so, that the proverb about horses and water was likely, in her case, to apply exactly.

He was not looking forward to the meeting, and not only because he expected her to resent him; he could also detect in himself the seeds of hostility. He imagined her a kind of Pavlovian liberal, the sort of shrill, tiresome woman to whom all policemen were pigs, the law a bludgeon wielded by money and power. It wasn't that he necessarily rejected radical politics; in fact, he approved the goodheartedness that often lay behind it. What he disliked were people who talked in slogans, who substituted blind idealism or reflex cynicism for the uncertainties of real thought. He was afraid she would turn out to be one of them, though in entertaining that fear, he recognized, he was close to thinking in labels himself. Perhaps, he consoled himself, he was wrong. Certainly Seligman, in the image he had formed of him, seemed unlikely to have attached himself to anyone simpleminded. Moreover, for both of them the relationship had involved contradictions between feelings and beliefs, whose successful juggling must have required some suppleness of mind. Nevertheless, as the time for the meeting approached he found himself dreading it. If she were reasonable, it would not be easy; if she were not, it would be a bitch.

First impressions reassured him. She was on time, and she was not wearing the uniform of the lunatic left. She was dressed in Levi's tucked into knee-length boots, a man's cotton shirt—originally pale blue, now almost white from laundering—and a pigskin trenchcoat, its collar turned up, draped across her shoulders like a cloak. The effect was informal, but casual rather than scruffy; it had been chosen, Sullivan guessed, not as a statement of protest, but because it suited her. The boots and coat looked expensive, their suggestion of offhand elegance confirmed by the fact that her hair had been cut, and cut recently, by someone who knew what he was doing. She wore no makeup, and this gave her an air of severity, which was enhanced, he guessed, by her dislike of the present situation. When she relaxed, he thought, she must be a strikingly beautiful woman. He found himself wishing they had met in different circumstances.

She'd entered briskly, preempting his secretary's attempt to announce her, and stood facing him in the center of the room. Getting up from his seat, he'd been on the point of offering to shake hands, but had changed his mind. It wasn't a courtesy she would welcome, he'd sensed.

Instead, he said, "Thank you for agreeing to see me, Miss Forrester. I appreciate it."

"Do you?" She stared at him. "I didn't know I had a choice."

"At any rate"—he smiled—"I'm grateful to you for making it easy."

Ignoring this, she glanced around the room.

"Cozy," she pronounced.

"That wouldn't be my word." Sullivan made a face. "Do you like it?"

"Nifty." The tone left her meaning in doubt.

"Thank you . . . Won't you sit down?"

He gestured to the couch, and sat in one of the chairs beside it.

"Let me begin by explaining my interest in Paul Seligman. I'm a special counsel appointed by the Senate Select Committee on Intelligence to investigate the circumstances of his death—or disappearance. My job is to discover what implications, if any, there may be for national security."

"To find out, in other words, if he was spying for the Russians."

"I see you've been reading the newspapers."

"How could I avoid it? It was on the front pages for days. Thank God they're losing interest at last."

He nodded. "Then you'll honor my request to keep the investigation confidential? I believe it's in everyone's interests, especially Paul's."

"Yes. Though I question how much you worry about Paul's interests . . . Not that he'd care anyway. And not that it makes any difference to him now."

"You think he's dead, then?"

She stared at him. "Don't you?"

"It's been suggested otherwise. There was some question about the police identification . . . I'm inclined to think he is."

"So what do you want to know?"

"Paul's death . . ." he began. "Look . . . I'm sorry if this is painful for you. I know it must be. You were close to him, weren't you?"

"We were lovers." She said it flatly. Let's call things by their right names, the tone implied. "What about his death?"

"Was it a shock to you?"

"Was it a shock . . ." She looked at him blankly. "What else would it be?"

"It's thought he committed suicide. Did he ever discuss that with you?"

"Never." She shook her head impatiently. "And he didn't do it."

"You seem very sure."

"We were lovers," she repeated. "Very close, as you put it. He enjoyed life . . . we enjoyed it together. He had no reason to kill himself."

"The police think he did."

"The police." Her tone dismissed them. "What do *they* know? *I* know he didn't."

"You were close." Sullivan changed tack. "Yet you didn't live together. You had separate apartments."

"Yes, we did. But in fact we lived in mine. He used his as an office." She paused. "I assume this is leading somewhere?"

"I think so . . . Then he didn't keep any papers in yours?"

"No."

"Just personal belongings?"

"Just a few clothes. Look, I wish you'd get to the point. You haven't asked anything I haven't been over, ad nauseam, with the police already. I didn't lie to them, you know."

"I'm not suggesting you did. And I'm sorry to take you over old ground. Unfortunately, I must. My interest here is not necessarily the same as theirs."

"So what *is* your interest?"

"I guess it's this: if you were close enough to Paul Seligman to know he didn't kill himself, were you close enough to have known, for example, if he was seeing someone? . . . Regularly, I mean."

"Look, I said we were close, but that doesn't mean we lived in each other's back pocket. He came and went as he pleased. He didn't have to punch a clock, for Christ's sake. He could have been seeing the whole Russian Army for all I knew. But . . ." She paused. "He wasn't."

Sullivan was silent.

"You're wondering how I know," she continued. "I knew him, that's how. He wasn't that kind of man."

"And there was never anything, in the light of what's happened since, that made you wonder?"

"Wonder?" she echoed. "What sort of thing?"

"Unexplained absences. Odd phone calls. Dates broken at the last minute. That sort of thing."

"Never." The reply was immediate and emphatic. But her eyes seemed to cloud momentarily, as though, even as she spoke, she recalled an exception.

"Then did he, perhaps, in the months before his death, seem worried about anything? Depressed, possibly, or unusually preoccupied?"

"He was always inclined to be moody." The eyes clouded again. "I didn't notice anything unusual.

"Look." She leaned forward. "I know what you're thinking. I know what they're saying about him. It's all lies. He wasn't a traitor. He couldn't have been. He was too straight, too loyal to that godforsaken agency of his . . ."

She broke off. It seemed to Sullivan that she'd abandoned the present conversation and returned, in her mind, to some other from the past.

"Loyal," she repeated. "God, was he ever loyal! He was loyal to the point of folly."

"To the point of folly? What does that mean?"

"It means . . ." She hesitated. "It means they didn't deserve him."

"Why not?"

"As if you didn't know." She spat the words at him. "They got rid of him, didn't they?"

"Got rid of him?" Sullivan was startled. "You mean they fired him?"

"Fired him, asked him to resign—whatever you want to call it. What did you think I meant?"

But this was not a line of speculation Sullivan wanted, at present, to pursue.

"Do you know why?"

"I don't have any idea."

Her look was defiant. Don't expect any charity from me, it seemed to say. I'm here under protest. Anything you get you'll have to work for.

Shit, Sullivan thought, this is going to get miserable. He found himself reluctant to continue. He didn't want to cross-examine her, or reopen wounds that were best left to heal. She was too vulnerable, she'd been through too much already. He didn't want them to end up enemies—if they weren't already . . . What he really wanted to do, he was surprised to discover, was comfort her.

She's lying to you. He used the suspicion to force himself back to reality. She's lying, and you're snowed by her looks. Stop behaving like a schoolkid and start using your head! You're going to have to get rough; she won't give a thing otherwise.

"I think you do." His voice was cold.

She stared at him, an angry flush spreading over her face.

"I don't particularly care what you think."

"Possibly not. But you may be interested in what I know."

"I doubt it. I'm sure it wouldn't surprise me."

"It wouldn't surprise you to know that the FBI has a file on you as long as my arm?"

"Surprise me? You've got to be joking. There was a time I couldn't go anywhere without running into those clowns."

"And you knew, of course, that once your association with Seligman became known the file would be passed to the Agency? You must have guessed, mustn't you, what that would do to his career? So my question is"—Sullivan fired it at her— "how much did you tell Paul?"

She flinched as if he had struck her.

"You think I didn't tell him everything? You seriously believe that?"

"I don't know what I believe." Sullivan was pitiless. "Did you, for instance, tell him about Ivan?"

"Ivan!" That did surprise her. "You know about him too?"

"I know . . . but did Paul? Did Paul know that your immediately preceding lover was a Russian intelligence officer?"

"Intelligence officer!" she gasped. "He was not! He was a diplomat. He worked for the U.N."

"Oh, come on!" Sullivan snapped. "You don't really believe that, do you?"

"I didn't know he was in intelligence. I honestly didn't. Anyway," she fought back, "I've only got your word for it."

"Take it or leave it. You still haven't answered the question. Did you tell Paul?"

She lowered her eyes. "No. I never told him. But it wasn't for the reason you think. He didn't want to know about my former lovers. They were past, he said, and it hurt him to hear about them. I'd told him enough about myself to make him aware of the dangers; it didn't seem necessary to mention Ivan. The rest was bad enough as it was . . . Look, Paul knew what he was getting into. It didn't make any difference to him."

"In other words, everything was open between you?"

"Except Ivan . . . Yes."

"So you're telling me, then, that Paul knew the risks, and you knew he had been fired, and yet you have no idea why? You never discussed it with him?" His voice was sour with disbelief.

"Oh, for Christ's sake!" she flared. "Of course I did. I felt like hell about it. Especially when he told me he resigned because he wanted to, that he was tired of working, that he needed more space, more time to really live in, more time to spend with me. I couldn't accept that kind of charity, so I nagged at him until in the end he gave in and admitted the truth. The Agency had forced him to choose, he said, so he had chosen.

"You must have known all this." The defiance had left her; its place had been taken by a kind of apathy. "Why make me go through it again?"

"I guessed." Sullivan, too, felt empty. "I wasn't sure. It helps me a lot to know it for certain." The words were more for himself than her.

"Help you to what?"

"The truth." He shrugged.

"You really care about that?"

"As a matter of fact, I do."

"Then I'll tell you. The truth is Paul Seligman was a decent, honorable man. One of the most decent and honorable I've known. The truth is"—here, quite suddenly, her voice broke—"he's dead."

She sat very straight, struggling with her tears, furious that her emotions had betrayed her to his sympathy. That was a fine job, Counselor, he told himself savagely. You carved her up nicely. You should be proud of yourself. You're an ornament to the Bar, Counselor. A fucking ornament.

"Please . . ." He moved across to touch her gently on the shoulder.

"Leave me alone!" She shrugged his hand away.

"Listen," he said. "I'm sorry."

"You're sorry." She let the words hang in the emptiness between them. "What difference does that make? . . . As if you really care anyway. As if you care about anything besides your fucking secrets."

"That's not true!" He was stung.

"Isn't it? Then why are you harassing me?"

"I'm not harassing you. I'm just—"

"You're just doing your job. Is that it? That's your excuse, isn't it? You, and the police, and the CIA and the FBI? You spend your time following me around, tapping my phone, interrogating me—me and anyone else who doesn't exactly toe the line. And when we call you on it, you just shrug your shoulders and smile your polite official smiles. 'We're sorry, people,' you say. 'We're not such bad guys really; we're only doing our job.'"

Sullivan said nothing.

"Well, your job stinks," she continued. "And even if it were necessary—which I don't admit for a moment—it still wouldn't excuse you. Because you enjoy it too much. You talk about the national interest, or national security; you hide behind those great big, comfortable, justifying abstractions, but what you really like is the power. 'We can do what we like,' you tell yourselves, 'because it's all for Uncle Sam.' But it's not. You do it for yourselves . . . like a bunch of closet Nazis.

"Well, deny it!" she challenged. "Go on, deny it!"

"I can't be bothered."

Now Sullivan was angry, overwhelmed, suddenly, by the desire to hit back, to wound as he had been wounded. Nazi? What the fuck did she know about Nazis? What right did she, with her trendy socialism, which rested snugly, no doubt, on someone else's money, have to sneer at national security and the other "big, justifying abstractions" when it was those abstractions precisely that guaranteed her the liberty to sneer?

What did she know about oppression, about brutality, about the real denial of freedom? And what did she know about the price, payable in work and lives, of keeping them at bay?

"I can't be bothered," he repeated. "You wouldn't listen anyway. It's not something you're good at, you people. You never do listen much, do you? You're too busy talking, standing on your soapboxes, proclaiming your monopoly on truth and justice. What time do you have to trouble your heads with the facts?"

"Facts." She dismissed them. "I know your kind of facts."

"Do you? Try this one. In 1969 you were working for an organization that calls itself Spywatch. Isn't that a fact?"

"What about it?"

"And isn't it a fact that Spywatch was set up to uncover and publish the names of CIA fieldmen abroad?"

"Certainly."

"Then perhaps you remember another fact? In August 1969 Spywatch published the name of Michael Walsh, the station chief in Athens. And ten days afterwards, some radical, or at least some little thug who called himself a radical, walked up to Michael Walsh in the street and shot him three times in the head." Sullivan paused. "Score one . . . for truth and justice."

"Listen," she said earnestly, "I—"

"No. You listen!" Sullivan cut her off. "I haven't finished. I have more facts. They're details, of course. Trivia. Not your kind of facts at all. But I want you to hear them anyway.

"Mickey Walsh was married to a Greek girl. Thea, her name was. They had two little girls—aged about three and four . . . It's hard to explain things to kids that young. It took Thea a long time to make them understand where their father was, why they wouldn't be seeing him anymore. It didn't get through at first. And when it did, they didn't cry; they just stopped smiling. I think it was weeks before I saw them smile again.

"Well, of course," he resumed, "they got over it eventually. And Mickey Walsh was just an ordinary guy. He liked parties, and Greek dancing, and sitting up over a bottle of wine, getting drunk and talking about books. He liked playing chess, and sailing, and surprising his kids with presents. But lots of people like those things . . . He wrote poetry, too, sometimes. Good poetry. Good, but not great . . . As I say, he was an ordinary guy—brighter than most, maybe, and nicer. But he wasn't going to shake the world, or change the course of history. And then, of course, he was on the wrong side. That makes a difference. I suppose, from some points of view, he was no terrific loss—just another closet Nazi.

"At least," he said, "I hope you can see it that way. Because you did it to him. Helped, anyway. Not intentionally, of course; I don't believe you ever think that far ahead. But you did help."

He got up and walked over to his desk.

"You're right about one thing, though, I am trying to do my job. I hoped you might help me. But it's pretty clear where you stand on that. So I don't think there's much point in going on now. I may have to bother you again, of course. But . . ." He looked her squarely in the eye. "I sincerely hope not."

He pressed the buzzer on his intercom, and almost immediately his secretary appeared in the doorway.

"Miss Forrester and I are through," he said. "Please show her out."

She had been sitting all this time, listening. Now she stood up and walked to the door. When she reached it, she turned.

"Good-bye, Mr. Sullivan," she said quietly. "I'm sorry about your friend."

The look she fixed on him was puzzled. It was as though, for the first time since she had entered the office, she was seeing him as a real person.

But Sullivan was in no mood to notice.

"I'm sorry too." He barely glanced at her. "But what difference does it make?"

III

By the time she had walked to her car, which was parked in an underground garage some minutes from Sullivan's office, Gael had recovered enough composure to attempt to put her impressions in some kind of order. She was still angry: angry at the ordeal he had put her through for no apparent purpose, angry at the way she had let herself be manipulated, angry at the abrupt manner of her dismissal, and angry, finally, at herself for becoming angry. But mixed in with the anger, she recognized, was also some regret. She didn't know the exact cause of her hostility to Sullivan, but she was uncomfortably aware that it had deprived her of communication she might, in other circumstances, have welcomed. For the questions he had asked her were precisely those that, in the days following the shock of Paul's loss, when the stories had first begun to circulate, she had asked herself. And the answers she had given then—and gave now in the privacy of her own thoughts—were not nearly as confident as the ones she'd given him. There had been questions about Paul's behavior in the month before his death, which, though they had not disturbed her at the time, now nagged at her. While one part of her would happily have buried them, another part demanded they be brought to light. Sullivan had offered her just this opportunity— but she'd rejected it.

Beyond anger and regret was bewilderment. She'd been, surely, on the point of telling him. He'd subjected her to a cross-examination she now recognized as rather skillful, provoking her into unguarded responses that enabled him to force from her admissions she wanted to avoid. But then, just as he'd been about to break down her resistance, he'd given up. Why? Because she had called him a Nazi? Hardly—unless he was a great deal more sensitive than people in his profession had any right to be. Perhaps, then, he had not understood the extent of his success? She doubted that. He struck her as knowing, in the matter of cross-examination, exactly what he was doing. Why then? To let her stew in the juice of her own guilt and contrition? To soften her up for some later occasion when he would squeeze it out of her? Possibly. But there was a risk in that—and one, moreover, he had no need to take. Guilt fades; on a later occasion he might find her as recalcitrant as ever.

Then what had he been up to? It was a question she kept returning to on the drive back to Georgtown. The answer, she knew, depended on the truth about him. But that was hard to uncover. He was either a secret policeman with a soul—an improbable combination—or an inquisitor masquerading as father confessor. His looks, certainly, provided no clue. He'd struck her originally as a straightforward heavy, his thick, construction worker's body slightly uncomfortable in its formal casing of gray worsted. But behind the pleasant, slightly battered face, behind the mild, puzzled-looking eyes, was a mind that cut like a diamond. So how much of the performance had been real? The anger, for example, had seemed real; the sorrow for his friend too deep to be other than genuine. But it was suspicious that he'd been able to pick out so unerringly the episodes from her past that had the most power to disturb her. Ivan, of course, had been in the file. But what about Michael Walsh? Could Sullivan have known that it was Walsh's death that had prompted her resignation from Spywatch? Had his display of grief been simply that—inspired acting on a script compiled from Walsh's dossier? Had he in fact known Michael Walsh at all?

There was no way of knowing. But though she understood this, the questions continued to nag at her. As she approached her house she noted, without breaking her train of thought, that a parking space was open on her side of the street, several doors up. She maneuvered into it mechanically, remembering, without thinking about it, to roll up the windows and lock the doors. She vaguely registered, as she walked up the short pathway to her front door, that a light was on in the upstairs bedroom. But it was not until her key was in the lock that she remembered that the light should not have been on and recalled, in a moment of perfect, frozen clarity, her impression of a shadow against the curtain that should not have been there.

She stopped dead. Stepping back a pace, she held her breath and listened, her senses unnaturally acute and focused. But all external sound seemed to have ceased; she could hear only the thudding of her heart. She took another step backward and looked up at the window. The shadow by the curtain had gone. She listened again, cocking her head to one side and closing her mind to all messages but those that might be coming from the upstairs room. Nothing. She could hear nothing.

Imagination, she thought. There never was a shadow. You're scaring yourself for nothing. You forgot to turn out the light when you left this morning, that's all. But before the thought could comfort her, she remembered that she had left the house at eight-thirty, when the sun had already been up two hours. And then, as if to underline the import of that memory, the light upstairs went out.

Help. She needed to get help. She turned and started up the path. She would rouse a neighbor and phone the police. But before she had gone a yard, she was pulled up short. There in the gateway, silhouetted against the glare of the streetlight, hands held in front of him and crouching slightly in an attitude of serious purpose, was a man.

"Shut up and don't move!" His voice was throaty, somewhere between a growl and a whisper. "I've got a knife."

She knew without looking that there was no chance of running. The narrow yard was walled on either side, and there was no way to the back except through the house. The key was still in the front door, but there was no hope of getting there before he reached her. Even if she succeeded, she would still have to face whoever was inside.

It was her training, not any conscious process of thought, that now took charge of her. She found herself in the side-fighting stance, Kim Sung's litany of instruction sounding in her mind, the words accompanied by images—almost cinematic visualizations of the moves. Knife attack . . . knife in right hand . . . cutting up from below. Block left, punch right. Go for the throat.

"Karate, no less." He moved toward her, keeping his face and hands in shadow, the voice still soft but stronger, a lazy, velvet chuckle of anticipation. "Tiger Lady?"

Then he lunged.

She let it come, pivoting as the knife point passed her left forearm, sweeping across to deflect the thrust just a fraction before the right straightened and locked. But he had given away the knife hand. Her block met no resistance. Her punch never landed. Even as she realized it, he whirled, his left sweeping around backhanded in a great scything arc. The side of his fist slammed into her jaw, jolting the bone almost out of its sockets.

IV

"That's all they took? Just those few things?"

"Yes," she said. "At least I think so. But I couldn't swear to it. It's hard to tell when everything you own is in a heap on the floor."

She broke off and stared helplessly at the wreckage. The couch was overturned; the upholstery had been slashed, handfuls of the stuffing torn out and strewn around the room. The armchairs were also gutted. Books and records, swept off their shelves, lay in a jumble beneath the bookcase. The bureau had been ransacked, the drawers ripped out, their contents dumped and scattered. There was water everywhere, soaking the books, turning the papers into wads of pulp, seeping, in dirty gray stains, into the carpet.

The devastation was almost total. It could have been taken for the work of some anarchic force of nature—an earthquake, perhaps, or a hurricane—except that in the center of the room, completely unharmed, almost disdainfully aloof from the chaos around it, stood a delicate spindly-legged table, and on it, in a vase—the only one left unbroken—a flower.

It was this, more than anything else, that frightened her. There was a whimsical cruelty about it, a chilly laughter, that made the hair rise on the back of her neck. You went about heedlessly, she thought, fitting snugly into the groove of your life, surrounded by order, the comfort of possessions, the warmth of friends, the security offered by streetlights and highway patrolmen, but underneath was this deliberate human violence, which ripped its victims at will; it had not ripped her yet, the flower seemed to say, only because it hadn't chosen to.

"Can you give us any idea of the value?"

"Value?" Her thoughts were still on the flower. Value? Who cared about jewelry and crummy pieces of silver when the real loss was peace of mind? What was the price on that?

"Yes, the missing articles. What would they fetch?"

She forced herself to think. A box of costume jewelry—the thieves had unaccountably missed the box containing her one real treasure, a Kashmir sapphire inherited from her grandmother—a clock, a fluted silver bowl, and a gold watch that had belonged to her father. That was it. It seemed pathetically little.

"I'm not sure . . . Eight hundred dollars. Maybe a thousand."

"Weird." Sergeant Austin shook his head. "Don't you think so, Mancini?"

"It's a contradiction." Officer Mancini nodded. "The whole place seems to be covered with prints—which is what you'd expect, since people don't normally go around at home in gloves—but the door handles seem to have been smeared. That suggests we're dealing with professionals, or at least not total morons. But then how come they took the junk and missed the good stuff? And how come the trashing? . . . Maybe it was druggies, looking for cash, who got pissed off when they couldn't find any and broke the place up out of spite?"

"No," Austin said. "It doesn't have that feel to it. For one thing, they had a lookout. He, at least, was a pro."

Gael felt her jaw. There was a big, tender bruise on the right side. Her head buzzed, and she was still subject to occasional waves of nausea. She felt as if she had a ten-martini hangover.

"He was an expert," she said. "I've done karate for years, and by ordinary standards I'm good. But he was better. Much better."

"I admire you for standing up to him, miss." Mancini smiled. "Not many women would. Not many men, for that matter."

"I didn't seem to have any choice. Besides, the training gives you confidence—misplaced confidence, in this case."

"You can't tell us any more about him?"

"Not really. He had his back to the light. He was black, that's all I know. Black, and about six foot, I'd guess. But he was crouching; it's hard to be sure."

"That helps," Austin said. "Black, about six feet, and a whiz at karate. We could maybe check the clubs."

He said it without enthusiasm. His station handled dozens of robberies a week. Most of them were never solved; there wasn't the manpower to pursue them properly. Claim on the insurance, he thought, and forget about it.

"Sergeant."

"Yeah?"

"Look. As a robbery it's a contradiction. Right? It doesn't fit any of the patterns. So maybe it wasn't a robbery at all. Maybe it was just meant to look that way."

"Meant? Why?"

"I don't know exactly." Mancini was hesitant. Austin was not fond of theories; he preferred procedure. And sometimes, Mancini thought, he was not too fond of procedure either. Right now it looked as if what he really wanted was to go home.

"There was something I noticed upstairs . . . all those clothes thrown around. It looked like more trashing, but was it? There was a man's coat and a pair of pants, I noticed, with the pockets turned out. It strikes me they may have been looking for something."

"Of course they were looking for something." Austin affected a weary patience. "Money. It's what they normally look for, isn't it?

It's easy to conceal, hard to identify, and you don't have to sell it at a discount."

"Sure, but when you don't find any cash, you go after jewelry, don't you? So how come they missed the sapphire?"

"Christ, I don't know . . . She surprised them, remember. Maybe they panicked and took off before they got to it. What are you getting at, anyway?"

"They took one box and left the other. Right? And they lifted a couple of other odds and ends of no particular value. So here's how I see it. They're looking for something, not money or jewels, but something specific. And they're junking the place to make it look like a casual rip-off. But then she comes back, and that scares them. So they grab whatever's in reach and take off."

"They were looking for something specific? Like what, for example?"

"Ah . . . now that I can't tell you." Mancini shrugged and spread his hands. The question, he implied, was unreasonable.

"Pity." Austin's voice was dry. "It is kind of vital to your theory." With a sigh, he turned to Gael. "How does that strike you? Was there anything like that in the house?"

"No." Gael looked blank. "At least, I can't imagine what."

"So much for that, then." Austin was about to drop it, but Mancini interrupted. It was his theory, and he wanted it to have its day in the sun.

"Look, Miss Forrester. Forgive my asking. But the jacket and pants—who did they belong to?"

"They belonged to a friend of mine."

"Belonged?"

"Yes. He's dead."

Her tone was forbidding, but Mancini was not to be deterred.

"Might I ask who he was?"

"I don't see what this . . . oh hell." She shrugged. "It's no big secret. His name was Paul Seligman."

And then it dawned on her. Of course! Sullivan. The apparently pointless interview, which had kept her away from the house. Suddenly she found herself trembling with anger.

Now Austin was interested.

"This Mr. Seligman," he asked, "wasn't he the one who was lost in the Bay recently?"

She nodded.

"And didn't the papers say he used to work for the CIA?"

"Yes."

She saw Mancini glance quickly at his superior. It was a sideways flick of the eyes, accompanied by the briefest of smiles. Then his face returned to neutral. But the look, while it lasted, had expressed pure triumph.

V

Sullivan was in bed reading when the phone rang. Reaching for the receiver, he glanced at his watch. Eleven-thirty. Who the hell could be calling at that hour?

"Sullivan here. Who is it?"

"Mr. Sullivan. This is Gael Forrester." Her voice was high and taut. "I'm extremely sorry to disturb you this late, but I thought you'd want to know your goons did a thorough job."

It was the hostility, rather than the words, that registered. Oh Christ, he thought, not her.

"My goons? Do you mind explaining just what the hell you mean?"

"My goons?" she mimicked savagely. "You had no idea, of course, that while I was downtown talking to you my house was being turned upside down and trashed."

"Your house has been burgled?"

"No, Mr. Sullivan, not burgled—searched. They took three or four things, of course; I imagine they wanted it to look like a robbery. But in fact it was systematically searched . . . and systematically devastated."

"And you think I had something to do with it?"

"Well, it does strike me as rather odd that it happened precisely when I was in your office, answering questions which, so far as I could see, had no obvious purpose. And it also strikes me as odd that the things they seemed most interested in were Paul's clothes."

"How do you know it happened while you were in my office? You came to me straight from work, didn't you? So how do you know when it happened?"

"Very quick, Mr. Sullivan. But it doesn't work. You see, I was lucky enough to arrive in the middle."

"Jesus! Are you all right?"

"Yes. As a matter of fact, beyond a bruised jaw and a few cuts and abrasions, I am. So I guess you can congratulate yourself. Everything ran smoothly and nobody was hurt. That must be a relief to you. I know how much you dislike it when anyone gets hurt."

"Miss Forrester, look . . ." Sullivan kept his voice level. He was tired of her and her silly accusations. But she'd been robbed, apparently manhandled, and was obviously scared. She was acting like a child, but she had some excuse; there was none for him. "Believe me, I had nothing to do with what happened to your house. For one thing, I don't have any interest in it. For another, I don't have any goons. As I explained to you earlier, I work for the Senate Select Committee, not the CIA, and my staff, at the present moment, consists of me . . . Now I'm sorry about your house, and I'm even sorrier you seem to think I was involved. But I really wasn't. I think you should call the police."

"I've already done so. In fact, it was they who suggested, since nothing of value was taken, that the motive was probably not theft."

"What did they think it was?"

"They didn't say exactly. But when they noticed the interest the thieves, or whoever, had shown in Paul's clothes, they asked me who they belonged to. It was at that point they started to see it as a search."

"Then they knew who Seligman was?"

"Yes."

"How did they react?"

"They looked at their feet and pursed their lips and examined their fingernails. Then they said they'd better be getting along. A forensic team would be around in the morning, they said, and perhaps I'd feel more comfortable spending the night in a hotel."

"Did you mention your talk with me?"

"Of course not. I'm not stupid. I know I can't prove anything. But that doesn't alter the facts."

"And the facts are that I arranged the interview to get you out of the way so my goons could search your house. Is that it?"

"Yes. That's it exactly."

Sullivan was silent for a moment. Then he said:

"Didn't work very well, did it?"

"Didn't it? I'd have said it worked just fine."

"Really? Then how do you explain the fact that you got home in the middle? I mean, if I'm the sinister fascist you seem to believe, and devious enough to dream up a stunt like that, then I'd hardly have let you leave my office until I was sure my goons were through, would I? Or am I giving myself too much credit? Perhaps I'm only a sinister, devious, *stupid* fascist? . . . But even then your theory doesn't work. Because since, as you'd already told me, you work until six every evening, I wouldn't have needed to detain you at all. I could simply have scheduled the break-in for earlier in the day, couldn't I?"

She said nothing.

"Well, couldn't I?"

The silence that followed lasted perhaps half a minute. Sullivan was tempted to hang up, but he remembered how their last conversation had ended. He'd been brutal then, more brutal than the circumstances had really demanded. The least he could do now was give her the chance to salvage some pride.

"Mr. Sullivan." Her voice was small and awkward. "I seem to owe you an apology. I've been stupid and tiresome, and I've jumped to some very hasty conclusions. I'm sorry. I hope you can forgive me."

She offered no excuses, he noted, though there were plenty at hand. She'd lost her lover, her house had been devastated, she'd been abused and manhandled, hectored and bullied. Yet she made no appeals for sympathy or forbearance. She simply acknowledged she'd been wrong and said she was sorry, opening herself unflinchingly to the rebuff he could easily deliver. There was a grace in that, a generosity, that struck him, under the circumstances, as extraordinary.

"Please," he said. "That's not necessary. I can't really blame you for what you've been thinking, and I'm not very angry about it. In fact, when I remember the provocation I offered, I'm rather ashamed."

She said nothing.

"Look," he continued, "why don't we just forget it happened. We began badly. I was tactless and you were . . . understandably prickly. Then we both lost our tempers. That never improves matters. Why don't we start over? . . . At least, I may not need to bother you again, but if I do, why don't we?"

She still did not reply.

"I think what you need now is rest. You've had a rough day, and you must be worn out. I think the cops had a good idea. I think you should find a hotel. You probably won't get much sleep at home."

"Mr. Sullivan . . . ?"

"Yes."

"Do *you* think the break-in had something to do with Paul?"

Sullivan considered.

"It's hard to say. It could just be coincidence, except, as you say, that they seemed very interested in the stuff belonging to Seligman. Let me ask you something. *Could* there have been something of his there they might have wanted? Did he ever keep papers there, for instance?"

"Not that I know of. In fact, I'm sure he didn't. He never talked to me about his work, except in the most general terms. I knew almost nothing about what he was doing. I wanted it that way—and so did he." She paused. "I'd like you to believe that."

"I do," he told her. "I really do."

He did. He was convinced, nevertheless, that the break-in was more than coincidence. It was another piece of the puzzle, but he had no idea where to place it. And, beyond that, he was left with the niggling feeling that there was something about it he had overlooked, something glaringly obvious that he'd failed to notice because his nose was too close to the ground. He lay awake, wondering, arranging and rearranging the pieces, struggling to distance himself from his assumptions. But he was tired, and his mind was cluttered. His thoughts tripped over each other. When he fell asleep finally, hours later, the pattern continued to elude him.

CHAPTER 7

I

Gael's first impulse, when she woke next morning, was to call a broker and put her house up for sale. Instinct told her to turn her back on it, to walk away from the memory of a visitation that would haunt her as long as she stayed. For though the signs of that intrusion could be wiped away, the mess cleared out, the gutted furniture re-covered, the spirit of its ugliness would linger. Never again, she felt, would she be able to cross the threshold without first pausing to wonder what she would find inside.

Second thought told her this was silly. It was morbid to brood over a catastrophe that was, after all, one of the normal hazards of city living. People got mugged all the time; houses got broken into; these were facts, and running away would not alter them. Fear, she told herself, was something the mind itself created; you either controlled it or it would control you. So she must start cleaning up, straight after breakfast. And the first thing to do was get rid of that stupid flower.

She was not, however, able to start quite as soon as she wanted. Shortly after her return from the hotel, the police reappeared with a fingerprint expert. Nothing must be touched, they told her, until he was done. The job seemed to take several hours, and the effect of his labors was to add significantly to the mess without subtracting from the mystery. The intruders had worn gloves, he announced, and they'd worn them all the time.

It was noon before she could get to work, and three before she felt she'd made any progress. By then her bedroom had been restored to order, the kitchen cleaned out, the books and records in the living room replaced on their shelves, the papers picked up, and the debris—several bags of it—dumped in the garbage. This left the more serious damage: she would have to call the upholsterer about the couch and chairs, the broken pictures would go to the framers, the stained carpets would have to be cleaned. She would also need to speak to her insurance agent—though she entertained no hopes of him—and arrange for the locks to be changed.

She decided to take a break. She would load the pictures and carpets into the car and drive into Georgetown to see about them. She would call in at the locksmith and make her report to the State Farm agent. She was surprised to find herself almost cheerful. It was amazing what a lift to the spirits a little brisk labor could give.

The feeling persisted through most of her errands. The locksmith was comforting, the State Farm agent unexpectedly helpful. But when she got to the cleaners she was jolted again by a reminder of the loss that rendered all the others, by comparison, entirely trivial.

The carpets were no problem, the cleaners said, they would be ready by Tuesday. In the meantime there was another parcel for her, which they'd been holding for nearly three weeks. Would she care to take it with her? She paid for it and took it, discovering only then that what it contained was a jacket and a pair of pants belonging to Paul.

The cleaning ticket was dated June 10, the day she'd last seen Paul. Reading it renewed, more sharply than ever, her sense of loss. It was history now, that ticket. Like some old letter preserved under glass, it documented an irrevocable past. When it was written Paul had been alive, on his way to Lusby or already on board the *Excalibur*, preparing, in the meticulous way she had called fussy and he seamanlike, for his departure. Now he was dead, and this scrap of paper, recording an insignificant transaction tangential to his life, acquired inflated value as part of the meager record of his passing.

She recalled the circumstances clearly. He had left before midday, telling her he was going to Lusby. He would sail if there was a breeze, or work if there wasn't. Either way, he would be gone overnight. She was used to his odd, solitary excursions, accepting them as springing from his need for privacy and wondering only occasionally—as they grew more frequent—if they might not also express an unconscious desire for freedom. So she had said nothing and resigned herself to spending the weekend alone, cleaning up and settling into the new Barbara Tuchman. After he'd left she'd found the jacket on the bedroom floor. It was a favorite of his, and though it was wrinkled and covered with stains, he could never be persuaded to part with it long enough to have it cleaned; it was too old and shabby, he claimed, to be worth the expense. On impulse, and perhaps out of pique at being abandoned once again, she had taken the opportunity to surprise him.

Later she had simply forgotten it. The events of the days following—the discovery of the sloop, the appearance of the body, the police interviews, the funeral, the ugly publicity—had crowded it out of her mind. Now that she had it back, she didn't know what to do with it. It would be morbid to keep it, impossible to throw it away. It was too much a part of Paul simply to be tossed into the garbage. She could give it away, but who could she think of who might possibly want it?

The question was no sooner asked than her mind, jogged by the memory of the previous night's events, rephrased it. Who would be *interested?* That was the real problem. And the answer was easy: the intruders, obviously, the people who had so thoroughly rummaged through Paul's other clothing. But what had they been looking for?

She wouldn't know that, of course, unless she looked for herself.

She found it eventually in the lining, half a sheet of typing paper, folded twice and rolled into a tube. There were no holes in any of the pockets, so clearly it had been deliberately hidden. Had she not been looking, she would never have found it. And now that she had, she wasn't sure how it helped.

It was a list, two columns of numbers, twenty-seven in all, each consisting of seven digits: a group of two, a space, a group of three, a space, and a final group of two. Some were in pencil, others in ballpoint—which accounted, no doubt, for their surviving the dry cleaning—and beside some of them, in Paul's writing, were various annotations. Next to the first group, for instance, was the letter *C*, a question mark, and, leading away from it, an arrow, which later branched and connected the group to several others. The whole thing looked to her like a code, the annotations being Paul's preliminary effort to solve it.

On reflection she abandoned this idea. She knew next to nothing about codes, but the little she had read of them suggested that modern systems were cracked, if at all, by mathematicians with computers, not by amateurs doodling on half sheets of paper. Then what on earth was it? She had no idea whatever. She could only guess it was important. Why else would Paul have taken the trouble to hide it? And why would somebody have taken the trouble to ransack her apartment to get it?

But the real question was what should she *do* with it? Take it to the police? She rejected that immediately. What would Sergeant Austin make of her scruffy list? She could see his shrug, his patient, skeptical smile, the amused glance he would exchange with Officer Mancini. "Yes, miss," she could hear him say. "We'll look into it. Don't you worry. It'll be taken care of." And having witnessed the reaction of that pillar of the law to her last mention of the CIA and Paul Seligman, she could imagine to what extremes of inactivity those reassuring phrases could be stretched.

Besides, what did she really want him to do? It was here she thought of Sullivan. If she gave it to him, she could count on his pursuing the mystery with energy and determination. Did she really want that? Who knew where it might lead? Sullivan evidently suspected Paul of being a traitor. Might this not be the evidence he needed to prove it? Was she willing to have that happen?

It took her some agonizing to decide that she was. She had faith in Paul. It would be disloyal to hold the list back for fear of proving that faith unfounded. Resolving doubts meant facing them, and if facing them meant the destruction of faith—so be it. In that case the faith had been misplaced to begin with. But she couldn't resolve her doubts alone. She needed to share them with somebody, somebody with the knowledge to interpret that piece of paper. That somebody was Sullivan. She must call him, then, give him the paper, and answer the questions she'd evaded previously. At this point she had no other option.

Now she recalled their last phone conversation. Her part in it made her squirm with embarrassment, but his gave her some reassurance. Something about his behavior then, his straightforwardness, his restraint under provocation, suggested he might be trusted. Perhaps it was only from need, but she found herself willing to trust him. He was her only option; but instinct told her he might not be a bad one.

When she called, Sullivan was out. Nobody knew where he was. The secretary at his law firm told her he was due to appear in court the next day to hear the verdict in an appeal he'd been arguing. The court was in Baltimore, but perhaps, if it was urgent and she was unable to contact him later at home, she could get in touch with him there.

It was urgent. Her possession of the list made it urgent. For she'd recalled by then another implication of the intruders' evident determination to get it. They'd broken in once—why not again? And perhaps they hadn't only broken in. Paul, after all, had been murdered—she was sure he had. And that meant . . . She did not normally think of herself as nervous, but she had to get that list to Sullivan as soon as possible.

II

Brady was not impressed with the bar Sullivan had chosen for their meeting. It was in Georgetown, for a start, which had forced him to hassle with the rush-hour traffic on Wisconsin. Then it was jammed, and with the trendy singles crowd he instinctively disliked and normally avoided. They were grouped three deep around the bar, in poses whose studied casualness, he imagined, had taken hours of practice to perfect. The air was thick with cigarette smoke and murmured invitations to romance.

Around the walls were backgammon tables, all occupied, some surrounded by kibitzers, or refugees from the skirmishing at the bar. He spotted Sullivan in a corner, leaning back in his chair, gazing with an air of mild curiosity at his opponent. Their game was watched by a girl who had turned her chair around, straddling it and resting her chin on her arms against the back. She was studying the board as though some profound mystery were hidden there.

At Brady's approach Sullivan looked up and smiled.

"Hey," Brady said, "I'm sorry about the time. The traffic on Wisconsin was a bitch."

"No problem." Sullivan pointed to a seat. "I found a way to pass the time. Have a drink."

Brady looked at the wall of bodies around the bar and made a face.

"How?" he asked.

"Good point." Sullivan laughed. "Tell you what. Let me finish this, and we'll find somewhere else."

"Suits me." Brady dropped into the chair opposite the girl. She paid him no attention whatever. Sullivan's adversary, a young man whose Levi's, checked shirt, and drooping cowboy mustache gave him the appearance of an extra from a cigarette ad, glanced up briefly and returned to contemplating his move. He had rolled five-three, Brady saw, and he was not happy about it. His face was screwed up in a frown of concentration, and his eyes had the unfocused stare Brady associated with complicated feats of mental arithmetic.

Eventually he moved, slapping the counters into place with an air of confidence at odds with his former expression. Sullivan waited for him to pick up the dice. Then he took the cube from the slot in front of him, turned it to four, placed it on the rim of the board, and pushed it with his forefinger across to his opponent.

The young man immediately shook his head.

"Why not?" the girl asked.

"I missed his blot on the bar point." The young man stood up. "Now he has twenty-four shots at a prime. This is backgammon, not charity."

"But twenty-four shots is two to one," she insisted. "You told me three to one was the break-even for taking."

"It is." His voice was testy. "But if he misses, I still need a six. The odds against that are worse than one in three. So my real chances are closer to one in nine . . . You have to look more than one move deep."

He pulled a wad of notes from his back pocket, peeled off a twenty, and dropped it on the table in front of Sullivan.

"Bad double," he said. "You should have gone for the gammon."

"Would have," Sullivan replied mildly, "but I have to leave." He picked up the twenty and stuffed it into his pocket. "You *are* off duty, I hope?" He grinned at Brady.

"Gambling?" Brady grinned back. "Hell, that's big stuff. Vice Squad business. You know me—I'm only Missing Persons." He nodded toward the retreating figures of the cowboy and his girl. "Where did you find the pigeon?"

"He found me. He hustles, I think. Uses the girl as a come-on. He offered me a friendly game and then suggested a small bet. 'Just to make it interesting,' he said. 'You call it,' he said. So I called it ten bucks a point—just to make it interesting."

"I take it you're good, then?"

"Misspent youth." Sullivan shrugged and grinned. "I make out."

There was a smaller, quieter bar around the corner. It had booths, mostly empty, along one wall, a counter along the other. There were one or two solitary drinkers at the counter. No one looked up as they entered.

"I meant to meet here in the first place," Sullivan explained, "but I couldn't remember the name. You didn't much take to that other joint, did you?"

"It's the swingles," Brady replied. "They're too young and too laid back, too hell-bent on having fun regardless. It could be envy, I suppose, sour grapes at missing out on the sexual revolution, but I find them hard to take."

"Me too." Sullivan slid into a booth. "Or at least I used to. Now I take a sort of anthropological interest in them. I think it's a sign of age."

They ordered beers and waited in silence until the waitress brought them.

"I found the money," Brady said.

"I thought you had." Sullivan nodded. "But I wasn't sure. You were cryptic on the phone."

"Capalletti was there. I figured it was easier to meet, anyway. It's a complicated story."

"I imagine it took some finding."

"No. That's the surprising part . . . one of them, anyway. It didn't. If he'd deliberately set out to lay a trail, for Christ's sake, if he wanted to lead us to the money, he could hardly have done it better. It was right up front. In the bank statements—in the tax returns even. He made no effort to bury it."

"In the tax returns?" Sullivan's eyebrows shot up. "You mean he paid taxes on it? You've got to be kidding!"

"He declared it, but he didn't pay any tax." Brady, gratified by the sensation his words had produced, felt inclined to prolong it.

"Didn't pay? How come? Did he have some kind of shelter?"

"No. At least, not in the ordinary way. What he did was give it away."

"What?" Sullivan was thunderstruck. "All of it?"

"Yup." Brady nodded. "Every last cent."

To this revelation Sullivan could find no adequate response at all.

"That came out ass-backwards," Brady resumed. "Let me back up and start from the beginning. I checked the bank statements for 1976 first. And until June there was nothing. Every month Seligman banked his CIA check—around twenty-five hundred through March, and about fourteen hundred thereafter; it dropped, I suppose, when he started drawing his pension. He also made occasional small deposits—fifty, seventy-five bucks, never more than a hundred. Dividend checks, probably, or something like that. Then, in June, I hit the first exception. A fifteen-hundred-dollar deposit made on the twelfth of the month. So then I went to the deposit slips . . . A very meticulous man was your Seligman, thank God. He had the slips in a folder, in neat chronological order. It was right there. June 12, 1976. Fifteen hundred dollars—cash."

"From then on it was regular as payday. Fifteen hundred, always in cash, deposited around the middle of the month. The last payment was made on May 15, this year."

"And he disappeared on June 10. So one assumes he never received the June payment?"

"Never received it, or never deposited it. We never found any money, so I guess he never received it."

"What made you go to the tax returns?"

"I don't know." Brady shrugged. "Curiosity mostly. The returns were there, so I looked. I suppose I couldn't really believe anyone taking handouts on the side would be stupid enough to run them through his account, so I wanted to see if he'd declared them for tax . . . Well, he did.

"In 1977, for instance, he declared a gross income of approximately fifty-three thousand. His gross pension was twenty-one five; he got another thirty-five hundred or thereabouts from investments, and he received a ten-thousand-dollar consulting fee from the CIA. That leaves around eighteen thousand unaccounted for. And that is equal to twelve monthly installments of fifteen hundred dollars."

"And he gave all that away."

"He did. I spotted it mostly by chance. As you know, the total amount of tax due is entered near the foot of the first page of the 1040. I noticed he only seemed to owe a couple of thousand, although as far as I could tell there'd been withholding only on his Agency pension. Two thousand seemed like an awfully small tab to pay on nearly thirty thousand of other income. I figured he had to have some pretty substantial deductions, so I looked. And there it was—contributions to charity, eighteen thousand five hundred dollars."

Brady grinned. "At that point I thought I was going crazy. Hallucinating or something. So I went to the '75 return. Charitable contributions in that year came to five fifty. So what it boils down to is this: he was getting fifteen hundred a month in cash from unexplained sources, and he was giving the whole thing away."

For a moment Sullivan said nothing. He leaned back against the partition of the booth and stared at the ceiling.

"It doesn't make any sense," he said at last.

"No," Brady agreed. "I thought for a while maybe the payments were legitimate. Consulting fees or something. But that doesn't add up. Legitimate consultants get paid by check. And besides, it's not as if he were rolling in money. I figure his disposable income in 1977—without the cash payments, that is—would have been around twenty-eight thousand. Maybe less. By my standards, that's more than comfortable, but he had payments to his ex-wife—she was into him for a thousand a month—and then there was that boat. Upkeep on those things can hurt you, I would think."

"No kidding," Sullivan murmured. "If it's not painting and scraping, it's engine overhauls or marina fees. It never stops. I figure mine runs me about sixty-five hundred. Maybe more."

"So between the boat and his ex-wife, there wouldn't have been much change from the twenty-eight thousand. And yet, with an extra fifteen hundred a month coming in, what does he do? He hands it all over to the United Way. That's irrational." Brady sounded pained.

"People are, mostly," Sullivan said. "It's only economists who think they're not. He needed the money—at least, we think he did—but obviously he didn't want it. But then why did he take it in the first place." He sighed. "I guess we'll just have to find out where it was coming from."

"We?" Brady cocked an eyebrow.

"Manner of speaking." Sullivan grinned. "You've done your bit. I guess it's my turn now. As a matter of fact, I have made a little progress. It's not much compared to yours."

He told Brady about the trashing of Gael Forrester's apartment.

"Why hers?" Brady asked.

"Quick, aren't you?" Sullivan gave him an approving look. "Much quicker than I was. It took me all night to come up with the same question. But it's obviously the right one. Because if the break-in was connected with Seligman's disappearance, and if, as the police believe, the intruders were looking for something, you'd expect them to search *his* apartment before hers."

"Perhaps they knew—whoever 'they' are—that we'd already been to his. I think it was in the papers."

"Well, if they knew that, they'd either have to figure we found it—whatever 'it' is—in which case why bother to search anymore? Or they'd have to figure we didn't; in which case his apartment would still seem like the best bet. So if the break-in *is* connected, the only logical alternative is this: whoever broke in *knew* that 'it' hadn't been found and that 'it' wasn't in Seligman's apartment. And that suggests we're talking about someone who knows what *was* found in Seligman's apartment—"

"And that means," Brady cut in, "either the CIA or the police."

Sullivan smiled. "Well, actually, I was going to give you guys the benefit of the doubt. The Agency was there first, remember. Patterson removed documents within a few hours of the discovery of the sloop."

"Here we go again." Brady groaned. "I'm beginning to think Rutherford was a prophet. Every way you turn, he told me, you'll run smack into the fucking Agency.

"The trouble is," he continued, "it's all so fucking speculative. We keep talking about 'it' and 'whoever broke in,' and we link everything together in a neat deductive chain. But the welds are pure assumption. We don't really know that there was an 'it' at all. We don't even know if Seligman was murdered. I *think* he was, but I can't prove it. All we really know for certain is that he disappeared in mysterious circumstances, that he left the Agency two years ago under a cloud, that he seems to have been on somebody's payroll, and that his girlfriend's house was broken into. You don't have to be a policeman to find all that suspicious.

There's enough mystery there for anyone. But you can't build on mystery."

"No, you can't. But in this case, you can't sit on it either."

"Give me an alternative. Find where the money was coming from? Just how the hell are we supposed to do that?"

"I doubt we can. But there are other options."

"Such as, for example?"

"We could shake the tree."

"What does that mean?"

"It's an old counterintelligence trick. You shake the tree and watch what falls out. You hassle the opposition and watch for their reaction."

Brady thought about this.

"Sounds fine in theory," he said at last. "But I see a problem. You need to know who the opposition is. Who do you have cast for the role?"

Sullivan hesitated. He'd admitted Brady to partnership, but how far did he want to confide in him? Brady was a cop—a good cop. But his concern here was with a relatively simple issue of law enforcement. He believed a murder had been committed and he wanted to bring the murderer to justice. How would he react if the result of his efforts was a case that could not be brought to trial for reasons of national security? On the other hand, there'd been a bargain. He'd asked Brady to go out on a limb. He owed him something for that. He owed him a great deal. And debts were something Sullivan believed in paying.

"I'm surprised you can ask me that," he said. "Who else would it be, if not the fucking Agency?"

CHAPTER 8

I

There were not many people in the gallery—fewer, probably, than were in the well of the court. On the far side, scribbling notes occasionally on a yellow legal pad, a soberly dressed young man wearing horn-rim glasses was following the proceedings with unwavering attention. A law student, probably, Gael thought, preparing himself for eventual prominence on the bench. Behind him were a couple of women whose tense, anxious faces suggested a more than academic interest in the verdict. They must be relatives of the defendant—the mother and the wife, to judge by their ages. The only other onlooker, besides herself, was an old man with white hair and a military-looking mustache, who sat straight as a ruler, resting both hands on his walking stick, staring ahead with the fierce, unblinking gaze of an old hawk. It was hard to relate the intensity of that stare to the casual, almost purposeless atmosphere of the proceedings; he must be staring, she imagined, into the past—an ancient legal warrior reliving some spectacular kill of his youth.

She found it hard to keep her mind from wandering. If this was the climax to a murder appeal, as the usher outside had informed her, it was curiously undramatic. It reminded her, rather, of a dissertation on some point of philosophy by an uninspired lecturer to an audience of apathetic students. In precise, unemotional phrases the judge was working his way through the tangle of precedent toward a verdict, but there was nothing in his words or tone of voice to suggest that the issue here was violent death or that a young man's liberty might hinge on the outcome. There was no mention of the human circumstances, no recognition of the underlying turmoil of wants and fears, no acknowledgment of the panic or desperation that could lead a man to kill. Instead, there were long, painfully qualified pronouncements on the intent of the Fourth Amendment and the significance, for this case, of recent Supreme Court decisions regarding the *Miranda* rules—pronouncements, she sensed, addressed not so much to the present as to the future, to the posterity of lawyers who would pore over them, interpret them, expound their significance in cases not yet assembled, dealing with crimes as yet uncommitted, with murders whose victims were not yet born.

Yet in all this there was a sense of security. She believed that the political system, of which this placid ritual was surely an essential part, was corrupt and uncaring, protective of the haves and indifferent, if not hostile, to the have-nots. But she felt safe here, free for a moment from the anxiety that had dogged her since the break-in. They could not follow her here; there was no need, in this temple of law and order, to keep looking over her shoulder, as she had done ever since her fingers had closed around that tube of paper in the lining of Paul's jacket. She could relax here, confident that her part in the vicious melodrama would soon be over, that the paper would be delivered to Sullivan, and that he, and the other custodians of the system, would see the thing through to its end.

And it was Sullivan's presence, she was not too surprised to find, that reassured her most. Sitting at the defense table next to his client, his shoulders hunched, his chin on his chest, listening in a trance of concentration to the words of the judge, he struck her now as existing at a slight angle to the system, as being in it but not of it. She had tried all last night to contact him, and with each failure the need had seemed more urgent, so by morning there had seemed no choice but to drive out to Baltimore and catch him as he came out of court. It was illusion, probably, a feeling generated by overstretched nerves and her gathering doubts about Paul, but she had come to view him, in the midst of so much fear and suspicion, as the one person she could hold on to—solidly, immovably, dependably *there*.

A sudden stir in the court returned her attention to the proceedings. The judge had wound to his conclusion.

"It is therefore the opinion of this court," she heard him say, "that the statement made by the defendant to the police at the time of his arrest was improperly obtained and should not have been admitted in evidence."

Sullivan's client, elation all over his face, leaped to his feet. Without turning his head, Sullivan reached out a large hand, grabbed him by the coattails, and dragged him back into his seat. The judge paused.

"The defendant will kindly restrain himself," he observed mildly.

"It is further the opinion of this court that, in view of the publicity surrounding the original trial, a retrial, free from the bias of this publicity, would not be possible. The conviction is, accordingly, quashed and the case against the defendant dismissed."

With that it was over. The court was adjourned; the prosecutor, tight-lipped, marched out of the courtroom. Behind her, the two women hurried from the gallery. The law student began stuffing his notes into a briefcase. The old man did not move.

Below, amid the bustle, Sullivan stood like a stone, staring abstractedly into the middle distance. A slight frown creased his forehead. He was paying no attention whatever to the ecstatic chatter of his client. If he took any pleasure in his victory, she thought, he was keeping it to himself.

"Incredible!" the young man exulted. "It worked out just like you said. The judge even used your words. 'Violated the spirit,' he said. Just like you did. But you had it all figured, didn't you? Right from the start."

He patted Sullivan on the back and held out his hand.

At that Sullivan seemed to collect himself. He turned and saw the hand offered to him. For a second he seemed to hesitate; then he grasped it, shook it once, quickly—an absent, perfunctory movement—and turned back to gather his papers from the table.

"Mr. Sullivan?"

Sullivan, coming out of the courtroom, stopped and waited. He neither smiled nor made any gesture of greeting; he simply stood there patiently, as though her sudden appearance were just another, slightly unwelcome, claim on his time.

"Did you get my note?"

He nodded.

He hasn't forgiven me, she thought. He's still angry—and I can't honestly blame him. Remembering, she felt suddenly awkward.

"Look," she said, "about the other night . . . I'm really sorry. I was scared, you see, and not thinking very well . . . I tried to call you yesterday. Several times. But you were never in. Your secretary told me you'd be here today, so I drove out. The thing is . . ."

But he was not looking at her, she realized, and at that moment she was interrupted by a voice from behind.

"You, sir." It was the old man from the gallery. He was shaking, she saw, and his eyes, though still fierce, were full of tears.

"That was a disgrace. A travesty of justice. That young man was as guilty as sin, and you know it. Yet you swindled him free on some damned technicality. You ought to be ashamed."

"I'm sorry." Sullivan's voice was gentle. "I know how you must feel . . . It's the law, you see. We have these procedures, the best we can devise, and we try to achieve justice. Somehow, we hardly ever do. What we get, mostly, is law. Sometimes we don't even get that. I think we got it today. I can understand that to you it doesn't seem enough."

But the old man was hardly listening.

"Law," he muttered. The word was loaded with contempt. He turned away and stumped off.

"Who was that?" she asked.

"His name's Faraday." He was gazing after the old man. "He's the brother of the woman who was murdered.

"What should have I have said to him?" He turned to her suddenly, perplexed. "What does he care about the Fourth Amendment? His sister is murdered, and the law, which didn't protect her, protects the man accused of doing it. Just what the hell is there to say?"

He shook his head angrily as though trying to break free of the problem.

"I'm sorry." He seemed, at last, fully to acknowledge her presence. "I seem to have been rude . . . I did get your note. Let's go and have lunch . . . and a drink. What I need most right now is a drink."

"I don't know what to make of it." Sullivan frowned. "You're sure it was deliberately hidden?"

"It had to be. There was no hole in his pocket. He must have opened the seam and restitched it. You think it's a code?"

Sullivan shook his head

"These numbers were written at different times, some in ballpoint, others in pencil—two or three kinds of pencil, by the look of it. But there are only twenty-seven groups—enough for one short message, perhaps, but not several. Besides, ciphers are designed to avoid obvious patterns. Yet here we have seven groups with a zero-four prefix, and five with a zero-two. If this is a cipher, it's not going to fool anyone for long."

"Then what is it?"

"I think it's what you said—some kind of list. The groups look like serial numbers, and the doodles suggest that Paul—or somebody—was trying to order them. But I've no idea what they stand for."

"Well." She shrugged. "Whatever it is, I'm glad to be rid of it. The truth is I'm scared. And I don't enjoy it. I want to go back to normal life. I want to stop spending nights in hotels because I'm too scared to sleep in my own house. I want to walk down the street without wondering about each set of footsteps I hear behind me. I want to stop dreaming about 'them,' the silent, anonymous thugs whose faces are always in shadow. I want out."

"I think you are out. I'm not even completely sure you were ever in."

"Well, then why was my house searched? You know it was—and for that scrap of paper. So why couldn't they have been watching me since? Maybe they saw me get Paul's coat from the cleaners. Maybe they've been following me. Maybe . . ."

She broke off and glanced around the restaurant. There was no one in earshot; no one seemed to be paying them any attention. The other diners seemed absorbed with their own conversations, or with their food.

"Maybe they're watching us now."

She had lowered her voice, involuntarily. When she turned back to him, he was smiling.

"You think I'm being hysterical?"

"Not in the least. But I don't think you have to worry. If they did see you get the coat and decided"—he searched for a suitable euphemism—"to follow up on it, I don't think they'd have waited. And if, for some reason, they did wait, then they'll know that this"—he pulled the paper out of his pocket and waved it at her—"is no longer in your possession."

Their waiter arrived with the food, and they let him serve them in silence. The paper lay on the table between them. Presently Sullivan picked it up and put it back in his pocket.

I wanted out, Gael thought, so he's letting me out. He's making it crystal-clear to anyone watching that it's he who has it, not me. She felt a wave of gratitude toward him. Her thoughts drifted back to the courtroom, to the moment of hesitation before he'd shaken hands with his client, to his gentleness with the old man . . . How wrong you could be about people. But how eagerly you rushed to judgment.

"Did you mean what you said back there?"

"Said? Where?"

"Back there outside the courtroom, to the old man. That we try for justice with the best procedures . . ."

"And all we get is law? Yes. I'm afraid I did."

"So you think the old man was right? That what happened in court was a travesty? Was that why you didn't want to shake hands with your client?"

"Noticed that, did you?" Sullivan frowned. "I was hoping nobody did."

"Why?"

Sullivan thought.

"It was a judgment," he said. "And it wasn't mine to make. Not in public, anyway."

"It's like this," he went on. "I happen to believe the man was probably guilty. But it's not my job to make that decision. My job is to argue his case, the best I know how, on the evidence and according to the law. As a lawyer, I believed that some of the evidence used to convict him was inadmissible. So I appealed the conviction—as I was obligated to do—and as it turned out, I won. Now privately I don't feel too good about that. I still think he did it, and I sure as hell didn't want to shake hands with the little bastard. But when I'm in public, he's entitled to expect me to keep silent—especially since I'm his attorney."

"But if you feel that way, why take the case in the first place? You didn't have to, did you? Apart from anything else, he doesn't look as if he can afford you. That *is* a very fat-cat firm you work with."

"Oh." He shrugged. "I did it for nothing. There's a firm of young lawyers downtown who believe people who need good representation should have it. So do I. So I do work for them sometimes. I don't choose the cases; I just take the ones they bring. It's my way of atoning, I suppose, for being a fat cat."

"I didn't mean that personally. It was your firm I meant, not you."

"No offense." He grinned. "I am a fat cat."

"Well." She smiled back. "You may look like one, but I don't believe you are. Not inside . . . In fact"—she was suddenly serious—"I'm beginning to see you as one of the special ones."

"Me? Special?" He pulled a face. "I doubt that."

"I think you are. I'm not very fond of the system; I've always thought we could do better. But I think you're one of the people who really try to make it work. I think you care about justice, Morgan Sullivan. I saw that today in the courtroom. I saw it in the way you spoke to that old man." She hesitated. "I'm only sorry I didn't see it sooner."

"Ah," he murmured, "the irony of that. Now I feel really bad . . . I take a few cases for nothing, because I feel maybe it shouldn't always be the rich who get my services—such as they are—and where do I end up? With another kind of injustice, apparently.

"You blame the system," he went on. "I think it's the other way around. The system is fine, in itself. It's the people who mess it up. Take this case, for example. If the cop who booked my client had gone by the rules, there'd have been no appeal. But he was angry, so he pushed my client around. Not much. Not enough to hurt him. Just enough to make the whole system miscarry. But I can't honestly blame him for that. To tell the truth, I can't afford to."

He seemed to hesitate.

"You called me one of the special ones." He looked at her squarely. "I'm afraid you're mistaken. I've done the same as that cop, you see. In fact, I've done much worse."

"Worse?" She studied him gravely. "I can't see you doing that."

How had they got here, Sullivan wondered, why was he talking about this? How had the conversation wandered into this shabby corner of his life? How was it all their conversations—even that first one—ended with their confronting each other, face to face, with the masks off? He didn't know. Nor could he explain to himself why it now seemed so important that she should see him without his disguises. He only knew that it was.

"I was with the CIA at one time. I joined in the middle fifties, in the days when it seemed like a good thing to do, a worthwhile service to give. The Cold War was at its height then; Russia had just got the bomb, and America looked like democracy's only hope. None of us were troubled by doubts in those days. It seemed to us self-evident that we were in the right, that what we were striving for was so vital that the means were unimportant—at worst a very minor side issue. Even the scandals—Cuba, Chile, and the rest, and they came later—didn't make me change my mind. They bothered me, but I still thought we were right.

"Then, of course, we got into Vietnam . . . Jesus. How I hated that place! I hated what we were doing, and I hated what I was doing. But I still stayed. I guess one part of me said it was wrong but we were in it and we had to see it through . . . I didn't listen to the other part that said it was wrong period. Then my wife got killed by the Viet Cong, and for a while I stopped caring about the ethics.

"It was one day not long after that. I was interrogating a Viet Cong defector, and I just seemed to go mad. He wouldn't say anything, you see. He just sat there grinning and smoking Camels and acting dumb. I kept seeing him as the man who threw the grenade at Charley. I just couldn't get that idea out of my mind. And something just gave. One minute I was sitting there patiently asking him the same question for the zillionth time—the next I knew they were pulling me off . . . He had a jaw fracture, a broken nose, and half a dozen cracked ribs. I nearly killed him.

"And of course he knew nothing about Charley. He couldn't have. He was out in Tay Ninh province, and he was probably press-ganged into the Viet Cong in the first place. But I didn't care about that. I wanted to hurt someone. He was the right color and he happened to be available . . . All of which is why I felt like a jerk walking into that court and arguing that some big bully of a policeman had terriorized my client. It's also why I support the system. I think we designed it in our saner moments to protect us from ourselves when the feelings start to run high. God help us if we didn't have it."

And that blew it, he thought. So much for the image of Morgan Sullivan, white knight, champion of justice. But had that not been his purpose in the first place, to do away with the disguises? What had he hoped for, for Christ's sake? That she would hear his confession, absolve him, and respect him anyway? How fraudulent that was. How do you hope to be honest with others, he wondered, when you're never honest with yourself?

"God knows why I told you that," he said. "It seemed important when I started. But now I really don't know . . ." He hesitated.

"Maybe I was trying to explain why I reacted so violently to some of the things you said to me when we first met. They were a little close to the truth, perhaps, a little too close for comfort."

"No." She shook her head. "They couldn't have been further from it. I think, if the circumstances are right, we all have in us the capacity to inflict pain. You know it and it bothers you; you try to guard against it. But Nazis—that was what I called you, wasn't it?—they know it, and they don't care."

She was silent for a moment. When she spoke again, it was to change the subject.

"What was she like?"

"Who? Charley?"

She nodded.

"A little like you. Not in looks, of course, but she had the same way about her—direct and honest. In a way, fearless."

"Fearless." She gave a wry smile. "I'm hardly that. I couldn't wait, remember, to give you that paper."

"I don't mean physically, though I suspect you're that too. I mean you seem willing to see things through. Take that paper, for instance. You must have realized it might help to incriminate Paul. You could have burned it, but you didn't. Instead you brought it to me. That's what Charley would have done."

"To tell the truth . . ." She frowned. "I did think about burning it. I thought about it quite seriously. But I decided no. Paul was worth more than that; he didn't deserve that kind of distrust.

"It's odd," she went on. "You say I remind you of your wife . . . You remind me of Paul. When you were talking about the Agency just now, it might have been him speaking. I've heard him say exactly what you did. How when he joined it was like a crusade, and then everything started to go bad . . . The difference was he never left. He couldn't leave, you see, he had too much invested in it. It had consumed too much of his life. So he soldiered along, pushing the guilt to the back of his mind, telling himself it was dirty but necessary. And, of course, he was an analyst. That helped; he was never involved in operations, so he never really had to get his hands dirty. But even so, he never stopped worrying about it.

"I suppose that's why he didn't resent me. I expected him to, because I was the reason they forced him to resign—me and my unsavory past." She wrinkled her nose, "But in some funny way he seemed relieved, almost grateful. It was as though I had taken

the problem out of his hands. He didn't have to think about it
anymore."

"But he went on working for them. Consulting, at any rate."

"Yes." She grew thoughtful. "I've wondered about that . . . I
still wonder. In fact, it's one of the things I wanted to talk to you
about. You remember the first time we talked how you asked me
if there'd been anything about his behavior that struck me as
odd?"

Sullivan nodded.

"And I told you there hadn't. Well . . ." She flushed slightly.
"That wasn't entirely true. There was something. He took to going
off by himself. Not regularly, but often. Twice in a week maybe,
then not for several weeks. The point is that usually when he went
out in the boat he'd take me with him. But on these occasions he
didn't. He had ways of making it clear when he didn't want me—
he needed to be alone, he would say, or he had work to do. But
he always took work to the boat, even when I was along, so it
never quite rang true.

"At first I didn't think anything of it. But then it got to be more
frequent. And he became increasingly moody. I thought maybe
he was getting tired of me, that he was trying to tell me something,
but that wasn't like him. If it had been that, he'd have come right
out with it. Then, when he went off that last time, and all the newspapers started asking questions . . ." She faltered. "I started to
wonder too.

"Then you came along. At first I wanted to protect him; I wasn't
ready to talk about it. But then, as I say, I came to see that wasn't
the proper way. Now I want to know—for his sake and mine both.
So I want you to promise me something."

"What?"

"Two things, actually. I want you to promise to get to the bottom
of this. I think you'll do that anyway. But when you do, I want you
to tell me. I want to know the truth about Paul—whatever it is.
Will you promise me that?"

"Yes." He met her eyes steadily. "I will. But in that case," he
added, "there's something else I need to know."

"Yes?"

He hesitated. Was it worth it? he wondered. Was it worth disturbing the intimacy precariously established between them for a
question whose answer might not resolve a thing? She'd said she
wanted the truth about Paul. But had she said it only in the con-

fidence that the truth would turn out to confirm her own belief? How would she take it if, as he was more than a little afraid, it turned out otherwise? Would she be able to forgive him for that?

"Bunin?" he asked. "Ivan Bunin. He left the U.N. in mid-1977. That was more than a year after the start of your relationship with Paul. The FBI file says you remained on friendly terms with Bunin. Did he ever, to your knowledge, meet Paul?"

She frowned. "Now you sound like a prosecutor again. Yes. As a matter of fact, he did. I introduced them, I think. At a party I gave in Georgetown."

"Did they ever meet after that?"

"Not to my knowledge. They may have. Paul liked him, I remember." Her eyes clouded. "I did too. He was an extraordinarily charming man. In fact, I find it very difficult to believe he was a spy."

"He may not have been. Nothing was ever proved against him. The FBI, however, believes he was a spotter."

"Spotter?"

"A talent spotter. Someone who identifies potential agents. People with the inclination and the access to be useful. The spotter steers them in the KGB's direction; somebody else does the actual recruiting. Spotters are often legitimate diplomats, and difficult to nail for that reason."

"And you think Ivan may have spotted Paul?"

"There's a good chance. But that doesn't mean Paul was recruited. Temptation is not the same as sin, thank God. They met, though; it's something to bear in mind."

"Something to bear in mind." She frowned once again. "I wish you didn't have to. I don't like to think of you . . . rooting around in my past."

"Believe me." Sullivan was earnest. "I don't like it either."

"I suppose not." She eyed him gloomily. "I think I like you, Morgan Sullivan. But I don't like your job. I wish we could have met in other circumstances."

"Me too . . . But is there any reason why we shouldn't?"

She hesitated.

"Maybe not. It's hard to say, under the circumstances. We'll have to see."

He let it go at that. It wasn't as good as a promise, but it was better than nothing.

II

When Sullivan got to his office the next morning, Roy Tyrell was there having coffee. As usual, he was sprawled on the sofa with his feet on the coffee table in front of him. Beside him was a cardboard box and a stack of file folders. He had been reading one of the files, but he put it down when Sullivan entered. "Aha," he drawled. "The man we love to hate."

"We do?" Sullivan stopped, puzzled.

"Michael Eglinton does. He's been breathing fire since you spoke to him. He feels you impugned the security of his division. He's tending to view you as a reincarnation of Spearman. Have a doughnut."

"Doughnuts?" Sullivan was temporarily diverted. "What are you doing with doughnuts? I thought you only ate protein."

"They're for you. A post-breakfast snack. If you had breakfast, that is."

"I did this morning." Sullivan grinned. "Tuna fish. I shared a can with Cooper. It's all he'll eat these days. He's getting very picky."

"Shared breakfast with a cat?" Tyrell's eyebrows rose. "You're becoming a slob, Morgan. You should find yourself a woman to civilize you."

"Possibly." An image of Gael passed quickly through his mind. He sat down on the couch beside Tyrell.

"So Eglinton finds me a pain?" he asked. "Who else does?"

"Everett's not crazy about you, but he's not crazy about anyone. He's pleased about Eglinton, though. He loves it when somebody goofs. He's ordered a procedures review of Eglinton's division. And he's put Patterson in charge. Eglinton is madder than a wet hen."

"Patterson," Sullivan mused. "I'm interested in Patterson. Tell me about him."

"Nothing to tell. He's what he seems. A one-man disaster area— mean, small-minded, disappointed in his ambitions, vindictive. Completely out of his depth."

"Out of his depth?"

"He's in the wrong business. Counterintelligence takes imagination, subtlety, finesse. I don't have to tell you that. Patterson is strictly a left-hemisphere man. A to B to C. That kind of thinking. Spearman despaired of him."

"Yet Spearman left, and Patterson stayed?"

"Spearman had too much imagination . . . I told you about that. But in his way he was magnificent. Did you know, for instance, he suspected the Sino-Soviet dispute was a gigantic con, designed to lull us into a sense of false security. He could argue it, too. Very persuasively. He had imagination, all right. On a grand scale."

"Go back to Patterson for a second. As I listened to your description, it struck me I was hearing the profile of a classic first-degree risk. 'Mean, small-minded, disappointed in his ambitions, vindictive.' "

Tyrell pursed his lips. He eyed Sullivan thoughtfully.

"Morgan." He sounded concerned. "You wouldn't be coming down with a case of Spearman's Disease?"

"No. Listen. Patterson never did explain properly what he was doing in that registry."

"He was stirring up shit," Tyrell replied promptly. "It doesn't make sense to you because you don't think that way. If you knew him it would."

"Everyone discounts Patterson," Sullivan murmured. "I wonder why."

"He's a lightweight—eminently discountable." Tyrell shrugged.

"No." Sullivan shook his head. "It's not that. Not entirely . . . Look, Roy." He leaned forward. "There's something bothering me."

"There usually is." Tyrell smiled. "What is it?"

"Everyone around here is too complacent. Everett, for example. He didn't spell it out exactly, but the meaning was clear. 'There is no mole. Seligman was OK. So write your report and get the hell out of here.' Eglinton even came right out and said it. It's the same story with Patterson. He's found in Eglinton's registry, right in among the crown jewels, he comes up with some utterly lamebrain story about checking security, and people practically fall over each other in the rush to believe him. Eglinton calls him trusted and reliable, and in the next breath says he doesn't have the balls to be anything else. You say he's mean and vindictive—and that makes his story true . . . I don't get it. There are grounds for concern about Seligman and Patterson both, but nobody's sweating. It makes me wonder if there's something you know and I don't."

"Like what, for example?"

Sullivan considered. This was a point of decision. He could try for a reaction by voicing Brady's suspicions, or he could play dumb. The former course might simply put them on their guard; playing dumb, on the other hand, would leave him exactly where he was. He decided to take the risk.

"I'm going to be hypothetical for a moment. If the Agency found itself with a mole on its hands, how would it deal with the situation? If it knew who the mole was, let's say."

"Hard to say." Tyrell shrugged. "It would depend a lot on the flap potential."

"Let's say that the flap potential was enormous. Is it possible the Agency might be tempted—how shall I put this?—quietly to take care of its own?"

Tyrell gave a long whistle. "Jesus, I was right about you. You are coming down with a case of Spearman's Disease."

"Am I?"

"Looks like it. You're displaying the classic symptoms."

"Such as?"

"Ignoring the obvious in favor of something impossibly sinister and complicated. Look, you're puzzled by the general complacency, you say. Nobody seems to be sweating. But be realistic. Nobody wants to be caught sweating. Nobody wants you here, and everyone has his axe to grind. Everett, for example, doesn't want any more mole talk. He's worried about the treaty; the President tells him to worry, so he does. Eglinton worries about his position: he doesn't want anyone suggesting the satellite systems have been breached. Patterson is generally pissed off: he wanted Spearman's job, didn't get it, and is now hitting out at targets of opportunity . . . There's no need to assume a conspiracy. People serve their own interests. I think it's as simple as that."

"So you're each marching to the beat of a different drummer?"

"Drummer?" Tyrell, in the midst of lighting a cigarette, was suddenly still.

"Yes. You're all following different beats, yet you're all amazingly in step."

"For now we are." Tyrell blew out his match and grinned. "We're all waiting for the word on Seligman. When we get it, of course, there may be some breaking of ranks."

Sullivan wondered if he'd gained anything. What Roy said made sense, up to a point. There'd certainly been nothing revealing about his reaction. But then, he hadn't expected anything from Roy. It was what happened when Roy passed it on. Shake the tree. It was what he had promised Brady, but was it what he'd been doing? Perhaps a more accurate description might be "floundering around."

"You never ate your doughnut." Tyrell's voice cut in on his thoughts.

"You're right. I didn't." He reached for the box, which he had placed without thinking on Tyrell's stack of folders. As he did, his eye fell on the top one, taking in but not really registering the stern official admonitions stamped on its cover. He took a doughnut and bit into it, replacing the box on the table beside the folders. Something stirred in his memory. He took a closer look at the cover of the top folder. In the upper right-hand corner was a number, the file number.

He read it, It was CSX 04 382 78.

And suddenly the pieces seemed to fall into place.

CHAPTER 9

I

As soon as Tyrell had left the office Sullivan got on the phone. The next ten minutes were spent explaining his needs to Registry, the rest of the morning waiting for the replies. By lunchtime they were in, and he was ready to tackle Everett. Here, however, he encountered an obstacle: despite the repeated promises of Everett's secretary, Everett did not return his calls. The Director of Central Intelligence evidently believed in the loneliness of power. By late afternoon Sullivan had had enough; he called and left a message that he was about to report to the Committee and felt obliged, as a matter of courtesy, to let Everett know. Within minutes he was in the Director's office.

"Wrapped it up already?" Everett looked up as he entered. "That was amazingly quick."

He was reading a report and made no move to close it. He personified the busy executive, Sullivan thought, unable to spare more than a few precious moments, and somewhat reluctant to spare those.

"I've made some progress." Sullivan parked himself, uninvited, in a chair opposite Everett. "I wouldn't say it was wrapped up exactly."

"No?" Everett frowned. "Then what's all this about going back to the Committee? I thought you'd agreed not to unless you had something to report."

"I do have something to report. I think Seligman was spying for the Russians."

Everett shut the report, but said nothing.

"And I think the integrity of the satellite systems is questionable."

Everett remained silent.

"I also think people in the Agency have been giving me the runaround. I therefore propose—"

"Wait." Everett came to life. "Are you saying my people are involved in some kind of cover-up?"

Interesting word, Sullivan thought. His word, not mine . . . Interesting set of responses, too. No comment on the news that his ship has been torpedoed; panic at the suggestion of wrongdoing by the crew.

"Cover-up?" he queried. "No. I'm not prepared to go that far—yet. I just don't think your people have been completely candid. So I'm asking the Committee for a broader mandate—a full security review, conducted by a team of independent investigators. And when I get it, I'm going to rip this place apart."

"Rip it apart? What kind of horseshit is that?" Everett's first instinct, as usual, was to browbeat. Then he caught the look in Sullivan's eye and thought better of it.

"But you came to me first?"

Sullivan nodded.

"Then this could be negotiable?"

"Possibly. What are you offering?"

"Depends on what you want." Everett's voice was wary.

"I want the story—the whole story."

"Which story is that?" Everett looked blank.

"Shit!" Sullivan pushed back his chair and stood up. "This is a waste of time. I came here as a courtesy. I didn't have to."

"Courtesy? Odd kind of courtesy. I'd call it blackmail."

"Blackmail, negotiation." Sullivan shrugged. "Call it what you like. I doubt if the Committee will care. They'll be too busy hitting the panic button. I think they'll authorize an investigation that will make previous efforts look like hunt-the-thimble—unless, of course, you persuade me it's not necessary." He remained standing.

Everett's response was immediate. "I can hardly do that unless I know what you're talking about."

"Well, I'm prepared to tell you, if you're prepared to listen."

"Then sit down." Everett reached for the telephone. "And hold your horses. I want Tyrell to hear this."

The waiting was conducted in silence. Everett pointedly went back to his report; Sullivan stared out the window. Shake the tree, he was thinking. See what comes tumbling out. Or should it, perhaps, be who? See *who* comes tumbling out. He wondered if it might not be himself.

Tyrell took in the situation as soon as he entered. He glanced quickly from one to the other, flashed a grin at Sullivan, and sat down in the chair at the opposite corner of Everett's desk.

"Somebody die?" he asked.

"Your buddy"—Everett stressed the second word—"is blackmailing us."

"Blackmail, bullshit!" Sullivan snapped. "I'm simply laying out options."

"He thinks Seligman was a mole," Everett cut in. "And he thinks we're covering up. So he's threatening to go back to the Committee unless we come clean. I wanted you to hear this."

It was your bright idea, his tone implied. And see where it got us.

Tyrell turned to Sullivan. "In that case, perhaps I'd better hear it. Go ahead, Morgan. Let's have the case against Seligman—prosecution's opening statement."

"I'm going to begin"—Sullivan found himself, perhaps in response to Tyrell's choice of words, using his courtroom manner— "by reminding you of what you know already. About two years ago Seligman was forced to resign from the Agency because of his association with a woman named Gael Forrester. For all kinds of reasons, including a liaison with a suspected KGB talent spotter, Gael Forrester was regarded as a risk, unsuitable company for a high-ranking Agency officer. This is all in the file. The record is somewhat cryptic, but I'm satisfied this is essentially what happened. Miss Forrester, incidentally, corroborates it.

"Shortly after his resignation, Seligman was retained as a consultant by the Agency. In this capacity he had continued access to classified material and key Agency personnel . . . I should add here, parenthetically, that I find this almost incredible. If he was risk enough to be fired, then continuing to allow him that kind of access strikes me as little short of criminal."

"Not really," Tyrell interjected. "We were short of analysts and missed his expertise. The consulting gave him access to general surveys only. Classified, but not very sensitive."

"Be that as it may." Sullivan frowned. "I'm not qualified to judge. In any case, it's a side issue. The main point is, what he was getting under the consulting arrangement wasn't all he was getting. Not by a long shot. He was getting more—a great deal more."

He waited for reactions. There were none.

"That doesn't seem to surprise you."

"I'll be surprised when I'm convinced," Everett growled, emphasizing the last word. "Suppose you tell us how you know."

"It's simple. Seligman had a list. A list of serial numbers. It took me a while to recognize them as Agency file numbers—the letter prefixes were missing—but once I'd made the connection, it was very easy to verify. I just took a random selection of numbers from the list and submitted it to Registry. Did they have any files, I asked, with numbers matching the ones on the list. It turned out they did—in every single case."

"Wait a moment," Tyrell interrupted. "Let me get this straight. Seligman had a list of numbers, you say, but without letter prefixes. And the digits in his numbers matched those of certain Agency files. And these files weren't among the ones passed to him under the consulting arrangement?"

"Exactly. I didn't give Registry all the numbers on Seligman's list—I didn't want to waste their time. And one match in seven you could conceivably write off to coincidence. But seven? No way. Seligman's list was a list of Agency files."

"That doesn't prove anything," Everett objected. "He could have made the list before he left, omitted the letter prefixes for security reasons, and forgotten all about it."

"I'm afraid not. The list was found sewn into the lining of one of Seligman's jackets. Which suggests that his reasons for having it, whatever they were, were hardly innocent. But the clincher is this— three of the numbers in the sample I submitted to Registry were for files opened after April 1976. Subsequent, that's to say, to his leaving the Agency. So someone—and someone, presumably, who's still here—was giving him those numbers. And what use would the numbers be without the files?"

"How did you get this list?" Everett asked.

Sullivan told him, omitting, however, any mention of the raid on Gael's apartment. Instinct and training both cautioned him against revealing his whole hand. He would give them as little as possible, the bare minimum to justify his stand, and see what they made of it. He could then use what he hadn't given them as a check on what they said. He'd asked Everett for the story; there were stories and stories, he knew, and he was not interested in fiction.

Everett, in any event, was not impressed by what he was given.

"I don't call that proof," he sneered. "It all rests on the word of the girl. And I can't think of any reason for believing *her*.

"Look at it this way," he argued. "Finding, or pretending to find, that list would be a perfect way of stirring up trouble for us. And she's been associated with more than one group devoted to doing just that. It ties in with what I warned you about. Someone is determined to keep this thing alive. And you," he accused, "are giving him every assistance."

"A good try . . . but no points." It was Tyrell, surprisingly, who responded. "What Morgan will counter, unfortunately, is that someone outside the Agency—whether Seligman or not doesn't much matter—compiled that list. And he can only have done that by receiving the information from someone inside the Agency. So the problem changes its shape, perhaps, but remains a problem. Am I right, Morgan?"

"Close enough."

Though grateful for the support, Sullivan was nevertheless puzzled by it. In ordinary circumstances Roy's delight in needling Everett might be explanation enough, but here the integrity of the Agency itself was at stake. Roy cared about that, probably cared much more than Everett, because for Roy the Agency was not merely an intermediate rung on the ladder of office, nor yet simply a career; it was nothing less than the cause to which he had dedicated his life. How, then, could he remain so cool?

The obvious answer was that he knew something, something he was confident would absolve the Agency. But why hadn't he admitted it before? He'd been forbidden, perhaps, by Everett. Compelled by duty to put obedience before friendship. Sullivan could understand that. But it didn't resolve anything. For what he couldn't understand, in that case, was why Roy had been so eager to involve him in this farce.

"You're close," he repeated. "And in strict logic I can't beyond doubt connect Seligman with the list. But I'm convinced it was his.

"He was on somebody's payroll." He brought it out abruptly.

"From June 1976 until the month before he disappeared he received fifteen hundred dollars a month in cash, over and above his normal income. Where did it come from? I don't know. What was it for? I can't be certain about that either. But in the light of what I've already told you, I can hazard a very educated guess."

"How did you discover it?" Tyrell asked.

"He put it in his checking account. Regularly. About the middle of each month."

"Put it in his account?" For the first time it seemed Tyrell was shocked. "What an extraordinary thing to do!"

Sullivan nodded.

"Don't ask me why. I can't tell you. There's a lot I can't tell you. It's what I *can* tell you that scares the shit out of me."

"Is there more?"

"A little . . . Seligman met Bunin, the suspected talent spotter. Gael Forrester introduced them. That may not mean anything, but the timing is bothersome. It happened, she thinks, in early May 1976. About a month, that is, before the payments started."

"Is that it?" Everett asked. He was quiet now, Sullivan noticed; all the bluster had evaporated.

Sullivan nodded. "Let me summarize it for you in the proper sequence. Seligman was fired as a risk. He was introduced to a suspected KGB spotter. He was subsequently rehired on a consulting basis. A month later he started receiving regular cash handouts. Now he turns out to have been in possession of a list of Agency files he shouldn't have known about, and couldn't have unless someone on the inside was telling him. To cap everything, he had regular contact with Agency personnel, and any of those contacts may—as Comrade Patterson's recent actions have demonstrated—have had access to the satellite manuals. The inference is obvious. He was selling secrets to the Russians. And among them, very possibly, were the satellite secrets."

For several seconds there was silence. Then Everett spoke.

"Two things," he said. "You've made a reasonably good case against Seligman, but you haven't explained how he died, or why. And where's the cover-up? You came in here complaining that we weren't being completely candid. Yet, as far as I can see, you've managed to build your case without any interference from us. What are you bitching about?"

"I think I can explain that," Tyrell said. "I think your points are tied in together. You see, Morgan here believes we're not worried enough. About Seligman, I mean. He thinks we should be sweating more. And he thinks the fact we're not suggests that we already know about Seligman—that we know he was a spy, that we know the extent of the damage, and that we've already taken care of the problem in our own inimitable way."

"Taken care of it?"

"Yes," Tyrell replied calmly. "I think he thinks we murdered him."

Everett, who had been doodling in the margin of his notes, was suddenly still. For a second he sat transfixed, his eyes unblinking, his pencil arrested in mid-stroke. He looked as if he had seen a Gorgon.

Slowly he raised his head to confront Sullivan.

"Is this true?"

"Poisoned wet suits for Castro . . ." Sullivan shrugged. "Why not weighted diving belts for Seligman?"

"And you think you have evidence?"

"Some," Sullivan bluffed. "Not enough to make it stick. But enough to bother me. Enough to make me go to the Committee and get a mandate to find out. Unless, as I said before, you can convince me otherwise."

At that, Everett seemed to come to a decision. He turned abruptly to Tyrell.

"I think," he said, "you'd better tell him the story."

II

"So what *is* the story?"

Sullivan studied the two men confronting him. Everett was leaning forward, his shoulders hunched, his head tilted slightly back, staring down his nose as if in a last-ditch effort at intimidation. Tyrell, on the other hand, was sprawled sideways in his chair, one leg draped over the arm and swinging gently to and fro. Even after a whole day in the office he still managed to look as if he'd just arrived. His shoes were unscuffed, his suit was unrumpled, his shirt was as fresh and crisp as when he'd put it on. In contrast to Everett, who was a study in tension, he looked completely at ease, untroubled by the confrontation, perhaps actually enjoying

it. Sullivan found him remarkable; he'd known many people who
thrived under pressure, but none who seemed to live on it in quite
the same way as Roy.

"I must congratulate you, Morgan." The drawl was as languid as
ever. "The hand has not lost its cunning. You've been remarkably
quick."

Sullivan shook his head. "I've been remarkably lucky. The list
and the cash were what did it. Without them, I'd be nowhere."

"Quick, lucky—whatever." Tyrell shrugged. "The point is
somehow you managed to put your finger on most of the pertinent facts."

"Facts, yes . . . But in what way pertinent?" Sullivan raised
his eyebrows. "*That's* what I expect you to tell me."

"Fine," Tyrell said. "But first let me confirm the facts. Just
so we all know what we're talking about."

He leaned slightly on the word "all," at the same time bestowing
a bland smile on Everett. He had the air, Sullivan thought, of a
schoolmaster encouraging a slightly backward pupil.

"First, you're right about Seligman. He *was* passing secrets to
the Russians. And getting paid for it. Second, we *did* know all
about it. Third, he *was* getting help."

"Ah." Sullivan leaned forward. "He *was* getting help? And I
suppose you know who was giving it to him?"

"Yes." Tyrell smiled again.

"Then I presume there'd be no objection to my knowing who
it was?"

"Not in the least," Tyrell said calmly. "I was."

For a moment Sullivan was beyond words. He sat back in his
chair, let his breath out in a protracted whistle, and raised his eyes
to heaven.

"Shit," he said at last. "An operation. I should have known."

"No reason why you should." Tyrell paused. "What I'm about to
tell you is at present known only to four people in the Agency . . .
three, actually, since I suppose we must assume the fourth is
dead . . . I need hardly emphasize that it is not to be mentioned
in any report you may make to the Committee."

"No," Sullivan said flatly. "No blind deals. I'll hear, then I'll
decide."

"And if you're satisfied our security's intact?"

"That's different. In that case, I'll tell the Committee so. But
without details . . . Is that good enough?"

Tyrell looked at Everett.

"I guess it'll have to be," Everett muttered.

"OK," Tyrell resumed. "What we're talking about here is an operation named Theta. Theta was a brainchild of mine . . . At least—" he smiled briefly at Everett—"since it doesn't seem to have been an unqualified success, I imagine no one will begrudge me the credit.

"Actually, it might be more accurate to call Theta a child of strife, conceived in the last tortured months of the Spearman inquisition. Morale, as I've told you, was very low in those days. People were running scared, worrying about their pensions, covering up papers when you walked into the room. Factions in the Agency wouldn't speak to one another. There was a Gadarene rush to take early retirement . . . a situation, in fact"—he cast a sidelong glance at Everett—"not unlike the present.

"At some point, I can't remember exactly when, I started thinking about the opposition. If they only knew, I thought; if they could only see us, they'd be breaking out the champagne . . . Then it came to me that of course they did know. I mean, apart from anything else, it was all over the cocktail circuit. Hints were even beginning to surface in *Time* . . . And it occurred to me that if I were my opposite number in the KGB, I'd be doing more than celebrating—I'd be out looking for ways to exploit the situation. After all, the victory of the masses is still some distance off, and fishing in troubled waters is a favorite hobby of theirs.

"And that's how Theta was born. They'd be out trawling for agents, I figured. It seemed only courteous to help them out."

"Then Theta was a misinformation exercise?" Sullivan cut in. "The classic ploy. You fix them up with an apparently disgruntled Agency officer, establish his credibility by giving him chickenfeed to pass, and then . . ."

"Exactly." Tyrell nodded. "Then you give them something to gag on. Pig swill preferably. Generously seasoned with broken glass.

"The problem, of course," he went on, "was to find an actor for the leading part. We had disgruntled officers in droves by that time, but they were genuinely disgruntled; it didn't seem wise to put temptation in their paths. Loyal subjects, on the other hand, are usually looking to make a career here. With them you face a reentry problem.

"You don't just ask someone to do something like that out of the blue. You can't. Because if he has the brains to be worth asking in the first place, he's going to know what it is you're asking. You can never bring him back, you see. You destroy his usefulness for anything else. While he's active you have to limit his access to what you can afford to lose, in case they catch him and put him through the grinder. And when he's blown, as they all are in the end, you can never quite bring yourself to trust him again—if he's still around to trust, that is—because you can never be certain he hasn't been turned."

He broke off then, his face clouding, it seemed, with memories. When he resumed, it was in a different tone, serious, almost somber, with no trace of his normal flippancy.

"Morgan, you said something once about what this work can do to people. And you were talking about the desk jockeys, case officers and the like. Well, I'm talking about the front line. Strange things can happen to your loyalties out there in the middle, in no-man's-land, taking orders—and money—from both sides. The boundaries start to get hazy; the old distinctions become blurred. Black isn't as dark anymore; white isn't as clean; everything is colored dirty gray. In the end, I suppose, the whole idea of sides loses its meaning. Friends, enemies—what's the difference? You're in it for yourself by then, for what you can get out of it—money, generally, or kicks. Usually both.

"It's an addiction, you see, and, like all addictions, ultimately self-destructive. A one-way street to nowhere. Not many want to take it."

There was an impatient movement on the other side of the desk.

"Are you dictating your memoirs?" Everett grumbled. "Or can we expect you to return to the operation at some point? I have a dinner appointment with Izakson at eight."

"Yes." Tyrell eyed him coolly. "God forbid the senator's steaks should spoil."

It was Spearman who'd solved the problem, he continued. Spearman, desperate for scapegoats, had fastened on Seligman, and Seligman had been axed. In a quite sympathetic and friendly way, with the knowledge scarcely concealed on either side that office politics had wielded the hatchet, and with the promise of a comfortable consulting job to smooth his path in the hereafter. And Seligman had been only minimally bitter, knowing the ways of this particular world, and knowing also that he had reached his limit anyway, that GS 17 was as high as he would go . . . At that point, Tyrell had sat back and waited.

"You didn't wait very long," Sullivan commented. "He left in April and was on their payroll by June."

"I never expected to wait very long." Tyrell's reply was prompt. "Spearman's parting gift was incredibly well chosen. Seligman had to be an inviting target for them, and the woman's circle of acquaintance made it almost certain he'd be spotted. I told him that before he left. And I also mentioned that I'd take it kindly if he would play along a little. I said that with a little luck we might be able to roll up a network or two . . . Wasn't strictly my business, of course; it was Spearman's. But he wouldn't have taken that kind of suggestion from Spearman at that point. Whereas from me he would."

"I'm surprised he'd take it from anyone."

"You didn't know him. He was almost a founding father—one of the Agency's Four Hundred. He'd been shafted, pleasantly, apologetically, thoroughly shafted, but his loyalty was absolute. To him the Agency was not a career, it was a duty."

"And he didn't know, when he left, what you had in mind for him?"

"Not altogether. I simply pointed out to him the more or less obvious fact that at some stage he'd be contacted, and asked him not to react like a frightened virgin when it happened. Play it cool, I told him; ask for time to think, and let me know."

"And how was he to do that? I mean, you would expect them to watch him pretty closely after the first approach. He couldn't just go running back to you. They'd simply have scuttled back into the woodwork, in that case. Besides," he added, "I wonder that he swallowed your story about rolling up networks in the first place. Networks my ass! The Russians are smarter than that. I doubt whether, even by the end, he could have given you a description of his principal case officer."

Tyrell smiled. "Well, of course, you know that. But he didn't. He'd never been exposed to the clandestine side at all, let alone counterintelligence. No. I worked out a simple signaling procedure. It worked around the pension checks, his one open channel to the Agency. Cash all the checks immediately, I told him, until you're contacted. Then hold the next check at least two weeks. And I instructed Accounts to notify me whenever a check of his was held."

"Well, that's fine . . . as far as it goes. But what then? You still have the problem of a pipeline. He's on the outside, and you're on the inside, and as soon as that line is crossed, the alarm bells start ringing all over Dzerzhinsky Square."

"Yes. But I had a solution for that—a thing of beauty, I believed at the time. I still do. As soon as the first check was held up, we were to activate the consulting arrangement. That would kill two birds . . . You see, he being strictly an analyst, the product they could expect from him in the normal course of things would be limited: who worked where, the current U.S. assessment of the Soviet nuclear stockpile, satellite timetables—the sort of stuff they could check for accuracy by taking a subscription to *U.S. News and World Report*. But the consulting arrangement would give him legitimate access to the Agency, meaning not only the potential for high-level product—very tempting for them—but also a cast-iron excuse for visiting Langley. Shit, he could come to my office whenever he liked."

"And it worked?"

It seemed that it had. Seligman had been very quickly spotted, Tyrell said, by Bunin or by somebody else, and contacted within a month. Tyrell had then waited awhile and activated the pipeline. Once that had been done, the whole proposition had been placed before Seligman.

"And he went along?"

He had done that too. After all, Tyrell explained, he was virtually committed before he left the Agency. After that it was only a question of sheep and lambs. If he were willing to go along for the sake of rolling up networks, he would hardly have been likely to draw the line at a little misinformation . . . And there you had it, Tyrell said. A classic misinformation exercise. Straight out of Hoyle.

"Except that something went wrong." Everett beat Sullivan to the punch. "And we were landed with a first-class scandal and a Senate investigation."

"Yes," Tyrell agreed. "Something obviously did go wrong."

"What?" Sullivan's question plopped like a pebble into the ensuing silence.

"You tell me . . ." Tyrell spread his hands. "I can guess, of course."

"He was blown." Sullivan supplied the answer. "And murdered—in a way deliberately calculated to create mystery and cast suspicion on the Agency."

"Something like that." Tyrell nodded. *"Pour encourager les autres* . . . A message from the management at Dzerzhinsky Square: 'Don't do it again.' "

"Well." Everett turned to Sullivan. "Are you satisfied?"

Sullivan stared at him, opposing the Director's belligerence with a cool determination.

"No," he said. "Absolutely not."

Everett was the first to recover. "Well, what more do you want?" he growled. "Color pictures, for Christ's sake? An affidavit from Brezhnev? These things aren't written down, you know. You don't keep files on an operation as sensitive as this."

"I know that." Sullivan kept his voice even. "I want details. Who decided what to pass? How did the mechanics work? What was the ultimate goal?"

"I can supply those," Tyrell offered. "Within reason, of course . . . The decision on what to pass was taken by Brayer and me. He ruled on the intelligence value of what was offered; I checked the danger to sources."

"What about the mechanics? You've already told me that the stuff he reviewed under the consulting arrangement was low-level, of no particular value to the Russians. So how did you supplement? I mean, you can hardly fire someone as a potential security risk and then turn around three months later and give him the run of the Agency. I can't see the Russians swallowing that. So what was the story?"

"We did it with the think pieces. They were generalized and low-level, as I said, but a good analyst could use them, nevertheless, to generate specific follow-up questions. Seligman would pass the think pieces to his contact, and the contact would later come back to him with more questions. Then Seligman would come to the office and tell us he couldn't possibly assess the think piece without such and such detailed information on the backup. Some of the time, of course, I'd refuse to play along. There's such a thing as being too willing. But often I'd allow him to see specific reports under direct supervision. He'd memorize them and pass them on."

"Sounds thin."

"Possibly. But you have to remember two things. One was that Seligman's cover story made him a scapegoat. We never really distrusted him, the story went, circumstances simply forced us to behave as if we did. And the consulting arrangement permitted us to play it both ways: we could continue to use him for the work he was really good at, and yet appear to have covered our asses security-wise.

"The second point is that the mechanics were really their idea. All we did was throw them an innocent, an analyst ignorant of tradecraft, whose present relationship gave him limited access to chickenfeed. We left it to them to figure out how to exploit the situation. They had to work out the details, supply the tradecraft, come up with the story. All he had to do was act dumb, and willing."

"And supplementary questions are what they came up with?"

"Yes. They were pretty good at them, actually. Their questions were always pretty scattered—they didn't suggest any obvious intelligence targets—and they were always authentic. I mean they were always the sorts of things Seligman might genuinely have needed to know in order to make a competent assessment. Also, I doubt that even the supplementaries were their primary target. They were very patient; they never pushed too hard. But they were always telling him to keep his eyes open when he was in the office. I guess they were figuring that in the end we'd get used to having him around and, if the cover story were really true, we'd start to get careless . . . which, of course, we did."

"How?"

"Oh, we started to leave stuff on the desk where he could see it. I'd get called out over some flap or other and leave him there for a few minutes—things like that. And that was when, from their point of view, the investment began to pay dividends."

"So he never really did have the run of the place? He was never in Eglinton's division, for instance?"

"Hell no." Tyrell sounded shocked. "He'd be escorted in by a guard and escorted out again. He was checked for cameras and suchlike, in and out. And he never saw anything that Brayer and I hadn't agreed he could see."

Sullivan considered. It sounded plausible, reasonably plausible. The kind of opportunity the Russians would try to exploit, and more or less in the way Roy had described. And yet there remained questions. What had it all been about, for instance? Why had the Agency been willing to go to these lengths? And why had the Russians, as it appeared, been so easy to trick?

"What was the target?" he asked. "I think I understand the operation—how it worked, that is. But what was it intended to achieve?"

Tyrell's reply was prompt and definite. "Sorry. I can't tell you that. It's not relevant to your inquiry."

"I'd like to be the judge of that."

"No. It involved agent protection. That's as far as I'm prepared to go."

"But the operation failed, for Christ's sake!"

"Probably," Tyrell conceded. "But we can't be certain of it. If the KGB murdered him, which seems a likely bet, then I suppose it did. But it hasn't been proved that they did, so I'm not willing to assume anything yet. You don't need to know the target, Morgan, and I'm not going to tell you."

Sullivan turned to Everett.

"Do you go along with this?"

From the corner of his eye he could see Roy's expression of surprise and resentment. It was dirty pool, he evidently thought, for Sullivan to try to exploit the antagonism between him and his overlord. But Sullivan felt no guilt. Roy had chosen his company in this matter, and Roy could live with it.

Everett hesitated. The urge to assert himself by overruling his exasperating subordinate, Sullivan could see, was very strong.

"Yes." Everett overcame it. "Look, Sullivan. You're empowered to conduct an inquiry into a specific occurrence—Seligman's disappearance. You are not entitled to poke your nose into any corner of the Agency's business that takes your fancy. You're way beyond your mandate here, and I'm perfectly willing to defend that position before the Committee."

"Fine." Sullivan accepted this with the appearance of equanimity. "Then there's another question I have to ask. And I'm sure even you will concede I'm entitled to ask it."

"Yes?"

"Just why the fuck"—he spat the words out, each one separately, like cherry pits—"didn't you tell me all this before?"

"Look, Morgan." It was Tyrell, unexpectedly, who answered. "You're still not sure whether you believe us, are you?"

"To be quite honest, no."

"And if we'd taken you to one side your first day here, before you'd even had a chance to look at the files, and whispered it into your shell-like ear, would you have believed us then?"

"I don't know." Sullivan thought about it. "Probably not."

"You're damn right you wouldn't. You couldn't go back to the Committee and say, 'Guess what? My old friend Roy Tyrell just told me the whole story and there's nothing to worry about.' You'd have to have checked some anyway. So you haven't lost anything.

"But that doesn't really answer your question," he continued. "I'm afraid the real answer is we didn't want to tell you anyway. Theta was sensitive. It still is. And the Committee leaks like a sieve. We didn't want to risk having it written up in your report to them, and appearing two days later on the front page of the *Post*. But then you got hold of that list and found out about the money, and we were forced to change our minds. It's as simple as that."

"You could have asked me to suppress the details. After all, I agreed to do that just about ten minutes ago."

"We could, but we chose not to. You know how it is in this business. You don't trust anybody if you don't have to."

"I see. So my investigation has been, as Eglinton said, a pointless charade?"

"Not entirely. We needed to get the Committee off our back." This was Everett's contribution.

"Did you?" Sullivan's voice was cold. He looked from one to the other. "And now you think you've done that?' Well, I shall have to disappoint you. I was here before, remember. I spent ten years here. When you live around stables, you learn to recognize the smell."

He turned to Tyrell.

"You asked me if I'd have believed you if you'd told me all this in the beginning . . . Well, I probably wouldn't. And for pretty much the same reason I'm suspending judgment now. There's no corroboration. There are no files, you say. No records. Nothing. The whole story rests on your unsupported word."

"I see." Tyrell's voice was quiet. "I can remember when that would have been enough."

"I know. It still is—in any area but this. But I know where your loyalties lie, Roy. Besides, as you point out, I have to convince the Committee . . . Seligman was a kind of double, you say, a licensed double. And the consulting arrangement was a pipeline. But even if all that is true, there's still something you can't be sure of. Doubles can be turned, you say, so why not Seligman? More may have flowed down that pipeline than you imagine."

"But if Seligman was turned," Everett objected, "why did they kill him?"

"I don't know that they did," Sullivan replied. "Roy made that point already. And you don't know it either . . . unless you know a great deal more than you were willing to tell the police."

Everett shut up.

"Corroboration," Tyrell mused. "You want corroboration. Documentary evidence . . . I think I can supply it."

"How?"

"Well, we don't have files, but we do have some documentation. We have a list, for example, of what we passed to him."

"How does that help?"

"You have a list too, remember. And I don't know what's on it. And since you only checked a sample from your list with Registry, I can't find out. Now the most damaging part of your evidence against Seligman was his possession of file numbers he shouldn't have had. Right? And we told you we gave them to him. So if you get our list and check it against yours, you can at least find out if he had anything we didn't give him. If he didn't, I'd say it was fairly convincing evidence that what we've told you is true, and that he wasn't turned. Wouldn't you?"

Sullivan considered.

"I might buy that," he said. "It wouldn't necessarily be conclusive, but it would certainly be reassuring."

The meeting broke up shortly after. Everett departed, with conspicuous lack of ceremony, to his dinner. Sullivan and Tyrell were left alone in the office. But a new constraint was between them. Too many things had been said, or implied, in the last half-hour; now they could not find words for their thoughts, or did not choose to. Presently Tyrell left to get his list.

It was on Sullivan's desk a few minutes later. Three columns, containing sixty-eight file numbers. A note at the bottom of the page in Roy's handwriting requested him to destroy it before he left the office. The note was not signed; it was simply initialed "R.T."

Not long after that, Sullivan was on his way back to Georgetown, wondering once again what the hell he had gotten into, why he had got into it, and when he would get out. For the fact was, apart from the letter prefixes missing from Seligman's numbers, the lists matched. There was no number on Seligman's list that was not on Tyrell's.

BOOK THREE

August 4, 1978–August 10, 1978

CHAPTER IO

I

The house was part of a terrace, two stories high and set slightly back from the street. In style, he supposed, it was Regency: the cream-colored façade dominated above by a pair of tall windows whose symmetry was only slightly marred by the air-conditioning unit set into the base of the left-hand one; below them, a shallow bay window, flanked on the right by the front door—black, with an imposing brass knocker—and, leading down from the door, a short flight of steps. In front was a patch of garden, walled on both sides and shielded from the street by a shoulder-high boxwood fence.

A pleasant little house, Foley thought, in a pleasant little street. Two or three bedrooms, he guessed, a couple of bathrooms, living room, kitchen, and den. Pleasant, but not special. In any other neighborhood, he figured, indulging for a moment his professional habit of pricing other people's property, it might be worth a hundred and twenty-five thousand. Maybe a hundred and thirty. But this was Georgetown, where the amenities might include not only easy access to the Capitol, but diplomatic or even congressional neighbors. Here it would fetch two fifty, minimum.

A pleasant little house in a pleasant little street. But Foley was not a realtor; he could see drawbacks. The hedge in front was not tall enough. And neighbors of any kind, congressional or otherwise, could not be considered an amenity. Worst of all was the front door. He hadn't, from a distance, been able to identify the lock, but that didn't bother him; he had a way with locks. What did bother him was the prospect of standing at the top of those steps, in full view of the neighbors and any casual passerby, *demonstrating* his way with locks. The front door, he told himself, was definitely out.

But if not the front door, then what? The back door could be reached only from the back. And since the house stood smack in the middle of its terrace, you got into the backyard, presumably, either from the house itself or from someone else's backyard. And if a strange man fiddling with the front door would attract attention, a strange man running an obstacle course through the neighboring backyards was liable to attract a great deal worse.

This was not the kind of job he liked to do in the daylight. If nighttime offered the disadvantage of making it difficult to see what you were doing, it more than compensated by making it very difficult for anyone to see you doing it. Stonemason, however, had been unyielding on this point. "Do it in daytime," he had said, "when we know he won't be there. We don't want you getting caught."

Well, Stonemason had a point there. Foley's own concern on that score was considerably greater than Stonemason's. But there remained the problem of how to get in. Stonemason hadn't offered much help on that. "You'll contrive something, no doubt," he had murmured, adding, as he was always careful to add, "You'll be on your own, of course. Completely on your own. You understand that, don't you?" Foley did indeed understand that. There had been no need for Stonemason to point it out; it was quite evident from the care Stonemason had taken to cover his tracks. There'd been the usual telephone contact, made by one of Stonemason's henchmen from a pay phone, the usual brief meeting in what Stonemason no doubt referred to as a "safe house." He'd been given his instructions, handed the discs and the first installment of his fee, and dismissed. Stonemason would call him later to confirm that everything had gone smoothly, and the balance of the money would be placed in an envelope and pushed under his door. After that, there would be silence—until the next time. In the jargon of Stonemason's trade, he was "disavowable."

He didn't mind. His understanding of his status was built, very handsomely, into his fee. What he did mind was the idea of doing time on Stonemason's account. So unless he could find some reasonable alternative to the front door, he would call the thing off and refund the fee—minus, of course, his out-of-pocket expenses.

He was halfway around the block when it came to him—a basement. There had to be a basement. The front door was well above street level; there had to be something besides earth under the first floor. If there was a basement, there might well be a basement entrance or basement windows. At least it was worth a look.

When he had finished circling the block he found that he had had a stroke of luck. A parking space had opened up right in front of the house. He eased the van into it, collected the box, which, since the van was painted with the insignia of the Acme Plumbing Service, he imagined onlookers would correctly deduce contained his tools, and let himself in through the gate.

A glance confirmed he was right. To the left of the steps leading up to the front door was a basement well. The windows were barred, but his dismay at seeing this was immediately dispelled by the realization that the flight of steps leading down into the well must, if it served any purpose at all, lead down to a door.

For the moment, however, he ignored the basement. First there were some elementary precautions to take. It would be wise, for example, to make certain that the house really was empty. He walked up to the front door, and was about to push the bell when he noticed it was connected to an intercom system. That was excellent. If someone answered his ring he would be all indignation at the blockheads at Acme Plumbing who had sent him halfway across town to the wrong address; if not, the intercom would serve nicely as a prop in the little charade he proposed to stage for the benefit of watching neighbors.

He pushed the doorbell, waited half a minute, and pushed it again. No response. So far so good. He leaned his head close to the speaker. "Acme Plumbing," he mouthed. "I've come about the leak in the basement." He put his ear to the speaker, went into a pantomime of listening, nodded, said something else, and took himself and his tools off to the basement, awarding himself an Oscar for the performance.

There were two locks on the basement door: a Yale—laughably simple—and a mortise of somewhat greater complexity. Neither gave him any problem, however. Within minutes, thankful that the door was not secured inside with a chain and hook, he was in the house.

Once there, he made a quick tour of inspection, taking care to wipe the door handles and stay away from the windows. There were three phones, he discovered: one in the living room, one in the master bedroom, the third in the den. He decided to take the bedroom first, then the living room, and to leave the den for last because it was in the basement and on his way out.

He put his box on the floor beside the bed. Inside, in neat compartments, were the implements of his profession: picklocks and tweezers, pliers and screwdrivers in various shapes and sizes, rolls of insulating tape and coils of hair-fine copper wide. In a separate compartment by themselves were five discs about half the size of a fingernail and no thicker than a shirt button. Stonemason had given him five to be on the safe side. "There's no telling how many extensions the man may have, and I want them all covered," he'd explained. "If it's less than five, you can keep the spares—they won't do you any good."

He cut himself a six-inch strip of tape. Then, having lifted the receiver from its cradle and placed it on the bed, he stretched the tape across the cradle, smoothing it onto the body of the phone at either end so the buttons that opened the line would be held in place while he worked. He made a mental note to remember to remove it when he had finished; he had forgotten it once, and it had cost him a client.

That done, he moved on to the receiver. The discs were very simple to install: you simply uncrewed the cap of the mouthpiece, placed the disc in the cavity behind it, fixed it in place with tape or epoxy, replaced the cap, and went on your merry way. The disc would then transmit any reasonable level of sound in the room to Stonemason's tape recorders, whether the phone was in use or not. When Stonemason's interest in the subject was exhausted, he would simply unhook the recorders. Probably the disc would never be discovered, but if it was, no great harm would be done. Mr. Sullivan would be indignant, of course—nobody likes to have his private life preserved on tape—but there would be absolutely nothing he could do about it.

He took one of the discs, wiped it carefully with his handkerchief, dabbed it lightly with epoxy, and placed it, epoxy side up, on the bed. Then he unscrewed the cap of the mouthpiece and laid it on the bed beside the disc. Picking up the disc with tweezers, he was about to glue it in place when something caught his attention.

He peered into the mouthpiece cavity, his expression changing, as he studied it, from curiosity to incredulity.

Then he put down the tweezers and began to laugh.

II

"They match, don't they?"

Sullivan looked up. Tyrell was standing in the doorway, a quizzical expression on his face. Without waiting for Sullivan's response, he went over and poured himself a cup of coffee from the Thermos Sullivan kept permanently on hand and parked himself on the sofa, resting his feet on the edge of the coffee table. Sullivan glanced at the clock above the sofa. He'd expected to see Tyrell earlier, felt sure he'd be in, eager for the verdict on the lists, as soon as he got to the office, but it was now past eleven. If Tyrell was anxious, he thought, he certainly wasn't showing it. His question, in fact, had been hardly interrogative; he knew very well what the answer would be.

"Well?" Tyrell said.

"They match." Sullivan nodded. "Up to a point."

"Up to a point?"

"There's no file on his first list that isn't also on yours," Sullivan explained. "But your list is longer than his. Nearly three times as long, in fact."

"You attach some significance to that?"

"Not necessarily. It depends whether the list you gave me listed the files in the order in which they were passed. Did it?"

Tyrell nodded.

"Then there may be some significance," Sullivan said. "But I won't know until I've read the files. The point is, you see, he didn't bother to list everything you passed him. His list isn't even a chronological section of your list. Some files apparently interested him more than others. One wonders why."

It was not a subject, however, that appeared to interest Tyrell.

"But at any rate," he said, "he doesn't seem to have anything he wasn't authorized to have. So we can stop worrying about him."

It was a statement, but a statement, Sullivan saw, with a hook in it. Roy was not quite as indifferent as he seemed. He wanted to know the drift of Sullivan's thinking, but he wasn't willing to come right out and ask. Instead he was fishing, throwing out statements that invited disagreement in the hope that Sullivan would volunteer something. But Sullivan wasn't biting.

"Were you worried?" he asked. "I'd never have guessed."

"Worried?" Tyrell pursed his lips, tilting his head from side to side like a pair of scales settling into balance. "That's a little strong, perhaps. I had to be open, let's say, to the unexpected . . . I always trusted him, of course. That goes without saying. But I'm glad to have my trust confirmed."

Fishing again. This time Sullivan decided to nibble.

"Is it?"

"Well, isn't it?" Tyrell cocked an eyebrow. "Don't tell me you still have doubts about him."

" 'Doubts' is a little strong, perhaps." Sullivan waggled his head and gave a passable imitation of Tyrell's judicious drawl. "I have to be open, let's say to a number of possibilities."

"Such as . . .?"

But that was further than Sullivan was willing to go. If Roy wanted information, he would have to be more confiding himself.

"You guys took a big risk with Seligman," he observed.

"How so?"

"Throwing him to the Russians like that. I mean it's all very well to talk about being able to limit his access to what you could afford to lose, but you mean after he left the Agency, don't you? What about before?"

"Before?"

"Yes. It isn't as if he were low-level. He was a Deputy Director, for God's sake. A walking card index of classified information. How could you be sure they wouldn't just whisk him off to Moscow and run him through the grinder? How do you know, for that matter, that they didn't? There was a body in the Bay, admittedly, but nobody's proved it was his."

"No." Tyrell was definite. "They wouldn't have done that."

"How do you know? Did you cut out his memory?"

"He was an analyst." Tyrell ignored the sarcasm. "With an analyst's access. He didn't know about operations or source identities or military secrets. His job was to take our reports on Soviet weaponry, troop movements, and the like and turn them into assessments of their military capability. His access, in other words, was to information the Russians already knew." He smiled. "At least one imagines they know their own military secrets. So the worst he could have done was tell them how much we knew about them. Most of that came out in the SALT talks anyway."

"He knew nothing about source identities?"

"Very little. Most of his data came from technical sources. Where the sources were human and sensitive he'd have had no more than a general description—'Well placed and usually reliable'— that sort of thing."

"Identities can be inferred from descriptions."

"Sure they can—if you can remember and correlate enough descriptions. But would he have been able to remember? He saw thousands of reports every year, don't forget, and it was content he was concerned with, not source description."

"Well . . ." Sullivan sounded doubtful. "It's surprising what you can get someone to remember if you go about it right."

"That's also true," Tyrell conceded. "But how long does it take? Months. Maybe years. With teams of interrogators, unlimited patience, and no guarantee of success. I'd hate to tell you how much time and money we've spent in the past few years on apparently promising interrogations, only to end up with so much garbage. Why would they go that route when there seemed so much more to be had by leaving him where he was?"

"Poking around in your office, in other words?"

"Exactly . . . Look, Morgan, stop reinventing the wheel, will you? All your questions are pertinent, I'll admit. Only they've all been asked before. We went into all that before Theta was ever approved."

"No doubt." Sullivan's voice was dry. "But since I wasn't around in those days, perhaps you'll bear with me a little. The Committee would want me to ask these questions, I think. They'd hardly have bothered to appoint me otherwise."

"I suppose not." Tyrell shrugged. "But since you mention the Committee, perhaps I could ask you a question?"

"Go ahead."

"What exactly was your mandate from them?"

"They empowered me to investigate the security aspects of Seligman's death or disappearance. To find out, in other words, if he had been disloyal. Why?"

"Precisely what evidence is there, at this point—now that you know I passed Seligman every file on his list—for continuing to doubt him? It seems to me Theta explains all the evidence you raised against him yesterday. What else is there?"

Sullivan thought about it. There was no evidence against Seligman. There was no evidence against anybody. There was nothing, really, beyond his disturbing intuition that the truth about Seligman—the whole truth—had yet to emerge. And, as Roy had just managed to remind him, his mandate from the Committee was limited; it was not carte blanche to poke around until he had satisfied his curiosity or indulged his intuition. The committee wasn't in the least interested in the whole truth about Seligman, as he and Brady were. The Committee was interested only in security, chiefly satellite security. So unless he could show definite grounds for believing that the truth about Seligman had some bearing on those matters, he had no justification for going on, no reason for withholding from the Agency its clean bill of health.

He ignored Tyrell's question. "You know, the wind changes a lot around here. Three weeks ago you were twisting my arm to get me in here. Now it seems you can't wait to get me out."

"It's not me," Tyrell said quickly. "The heat comes from above. I merely reflect it. It seems Everett had another call from the White House this morning, so he called me, and so . . ."

"And so here you are."

"Yes," Tyrell said, "here I am."

"And the message, I take it, is 'put up or shut up'?"

"Yes," Tyrell said. "I think it is."

"Well, I have nothing to put up—to answer your original question. So what are my choices?"

Tyrell did not bother to give him the obvious answer. Instead he said: "You're pissed off, aren't you?"

"You might say that." Sullivan smiled a tight, humorless smile.

"Well, I am too—if that helps at all. I got you in here, in good faith. And then they tied my hands; they wouldn't allow me to brief you about Theta. So now when it all comes out it looks as if I deliberately misled you. I'm not happy about that."

"No," Sullivan said. "I imagine not."

"But you do understand, don't you? You do know that I didn't deliberately use you?"

Sullivan was silent for a moment. He would rather have been asked that question earlier, he thought. He would rather have received Roy's assurance, his oblique apology, at the beginning of the conversation. He would have much preferred, in fact, not to have had to receive it at all.

"Yes," he said at last, grudgingly. "I suppose I do."

When Tyrell left, shortly afterward, Sullivan sat for a while going over the conversation in his mind. It was put up or shut up, Tyrell had said, and if he had nothing to put up, then as far as they were concerned the matter was closed. But then, as far as they were concerned it always had been closed, hadn't it? Everett had hinted that, Eglinton had said it, and now, it seemed, Tyrell was confirming it. He'd been brought in to soothe the Committee, that was all. He'd been given a temporary license to poke around, been encouraged, it almost seemed, to rake up just enough doubt as they could easily satisfy, just enough to make the investigation seem real—but that was it. The license was now revoked, apparently; the poking around must now cease. Unless, of course, he could find something to put up.

But did he really want to? And why? Was there anything behind his reluctance to give up the hunt but egotism—resentment at being made use of, or distaste for the prospect of defeat? And was the sense of failure reasonable, the resentment altogether fair? For although he unquestionably had been made use of, it hadn't necessarily been done cynically. The Agency, after all, had a need to protect itself against people who, in the name of the national interest, built careers out of making its life difficult, and there were several of these on the Committee. So could he really blame Everett and Tyrell for grabbing any means at hand to avoid giving such people the details of Theta? Did he really begrudge them a few weeks of his time?

It was not easy to answer these questions; they called for a degree of introspection he was not, at present, prepared to give them. So, leaving them unanswered, he gazed for a moment out the window, letting his thoughts drift while his eyes wandered over the trim lawns and walkways, the bland institutional architecture of the Agency campus. It looked so green and pleasant in the morning sunshine, so innocent; for all the world, he thought, like a small rural college. And the two men sprawling on the grass below, one gesticulating earnestly while the other nodded and puffed at his pipe, could easily, he thought, have been lecturers, arguing some point of quantum mechanics or the Theory of the Firm. Seligman had been like them, probably. A natural academic, content to potter among his charts and statistics, engrossed completely by theories and predictions. Or he had been, at least, until the lethal competition that so absorbed his interest had torn him away from his charts and statistics, had set him down instead in the midst of a battlefield, and then, almost casually, it seemed, had killed him.

But if it had killed him, who exactly had pulled the trigger? Had the Agency done it to punish his treachery without provoking a scandal? Or, as Tyrell maintained, had the Russians found out about Theta and taken a vicious revenge? The balance of evidence certainly now seemed to favor Tyrell. But there were problems nevertheless. Why, for example, had Seligman compiled that list? What pattern in the apparently random selection of information that passed through his hands had caught his analytical eye? And why, if he saw or thought he saw a pattern, had he spoken to no one about it? Why had he hidden his suspicions instead, in the lining of his coat?

He didn't trust anyone—that was the obvious answer. Whatever he thought he'd discovered was something he'd been afraid to mention even to his masters. And that, if true, implied something else: he hadn't mentioned it, presumably, because what he'd discovered was in itself the cause of his distrust.

Then Sullivan caught an echo of what he himself had said about Theta. If Theta was a pipeline, he'd told Everett, then more might have flowed down it than its makers intended. Was it possible, he wondered, that Seligman had reached the same conclusion? Had he come to suspect that somebody involved had turned Theta inside out, that it was no longer a misinformation exercise aimed at the Russians but, on the contrary, a Russian operation with the Agency as its target? And if he had suspected that, what had he done about it? What, indeed, could he have done about it? Seligman would have been caught in the middle, unable to voice his suspicions for fear the real culprit might shift the blame onto him. And that, certainly, might not have been very difficult, for Seligman's situation was decidedly awkward; after all, he had actually passed the documents, without any written authority; he had pocketed the Russian cash . . . Pocketed the cash? It seemed to Sullivan that his head was alive with echoes. Brady's words came back to him; he could almost hear the incredulity in Brady's voice. "If he'd deliberately set out to lay a trail, for Christ's sake, if he wanted to lead us to the money, he could hardly have done it better." Perhaps he had been trying. Perhaps, as his suspicions had started to harden, he'd wanted to be able to document that he hadn't pocketed a dime.

And of course there was the break-in. Now Sullivan's thoughts seemed borne along on a surge of revelation. As Seligman had started to worry about Theta, someone evidently had started to worry about him. Even after he'd been killed, someone had worried enough to break into Gael's apartment to recover whatever he'd left behind. And, as Brady had figured out, whoever had done that had known beforehand that there was no point in searching Seligman's own apartment. And they'd known it, obviously, because they'd already searched there. Which meant, of course, that "they" were the CIA, or, to be more specific, Patterson.

So he was back, it seemed, to Brady's original theory—but with a twist. Someone in the Agency had killed Seligman, though not because Seligman had been a traitor, but because the killer himself was. And that narrowed the field of suspects down to the three men who'd been actively involved in the operation: Brayer, Patterson, and Roy Tyrell. One of these men, if the reasoning was correct, was Spearman's mole.

The only problem, of course, was that the reasoning might be off by a mile. Though it had the merit of tying together all the loose ends, it suffered from the crippling weakness of being backed by very little hard evidence. It was entirely possible, for example, that the trashing of Gael's apartment had nothing to do with Seligman. It was also conceivable that Seligman's eccentric treatment of the money had been prompted by simple honesty, the innocence of a man with no training in the finer points of espionage. As for the list, there could be any number of explanations—though Sullivan could not, offhand, think of any—why Seligman had made it.

The trouble was, Sullivan reflected, that people in general, and lawyers in particular, had a bias toward order. A theory that tied everything together was always preferable to one that left loose ends. Yet people's actions were almost always less tidy than their minds. They acted on impulse; they did things for reasons that to them seemed compelling but to anyone else might make no sense at all. Human behavior was naturally chaotic, so any theory that attempted to sort its disorder into neatly labeled boxes ran the risk of forcing much of the clutter into the wrong box. More than likely, he thought, he was making that mistake. And it was a mistake he was very eager to avoid, because his neat, orderly, completely speculative line of thinking had led him to place his friend on the short list of suspects for crimes including treason and murder.

Roy Tyrell a traitor and a murderer? Instinctively he rejected the idea. Logically, perhaps, it was possible; intuitively it wasn't. And even logically it made no sense to set a shaky line of speculation against his ten years of friendship with Roy. He *knew* Roy; that was the point. The outlines of Roy's personality were almost as familiar to him as his own. And though he would never claim with certainty to know exactly what anyone—including himself—might do in any given set of circumstances, he was absolutely confident that there were certain things that Roy would not do. Treason and murder were among them.

But what about Brayer and Patterson? He'd seen Brayer only once and had been unable to form a clear opinion of him. His impression was of a small, gnomelike man who puffed constantly on his pipe, kept his thoughts to himself, and viewed the world with an affectionate cynicism. He would have to question Brayer, obviously, ask him about his role in Theta. Patterson, too, would bear further looking into. He had the psychological profile, if reports were accurate, of the classical security risk. Moreover, the reason he'd given for being in Eglinton's vault among the satellite secrets still struck Sullivan as very lame. Patterson had also headed the team that searched Seligman's apartment. Patterson would definitely bear looking into.

They would all bear looking into: Patterson and Brayer because they were both still question marks, Roy because fairness demanded it. But where should he look? Inquiries into the details of Theta, Roy had made clear, would get no further response. And if his theory was correct, asking any of the three participants would in any case be pointless, because he could hardly expect them to incriminate themselves. He would have to attack the problem from another angle.

It took him another hour of thinking to come up with an idea. His theory, he reasoned, implied the existence of a mole. So instead of speculating in the abstract about Theta, shouldn't he go back and try to link his inquiry with the earlier mole investigation? Wouldn't it make sense, at this point, to go and talk to Spearman?

Yes, he decided, it would. He would see Brayer first, to obtain some corroboration of what Tyrell had told him about Theta. Then he would get the outsider's view: he would talk to Spearman.

III

"Theta?" Martin Brayer said. "Frankly, I never paid much attention to it. It was one of Roy's babies."

He placed a certain sardonic emphasis on the word "babies." If the world was divided into thinkers and doers, Brayer, Sullivan guessed, was unashamedly classed with the thinkers. And he was one of those rare thinkers, evidently, who had no hankering for the world of action. Short, stout, bespectacled, resolutely unathletic, he would sit and watch the movers and shakers, deriving a mild amusement from their activities without the slightest desire to join in. That, at any rate, was the impression he seemed determined to create.

"But you *were* involved?" Sullivan insisted.

"Involved?" Brayer raised his eyebrows. The notion of being involved in anything seemed to strike him as faintly absurd. "I wouldn't say that. I was consulted, from time to time . . . No," he corrected himself, "I wouldn't even say that, since 'consulted' implies some interest on Roy's part in my opinions on the matter. 'Informed' would be more accurate, I think. I was informed, from time to time, that certain things would happen."

"What things?"

"Well . . ." Brayer smiled, a shade sourly, Sullivan thought. "I was informed, for example, that my department would hire Paul Seligman as a consultant, and find things, if necessary, to consult him about. It was fortunate, I suppose, that things to consult him about weren't hard to find, his resignation having left us rather shorthanded in his area."

"But you knew why Roy wanted him hired?"

"Pump priming." Brayer nodded. "They were setting him up for some misinformation ploy or other. Roy was kind enough to confide that."

"Did you know the purpose of the operation?"

"No." The tone implied a decided lack of curiosity.

"But you did know that the papers Seligman had access to were finding their way to the KGB?"

"Of course."

"And you *were* Seligman's official contact in the Agency?"

Brayer nodded. "Since I was the person hiring him to consult, I was naturally his contact. If you set up a cover, you should go through the motions of maintaining it, I assume."

"And you and Tyrell jointly decided what he should receive?"

"Not exactly. Roy decided what should be passed in furtherance of Theta and consulted me as to whether I had any objections. Since the material was essentially chickenfeed and came from his sources, this was largely a matter of form—soothing my ruffled sensibilities, I expect; I never looked at the stuff very closely. On the other hand, however, when it came to his role as a consultant, I decided what Seligman should see, and where the sources were possibly sensitive, I consulted Roy. It was assumed, you see, that everything Seligman got would be at risk."

"And you kept a list of everything?"

"Yes, we did . . . or rather, Roy did. It didn't seem wise to have more than one copy."

"I see . . . Then if I read you correctly, you're saying that what Seligman was doing for you was separate from what he was doing for Roy?"

"Separate but parallel," Brayer qualified. "For me he was genuinely consulting, most of the time. I really don't know what he was doing for Roy."

"And you never cared to find out?"

"No." Very emphatic.

An obscure, tangential memory passed through Sullivan's mind. Some characters in a Steinbeck novel, he recalled, had once sat with their backs to a brass band playing fortissimo, and no one had turned around to look. Brayer's indifference, he thought, was at least on a par with that.

"You know," he observed, "I find your lack of curiosity rather surprising."

"I find your question rather surprising." Brayer looked down his nose. "Curiosity, at least about matters that don't concern one, is not much encouraged around here. It's a security principle, you see; it's called need-to-know. I'm surprised you haven't run across it."

"But Theta did concern you, surely? The operation involved obvious risks."

"Not to me." Brayer grinned suddenly. "The intelligence value of the information Seligman received was very low. If anything was at risk, it was sources. They were Roy's department."

"You're saying, then, that the responsibility for Theta was Roy's?"

"Oh yes." Brayer grinned again. "Entirely."

"I'm not sure I agree." Sullivan was getting irritated by Brayer's Pontius Pilate impersonation. "You passed the stuff, after all, and you consulted with Roy on the choice of material. So the distinction you seem determined to draw between the consulting and the operation exists, I would say, entirely in your mind. If it turns out that Seligman was passing more than he was authorized, you and Roy will sit in the hot seat side by side."

"I see." Brayer didn't seem very concerned. "There's some question, is there, of Seligman doing a bit of dealing on the side?"

"I don't know yet," Sullivan said carefully. "There very well may be."

"And if he was, you're saying, then he got the goods from Roy or me? Or Roy *and* me?"

Sullivan nodded. "You do seem the obvious choices."

"Well then . . ." Brayer shrugged. "We'll just have to keep our fingers crossed, won't we?"

That curious lack of concern again. Were they really not sweating? Or was it, as Roy had suggested, that nobody wanted to be seen sweating? Was Brayer really as indifferent to Theta as he made out? Did he really regard it as some juvenile gunpowder plot, not worthy of his attention? Or was he backing away from it fast, scared that it might blow up in his face?

IV

As he approached the turnoff, Marvin Nichols cut his speed back to thirty and slipped the Corvette into third. Take the turnoff to the canal, they'd said. About a mile after the turnoff is a dirt road turning left off the blacktop and down to a stone cottage beside some lock gates. Wait there, they'd said. Park between the cottage and the canal, switch off your lights, and wait. We'll be there by eight with the money.

Cloak-and-dagger bullshit. Marvin smiled. Pay-phone contacts, passwords, meetings at dusk in deserted houses on lonely canal banks: it was all typical of them, and a complete waste of time. They owed him money was all. He'd done a job and they owed him. So why not just meet him in a bar somewhere and slip him the cash in an envelope? It was habit, he supposed. They clung to the habits of their profession, just as he clung to the habits of his. And besides, they were paying; that gave them, within limits, the right to make the rules.

Within limits. It was an important qualification. He was a reasonable man, an accommodating man, but there were still limits. It just wasn't smart to let them make all the rules. For one thing, they were honkies and therefore by nature untrustworthy. For another, the job hadn't worked out exactly as planned. It wasn't his fault—he'd done what he'd promised—but in his experience people seldom paid for excuses. "No goods, no pay" was the rule in his profession; it was unlikely, he imagined, to be different in theirs. Which was why he had insisted, originally, on getting half the money in advance. And it was why, earlier in the afternoon, he'd sent Otis out fishing—along the canal bank—and why he'd told Otis to take along his gun.

The necessity made Marvin uneasy. He was inured to the minor violence of his profession, but guns made him nervous. So did Otis. Otis was excitable, and Otis was a bomber, Basically Otis didn't give a shit. Put Otis behind the business end of a snub-nosed .38 and Otis was liable to pull the trigger. For this reason Marvin had almost sent Otis to negotiate and taken the gun himself. But that would be stupid, he'd decided. For all his other talents, Otis could no more reason than fly to the moon. And reason, plus a little persuasion, was what the situation demanded. So, with misgivings, he'd sent Otis along the canal bank, with instructions to hide up in the bushes near the cottage and not to show himself, or the .38, unless it became necessary.

"And remember," he'd warned, "the piece is for persuasion. You don't use it unless you have to. Unless it's them or us. We're only talking two thousand dollars, remember. And killing those guys is murder one. I don't buy that kind of trade-off. It just isn't rational."

He glanced at the odometer—nine tenths of a mile since the turnoff. The dirt road should be coming up soon. When he looked back to the road he saw it: a break in the shoulder some eighty yards ahead. He looked at his watch. Seven-fifty. It was beginning to get dark, but the light would hold, he figured, for about twenty minutes. And that was important. Because if things got nasty and Otis had to shoot, he wanted to be sure Otis could see who he was shooting.

The dirt road led, as promised, to a derelict cottage almost hidden among willows and sycamores. When the canal had been operating, he guessed, the cottage had housed the gatekeeper. But the lock gates were idle now, their timbers rotting, the ironwork crusted with corrosion. The cottage itself had evidently been empty for many years; the structure was still intact, but there was no glass in the windows and half the slates were off the roof. On the wall nearest the canal someone had spray-painted a peace symbol and, underneath, the exhortation MAKE LOVE, NOT WAR. Seeing it, Marvin grinned. He'd spent a reluctant year in Vietnam himself, in the late sixties, dealing drugs and avoiding combat duty, and the sentiment was his exactly. Make love, he thought. If the cottage were used by anyone now, it would be for that purpose. Kids, probably, with nowhere else to go. He hoped none of them planned on using it tonight.

There was no sign of another car, but it was not quite time. He parked the Corvette close to the wall, somewhat back from the one window, lit a cigarette, and settled down to wait. It would be reassuring, he thought, to make contact with Otis. But he wasn't dumb enough to try. The fact that he couldn't see them didn't mean, necessarily, that they weren't there.

He slid farther down into the seat, leaning his head against the door frame so he could gaze up at the patch of sky framed by the sycamore branches overhead. It was pale silver, touched here and there with gold, and so still and sultry that the leaves silhouetted against it were barely moving. Then his eye fell again on the peace symbol and the slogan beneath it, and his thoughts drifted back to the long throbbing summer evenings of his adolescence. He'd come a long way since then, he thought complacently, fingering the heavy gold chain he wore around his neck. And he planned to go a lot further.

"Nichols?"

Marvin turned his head. The whisper had come from the window. They were inside the cottage.

"Yeah?"

"We're inside . . . in the cottage."

"Yeah?" He took a pull at the cigarette and let the smoke drift lazily out through his nostrils. "Well, I'm out here."

"It's better inside . . . safer."

"Safer for who? I feel safer out here."

Silence.

"Do you have it?"

"Sure." He took another drag. "But if you want it, you'll have to come outside."

Trying to be cute, he thought. Come inside, Mr. Nichols, so we can knock you on the head. But they'd outcuted themselves. He wouldn't go in, so they'd have to come out. He could wait as long as they could.

He waited for maybe a minute. Then he heard the creak of a hinge, followed by footsteps on gravel. A figure edged around the corner of the building, followed, two seconds later, by another.

They stopped just beyond the corner, about twenty feet from the Corvette. It was almost dark but he could make them out well enough. They wore dark business suits, just as they had at the first meeting, white shirts and dark ties, hats pulled well down over their faces. Their features were lost in shadow. Only the difference in their height distinguished them. There are black men and white men, Marvin thought, and now these. Faceless wonders. The original gray men.

"So we're out," the taller one said. "Now it's your turn. Get out of the car."

Marvin hesitated. Had they left someone inside? He was close to the wall and back from the window; so long as he stayed put he was in cover, whereas they were sitting ducks for Otis. If he got out, on the other hand, he could be zapped from the window. But shit! he thought, it's only two thousand dollars. Peanuts to them. He climbed over into the passenger seat and got out, taking care, however, to stay back from the window.

"Where is it?" the tall one asked.

"Good question." Marvin shrugged. "I can tell you where it isn't. It's not in the house. We looked everywhere and we looked good. We tore the place apart. It wasn't there."

They digested this in silence.

"We looked all over," Marvin repeated. "We kept our end. And . . ." He paused. "We're looking to get paid."

Again there was no reaction.

"You told us to look," Marvin insisted, "and we did. It's not our fault it wasn't there."

"Did you follow instructions?" This from the small one.

"Instructions? What instructions?"

"To make it look like a burglary. Did you steal something?"

"Sure we did." Marvin grinned. "We looted the fucking place."

This time the silence was much longer.

"Costume jewelry," the small one said. "A silver bowl. An electric clock . . . Some robbery."

"How the hell—"

"The girl saw you," the tall one cut in. "She came back and saw you. Now the police have your description. You fucked up and you didn't get it. But you still think you deserve to be paid."

"Sell the clock," the small one added. "It's about what you're worth."

Shit, Marvin thought. Problems. Get your gun out, Otis, and give them a good look at it. Only take it easy, for Chrissake. No shooting.

"Look . . ." He spread his hands and took a step forward, talking to distract them, to provide an opening for Otis. "She never saw me. I kept myself in shadow. So there's no need to panic. Now just hand over the money and I'll be on my way."

"Why should we?" It was not a question but a challenge.

Marvin waited, keeping his eyes on the two men and his ears on the bushes from which Otis would be emerging, but there was no movement from the bushes. Dumb nigger! he cursed inwardly. Come out of the frigging bushes and show them your frigging gun!

"Two reasons," he said finally. "One, my buddy Otis is over there in the bushes. With his gun. It should be pointing at you right about now."

He raised his voice a fraction on the last words, but there was still no movement from the bushes. Nor, he noticed, did they react to his threat. And that was odd, he thought, suddenly uneasy. They should at least have looked.

"You said two reasons," the small one asked. "What's the other one?"

He's not there. The realization struck Marvin like a kick in the stomach. The dumb fuck went and got lost. He'll pay for this, he promised himself savagely. I'll kick his black ass for this.

"It's very simple." He forced himself to speak calmly, affecting the nonchalance of one who holds all the cards. "You see, I know who you are.

"You probably figure you're cute with that cloak-and-dagger routine," he went on. "But it doesn't work with me. I know who you are, and if I don't get that money in about fifteen seconds, I'm going to get in my car and drive home. And when I get there I'm going to get on the phone to my congressman. And when I do that"—he paused—"the shit will hit the fan."

What happened then surprised him.

"All right," the tall one said. "We'll give you the money."

He put a hand in his pocket and drew out a thick envelope. With a flick of his wrist he tossed it onto the gravel at Marvin's feet.

"Pick it up," he said. "Count it. It's all there. Yours and your friend's. Go ahead. Pick it up and count it."

For a second Marvin stood there, poised between suspicion and relief. Then he stooped down. As he did he sensed a movement, heard it rather than saw it. When he looked up, the small man was holding a gun.

"Now wait. Wait just one second." Marvin spread his hands and spoke very deliberately, a reasonable man dealing calmly with other reasonable men. "That isn't necessary. You don't want to pay? So OK. Don't pay. Put the gun away and take back the fucking money."

He pitched the envelope back to them.

They didn't move.

It came to him that they were going to kill him. For two thousand lousy dollars. No. Not even for that. For no reason. Christ, he thought. It's stupid! It's just plain fucking stupid! But then he understood. It was he who was stupid, not they.

"Listen," he said, "that was all bullshit what I said. I was bluffing was all. I don't know who you are, and I don't give a shit. And even if I did, it wouldn't help. I can't tell anyone, don't you see. I'm in it too."

They said nothing.

"Otis," he said. "Otis knows where I am. He'll go to the cops. You won't get away with it.

"Christ!" he said. "Don't you fuckers understand? There's no reason for this. This is murder you're doing, and it's totally fucking senseless. It's—"

But the gun came up anyway. He heard the cylinder rotate, the rasp and click of the hammer sliding into the cocked position.

"No! Don't!" It was all he could think of now. "Please."

Instinctively he flung up his hands to protect his face. His lips started to form another syllable, another protest against the monstrous irrationality now facing him, but it was never uttered because the slug caught him first, caught him in the center of the forehead and took the top of his head off, trapping the word forever between tongue and teeth.

The small man came over and inspected the body. He didn't need to look closely; Marvin was obviously dead.

"I wonder . . ." he said.

"Don't." His companion came over to join him. "Go do the other one . . . Ours is not to reason why," he added. "Hanged for a sheep, hanged for a lamb. Go do it."

"Perhaps it wasn't needed." The small man didn't move. "Maybe he really was bluffing."

"Better safe than sorry." The tall one shrugged. "We had no choice. We still don't. So go do the other one!"

The small man stared at him for a moment, then nodded and went toward the cottage. The door creaked. Silence. Then a snuffling sound, a frenzied straining noise somewhere between a grunt and a scream. Then a muted detonation. Then nothing . . . The door creaked again, and footsteps sounded on the gravel.

"Don't just stand there," the small man snapped. "Get the dope and put it in his car. I have to get rid of the gun."

He started to take off the silencer.

"The muffler, too," the tall man said. "And not here. Not in the canal. It's the first place they'll look."

"They won't look. Not when they find the dope. They'll think they were dealers. They don't mind if dealers shoot each other."

"Better safe . . ."

"Proverbs again." The small man sounded testy. "With you it's always proverbs. Can't you think of anything better?"

"They're the wisdom of the people," the tall man said. "What could be better than that?" He pointed at Marvin. "He should have remembered his proverbs."

"Which proverb?"

" 'A little knowledge is a dangerous thing.' "

"It's not 'knowledge,' " the small man objected. "It's learning' . . . ' A little learning is a dangerous thing.' If you're going to say them, you should get them right.

"And besides," he added, "there's a better one."

"What?"

" 'Half a loaf is better than no bread.' "

The tall man considered.

"I get it," he said. "It's not better, but it's not bad. Not bad at all."

And he started to chuckle.

CHAPTER II

I

Spearman lived on the upper reaches of River Road, on the fringes of what Sullivan, with the city dweller's disdain for the pretensions of suburbia, called "hunting country." Sullivan's dentist lived there, slightly closer to town, and on his biannual visits for checkups Sullivan had always been amused at how, as the houses began to thin out, their architecture labored to suggest the ante-bellum South. Doric columns supporting heavy pediments lent dignity to structures that could not have been built, he guessed, before 1960; and the half acre or so of grass that fronted these mansions was apt to be surrounded by white rail fences whose style implied that the area enclosed was actually a paddock. In some cases the owners, fearful perhaps that the message of columns and fences had been too subtly stated, had placed life-size plaster figures outside the gateway. These figures, of plump, jolly black men dressed as jockeys, contrived to hint at a lifestyle built around servants and horses.

It was an odd environment, he thought, for a retired spy catcher. But then, nothing he'd so far heard about Spearman suggested the conventional. And what setting, indeed, *was* appropriate for a man of Spearman's former profession? An apartment in Watergate? An attic in the State Department? Perhaps hunting country, with its elaborate surface, its faint air of unreality, was as good as any.

Spearman, in any case, had not been eager to have his environment invaded by the past. "I've served my time," he'd observed somewhat plaintively when Sullivan called. "I'd rather hoped to be able to enjoy my freedom in peace." But when Sullivan started to explain in detail the purpose of the call, he'd changed his mind. "Not now," he'd cut in. "Not on the telephone. If we must discuss these matters—and I suppose we must—come and see me tomorrow . . . But not first thing in the morning, if you don't mind. I rise late these days; it's one of the few benefits of retirement."

Spearman's house, Sullivan observed when he pulled off the highway and got out of the car to open the gate, was at once larger and less pretentious than its neighbors. It was set well back from the road on a small hill and surrounded by several acres of land. But there was no rail fence enclosing the fields, no plaster jockey to welcome visitors, and the house itself was simply a large, white, stylistically nondescript building, shaded on either side by beeches and elms. The entrance to the driveway, on the other hand, was protected by iron gates set in heavy stone pillars, and the boundaries of the property were guarded by an untidy but impenetrable-looking hedge. Spearman, he thought, was evidently someone who valued his privacy and could afford to pay for it.

This impression was confirmed when he approached the gates. They were operated electronically from the inside, a small notice on the near pillar politely informed him, and callers were requested to use the telephone in the box beneath the notice to inform the house of their arrival. Sullivan did so, and was answered by a woman.

"My name is Morgan Sullivan," he said. "I believe Mr. Spearman is expecting me."

"Please hold on a minute." The voice was pleasant but not particularly welcoming. "I'll let him know you're here."

She was back presently to say that Mr. Spearman was indeed expecting him, and if he would return to his car, she would open the gates. She sounded like a secretary, or a housekeeper. Spearman evidently kept himself in some style, Sullivan thought, recalling something Roy Tyrell had said about Spearman having a lot of money of his own. It was one of the reasons, Roy said, why Spearman had not cared much whom he antagonized.

The front door was opened by a tall thin man in some of the most eccentric clothes Sullivan had ever seen. He wore gardening gloves, tucked into the sleeves of a checkered Fair Isle sweater; baggy flannel trousers supported at the waist by a striped necktie; gumboots; and, as a crowning touch, an old homburg hat, originally black but now almost green with age, surrounded by what looked like a mourning veil of black net, pushed back onto the brim in front to reveal his face. That face, Sullivan observed when he had recovered sufficiently from the outfit to focus on it, was broad yet fine-boned, with a wide, thin-lipped mouth and penetrating greenish-yellow eyes.

"Tom Spearman," the apparition said.

He held out his hand, noticed it was still gloved, and withdrew it to remove the glove before offering it again.

"Bees," he said, by way of explaining the gloves and the rest of his outfit. "I've been stealing their honey. It's what I keep them for, but they always seem to resent it."

Sullivan, who could think of no suitable reply, smiled and nodded.

"Sorry about the gates," Spearman went on. "Rather unwelcoming, I'm afraid. I had them installed when I left the Agency. The press pestered me for a time, you see, and it was either that or have those people camping on the doorstep. They leave me alone now, but I kept the gates. It's always nice, don't you think"—he fixed Sullivan with a bland stare—"to know in advance whether your visitors are welcome?"

He led the way into the house.

"We'll talk in the garden, I think. The bees should have calmed down by now. In any case"—he glanced back over his shoulder and gave Sullivan a wisp of a smile—"given the subject of our discussion, we have less to fear from the bees in the garden than from the bugs in the house."

"Bugs?" Sullivan was startled. "You think that's likely?"

"Oh, I don't know." Spearman shrugged. "Perhaps I'm over-cautious. But I left the Agency under something of a cloud, as you're no doubt aware, and I still keep in touch with a number of my former colleagues. They'll have noticed that, of course, and probably wonder what it is we discuss. I wouldn't put it past them to indulge their curiosity."

" 'Them'?" Sullivan queried.

"You know who." Spearman looked at him sharply, as though to assure himself he was not dealing with a moron. "They *do* do such things, you know."

Them? . . . You know who? . . . There was something disquieting, Sullivan thought, about the choice of words. It implied the existence of a large number of people with nothing better to do than keep an eye on Spearman. Yet Spearman had been retired for two years and, as far as the Agency was concerned, was dead and buried, existing only as an object lesson or an entertaining legend. Overcautious? The man was paranoid.

But was that really so surprising? Spearman had spent almost a lifetime compiling a catalogue of the types of treachery, tracking an enemy who never showed his face, whose most formidable weapon was the bewildering variety of his disguises. And he'd ended in the conviction that he'd failed, that the enemy had undermined his defenses and contrived his downfall. So was it surprising that his necessary professional skepticism had become, in time, an obsessive, consuming suspicion? It was a malady, Sullivan now remembered, that Tyrell suspected *him* of having. Spearman's Disease.

"Why don't you check?" he asked.

"I do check." Spearman seemed to find the question astonishing. "I check regularly."

"And have you found anything?"

Immediately he regretted asking. It would embarrass Spearman, he realized, and since he had come to get Spearman's help, that was stupid.

But Spearman apparently was too committed to his own reality to notice its conflicts with the world of common sense.

"No," he said firmly, "And that's what bothers me. They're getting much too good at it. They're getting better all the time."

He led Sullivan through a tiled patio, down a flight of steps, and out into a small orchard. In the middle of the orchard, shaded by apple trees, was a garden and two comfortable-looking wicker chairs.

"Do you like Bloody Marys?" he asked. "My daughter will be out presently with a pitcher. Or, if it's too early for you, I can ask her to make you some coffee."

Sullivan said Bloody Marys would be fine.

"Well then." Spearman smiled. "We'll wait for the drinks . . . And then you can tell me what you're doing in that rat's nest over there."

"One thought," Spearman said, "has always haunted me. It haunted me when I was in charge of Counterintelligence, and it haunts me still. We are the only major intelligence service in the West that has never had a mole.

"We've had our share of traitors, of course: venal little men who acquire a taste for caviar and turn to spying to support it, or the unfortunates whose sleeping arrangements expose them to blackmail. But we've never had a real mole—the kind who's recruited in college, trained specially, inserted into the service, and allowed to lie dormant for ten, maybe fifteen years while he burrows his way to a position of trust. We've never had one of those . . . Or not so far as we know."

Sullivan was silent. Spearman's style of conversation was leisurely, even rambling. He seldom answered a question directly, preferring to come at it from an angle, to encircle it with coils of implication and qualification, to avoid confronting it until he had it thoroughly surrounded. But it was better, Sullivan had discovered, not to prompt him. It took patience to follow the spiral of his thought to its conclusion, but it could be illuminating.

"Think abut it," Spearman said. "The French have had one; the West Germans have had one; the British have had several— Philby was only the most celebrated—but we haven't. Why?

"Think about it," he insisted. "We are the major target, their number one enemy, the backbone of resistance to their dismal ideology; they have only to sever us and all the limbs are paralyzed . . . And consider this, too. Consider their persistence, their incredible patience, their willingness to wait decades, even generations, for their plans to mature. Then ask the question again. Why not us? Why, when they recruited all those bright young men from the universities of Europe after the war, did they make such an amazingly generous exception for us?"

He broke off and waited, staring at Sullivan almost accusingly. The question was no longer rhetorical, Sullivan realized; he was expected to respond. Spearman, it appeared, was reenacting the great conflict of his final years at the Agency. He needed an adversary, and Sullivan was cast in the role.

Reluctantly Sullivan accepted it. "Obviously they didn't. But perhaps they were unlucky. Maybe they could never find an American Philby. It *is* a position that requires unusual talents."

"Ah." Spearman's lips twitched. "Are we more patriotic . . . or less talented?"

"Neither, necessarily. Perhaps our security procedures were just more effective."

"Have you had any dealings with the British?"

"No," Sullivan conceded. "I can't say I have."

"I have. It's been fashionable in recent years to belittle them, because of Philby and the others, but that's a mistake. In fact, the British are the professionals in this business. They should be— they've been at it since before the *Mayflower*. I seriously doubt whether our procedures are any better than theirs. I'd be surprised if ours were even as good. To tell the truth, I often wonder if the reason they seem to have had more than their fair share of moles isn't simply that they're better than the rest of us at catching them."

Sullivan thought about this. The logic struck him as similar to that used to justify Spearman's suspicions about the bugs: the absence of evidence being taken, in itself, as proof of the diabolical cunning of the enemy.

"I don't think so," he said gently. "Take Philby, for example. You were on to him years before they were, but they wouldn't listen. Not old Kim, they said. You can't expect us to swallow that. He's one of *us*. A lifetime member of the club . . . Snobbery," he continued. "It's always been their blind spot. They can never bring themselves to think ill of a member of the club."

"And we, of course, don't have a club?"

"We do, but not to the same extent. And not in the same way. You earn membership in our club; you don't belong by birth."

"I could argue that"—Spearman smiled—"but I won't. Because even if the requirements for membership are different here, the effects are the same. If you belong, you're special. Club members are privileged. They're above suspicion. Why?

"I'll tell you why." He leaned forward, stabbing at the tabletop with his middle finger. "Because they run the place, that's why. Because they've been around so long we take their loyalty and dedication for granted. And in the Agency's case, they're mostly members of the founding generation, or the one after it. They went through college in the late forties and the fifties. In the Golden Age, that is, of the mole."

With this, he seemed to consider his point sufficiently made, for he relaxed suddenly and smiled, addressing himself at last to the question Sullivan had asked fifteen minutes before.

"But of course this is abstraction. Background. The premise, if you like, on which Counterintelligence operated when I was in charge. What you asked, I recall, was when and why I first started to believe in the existence of an Agency mole, not as a theoretical probability but as brute fact.

"It wasn't any one thing at a particular time. Things came together gradually, as they always do in this game. They formed a
pattern, a weave in which no one thread stood out; it was the whole
that mattered. I suppose the first inkling was when we started to
lose agents at a faster than normal rate. There's always attrition, of
course, because an agent lives a lot on his luck and his luck usually
gives out eventually. But in Eastern Europe in the early seventies
it seemed that everyone's luck ran out at the same time. And it
wasn't just an epidemic of carelessness, for they were mostly good
men, professionals whose tradecraft was reflex, whose cover was
so instinctive it was part of their real identities. So I ordered investigations. But these things are always hard to track, and we
got nowhere. The statistical evidence was there, and there was no
satisfactory explanation of how the men had been blown, but
beyond that there was nothing to support a mole thesis. We were
simply up in the air.

"Then, one day in April 1975, an East German on vacation
walked into our embassy in Vienna. He said he was a colonel in
the security division of the Volkspolizei and he wanted asylum in
the U.S. He also wanted a new identity and money—a lot of money.
In return, he offered us everything he knew about Vopo counterintelligence operations, including a piece of information which
he said was bound to be of interest. The man's name, oddly enough,
was not German but Russian. It was Zukovsky. Alexander Zukovsky."

II

At about the time Sullivan was sitting down to Bloody Marys with
Spearman, Brady was in the morgue in Baltimore, being sick.

He'd hoped to do it discreetly, excusing himself quietly as the
queasiness swept over him, but as usual the swiftness of the spasm
took him by surprise and reduced him to ignominious flight.
Doubled up, a hand clasped firmly over his mouth, he galloped off
in quest of the nearest relief, a men's room whose location he'd
noted, against such a contingency, on entering the building. There,
under the detached but not unsympathetic gaze of the elderly
black attendant, he parted company with his breakfast.

"Something gruesome, was it?" the attendant asked.

Brady nodded. Then, partly from the aftertaste of semidigested breakfast and partly in memory of what he had seen on the slabs, he shuddered. "Gruesome" was right, he supposed, but it totally failed to do justice to the day-old corpse with half its head missing and the remainder churned to a pulp of mangled flesh and splintered bone. Yet it was not the sight of the corpses, horrible though that had been, that affected him most; it was the surroundings: the penetrating chill in the refrigeration room, the cheerless light, the smell of formaldehyde, and the pervasive, desolating sense of loneliness. What, he thought, a place to end your life.

"Yes." The attendant inclined his head judiciously. "We do see a world of ugliness down here. Well . . ." He turned and shuffled toward the towel dispenser. "Look at it this way—it could have been you on the slab in there. Or me. But I'm here drying my hands, and you're over there throwing up . . . That make you feel better?"

"No." Brady shuddered again. "But thanks anyway."

Hollowpoints, the Chief Medical Examiner had said, and from a powerful weapon, .357 magnum, probably. They mushroomed on impact, doing more damage than a double charge of buckshot, and they offered the killer the additional advantage of leaving Ballistics almost nothing to work with. Beyond that, he had little to offer. A gunshot wound in the head obviously had been the cause of death, and the victim had been an adult male Negro, about 6'1", 185 pounds, who had been in exceptionally fine physical shape. The only odd thing, considering the circumstances in which the bodies were found, was that the autopsy had revealed no traces of cocaine. This confirmed the findings of the forensic lab, which had found no traces of the drug in the victims' clothing, either. An unusual case, the CME had suggested, of dealers who were not also users.

The information had not surprised Brady. He was quite sure Marvin Nichols had not been a dealer. Housebreaking had been his line, with a little violence thrown in when necessary. The computer showed two arrests and one conviction. The first arrest had been in 1972, a robbery in Bethesda that turned sour for Marvin when the police traced the stolen goods and the receiver made a deal with the prosecution. The second had never reached court, because the young woman whose apartment in Georgetown Marvin had trashed was too impressed by that display of violence to risk another. Otis Taylor's record was longer, but he too had no history of dealing. Brady was satisfied that the record was accurate in his case also, because dealing cocaine, at least in quantities large enough to get killed for, put you in a different financial league than burglary. No dealer in his right mind would stoop to theft when the risks in his own trade were so much smaller and the rewards so much greater. No, Brady thought, Marvin and Otis were small-time thieves with no links to the world of hard drugs. Then what had they been doing down there by the canal with a packet of cocaine in the glove compartment of their car? And what had they done to get themselves shot?

Brady's interest in Marvin and Otis, his presence at the morgue, was the result of a call he'd received earlier from Sergeant Austin. The bodies had been found by the canal, Austin had told him, both had records for housebreaking, and one of them, to judge from a business card found in his wallet, had belonged to a kung fu institute in D.C. Perhaps, Austin had suggested, these were the men Brady was interested in talking to about the Forrester burglary. He'd given Brady the number of the kung fu institute, recommended he get in touch with the CME in Baltimore, and hung up.

The men *he* was interested in talking to? Brady had been left staring in outrage at the receiver. It was Austin's case, for Christ's sake. The break-in had occurred in his territory. Austin should be the one to call the kung fu place and make the trek out to Baltimore! But Austin never had shown much enthusiasm for the case. If it was a simple matter of housebreaking, he'd told Brady originally, he couldn't afford to waste time on it; and if, as Brady seemed to think, it had some connection with the dead spook, then he, Austin, knew better than to futz with it. The best he could do, he'd said, was to promise to call Brady if something turned up. This he had now done, his manner on the telephone clearly implied; the rest was up to Brady.

So Brady had called the kung fu place and become embroiled, for his pains, in a semantic misunderstanding with the Korean proprietor. The confusion concerned the word "good." Brady had used it technically and the Korean had taken it morally. No, he'd said, Mr. Nichols had not been good at karate; he'd been very bad at it. He'd understood nothing about it. It had taken some time to get the confusion cleared up. What the Korean had meant was that Mr. Nichols had believed that karate was a technique for hurting people, whereas in fact it was exactly the opposite. But yes, he'd agreed, though continuing to object to the use of "good" in this context, Mr. Nichols had been very good at hurting people. He had been a black belt, second degree.

After that it had been Dr. Daniel. The Chief Medical Examiner was still doing the autopsies when Brady called, and he immediately suggested Brady come on out so he could see for himself. Brady did not have the least desire to do so, but there had been an undertone of malice, a hint of challenge, in the invitation that had touched his pride. So he'd gone to Baltimore and seen things for himself, and, as he'd known he would be, he'd been sick.

And of course, to add to his embarrassment, Rutherford had been there too, with a couple of detectives from Homicide. They'd listened gravely to his explanation of his interest in the two dead burglars, and at the end thanked him politely for his help. A shade too politely, he'd thought, sensing in Rutherford's manner a touch of mockery. But he'd been grateful that at least Rutherford had refrained from asking awkward questions about his authority to pursue the Seligman inquiry. So he'd held his peace when Rutherford had announced his intention of following up on the drug angle, and he'd also managed to resist the very powerful temptation to suggest to Rutherford that the best course might be to stick to Homicide's established procedures and attribute the deaths to a suicide pact.

But what did it all add up to? He stared into the mirror at his pallid, grayish features and waited for his stomach to stop misbehaving. Marvin and Otis had probably broken into the woman's house, and the motive had probably not been theft. Now Marvin and Otis were dead, for reasons that almost certainly had nothing to do with cocaine. But was there a connection between the events? And if so, did it relate to Seligman?

He shrugged. Stick to the facts, he told himself. Give them to Sullivan and let *him* work them out. The Seligman case was a mess and getting messier all the time. Nothing about it was certain, not a single goddamn thing. The only thing certain, he thought, retching a little at the notion, was that Sullivan now owed him a breakfast.

III

"I've often thought," Spearman said, "that Counterintelligence should adopt a coat of arms. The device would be a package, postmarked Moscow, all tied up with bright red ribbon. The motto would be a quotation from Virgil: '*Timeo Danaos et dona ferentes*' . . . 'I fear the Greeks when they bring gifts.' Or to put it another way, things are almost never what they seem.

"You have a defector, let's say, with impeccable credentials, who brings you evidence of something you've always suspected. But just as you're congratulating yourself on your luck and preparing to go to work, a disturbing thought intrudes: is he real?

"You see," he continued, "thinking you have a mole is almost as bad as having one. You have to act on the suspicion, and your actions, justified or not, injure you. There's no way, for example, you can investigate yet keep your suspicions quiet. The investigation destroys trust, and without trust you're out of business. Agents start worrying about their case officers, case officers about their desk officers, and so on up the line, and pretty soon you're not gathering intelligence anymore, you're sitting around examining your navel. You're no longer an effective service, you're a debating society.

"Beyond which, of course, there's the waste of resources. The hunt takes time and energy. You neglect essential tasks, you pull people away from productive work, you spend so much time worrying about what may be an imaginary danger that you overlook real threats. All in all, I'd say it's a classic example of the treatment being worse than the disease."

"And that was the problem you faced with Zukovsky?"

"Part of it." Spearman nodded. "He arrived right on cue with just the evidence I needed. But the timing was a shade too perfect, the evidence fell too neatly into place. And since the implications, if we took him at face value, were going to shake the Agency to its foundations, it seemed more than usually necessary to look the horse in the mouth."

"What was the rest of the problem?"

"Zukovsky himself. His motive, for one thing, was too frankly commercial. And his story, when he came to the nub, was very short on facts. His key point, you see, was that four of the agents we lost in East Germany were betrayed—not by someone local, but by someone in Langley. The trouble was his evidence was entirely circumstantial, and almost entirely unconfirmed. What he told us boiled down to this: the men were arrested on a tip from the local KGB Resident, and the Resident let slip to Zukovsky that the tip had come from Moscow. From this, and the Resident's request that they time the arrests to make it look as if the first agent confessed and fingered the others, Zukovsky figured that the source they were trying to protect was not in Moscow but in Langley. It was a reasonable inference, but there was almost no support for the story. Nothing, in fact, except that the arrests did occur as he described and our own inquiry into them had come up empty."

"You can see what I'm getting at, can't you? Zukovsky ordered the arrests, so he was bound to know about the timing. But the rest of his story, the part about the Resident and the tip-off from Moscow, could easily have been invented, either by the KGB and the Vopos, in the hope of throwing us into a tailspin, or by Zukovsky himself."

"Zukovsky himself? Why would *he* want to do it?"

"Money. As I said, he was very frank about his motives. He was tired of life in East Germany and tired of hearing about the Era of Plenty awaiting his grandchildren. What he wanted, before he got too old to enjoy it, was a little plenty for himself, and he counted on us to provide it. Now he wasn't stupid; in fact he was very much the reverse. He knew perfectly well that, apart from the story about the Resident, he really didn't have very much to offer. Not enough, at any rate, to justify what he was asking. So it wasn't beyond the bounds of possibility that, to increase his value in the marketplace, he had made that story up."

"So what did you do?"

"What could we do"—Spearman shrugged—"except the usual? We put him through the grinder. We got the whole story on tape, took it apart, and went over it with a microscope, detail by painful detail. We took everything he told us about himself and the Vopos and checked it against what we knew. We asked him the same question sixty-four different ways and compared his answers for consistency. If he mentioned a person or a place we demanded detailed descriptions. We even asked him about the weather in Berlin on the day he received the tip-off. He had it pat. He had it all pat. In seventy-three days of interrogation, ten hours a day, seven days a week, he never faltered, never contradicted himself on any question of substance."

"Which in itself," Sullivan put in, "is a little disturbing."

"It is," Spearman conceded, "until you remember he was in the trade himself. He was an experienced interrogator and a trained observer. He was used to remembering things And of course he did get them wrong sometimes. He made about the number of errors you'd expect from someone with his training telling the truth about events that had happened some months before. But the mistakes were always minor. Never anything that cast serious doubt on the essentials. I suppose what it boiled down to after seventy-three days was this: either he was real or he was the best-prepared liar in the long history of the art."

"So what happened?"

What happened was that I got tired. I went to the then DCI and laid the facts before him. Either Zukovsky is lying, I said, or he isn't. I happen to think he's not, but be that as it may, we can't afford to ignore him.

"There followed"—Spearman pulled a face—"what came to be known as the Great Zukovsky Debate. The DCI called in the Deputy Directors and the heads of the larger sections. What he hoped to get, being the kind of man he was, was a consensus. What he got was a dogfight. We split into factions. One faction argued that Zukovsky was an obvious KGB plant, another that he was a fiction writer, hyping his story to increase sales; the third supported me. And in the end . . ."

"In the end," Sullivan supplied, "you won."

"No," Spearman said quietly, "I didn't. There was an investigation, certainly, A full-scale security investigation of everyone remotely connected with those four agents. I forced them into that. I outsat them and outshouted them until, from sheer weariness, they gave in. But I didn't win. I lost. I lost all the way down the line."

He was silent for a moment, remembering. The life had gone out of his eyes, and his features were set in a mask. Suddenly he seemed very old. He was still wearing the ancient homburg with its absurd mantle of black net, but in spite of this clown's headgear, in spite of the hints of paranoia that surfaced occasionally in his conversation, he achieved, at that moment, an extraordinary dignity. It was impossible for Sullivan not to take him seriously.

"You found nothing?"

"Practically nothing." With a visible effort Spearman returned to the present. "I had hopes, in the beginning, that elimination might work. The four agents were part of a network, so they knew about each other, but for security reasons each had a different case officer. That, unless you were willing to assume collusion, eliminated the case officers. Then their were two desk officers involved; the same went for them. And so on. Using that approach, I narrowed the field of suspects down to a handful of people in Plans. But then the boat sprang a leak."

"How?"

"Faulty assumptions. I realized, at that point, that I was wrong to limit myself to people who had direct knowledge of the agents' identities. Their names could have been leaked indirectly."

"Indirectly?"

"Yes. The mole didn't necessarily need to know the names. If he leaked enough of their reports, the KGB could have worked the identities out from the source descriptions. What that meant was the list of suspects had to be widened to everyone who'd seen those reports. And that was more than a hundred and fifty people."

"But you persevered?"

"Of course." Spearman frowned. The question evidently struck him as frivolous. "I went throught their personal files from A to Z. I hauled them all in for interviews. I even gave polygraphs where circumstances seemed to warrant. And in the process I made a lot of enemies."

"Ah." Sullivan smiled. "There was wailing and gnashing of teeth?"

"There was worse than that. There was practically an insurrection. A 'Dump Spearman' movement was formed and quickly gained general support. It became a question of either or. Either I came up with a mole in fairly short order, or I packed my bags and left. In the end . . ." He broke off, smiling his wispy smile.

"But of course," he said, "you know the end."

"What about Seligman?" Sullivan asked. "What happened with him?"

"Seligman?" Spearman was temporarily nonplused. "Oh yes . . . Seligman." He hesitated. I'm afraid Seligman is a stain on my conscience. He was on the circulation list for the agents' reports, you see. Then that business about his girlfriend came up. You know about that, don't you?"

Sullivan nodded.

"He was an accident," Spearman continued. "The proverbial innocent bystander who catches a stray bullet. I could never suspect him with any conviction, but I had to go after him. So long as he persisted in his relationship with that radical he was a security risk, at least on paper. So he had to go. It was a shame, but he left us no choice. And you say that after he left he got mixed up in some misinformation scheme dreamed up by Tyrell?"

"Yes."

"Then I think it's time you told me about it."

So Sullivan told him.

"It fits." Spearman nodded thoughtfully. "It certainly fits."

Sullivan was gloomy. "It may fit, but that's not going to help much. It's all conjecture, everything I've told you. Based on facts which are open to a wide variety of interpretation. And unfortunately yours are the same. Zukovsky might indeed have been lying, and the unusual loss of agents that started you off in the first place might simply have been an abnormal run of bad luck.

"It's not that I discount your intuition," he added quickly. "But I can't rely on it. I have to think like a lawyer. Unless I can build a case that would stand up in court, I'll end up, if you'll forgive the expression, another voice, crying in the wilderness. And we can't afford that—especially if you're right—because each time we go mole hunting and come back empty-handed, the harder it is to get a license next time."

"I take your point." Spearman nodded. "But you haven't heard all my facts. There were other developments. After I left.

"It started up again," he went on. "They were quiet while I was investigating—the agent attrition rate dropped down to normal—but about a year later there was another rash of arrests. The inquiry was dead by that time, of course, and Zukovsky had disappeared into civilian life. I suppose they thought it was safe. The interesting thing is that it happened only a few months after the start of Roy Tyrell's misinformation scheme.

"Don't ask me how I know," he added sharply. "I'm not going to tell you. You can make an educated guess, no doubt, and I'd rather leave things that way. Just take my word for it. Or better still, check it out for yourself when you get back."

He paused briefly, fixing Sullivan with his feline stare, and again Sullivan felt the weight of personality behind the donnish manner.

"There is a mole," he said. "I don't think like a lawyer, perhaps, but you can't spend thirty years in this business without developing a kind of feel. Call it intuition, call it a sense of pattern, call it what you like, but your facts mesh too neatly with mine for me to write it all off to coincidence. There is a mole. He's undermining the foundations of the Agency. If he's not stopped, the place is going to collapse. And in spite of anything the radicals may say, we need it. We need it more than ever. But this time we're *going* to nail him, because this time we're not dealing with a hundred and fifty suspects; we've got it down to three. Two really, because one of them you can almost certainly discount."

"Tyrell?"

"No." Spearman blinked. "Not Tyrell. I'd say he was rather the favorite. I was thinking of Patterson."

"Patterson!"

"Yes. I have my reasons for saying so, but I'm not going to tell you them either . . . So it's Brayer or Tyrell. Now all you have to do"—he grinned wickedly—"is figure out which."

"Of course. No problem," Sullivan said deadpan. "What could be more straightforward? I'll just have them marched into my office, look them straight in the eye, and call on one of them to confess. Then, if he doesn't, I'll . . . well, I'll be at something of a loss, won't I? I'll be in the position of prosecuting a murder case without a corpse. No evidence to convict, and no certainty that a crime has even been committed."

Spearman was silent.

"Look," Sullivan said. "Understand my position. I don't have the freedom you had, or the knowledge of how that place works. I'm an outsider, stumbling about in an organization where the right hand doesn't know what the left is doing, and even the right hand knows a hell of lot more than I do. If there is a mole, he can cover his tracks much quicker than I can follow them. So what do you suggest I do?"

Spearman continued to stare at him, his face completely expressionless. There was something almost reptilian, Sullivan thought, in that coiled immobility.

"Roy Tyrell," he said at last. "He's a friend of yours, isn't he?"

"Yes. He is."

"I see," Spearman said. "That makes it difficult, doesn't it?"

"Yes." Sullivan returned the stare frankly. "It does. But you're wrong about him. Apart from anything else, it was his idea to get me involved in this thing."

"Was it?" Spearman said. "That's very interesting. I wonder why he did that."

IV

After Sullivan left, Spearman sat for a while, finishing his drink. Then he got up and went into the house. A little later, having changed his clothes, he emerged from the front door and climbed into the ancient Mercedes that stood outside on the gravel. For half an hour he drove, apparently at random, through the maze of side roads that skirted his property. Eventually, satisfied that these maneuvers had served their purpose, he headed into town.

When he reached Georgetown he parked in a side street, next to a pay phone. Entering, he dialed a number, let it ring five times, and hung up. Then he returned to the car and drove to another phone two blocks away. He waited.

After two minutes the phone rang. He got out of the car and answered it.

"Yes," he said. "I saw him. It's as I thought."

He listened for a while, then spoke again.

"Yes," he said. "That might help . . . I don't think we need worry about him, though. I think we have him headed in the right direction."

CHAPTER 12

I

Ordinarily Sullivan avoided the center of Georgetown. There was something about the place, especially on a Saturday in midsummer, that reminded him of Babylon. It was too crowded, he thought, stepping into the street to avoid a group of teenagers who were blocking the sidewalk . . . too noisy . . . leaping out of the path of a sports car that bore down on him murderously, blaring the horn to assert its right of way . . . too trendy . . . forced back into the street by the overspill from a boutique that sold exotic clothes at barbaric prices . . . and . . . glaring at the lines outside a movie house whose current attraction, the billboards informed him, was Fellini's *Satyricon* . . . too mindlessly given over to the pursuit of pleasure. He wouldn't be there, he told himself sourly, but for Cooper and that damned Spearman—Cooper because they were out of tuna and the cat insisted noisily on two square meals a day; Spearman because his insinuations had made Sullivan forget to stop at a supermarket on the way home.

But Spearman, more than Georgetown, he recognized, was responsible for his sour mood. The man had disturbed him. He was obsessive, no doubt, suspicious to the point of paranoia, and his preoccupation with moles obviously stemmed as much from a desire for vindication as from a sober assessment of the facts; beyond that, it was clear that his evidence as to the events after his departure from the Agency was supplied by a crony and had therefore, presumably, been slanted to suit him; yet, in spite of all this, he was oddly compelling. He had sat there in fancy dress, talking in circles, plastering the cracks in his case with a mixture of generalization and gossip, and had somehow persuaded Sullivan not only to think the unthinkable, but also—very nearly—to act on it.

In fact, he knew he would have to act on it. He had no choice. Not because Spearman—very cleverly, as he no doubt believed— had called his motives into question, but because the unthinkable, once thought, could not be lived with. In theory he could still walk away from the thing: accept the official version of Theta and report to the Committee that Seligman's death, however caused, had no apparent implications for national security; but in practice he would not thereafter be able to look Roy Tyrell in the eye. He would be even less comfortable with himself, knowing he had entertained these doubts about his friend and lacked the faith and courage to resolve them.

But how to resolve them? The details of Theta were buried in the memories of three men. And only one of them, if Spearman's suspicions were correct, knew *all* those details. And that man—

"Watch where you're going!"

He glanced up. A middle-aged woman, built like a truck and carrying before her a large, sharp-cornered package, which she evidently intended to use as a battering ram, was barring his way. Instinctively, without looking, he stepped aside into the street.

What followed were separate events, but they were fused by his startled perceptions into one. There was a squeal of brakes, followed instantly by an angry honking; he leaped a foot in the air and landed on the sidewalk, almost on top of the woman with the package. She, in turn, stumbled into another pedestrian, dropping her package in the process. It took him several moments to collect his wits, recover her package, and hand it, with muttered apologies, back to the woman. He was still slightly in shock, though about to continue on his way, when he heard someone calling his name. Turning, he saw that the car had drawn up beside him and a woman was leaning out the driver's window. It was Gael Forrester. She was grinning.

"I'm sorry," she said. Then, leaving doubt as to whether the apology was intended to cover the near miss or the grin, she added, "But you did look funny. You jumped like a jackrabbit."

"Yes." He managed a half smile. "I suppose I did."

"It's amazing." She seemed oblivious to the traffic backed up behind. "I was just thinking about you, then there you were, right under the front bumper."

"Thank God for your reflexes."

"Buy you a drink," she offered. "In atonement."

"I don't deserve it. But I'll take it."

"Get in then. I have to find somewhere to park."

That proved easier said than done. After fifteen minutes of unsuccessful cruising, they were back where they'd started. Since his house was only a block away, Sullivan then suggested, it might be simpler if he were to buy her a drink. After all, he said, it was a moot point who should atone to whom for what.

"Mmm . . ." She surveyed the study, the walls lined with books, the Eames chairs facing each other across the fireplace, the Calder above it, and the gleaming grand piano in the corner. "This is nifty."

"That seems to be a favorite word with you." He walked over to a cabinet and got out a tray of bottles. "It's what you called my office. I hope you don't mean it the same way."

"'Different tone of voice." She smiled. "Pangs of conscience apart, though, the law does seem to have its compensations."

"I told you, I'm a fat cat. And largely unrepentant."

"That again." She pulled a face. "Well, if you are, you're not the only one."

She pointed to the doorway. Cooper entered, complaining softly. He eyed her coldly as though he had heard the remark; then, finding her worthy of no further interest, he stalked over to one of the chairs and settled himself into it. Fifteen pounds of majestic feline indifference.

"That's Cooper. Probably afraid you'll steal his chair."

"Cooper?"

"After the marmalade. Cooper's Oxford . . . He wandered in off the street several years ago, liked it, and decided to stay. Since then, he's done nothing but eat."

"He *is* huge."

She drifted over to the piano. On the lid there was a stack of music: Gershwin, Scarlatti, and Haydn, a tattered copy of Hanon, *Selections from My Fair Lady*.

"I take it you play."

"I struggle." He handed her a gin and tonic. "I hope that's OK."

"Thanks. It's fine." She leaned over the keyboard and touched a key in the bass, releasing a velvety growl that seemed to take minutes to die away.

"My god," she murmured. "It's gorgeous."

"A Bösendorfer." He nodded. "The Rolls-Royce of pianos— though Steinway might disagree. It's an extravagance, really. Too good for me. It shames me whenever I touch it.'

"Play something."

He hesitated, wondering, evidently, whether the request was merely polite.

"If you like . . . What?"

"I don't know." She considered. "Something peaceful. You choose."

He picked through the stack until he found what he wanted, placed it on the music rest, and settled himself on the stool. Then he took a pair of reading glasses from his pocket and perched them on the end of his nose as if he intended, most of the time, to peer over them. They made him look owlish, she thought; owlish and rather severe.

The piece was slow and touched with sadness. A grave, arching melody, stated without accompaniment in the bass, was taken up by the right hand and elaborated with a tracery of deft ornaments. The harmonies darkened; passing from hand to hand, melody and counterpoint were extended and transformed until they merged, finally, in a passage whose restraint and grief were heartrending.

"What was it?"

"Haydn. The slow movement of a sonata."

"It's beautiful. Like a leave-taking between old friends: a few quiet phrases, a last embrace, then silence . . . You played it beautifully, too. No suspicion of struggle."

"Ah." He smiled. "I cheated with the ornaments in the left hand. Do you play?"

She shook her head.

For a while, still hearing the music, she sipped her drink in silence. Then she asked: "Have you made any progress? With the inquiry, I mean."

He thought for a moment.

"Some," he said. "I was wondering whether to tell you. I'm not certain of anything yet—that's why I hesitated—but I don't believe Paul Seligman was disloyal to the Agency."

She didn't respond immediately.

"I should be pleased, I suppose," she said at last. "It helps a little. I guess it's good to hear I wasn't mistaken about the Paul I didn't know. But it's the Paul I did know I miss."

"You asked me to tell you."

"Yes. I did. I don't mean to be ungracious. And it does help me, what you've said. I feel . . ." She frowned. ". . . . not relieved exactly, because I never really doubted, but . . . lighter. People say things, you see, and you don't believe them, but you can't ignore them either. It's like a trial, I suppose. The judge orders something stricken from the record—is that the phrase?—and instructs the jury to disregard it; they may try, but you know they'll never quite succeed. Do you understand?"

"Yes," he replied. "I do."

Something about the way he said it turned her attention from herself to him. He was not speaking, she sensed, from his experience of trials.

"You're not happy about the way the inquiry is going?"

He shrugged. "My instinct told me to stay clear of the damned thing. I wish I'd followed it. But they twisted my arm, you see. And then, of course, I got intrigued. It was a puzzle and I wanted to solve it. Now . . ."

But here he broke off, reluctant to continue.

"You'd rather not discuss it?"

"I shouldn't, I think. At least until I know more.'

Again they were silent. His last reply inhibited the questions she wanted to ask, and his own thoughts evidently were turned inward. At a loss, temporarily, for suitable small talk, she turned her attention to the bookcase beside her.

"You know," she began presently, "you're supposed to be able to read someone's character in the books he owns. I find yours baffling."

"Books or character?"

"Both. I see Dorothy Sayers and Agatha Christie. That figures. Books on chess and backgammon, the *Sunday Times Book of Crossword Puzzles*. All fairly consistent and predictable. But then I find ghost stories, Jane Austen, the Tibetan *Book of the Dead*, and finally poems by Edward Arlington Robinson. No pattern at all."

"A shapeless character," he suggested. "Or perhaps a grab-bag mind."

"Possibly." She smiled.

"In any case, they're not all mine. Those poems, for example. I think they were bought by my father. I've certainly never read them."

"Never read Robinson?" She sounded shocked. "Not 'Miniver Cheevy' or 'Richard Cory'? I thought everyone got *them* in school."

He shook his head. "Deprived childhood."

"Odd you should have that book," she mused. "Paul liked Robinson. Especially 'Richard Cory.' He said it reminded him of Roy Tyrell."

"Tyrell?" He sat up abruptly. "You know him?"

"Not really. I met him once. Paul introduced us . . . 'And rich he was,' " she quoted:

> "Yes. Richer than a king,
> And admirably schooled in every grace.
> In fine, we thought that he was everything
> To make us wish that we were in his place.

You don't know that poem?"

He shook his head. "How does it go on?"

> "So on we worked, and waited for the light,
> And went without the meat, and cursed the bread.
> And Richard Cory, one calm summer night,
> Went home and put a bullet through his head."

"And *that's* Roy Tyrell?"

"Oh. I don't know. As I said, I only met him once. He didn't strike *me* as suicidal. In fact, he looked pretty sassy. But Paul insisted he was Richard Cory. He had too much, Paul said, so he had nothing, and he would realize it in the end . . . Is he a friend of yours?"

"Yes," Sullivan said. "And I know what Paul meant. He was wrong, though. Roy has plenty, but I'm sure he can handle it."

The silence that followed was broken by the telephone.

Sullivan answered it. "Brady?" He listened for some time without speaking; then he said, "There've been developments at my end, too. I haven't sorted them out yet. It may take a few days. I'll call you next week sometime. Maybe Wednesday . . . You'd rather call me? OK. But don't call there; call here. If I'm not here, there's a recorder gizmo on the phone that'll take a message. And thanks."

He hung up.

"This inquiry," he said, "it's like trying to break a combination. There are *n* alternatives, each equally possible. All you can do is twiddle the dial, listen carefully, and hope to hear the tumblers as they click into place."

"Something just click?"

"I'm not sure," he said. "But I think so."

II

"Another day of this," the woman from Registry said, "and I'll have to ask Supply to lend me a wheelbarrow."

Her smile was not altogether good-humored. She'd made four trips already this morning, and three of them, she clearly thought, had been unnecessary; eighty-six files surely was more than any reasonable person could need at a time.

"I hope there won't *be* another day." Sullivan, peering over the stacks as if from behind a barricade, tried to exert charm. "I'm really sorry for all the trouble I've put you to, but I thought if I got them all at once it would save you running back and forth all day. I didn't realize they'd be so heavy."

He was sympathetic, but not very. She obviously suffered from the delusion, common to back-office workers, that the organization existed for her convenience and would fold up without her. Transporting files was her job, after all, and transporting them, he was prepared to bet, was far less of a chore than reading them.

"Lunch will be a problem." She said it with satisfaction. "Most of these folders are Top Secret. You can't leave them lying around here when you go out. Not even with the door locked. Just be thankful you have a private bathroom."

She turned to go, pleased with her exit line, but he stopped her.

"One more thing . . . Would you update me on the indexing system? It's been years since I worked here; I'm not sure I remember."

She hesitated. He'd been wise, he thought, to remind her he'd once belonged here himself. Otherwise she'd undoubtedly have hemmed and hawed and referred him to someone else for an answer. That would have been tiresome; the day promised to be long enough as it was.

"It's really quite simple." Her voice took on a schoolmarmy note: patient but not optimistic about her chances of being understood. "The letter prefixes denote country of origin. The first two digits identify the originating case officer; the last two indicate the year of origin; the middle three number the report in the chronological sequence originated by the case officer in that particular year . . . CSX 04 015 75, for example"—she took the top folder from the stack nearest her—"is the fifteenth report originated by Case officer 04 in Czechoslovakia in 1975."

"Thank you." He gave her his best smile. "That was a model of clarity. You'd make an excellent witness."

"God forbid I should have to. Well, I'll leave you to your researches. Have fun."

Fun? He doubted it. There might be three hundred pages of reading ahead of him, and though he was a reasonably accomplished skimmer—you had to be to survive law school—he lacked enough curioisity about the subject to sustain him in the task. The best he could hope was that it would prove illuminating, and that hope, he recognized, might well be unfounded. Seligman, possibly, had seen a pattern, but Seligman had been a specialist, as absorbed by the details of military logistics and hardware as a baseball fan by batting averages. A pattern glaringly obviously to Seligman might elude him completely.

He doubted, however, that the pattern he sought would relate to military information. Roy Tyrell, after all, had told him that what Seligman had passed to the Russians was chickenfeed—a claim he would hardly have made if a glance at the files were enough to refute it—and Spearman had spoken of agents exposed and destroyed while Theta was in operation. So it seemed reasonable to assume that the files' significance would lie, not in what they told him about tanks and missiles, but in what they revealed about the sources of that information.

Source protection, he now remembered, was indeed the main reason for the high classification given to most intelligence reports. The intelligence itself was often trivial, seldom anything whose disclosure would cause, in the words of the statute, "exceptionally grave damage to the interests of the nation." What was vital was the fact that the Agency had *obtained* the intelligence, for knowledge of this might enable an opposing service to identify and destroy the source. For example a report that Brezhnev had been taken sick at a particular meeting of the Politburo would interest the KGB only because it revealed that someone present at the meeting had talked out of turn. And, given knowledge of a sufficient number of similar reports, they might easily be able to deduce whose tongue had been wagging.

Examination of Seligman's list seemed to confirm that he had been thinking along the same lines. Seligman had arranged the numbers into five groups, each originated by a single case officer but spanning in most cases several years. The only exception was a single group, the CSX 04 group, which contained a file which appeared to have been originated by a different case officer in a different country. Sullivan decided to study this group first, partly because it was the largest—eight files in all—and partly because the anomaly intrigued him. He arranged the files in chronological order and went to work on the first.

"Subject: Proposed changes in the command structure of the Warsaw Pact forces," the title page informed him. "Date: 10/15/ 75. Source: Extremely well placed; unproven."

Source descriptions, he remembered, were essentially indicators of reliability. "Extremely well placed" meant that the source unquestionably had access to the type of information reported; "Unproven" meant either that the information had not been confirmed by another source or that the source was newly recruited and had not yet established his credibility. Unconfirmed intelligence was always suspect, but once a source had established a track record, his reports, confirmed or not, might be upgraded to "Reliable."

The substance of CSX 04 015 75 was two pages of detail on the proposed changes, containing many acronyms and abbreviations whose meaning was obscure, and it told him much more about the subject than he really wanted to know. The gist, he gathered from the paragraph of source comment at the foot of the report, was that Russia was tightening its grip on the forces of its allies. The next report, also classified Top Secret, dealt with logistical problems anticipated by the Warsaw Pact forces in the event of a war in Europe. It was dated 12/2/75, and its source description was the same as the first report's. The third file was the anomaly. Indexed HUX 02 006 76 and dated 2/16/76, it concerned "Recently implemented changes in the command structure of the Warsaw Pact forces." Its source was described as "Well placed; reliable." It confirmed the information reported in the first file and had led, apparently, to an upgrading of the first source, since in the fourth file "Extremely well placed; unproven" had become "Extremely well placed; believed reliable." In subsequent reports Mr. Extremely Well Placed Believed Reliable underwent further transformations, achieving in the final one the simple dignity of "Authoritative." This was the ultimate accolade, reserved for sources whose value, access, and reliability were established beyond serious question. There were, Sullivan recalled, very few of them.

It was tempting to infer that the sequence of CSX 04 reports recorded, among other things, the evolution of a source; but the inference rested, unfortunately, on a large assumption: namely, that the source for all the reports was the same person. If that were true, then the reports, once in the hands of the Russians, might well have been enough to nail him. The KGB would simply have had to list the people in Czechoslovakia who received advance notice of the changes in command structure and compare that list with the lists of those having access to the information in the other six reports. By eliminating any names that failed to appear on all seven lists, they could have reduced the suspects to a manageable number—perhaps even to one. It was the kind of thing, he reflected, that a desktop computer could do in its sleep; a microsecond of real time could well have placed Mr. Extremely Well Placed in a cell in Lubyanka. But the process would work only if the source were always the same. If not, the mathematics were far less promising. And since the range of possible source descriptions was limited—five or six altogether, he recalled—it was not altogether improbable that Case Officer 04 had controlled more than one source meriting the same description. In that case, what seemed like a pattern might have no significance at all.

But how to discover the number of sources involved? He could ask the case officer—if the case officer could be traced—but tracing him would mean asking someone in Plans. Whoever he asked would no doubt refer him to Roy Tyrell, so he might just as well bypass the case officer and go to Roy direct. The trouble with that was that Roy might very well question his need to know, and he could establish that only by revealing the drift of his thoughts. He was anxious to avoid that, not only because to do so prematurely would be the very essence of bad strategy, but also because the drift of his thoughts, when he examined it closely, made him rather ashamed.

The only alternative was a long shot. If it worked, he would avoid the confrontation with Roy; but it might not work, because the logic involved, even if he were lucky, was somewhat circular. It also meant plowing through more files. He would have preferred to avoid also another skirmish with the harpy from Registry, but life was imperfect, he reflected stoically; you couldn't have everything. He had to steel himself, nevertheless, to pick up the telephone.

"Miss Lawrence, please."

She came on the line.

"Miss Lawrence, I make this request with great trepidation and only from extreme need: could you possibly bring me all the files in the CSX 04 series after June 21, 1977?"

He meant it to be light and charming, but it came out sounding sarcastic. He was rather surprised to hear her agree at once, and cheerfully.

"Of course, Mr. Sullivan. It may take a while to log them all out. Would half an hour be all right?"

"It would," he said. "And thank you very much."

He spent the time looking at two more of Seligman's groups. It was possible, he concluded, that the pattern he seemed to discern in the CSX 04 files was repeated in the SRX 07 and HQX 03 groups also, but in these too it was unclear whether he was dealing with a single source. He hoped to hell he wouldn't have to ask for the subsequent files in those series as well.

Twenty-five minutes later there was a knock at the door. Miss Lawrence entered with another woman, each bearing twenty or thirty folders.

"Miss Lawrence," he began. "I'm extremely sorry to cause you—"

She cut him off.

"Mr. Sullivan, there is absolutely no need to apologize. You are entitled to ask for as many files as you wish, and our job is to bring them. Besides . . ." The corners of her mouth turned up in a tight little smile. "I believe I have solved the problem of getting them back to Registry. There will be no need for a wheelbarrow. When the time comes, instead of returning these files to Registry, I'll simply transfer Registry, lock, stock, and barrel, up here. Believe me, it will be much easier."

With that, she marched out, triumphant.

And Sullivan was content to let her triumph, because, though he was not inclined to call it that, he was having a triumph of his own. None of the sources in the files she'd brought was described as "Authoritative." Mr. Authoritative, whoever he was, had enjoyed a very brief moment of glory. Since June 21, 1977, it seemed, he'd been as silent as the grave.

III

"Roy," Sullivan said, "tell me about Zukovsky."

"Zukovsky?" Tyrell stared. "Where did you hear about him?"

Sullivan didn't answer.

Tyrell thought for a second or two.

"Spearman," he accused. "You've been talking to Spearman, haven't you?"

Sullivan nodded.

"Shit!" Tyrell said.

"What was wrong with that? I know he's not exactly persona grata with you guys, but since you guys haven't been very forthcoming, he seemed a good person to see. So I did see him, and he was very helpful."

"Helpful?" Tyrell sneered. "I'll bet he was."

Sullivan was irritated by the tone.

"And what exactly," he asked coldly, "do you mean by that?"

They were sitting under an awning in the stern of Sullivan's boat, anchored a couple of hundred yards offshore in the lower reaches of the Bay. Ostensibly they were fishing—hand lines were set and fastened to bamboo poles within easy reach of their chairs—but in the hour they'd been out they'd caught nothing and had seldom glanced at the poles or hauled in the lines to check the bait.

The time had passed in virtual silence, broken only by the occasional grunted remark or the pop of a beer can being opened. But the tranquility normally induced by the absence of weekend sailors and the comfortable sense of lounging around while the rest of the world worked was missing, destroyed by the knowledge that, in spite of the camp chairs, the ice chest, and the pretense at fishing, the purpose of the trip was not pleasure. They both knew what the purpose was, and each had been waiting for the other to begin.

Odd, Sullivan thought, how he'd instinctively shied away from the notion of having this confrontation at the Agency. Odd, too, that Roy had agreed so readily to take the day off. Perhaps both of them, conscious of the shadow the Agency cast on their friendship, were anxious to play this scene in a different setting, hoping in that way to recover the old trust. They didn't seem, however, to have gotten off to a very good start.

But it would be here if anywhere, he reflected. They'd taken many fishing trips together, but never in better conditions. The day was brilliant—hot, but with a slight breeze to disperse the humidity—the quiet undisturbed except by the patter of waves against the hull and the far-off drone of a powerboat. Out in the bay a flotilla of dinghies, only their sails visible, were bobbing and weaving with a random grace that reminded him of butterflies in a meadow. The whole scene—the dazzle of sunlight on water, the treetops stirring gently at the shoreline, the horizon rising and falling with the easy rhythm of sleep—seemed utterly remote from the world they'd left at the Agency. Yet it was here almost exactly, he couldn't help remembering, that Seligman had met his death.

He waited for Tyrell to answer, but instead Tyrell sat up and pointed to the pole behind Sullivan's chair.

"There's something on your line."

The pole was bent like a bowstaff, the tip whipping in rapid, uneven jerks. Tyrell walked over and hauled in the line. On the hook was a good-sized bluefish, which he released from the barbs and tossed onto the deck. It lay on its side, gills pumping, drumming its tail against the deck every few seconds in a convulsive effort to regain the water. Once, righting itself for a moment, it managed to slither a few feet toward the cockpit in a flurry of desperate swimming motions. Presently, when he had baited and reset the line, Tyrell came over and smacked it on the head with an empty beer bottle. It quivered and stiffened, the stripes on its side already beginning to fade. Tyrell hooked his fingers into the gills, took it to the side, gutted it, and dropped it into the ice chest.

"Did you tell Spearman about Theta?" he asked.

"A little." Sullivan nodded. "Not the details, just the essentials."

Tyrell frowned. For a while he didn't speak. He just sat there, apparently lost in thought.

"I guess it's my fault," he said eventually. "I should have warned you about him. I thought I had, actually, but I should have been more explicit."

He paused, wondering how to begin.

"Do you remember," he asked, "my saying once that Spearman had done us so much damage he might as well have been drawing his paycheck in rubles?"

Sullivan nodded.

"Well," Tyrell said carefully, "there's a school of thought in the Agency believes that he *was*. I don't necessarily subscribe to it, but I can't discount it, either. It has a circumstantial plausibility to it that's rather disturbing. The case rests, you see, on two fairly solid foundations: one is the undeniable damage caused by his mole investigations; the other is the inconsistency in his treatment of various defectors—chiefly Zukovsky.

"Zukovsky, you understand, was not our only recent defector. There were others. The important ones were a man named Panov and another named Kyrilenko. Panov and Kyrilenko were both KGB. They brought us valuable intelligence about KGB operations and personnel—but no mention of a mole. They were good. Research was thrilled with them, I was thrilled with them, everybody was thrilled with them—except Spearman. Spearman claimed they were plants and did his best to chop them into small pieces. Panov spent more than a year in the grinder. With Kyrilenko it was more like two. But when Zukovsky came along with a bunch of chickenfeed about the Vopos and some half-baked story about an Agency mole, Spearman practically fell over himself in his eagerness to believe. Zukovsky spent a bare ten weeks under interrogation before Spearman declared himself satisfied. Do you see what I'm getting at?"

"Yes," Sullivan said. "Spearman attempts to discredit the genuine defectors yet works to establish the plant."

"Correct. The debriefer who did most of the work with Panov and Zukovsky even went so far as to make the case in writing. He was axed for his pains, of course, but the thought stuck. When Spearman himself was fired, not too long afterwards, the DCI denied that those accusations had anything to do with the decision, but no one really believed him. We all felt more comfortable with Spearman no longer around."

He paused and waited for Sullivan to draw the obvious conclusion.

Sullivan did.

"So you're saying, in effect, that I may have given the substance of Theta to an active agent of the KGB?"

"Yes." Tyrell nodded. "That's what I'm saying."

Mirrors, Sullivan thought, an acid trip in a hall of mirrors; every fact capable of diametrically opposed interpretations, every story a surface hiding another underneath.

"It's plausible," he said. "But what Spearman told me was also plausible. And his theory at least was backed by documentary evidence."

"What evidence?"

"The files."

"Tell me about the files," Tyrell said.

Sullivan told him.

"Assuming quite a bit, aren't you?" was the comment when Sullivan had finished. "Item: all the CSX 04 reports were from the same source. Item: the Russians were able to use the reports to get a bearing on him. Item: they nailed him, and that's why we never heard from him again. All of which are questionable—especially the last. You don't really know, for example, that we *didn't* hear from him again. He might have been transferred to another case officer—that happens sometimes when a source is upgraded. Alternatively, he needn't have been an agent at all, necessarily, just an unknowing contact who flapped a bit at the mouth. We have a lot of those, you know."

"That kite won't fly." Sullivan shook his head. "He wasn't a casual contact; the reports were too detailed. As for the rest"—he shrugged—"you may be right. It may be a mistaken assumption. That's why I'm asking. Is it?

"If it is," he added quickly, "I'll be looking for documentation. I've had too much unsupported testimony on Theta already."

Tyrell stared at him for a moment without speaking. Then he leaned back in his chair and smiled faintly.

"I see."

"I don't think you do see." Sullivan's voice was sharp. "I took this thing on at your urging. I expected, therefore, to get your support. Instead, you kept me guessing from the start. I've had to squeeze the facts out of you, drip by drip. So if I'm treating you now as a hostile witness, you can hardly bitch about it. I'd say it was more than deserved."

Tyrell let that go without comment.

"What I'm saying," Sullivan went on, "is I want to know whether those sources were the same, I want to know if he was blown, and I want the answers supported, either by documents or by the case officer. And if it's the case officer, he'll be under oath and informed very clearly about the penalties for perjury. I'm through messing around, Roy. I want that clear."

"Oh, it is." Tyrell didn't sound terribly impressed. "It couldn't be clearer. The only thing is, you should be talking to Everett. He's the one who calls the shots."

"Fuck Everett!" Sullivan snapped. "He doesn't know shit about this, that's obvious. I want the answers from you, Roy. I want them now."

"Under oath, no doubt?" Tyrell's smile was infuriating. "After a solemn warning about the penalties for perjury?"

"Look." Sullivan made an effort to control himself. "We've been friends for ten years, and all the time we've been straight with each other. Now, all of a sudden, everything's changed. You hedge around, you prevaricate, you say you're not permitted to trust me—Everett's orders—but the simple fact is, you won't. How am I supposed to feel about that? What am I supposed to *think*, for that matter?"

"You talk about trust." Tyrell met his gaze squarely. "But with you it's a one-way street. You want me to trust you, but you won't reciprocate. And furthermore, when I *did* tell you about Theta you charged straight off to Spearman, who may very well have charged straight off to tell the Russians. You don't inspire confidence, Morgan. You really don't."

The reminder calmed Sullivan. Roy was wrong about trust, he thought; *he* had been the first one to forfeit it. About Theta, on the other hand, perhaps he was right. If Spearman *was* a KGB agent, Theta was certainly blown. But in that case, surely Roy's reaction should have been stronger. He should have made more, shouldn't he, of the carelessness that might have destroyed his operation? Instead he'd let it slide to pursue the reasons for Sullivan's interest in the files.

"About Spearman and Theta," he said. "You don't seem much bothered about that."

"I'm not."

"You're not? Why not?"

"Because I don't think you've done any damage. In fact, inadvertently, you may very well have helped."

"You'll have to explain that."

"Will I?" Tyrell gazed out toward the horizon, frowning. When he turned back to Sullivan his eyes were troubled. When he spoke, it was to make an appeal.

"Look, Morgan. Ten years ago you quit the Agency because you didn't like what it was doing, or what you were doing in its name. Things haven't changed; we're still doing things you wouldn't like, and this is one of them. So I'll say this one more time: you don't need to know, and you won't like it if I tell you. Why not leave things as they are?"

"I can't." Sullivan shook his head. "You know I can't."

"Yes." Tyrell nodded sadly. "I suppose I do . . .

"You asked me earlier," Tyrell began, "if sources had been blown by Theta, and if the authoritative source from the CSX 04 was among them. The answer is yes, to both questions."

"So you gave up sources." Sullivan's voice was grim. "And they were probably shot. How do you justify that?"

"You have to think of it as war," Tyrell said. "And war demands hard choices. You send people to get killed to further strategy which you know very well may have to be abandoned later. Every commander faces those choices, though he doesn't like to dwell on them. Theta was like that.

"We had a source," he continued. "Very high up in the Soviet Army. We picked him up in Eastern Europe in 1972 when he was Military Attaché to one of their missions there. We developed him slowly at first, used him sparingly, because we thought that, good as he was, he'd be better later. He was obviously going places in his career, so we let him sleep for a while in the hope that when the time came to wake him he'd be another Penkovsky.

"It was good strategy. In mid-'74 he was promoted and posted to Moscow with a key job in the Planning Division of the Soviet General Staff. He began to produce intelligence of superb quality: weapons data, transcripts of Planning Division sessions, blow-by-blow accounts of the political infighting at the Kremlin. It's no exaggeration to say, in fact, that he was worth more to us than the rest of our Bloc sources put together.

"But late in '75 it all stopped. He clammed up completely. No product. No contact. Just six months of total silence. At first we assumed it was because he had nothing for us. We couldn't do much about it anyway, for fear of jeopardizing him. Then, as time went on, it seemed clear that he'd been blown. We didn't know how, and it wasn't safe to try to find out, so we sat tight and waited, but without much hope.

"It turned out we were wrong, or half wrong, at any rate. In June 1976 he got back in touch. The GRU suspected a leak, he told us, and the heat was turned up high. They'd been leaning on everyone with access, particularly him. He hadn't dared contact us before, and he was taking the risk now only because he had no choice. They were closing in, he said. Unless we could do something to distract them, he was dead."

"Couldn't you have pulled him out?"

"We might have." Tyrell shrugged. "There were plans for it, at any rate, though God knows whether they'd have worked. It's not easy to kidnap a Russian general, even when he's willing. And the problem was he didn't want to leave. I think he figured that with help from us he might be able to ride things out. He wasn't in it for money, you see; he was acting from conviction. He was also, though it hardly seems necessary to say it, an incredibly brave man.

"Of course, 1976 was when Seligman fell into our lap. By June the Russians had made their first overture to him and the mechanics of Theta were already set up. But we hadn't decided on a target. The situation in Moscow decided for us.

"You'll remember," he continued, "that when I first described Theta I mentioned the supplementaries: follow-up requests for information inspired by the reports that Seligman passed."

Sullivan nodded.

"Well, when the first supplementaries came in it was obvious that the KGB was primarily interested in sources. That gave us our opportunity. They wanted to use Theta to trace and plug their leak; we would use it to make sure they plugged the wrong one."

"By doctoring up what you passed, in order to point them in the wrong direction?"

"In essence that was it." Tyrell nodded. "But the details were a little more complicated. To begin with, there was a credibility problem. Seligman was new and untested—to them, naturally, an object of great suspicion. We couldn't risk trying to fake things first time out. They had to believe in him before we could use him to mislead. That's what I meant when I spoke of hard choices."

"I see." Sullivan kept all expression out of his voice. "To protect a major source you sacrificed some minor ones—Mr. Authoritative from the CSX O4s being a case in point."

"Among others." Tyrell nodded. "We couldn't afford to do things by halves; there was too much at stake. Fortunately for us, however, the GRU moved with caution. They had to, really; our source was rather . . . eminent. Anyway, it wasn't until the fall of '77 that they'd narrowed the suspects down to a handful—with a short list of two—and seemed ready to go after our general. By then Seligman's credentials were fairly solid . . . or as solid as they were ever likely to get."

"And you gave them the misdirect?"

Tyrell nodded.

"But it didn't work, did it? You sacrificed all those agents to establish Seligman, but they got on to him anyway. Theta was a failure, just a very expensive failure. And that's what continues to baffle me. Why, in that case, the big mystery? Why all the crap about security and need to know? The operation bombed. There's nothing to protect anymore."

"It didn't bomb," Tyrell said quietly. "On the contrary, it succeeded magnificently."

Sullivan stared at him, dumbfounded. Tyrell, seemingly indifferent to the consternation he'd produced, went over to the ice chest to get himself a beer.

"Think about it." He opened the can and took a long swallow before resuming. "You were in Counterintelligence, so put yourself in their place. Remember the spy catcher's first commandment: 'Thou shalt not trust.' Think about the grinder and what happens to every defector who walks through its doors . . . Come to that"—he smiled—"take a look at yourself.

"You're all skeptics," he continued. "You have to be; the mentality comes with the job. To you every letter you receive is from the IRS, every package is potentially a bomb. If the Archangel Michael showed up in your office, you'd put him through the grinder—just to be sure he wasn't working for the devil. And if there's one thing you distrust more than all the others, it's a double—like Seligman. However long he works for you, however good the product, there's always that sneaking suspicion at the back of your mind . . . He finked on them, you tell yourselves, why not on us?

"That was the key to Theta. Distrust may be the armor of counterintelligence, but like most armor it has a chink. You're skeptics about almost everything, but there's one thing you can be counted on to believe, and that's the worst. You rush to that judgment like lemmings. Seligman was a double, automatically and irretrievably suspect. We could never hope to establish his credibility beyond question. But what we could do—and it would serve our purpose just as well—was destroy it absolutely."

He paused, as if expecting a response, but Sullivan said nothing. He knew the rest of it now, knew exactly what Roy was going to say, but the knowledge left him empty. He could summon no outrage, anger, or even pity, because these feelings—any feelings, in fact—were simply beside the point. He was now in a world where feelings, to the extent that they existed at all, were simply vulnerabilities, chinks in your armor where the enemy's knife might enter. And the discovery that Roy belonged to this world, created and perpetuated it, was not really discovery but recollection—something always dimly known, but up to now ignored. So he could only sit there, knowing what was coming, and in a perverse, masochistic way wanting to hear it.

"We blew him." Tyrell brought it out abruptly. "We spent months establishing him, we passed information wholesale, we destroyed half a dozen agents in the process—no wonder, incidentally, he began to get suspicious—then we made a deliberate slip. Nothing obvious, of course. Nothing crass or heavy-handed, just a minor inconsistency in one of the reports we gave him to pass, something that might have passed unnoticed by anyone not looking very hard. But they *were* looking hard, as we knew they had to be, and it was enough to explode him—him and all the information he had passed.

"And it was all true," he concluded. "Everything they got from him, except the deliberate inconsistency, was genuine. It all pointed to the real leak—our general in Moscow. Only by that time they wouldn't have touched it with a ten-foot pole. And that, of course, is why it doesn't matter much what Spearman may or may not tell them. Because if he does go to them, it will only confirm what they think they already know."

Something about the way he said it, something self-congratulatory, almost gleeful, struck a spark of anger from the lump of Sullivan's apathy.

"Very ingenious." His voice was as dry as the Sahara. "You took him, and others—people who worked for you and trusted you—and you sacrificed them on spec. I think that's the phrase I want, isn't it? And that makes it so much more remarkable; you couldn't even be sure the sacrifice would work."

"You never can be." Tyrell brushed this aside. "You just do what you can with the means at hand. I had to do something, and Theta was available. Besides, it did work. Our source is in place and sitting pretty. Some other poor bastard is in Lubyanka."

"And Paul Seligman is dead."

"Yes. And so are the others, I guess. I didn't think the KGB would react that way with Paul, but they did. And if you ask me would I do it again, knowing what I do, the answer would be yes—I'd do it every time. You establish your priorities and you make the hard choices. You have to; there's no other way to do it."

"Hard choices?" Sullivan challenged. "I think that's what bothers me most. How hard are they really? Tell me, Roy. How much agonizing did this one cost you?"

"You want me to feel bad about it?" There was an edge of scorn to the words. "Suppose I do. How does that help? Does it help Seligman, for instance?" Tyrell shook his head. "No. Sentimentality is what that would be."

Sullivan said nothing.

"I said you wouldn't like it, but you wouldn't listen. You didn't need to know, but you insisted. Well . . ." Tyrell gave a half shrug. "Now you know."

BOOK FOUR

August 12, 1978–August 15, 1978

CHAPTER 13

I

They were two hundred yards from the marker now, beating up toward it on the windward leg, the little boat not so much sailing as hurling itself through the water, plunging through the crests and crashing, in bursts of spray, into the troughs.

"We're not going to make it," Procter said.

The boy did not answer, did not seem to have heard. Leaning out almost parallel to the water, indifferent to the cramp in his hand and the pain in his legs where the edge of the cockpit cut into them, indifferent to the spray that drenched him head to foot, he was staring out over his right shoulder as if nothing existed but the marker and nothing mattered but clearing it to windward.

Racing conditions, Procter had specified: a trial run over the two-mile triangular course they would race later in the season. He had bet the boy five dollars that on the last, windward leg he could not clear the marker on the first tack. Now he was starting to regret it, not only for the money, which the boy could not afford and would insist on paying if he lost, but because in his effort to win the boy was pushing the boat, and himself, to the limit. He would shortly, Procter feared, push beyond.

But he had made the bet and set the rules, and he could not, for the boy's sake, back out now. It was not a question of money, or even of winning; it was a simple matter of pride. And the pride came from making choices and taking consequences. If he called the bet off he might save them a dunking, but in doing so he would be condescending—refusing to hold the boy to his choices and treating him, in consequence, as a child. He didn't believe in that. The boy did not deserve it. For in spite of his years and his size, he was not, Procter knew, a child at all.

The wind had freshened in the last minutes. It was gusting strongly now in long, dark streaks that swept over the water toward them, smudging the bright surface with trailing brushstrokes of gray. The boy was using the gusts, as Procter had taught him, to make up leeway. As each one hit, he eased the tiller a little, veering up into the wind. But as the boat veered it also heeled more sharply, and the water slid over the half deck on the leeward side, dangerously close to the cockpit.

They were on the edge, Procter knew, and he realized the boy knew it too and didn't care. It was total commitment, Procter thought, sailing with passion. And suddenly, in spite of the common sense that told him to back off before they flipped over, he was caught up in the same exhilaration. The hell with it, he thought; if we flip, we flip. They were wearing life jackets and the boat had flotation tanks; they would right her easily enough. But as he made the decision he knew that none of these calculations had entered the boy's head. The knowledge was slightly humbling. He had never been what anyone could have called a cautious man—the Coast Guard was not the place for cautious men—but in the boy, he realized, he had encountered a spirit harder and fiercer than his own.

They were closing now and he could see it was touch and go. One moment the marker would bob up to starboard, then it would vanish behind a crest, reappearing a second later directly ahead. They would either run right over it, he guessed, or have to fall off at the last second to avoid it. It would not hurt if they hit it—the marker was plastic and would not damage the hull—but racing conditions were racing conditions. Touching the marker meant disqualification.

Another gust might do it, he thought, might buy them the leeway they needed to bring them clear. And with the thought, the gust hit them. It was stronger than the others, pressing on them with a weight that made the boat lurch over, but the boy did not give a millimeter. The boat veered, heeled over, kept heeling; water rushed over the half deck, poured into the cockpit. And in that instant, with the boat teetering on the fine edge and Procter tensing himself for the shock of the water, the marker surged past, so close he couldn't tell if they had touched it or not. Then the boy let go of the mainsheet and the boat shook free and came up into the wind, sails flapping but past the marker and still right side up.

"Jeeesus!" Procter whistled. "You don't quit, do you."

The boy did not reply. Instead, he gazed astern at the marker, head on one side, brows knitted, as if he were trying decide about something.

"We touched," he said at last. "I felt us touch."

"I don't know." Procter considered. "It was close. Maybe we did, maybe we didn't. Who cares anyway? You made a hell of a run at it. I never gave you a ghost of a chance."

"I owe you five dollars." The boy was not to be sidetracked. "I'll pay it when we get back."

"Now hold on," Procter objected. "I don't know about that. I'd say it was too close to call. I don't give charity," he added carefully, "and I don't take it, either."

The boy stared at him, eyes narrowed.

"If it was a race," he demanded, "a real race, how would *you* call it? Remember," he cautioned, "if you cheat, you cheat yourself."

Procter hesitated. The boy was using his own words against him, the same words with which he'd explained how racing was largely self-policed, the rules a matter of honor for each competitor.

"If I weren't sure," he admitted, "I'd have to call it against myself."

"Then that's how I call it," the boy said.

Procter didn't argue; he knew the boy too well. It had been the same thing with his proposal to find the boy a corner in the Coast Guard station to save him from camping on the beach. The boy had agreed, but only on the understanding that he would work in return. And he *had* worked, worked like a beaver at all kinds of scut work, to the point where the deal had become entirely one-sided and Procter had been desperate for a way of evening things up. The sailing had been his solution for that one. No doubt, he consoled himself, he would find some way of returning the five dollars.

"Let's sail for fun now." He changed the subject. "I need some relief from the tension. That whole last leg I was expecting to have to swim home. Let's head over there." He pointed to an inlet some way ahead. "You almost swamped us with that last maneuver. A little bailing wouldn't come amiss."

The inlet was a quarter mile long, narrowing toward the head and wooded on both sides almost to the water's edge with big trees whose dense foliage, forming a canopy that shut out the evening light, seemed to enclose a brooding darkness. The ground rose steeply on either side, and the surface of the water, largely sheltered from the wind, looked like a sheet of minutely wrinkled silver foil. There was no sign of habitation; the place had a somber, eerie quality—tranquil but lonely, somehow slightly ominous.

They sailed up the reach and, finding a small gravel beach at the head, decided, instead of bailing, to run the boat up on the shore and let the water drain out of her. While they waited Procter smoked a cigarette and the boy amused himself tossing pebbles into the water. At length he tired of this and started to look around, inspecting the surroundings with a thoughtful, measuring eye.

"A good harbor for smuggling," he pronounced. "You anchor out there in deep water and land the stuff on this beach. A man waits on the headland," he added, completing the picture, "to guide you in with a flashlight."

"Going into business?" Procter grinned. "What would you smuggle, for example?"

"Dope." There was no hesitation about the answer.

"Dope?" Procter raised his eyebrows. "You mean marijuana?"

"No way." The boy gave him a pitying look. "My brothers grow *that* in the yard. Real dope, I mean. Cocaine or heroin."

He noted the disapproving frown on Procter's face.

"People do it, you know."

"Yes," Procter conceded. "I do know. There was a big stash of it taken by Customs a few years back, I recall. But not here. It was farther north. The Bay's too busy, I think."

"Busy is good." The boy's face wore a look of sententious gravity. "If I wanted to do something and not be noticed, I would go where there are plenty of people."

"You have it figured out, I see." Procter smiled. "I hope you'll cut me in on the profits."

There was no answer, and he assumed the subject was closed. But presently, after he had walked over to the boat to see how the draining was going, the boy took it up again.

"You remember the *Excalibur*?"

"*Excalibur*? Wasn't she the sloop I pulled off Rodo Beach?"

"The one I found with nobody on board." The boy nodded. "Mr. Seligman's boat. He was shot, remember, and they found him in the Bay."

"What about her?"

"Not her, him. Mr. Seligman . . . I think he was a smuggler."

"You *think*." Procter leaned heavily on the second word. "That's quite an accusation. What makes you think?"

"Not just think." The boy answered a little stiffly, offended that his statement had been questioned. "I also saw."

Details of the Seligman case came back to Procter. They had called it suicide, he recalled, but they were clearly unhappy about it. The ID had not been positive, and there were unresolved questions about secret documents and all that radio equipment. The press had raised a stink about it, he remembered, but their suspicions had centered on spies and satellites. No one had mentioned drugs or smuggling.

"What did you see?" he asked.

The boy thought for a moment.

"It was when I slept on the beach," he began. "Before you let me sleep in the Coast Guard station. There was a place I used to go sometimes, about two miles from the Wharf, maybe. Trees, a beach, not too much wind—a place like this." He gestured at their surroundings. "But with a house on the beach, and a place for boats." He shook his head, frowning. "What do you call those places?"

"A boathouse?"

"No. Not a house . . . It stands on legs in the water. Like a wharf, only smaller."

"A jetty?"

"Yes. A jetty." He stumbled slightly over the word. His English was almost perfect, but he still had a problem with *j*'s. "There was a rowboat tied up to it.

"I used to go there a lot," he continued. "Specially in the spring, because it was windy then and warmer under the trees. I went after dark because I didn't want to be seen. There was a sign on the fence, you see. It was not permitted to be there."

He broke off and glanced quickly at Procter, not quite sure, evidently, that this would be approved.

"Go on." Procter grinned. "What happened?"

Telling it now, almost three months later, the boy found it still vivid in his mind. A clear night, he remembered, with a three-quarter moon and almost no wind. Not quite freezing, but near enough to give him a miserable six hours. In spite of the poncho and two sweaters, he had slept little, shivering through long intervals of wakefulness, watching interminably for the dawn.

It had happened shortly after midnight, in one of the periods of half sleep when the impressions of his senses—the wind stirring among the branches, the splash of a wave on the shoreline—had merged into the setting of a dream. Something—something quite clearly not part of the dream—had startled him awake . . . Footsteps coming toward him through the undergrowth. The beam of a flashlight cutting through the darkness, playing erratically on the branches overhead.

His instinct, in the moment before his thoughts achieved coherence, had been to run. Trespassers would be prosecuted, the sign on the fence had told him, and though not entirely sure what a trespasser was, he had no doubt the words referred to him. But he hesitated just long enough to find the sense to resist the impulse. They couldn't have spotted him from the house, he realized. Probably it was only one of the occupants, unable to sleep, taking a stroll in the moonlight. So he'd stayed put, flattened into the undergrowth like a small animal, while the flashlight searched the bushes and the footsteps drew closer, crunching through the carpet of dead twigs and pine needles, till it took all his will not to break from his covert and hurl himself blindly into the sheltering darkness. But then, just as it seemed he *must* run, the sound had receded, passing by several yards to the right and heading off in the direction of the point.

A man—a glimpse of the silhouette confirmed the suggestion of the footsteps—and not strolling at all but moving briskly, with an air of purpose. At the time, however, he had been too relieved to wonder what purpose it might be that would drag someone out to the point at that hour of the night. What concerned him much more was when, and by what route, the man would return.

He had waited half an hour, maybe longer, ears straining for any sound of the return, but there were only night noises—birdcalls, the unexplained crack of a dead branch, a continuous rustle of small creatures hunting in the undergrowth. Then, from out in the Bay, so faint at first he was not sure it was real, swelling and dying away but each time closer and closer, the pulsing growl of a marine diesel.

Someone out fishing. He'd made no connection at first between the boat and the man who'd gone out to the point. But the boat had approached steadily, the engine noise suddenly louder as it was trapped by the walls of the inlet, changing abruptly to a softer throb when the helmsman cut the throttle. Then, above the sound of the idling motor, the footsteps again.

The man was moving more slowly this time, closer to the shoreline, letting his flashlight wander along the margin. And with him, keeping pace, a sleek black shadow edging in toward the jetty, was the sloop.

"A thirty-footer," the boy said. "Tall mast. Beautiful lines. An ocean racer. Just like the *Excalibur.*"

"*Like?*" Procter grunted. "There must be a dozen like her in this part of the Bay alone. How do you know it was her?"

"Let me finish first. Then, if there are questions, you can ask."

"Go ahead." Procter grinned. "It's your story. Tell it your own way."

About fifty yards from the jetty the sloop had cut her engine and dropped anchor. The man with the flashlight had rowed out and gone aboard. He'd stayed only a few minutes. Afterward the boat had departed, guided out to the point by the man with the flashlight.

"What else?" Procter was gowing impatient with the accumulation of detail. "How does all this tie in with Seligman?"

"Why in the dark?" The boy ignored the question. He was determined, Procter saw, to build his case like an attorney, brick upon brick and each in its proper place. "If you want to visit someone, you do it in the day, not at night when you can't see where you're going. Unless you don't want anyone to know."

"I see *that*. But what I don't see is how you bring it back to Seligman. So you see a sloop like his in slightly suspicious circumstances. But only once, and it might not even have been his. That's not exactly proof."

"Not only once." The boy shook his head. "Four times . . . Four times when I was watching. And each time the same thing. The man goes out with the flashlight, the sloop comes, he goes on board for a little, and the sloop leaves."

"You kept going back!" Procter sounded incredulous. "Did you ever think what might have happened if they'd found you? If they *were* smuggling, I doubt they'd have wanted a witness."

"I thought of it." The boy nodded. "But I was interested, you see. I wanted to find out more. And in the dark, among the trees, how was he going to catch me? No way, I think."

"Maybe not." Procter shrugged. "So you did find out more, I take it?"

"The last time, the sloop was late. The man stayed on the point, waiting, for maybe three hours. When the sloop came finally it was beginning to get light, so I saw her clearly that time. It was the *Excalibur*—I could read the letters on the stern. *Excalibur—Annapolis*. And when the man came back I could see he was carrying something. A packet." He made a frame with his hands to indicate the dimensions. "Like a big envelope . . . about so."

"And so you figured they were smuggling something?"

"Dope." The boy nodded. "What else is small enough to fit in a packet that size?"

Procter had several suggestions, but he didn't make them. They were speculation, anyway, and no better than the boy's. And the main point was incontestable: Seligman had been involved in something—something very weird.

"Did you ever tell anyone about this?"

"Why should I?" The boy shrugged. "If they were smugglers, it was their business, I think."

"Maybe . . ." Procter sounded doubtful. "But when the sloop ran aground at Rodo, the police took a statement from you, didn't they? Why didn't you mention it to them?"

"Police." The word was loaded with contempt. "They never asked. I was a kid to them. Just another little wetback. All they asked was if I took something from the boat."

"Brady asked that? I'm surprised. He struck me as pretty decent."

"Not Brady. The other one. The one with the big belly and the voice like a woman."

"He insulted you, so you told him nothing?"

"I told him what he asked." The boy was defensive. "Why tell him anything else?"

Procter thought for a moment. The case was closed, of course. And the cops would probably not welcome the prospect of having to reopen it. But did that make any difference to his obligation? No, he decided. He now knew something—for he had no doubt whatever that the boy was telling the truth—and it might have some bearing on Seligman's death. He must tell the police about it. What they did afterward was their business.

"This man," he asked, "the one in the rowboat—would you recognize him if you saw him again?"

"I don't know." The boy considered. "I saw him only once in the daylight and quite a long way away. Maybe. Why?"

"Because I think we have to tell the police."

"No." The boy's face set. *"Guardia Civil . . ."* He muttered something under his breath in Spanish. The words were unclear but their meaning unmistakable. "I don't talk to those people."

"Did you know Seligman?" Procter knew better than to tackle Latin obstinacy head-on.

"A little. I did things for him sometimes at the Wharf . . . A nice guy, I think."

"A nice guy is now dead." Procter kept his voice expressionless. "Shot in the head, weighted down with diving belts, and dumped in the Bay. Maybe he did it to himself, of course. But then again . . ." He paused. "Maybe not."

The boy digested this in silence. Then he got up and walked to the water's edge, collecting a handful of pebbles on the way. He began to hurl them, viciously, one after another, into the water, punctuating the action with mutters in which the words *"Guardia"* and *"ladrones"* were clearly audible. He had an imaginary target, Procter understood, and there were no prizes for guessing who it was.

"OK." The boy hurled the last pebble and turned back to Procter. "But not the fat one, you understand. Only Brady."

CHAPTER 14

I

The invitation was for 7:00 P.M., so Sullivan arrived at eight. His purpose was not to be fashionably late—he had no idea how late that was, anyway—he simply wanted the protection of a crowd. By eight the party would be in full swing, and no one would notice if he left almost immediately, as he was planning to do if the gathering turned out to be a waste of his time.

He suspected it would. Parties to which the host's social secretary invited you by telephone at the last minute usually did. He would have refused the invitation out of hand had the secretary not followed it with what she portentously described as a "personal message from the senator." The senator hoped Mr. Sullivan would be able to accept, she said, because there would be someone at the party he was anxious for him to meet. Sullivan did not know Senator Izakson socially, had wondered why anyone might imagine that the senator's anxieties would interest him until it struck him that Izakson chaired the Senate Select Committee on Intelligence. He'd inferred, therefore, that the invitation must somehow be connected with the Seligman inquiry, and not, as he'd first suspected, with getting him to contribute to the senator's campaign fund. What was *not* clear was why the promised meeting could not have been arranged in some less roundabout way. But that question could best be resolved by going to the party.

His arrival, however, did not immediately resolve it. The social secretary, who met him at the entrance to the senator's Neo-Gothic schloss in Chevy Chase, murmured something about how pleased

the senator would be that Mr. Sullivan had been able to make it
after all—the "after all" implying that he was perhaps a little more
than fashionably late—and whisked him off to meet her master.
The senator, a tall, angular man with ash-gray hair, a Florida suntan, and watery blue eyes whose stare was so unblinking that
Sullivan couldn't decide whether it was hypnotic or merely vacant,
received him with vague cordiality. His manner suggested he had
no idea who Sullivan was but was pleased to see him anyway. Then,
abandoning Sullivan to the secretary, he turned back to his en-
tourage and resumed, at the exact place he'd broken off half a
minute earlier, his monologue on the leadership vacuum in the Republican party.

"Why don't we get you a drink and introduce you to some of
these nice people?" The secretary, evidently anxious to get back
to her post, frog-marched him to the nearest waiter.

"Didn't you mention there was someone the senator wanted me
to meet?" Sullivan was not reluctant to be ditched—she reminded
him of a dental receptionist—but first he wanted to clear up the
mystery of the invitation.

"Yes." Her smile became a shade distracted as her eyes wandered over the throng. "I can't seem to spot him at the moment.
He's here somewhere. No doubt you'll bump into him shortly."

With that, she thrust a drink into his hand and steered him
toward the nearest group.

"Now here are some people I *know* you'll want to meet . . ."

There were three in the group: a middle-aged woman of strik-
ing, if rather predatory, good looks, who repeated his name carefully after the introduction as if determined to remember it; a
journalist; and a British diplomat, who shook hands, nodded, and
smiled with lazy affability, but remained silent.

"We were speaking of the presidential nominations." The
woman wasted no time on ordinary small talk. "Such a pity the
senator won't run, don't you think?"

"Senator Izakson?" He smiled innocently. The leadership
vacuum seemed to be the theme of this party. "It is indeed, particularly for us Democrats."

"Don't tell me you're one of *those*." This in accents of pure
horror. "And here I was thinking you looked so nice and intelligent."

They went on in this vein for a while. After a few minutes the journalist wandered off, and presently the woman was detached by someone who had someone who was simply dying to meet her. This left Sullivan in desultory conversation with the diplomat. For lack of any more promising topic, Sullivan mentioned that he was a criminal lawyer. The diplomat commented that he'd once contemplated the law but it was too much like work. Then the diplomat told Sullivan of a technique for avoiding tiresome acquaintances at cocktail parties. The trick was to carry two drinks at all times, he said. Then if you met someone you didn't want to talk to, you explained you couldn't stop because you were fetching a drink for someone else. The technique offered the added advantage of allowing you to drink twice as much, he said, but it was difficult to manage if you smoked.

He then noticed his own drink was getting low and sauntered off to get a refill.

To make his isolation less conspicuous, Sullivan retreated to a corner. From the fringes the party reminded him of a straggling galaxy made up of planetary systems in which a major luminary was orbited by a host of lesser lights. In the middle, Senator Izakson, the great sun himself, cast beams impartially on all the satellites. The conversation was an uproar in which anything over two feet was shouting distance, but isolated snatches nevertheless would occasionally, by some trick of the acoustics, filter over to Sullivan's corner.

". . . Say what you like about that nasty little business, I still think Dick was one of the great Presidents . . ."

". . . You mean there are people who actually *read* the *National Enquirer*? . . ."

". . . My dear, he was like a rabbit. Lolloped in, turned me on my back, did the foul deed, and lolloped out. When I asked him later to what I owed the honor, he said it was halftime. Don't talk to *me* about Monday-night football! . . ."

Hell, Sullivan thought, trapped in Gomorrah. He couldn't leave while the social secretary stood guard at the door, and he was still curious about the meeting he'd been promised, but drinking alone depressed him, and none of the conversations offered much inducement to join in.

It was then, to his great surprise and relief, he caught sight of Gael Forrester. She was on the far side of the room, talking to a young man whose sleek looks and air of self-importance proclaimed him an aide to one of the political dignitaries. Her expression as she listened to him was quizzical: half amused, half tolerant, the look of a well-mannered atheist at a revival meeting. She had put her hair up and was wearing a linen shirtwaist dress, belted, whose crisp simplicity made her look fresh and elegant. To Sullivan, at that moment, she was extraordinarily attractive.

He stared at her, willing her to glance in his direction, but she didn't. He began to edge his way through the crowd.

"You're Sullivan, aren't you?" The murmur from behind checked him in mid-stride.

"Yes, I am." He turned to face the speaker.

"Izakson said you'd be here." The voice was flat, with a faint echo of the Midwest. "If you can spare a minute, I'd like a word with you . . . privately."

Damn, Sullivan thought, it was the man he'd come to meet. But why the hell did he have to surface at this particular moment?

"Privately?" He stared pointedly at the revelers around them. "Here?"

"Izakson's study. It's off the front hallway. The passage on the left, first door on the right."

"Fine." Sullivan started to turn away. The man's tone was a little peremptory for his taste. "In five or ten minutes. There's someone I want to say hello to first."

"OK." The man nodded. "It's better we go separately, anyway. Five minutes, then."

Gael spotted Sullivan when he was halfway across the room. Her first feeling was relief—the smug self-absorption of her present companion was beginning to grate on her—but mixed in with the relief was a good deal of pleasure. She liked Sullivan, liked his big-man's gentleness, felt a wave of something close to affection now as she watched his burly figure picking its way through the crowd with the forbearing patience of a wolfhound among a kennel of pups; but beyond that she found him formidable, and therefore exciting. It was not for his intelligence and honesty, though she respected those, nor yet for his physical presence, but because underneath the soft voice and the courtesy she could discern a core of granite. He would do what he set out to do, would Mr. Sullivan; it would take a Sherman tank to stop him; and it was this quality, rather than looks or even brains, that for her defined a man.

"Morgan." It was the first time she had used his Christian name, and she did it a little self-consciously. "What are *you* doing here?"

"I slipped the bouncer a twenty." He grinned. "And he looked the other way. But what about you? I shouldn't have thought it was exactly your scene either."

"Oh." She shrugged. "The senator and my father are sort of cousins. He invites me from time to time, and once in a while I accept . . . This is Dick Talbot." She indicated her companion. "Dick, Morgan Sullivan."

The two men shook hands, covering their wary inspection of each other with perfunctory smiles.

"Morgan is a lawyer," she explained to Talbot. "And Dick"— she turned to Sullivan, smiling, he thought, a little wickedly— "does something important for the senator."

An awkward pause followed the introductions. Gael broke it by turning to Talbot.

"Would you be very kind and get me a drink? I've been chewing on ice for the last ten minutes. The waiters seem to have decided to boycott this side of the room."

He smiled a little ruefully and trotted off. Gael turned back to Sullivan.

"What *are* you doing here?"

"Here?" He waved airily at the assembly in general. "Or here?" Pointing at the spot where they stood.

"Both." After twenty minutes of solid politics, she welcomed the prospect of a little light flirtation.

"Well, as to the larger question, it's still something of a mystery. But the other is easy. There are three answers. I came over first"— he paused—"because you are the only person I know here."

"*Not* very flattering."

"I can do better," he offered. "Shall I?"

"Yes." She smiled. "I think you'd better."

"I came over to dispute the Republican party's monopoly on youth and beauty."

"That *is* better." She inclined her head graciously. "What else?"

"I came over . . ." He hesitated, dropping his bantering manner. ". . . to ask you if you'd like to have dinner with me."

"Tonight?"

"Yes." He was suddenly awkward. "But you must have other plans. Perhaps another time. Perhaps—"

"I don't have other plans." She cut him off. "And I'd very much like to have dinner with you."

"Good." He was easy again. "But there's someone I have to talk to first. Can you give me fifteen minutes?"

It appeared she could, though the prospect of listening to Mr. Talbot for that much longer, she gave Sullivan to understand, was not appealing. Then Talbot returned with her drink, and Sullivan, feeling guilty but for the first time good about the evening, left to keep his appointment.

Izakson's study was a tall, cavernous room furnished like the library of a small private club: leather couch and armchairs, low table covered with newspapers and magazines, heavy velvet curtains, and shelves lined with the sort of books nobody ever reads. The curtains were drawn; the only light came from a single table lamp beside one of the armchairs, in which sat the man Sullivan had come to meet. He was holding a glass of the senator's bourbon and reading the *Wall Street Journal*.

When Sullivan entered he looked up, folded the paper carefully, and laid it aside.

"Drinks are over there." He pointed to a cabinet on Sullivan's right, but otherwise made no move to greet him. "If you like bourbon, it's in the square decanter . . . Kentucky. Twenty-five years old. A cut above the stuff they're serving outside."

"Who are you?" Sullivan ignored the invitation. "What's this all about?"

"My name's Stonemason." The man produced a wallet from his inside pocket and flipped it open for Sullivan's inspection. "I'm with the Defense Intelligence Agency."

Sullivan barely glanced at the ID. Instead, he studied its owner. Stonemason was heavily built, on the tall side of medium height, with short-cropped hair and features that were regular and definite but aesthetically neutral, neither pleasant nor the reverse. He had the kind of eyes, dark brown and set close together, that took everything in but let little out. It was difficult to guess his age; his face had probably looked much the same at twenty as it did now. It would continue to look that way, Sullivan guessed, well into late middle age, completely unmarked by years or emotion, until one day, quite suddenly, senility would lay hold on it and crumple it, like an empty paper bag. The clothes, too, were neutral—bureaucrat's gray suit, white button-down shirt, unenterprising tie. Only the shoes looked out of place: black and heavy, shaped like flat-bottomed barges, they were the kind worn by house detectives or waiters, people whose work involves a lot of walking.

But Stonemason clearly was no foot soldier. For one thing, he spoke like a man accustomed to giving orders. Besides that, there was his casual requisitioning of the senator's study and best bourbon, the habitual omission of the respectful "Senator" when he mentioned Izakson's name. Whatever he did at the DIA, Stonemason evidently cut a lot of ice with the senator.

Seeing the lack of interest in his ID, Stonemason put it away.

"These things can be faked, of course," he murmured. "But I imagine Izakson's credit will cover me. If not, I can give you a number to call."

"I'll take the number," Sullivan said flatly.

"That makes sense." Stonemason didn't appear put out. He took out a notebook, tore off a page, and scribbled the number on it.

He handed the page to Sullivan. "When you call, use a pay phone. Don't call from the Agency or use your home phone. Your home phone is bugged."

Sullivan stared at him, longer this time.

"Bugged?" he asked coldly, anger beginning to rise in him. "And just how the hell would you happen to know?"

"How do you think?" If Stonemason was intimidated by the stare or the tone of voice, he didn't show it. "We found it when we tried to install one of our own."

It was the matter-of-fact tone, the complete lack of embarrassment, that most infuriated Sullivan. Suddenly he was sick to death of these agencies, these colorless, buttoned-down organization men with their placid assumption that the law was just a fiction, dispensable whenever it suited their dubious purposes. He'd had it with all of them, and particularly with this cardboard creep.

"You bastards never learn, do you." He stood up, buttoning his jacket, his voice smoking like dry ice. "Well, it's time you did. You'll be getting a call from Justice in the morning, so in the meantime get yourself a good lawyer. Your buddy Izakson won't help much with this. In fact, from now on I doubt that he'll touch you with a pole."

"Shit." Stonemason didn't raise his voice; he just sounded weary. "Let's dispense with the histrionics, shall we? You have no proof beyond my admission, and that can easily be retracted. Why don't you sit down and listen?"

Sullivan hesitated, his anger cooling. The man was right, of course. He could call Justice and scream invasion of privacy, but where would that get him? Justice would tut-tut sympathetically, bemoan the lack of hard evidence, and sit firmly on its hands. Anger was useless against realpolitik.

He sat down.

"Well, at least have the courtesy to explain why you found it necessary to tap my phone."

"What would be the point?" Stonemason shrugged. "We were interested in your investigation, obviously. But I doubt that you'd find our reasons compelling. That's history, anyway. The main thing is"—he leaned forward—"someone besides us is interested. It could be the Agency, trying to keep tabs on you, or it could be someone on the outside. Either way, it should tell you something. You're making someone uneasy, obviously. And why would anyone be uneasy—unless he has something to hide?"

"You don't know who it is?"

Stonemason shook his head. "They used microtransmitters. No wires, no listening posts—no way of tracing. We might, however, be able to figure it out." He added carefully, "If we pooled our information, that is."

So that was it. Stonemason had volunteered information about the bug in the hope of learning something in exchange.

"No," Sullivan said flatly. "To start with, I don't know who you are or what your interest is. All I know is what you've told me, and I can't pretend to be very reassured by that. I'd have to check your credentials and satisfy myself on your need to know. Then, maybe, we could talk."

"Very proper." Stonemason gave a faint smile. "Well, I can't argue the point, so I won't try. All I can do is make a suggestion. . . if you're willing to listen, that is."

"I'll listen. I won't promise to take it."

"Leave the bug in place. Remember it's there and guard against saying anything you wouldn't want overheard, but don't touch it. Sooner or later someone—the guy who put it there—may let slip something he shouldn't have known about. And that may tell us a lot."

"Us?" Sullivan queried. "I don't see that you have any standing in this thing."

"Suit yourself." Stonemason took this, like everything else, calmly. "You may change your mind later on. If you do, or if at some point you decide you need help, you have my number. Any time of the day or night, it'll always reach me."

He stood up.

"It's time we rejoined the in-group. Not that they'll have noticed our absence . . . I'll go first, if I may. Give me a couple of minutes before you follow."

When he reached the door he stopped and turned.

"In the meantime," he said with a smile that was almost engaging, "you really should try some of Izakson's whiskey. It's amazingly good."

II

Gael leaned back and sipped at her wine. The waiter had cleared their table, leaving only the wineglasses, and was now bustling about straightening chairs and rattling silver: conspicuous, unproductive busyness whose real purpose was to tell them to go home. Yet in spite of this, and though Sullivan had paid the bill fifteen minutes earlier, she was disinclined to move. She rolled the wine around on her tongue, savoring it slowly because she knew it was the last, comfortable with the silence they had fallen into because it was not just emptiness but the companionable quiet of people who have talked to each other and therefore have something to digest.

It was her first real date since Paul had died. She'd approached it with misgivings, pleased that Sullivan had asked her, but disturbed too because some part of her felt guilty about wanting to accept. Sullivan attracted her—that was the truth behind the rationalizations she'd invented for herself—and she knew she attracted him also. But it was too soon; Paul was too strong a memory; she should not foster something she wouldn't be able to go through with. Yet she'd accepted anyway, had enjoyed the evening, and was reluctant to bring it to an end.

For this, she recognized, Sullivan's tact was largely responsible. As if he'd sensed her unease, he'd steered the conversation into impersonal subjects—music, their dislike of Republican politics, shared enthusiasms for P. G. Wodehouse and the Civil War—that enabled them to explore each other without ever coming too close to the boundaries of self. She was grateful for that; grateful, too— though it let light through her rationalizations—that they had not spoken of Paul. She missed Paul, missed him terribly, but since Sullivan had relieved her doubts about him, the quality of her feeling had changed. The urgency had lessened; the raw pain had diminished to an ache; she was almost ready to start letting him go, to receive now, like sleep, the forgetfulness with which the living accommodate the dead. Wounds, she was beginning to find, heal better when not constantly reopened.

She glanced across at Sullivan. He was gazing absently at some spot over her shoulder, as if he'd abandoned her for the moment and retreated to some private region of his thoughts. What he found there seemed to bother him, for his frown was too deep to be produced by concentration. Once or twice, in the short pauses that broke up their conversation, she'd been troubled by that frown and wondered about its cause. At first she'd mistaken it for boredom, but his obvious delight in her company had dispelled that fear. Now she saw it as something deeper, a continuation of the abiding worry she'd sensed in him when she'd visited his house.

"A penny for them."

It was a measure of how quickly their friendship had developed that her curiosity struck neither of them as intrusive.

"A bad bargain." He smiled. "They're not nearly worth it."

"Business?" she queried. "Back in the grim corridors of the CIA?"

"Close," he conceded. "But let's not spoil a pleasant evening . . . Speaking of which"—he jerked his head in the direction of the waiter—"our friend seems ready for us to leave."

" 'Our revels now are ended.' " She felt a stab of disappointment. "He's pocketed the tip and now he wants to go home and put his feet up. You can't blame him, of course. But all that banging around does nothing for the atmosphere."

"Shall we then . . . ?"

She pushed back her chair.

"Thank you for dinner, Morgan." She felt formal with him again for the first time in hours. "I enjoyed it a lot. In fact, it was just what I needed."

He drove her home in silence. The intimacy they'd established did not survive their departure from the restaurant, and they were left feeling slightly awkward, as though they had advanced too quickly toward each other and needed to retreat a little and take time to consider. When they reached the house, Sullivan got out and opened the car door for her, but hesitated perceptibly before he walked her to the gate. There he turned and held out his hand.

"Good night." He was evidently anxious not to give the impression of wanting to hang around. "I'm glad we met up at the party. I hope we can do this again sometime."

She didn't want to leave things like that. His words sounded flat, unexpectedly distant. The evening had promised more, she felt; it had seemed like the prelude to something—she didn't know what and wasn't prepared yet to be specific—but something, at any rate, more definite than that vague "sometime." And whereas before, in the car, she had worried a little about whether she should invite him in for a drink—how he would take it if she did; how he would take it if she didn't—now, when he'd made it clear he didn't expect her to, she felt, perversely, deserted.

"A nightcap?" The offer came out sounding to her ears more like a plea.

Again he hesitated.

"It's late," he hedged. "You must be tired."

"It's not that late." She shook her head, slightly impatient. There was such a thing, surely, as too much tact. "And I'm not at all tired. Come in if you want. I'm not just being polite."

He studied her for a moment, then nodded.

"In that case, yes. I would like to."

With a last flicker, diminuendo, up the keyboard, Scarbo vanished . . . Silence . . . The stylus rumbled back and forth along the final grooves. Gael got up and replaced the record in its cover.

Her attempt to recapture the mood of the restaurant had failed. His preoccupation with whatever was worrying him had resisted her efforts to banish it, and the conversation had languished. The silences had become longer and more frequent, had seemed taut, finally, with their uncomfortable awareness of the hour and circumstances. To cover the unease, she had suggested music. That had given them, at least, an excuse for not talking.

But with Scarbo's departure they were alone again, and Gael was left fishing around for something to say.

"Very spooky." Her opening effort struck her as lame, but she could think of nothing better. "Who was Scarbo, exactly? I've often wondered."

"A goblin." Sullivan sniffed his cognac. "To amuse himself, he would appear by your bedside at midnight and play terrifying tricks on you. Ravel found him in a poem and turned him into music."

"A poem?"

She hardly thought about what she was saying. Her mind seemed split into compartments: one wished he would go home and put an end to this awkwardness; another was afraid he would go and looked desperately for ways of bringing the conversation back to life; a third, aloof from the other two and flatly resisting her efforts to censor it, studied the hand in which he cradled the brandy glass, guessed at the strength in the broad fingers and, recalling their deftness of touch at the piano, wondered how they would feel on her skin.

"A prose poem. 'How often have I heard the scratch of his claw against the silk curtain around my bed.' " As he quoted, his voice became a cold, dry rustle.

"Sinister." She affected a shudder. "I imagine him sea-green and scaly, with red eyes and a laugh like the rattle of earth on a coffin. I'll probably lie awake all night listening for him."

"Don't worry. He doesn't get out much nowadays." Sullivan smiled. "He went into retirement at the end of last century. We've invented other horrors. Well . . ." He drained his glass and stood up. "I guess it's time I was going."

She said nothing. The loneliness she'd been fending off for the last hour took hold of her. Goddammit, she thought, what had made them this way? It was ridiculous. They'd been so comfortable with each other before; now they were like adolescents on a first date, wondering if they dared touch and who would make the first move.

"Yes," she said at last, wearily. "I suppose it is."

He followed her out into the hall and up the short passageway that led to the front door. She opened the door for him and stood aside to let him pass.

He stopped and turned toward her. They were barely a foot apart, and the space between was alive with tension. Standing there in the half light cast by the streetlights, he seemed, for the moment, unable to speak or move, as if caught between two perfectly balanced forces and waiting for one of them to exert the stronger pull.

"What is it?" she asked.

He said nothing.

"Then what are you waiting for?" The words came out unbidden, in a sudden rush of anger directed partly at him, for his apparent determination to leave all the decisions to her, and partly at the circumstances, the situation they'd backed into, where the choices were forced upon them before they were ready to choose.

"Go . . . or whatever. Do *something*. Don't wait for me to make up your mind."

His head went back as if she'd struck him across the face. Instinctively, as though she really had hit him, she reached out and touched his cheek.

"I'm sorry, Morgan," she whispered. "I'm so sorry . . . I can't think what possessed me to say that."

She had said it, however, and as the implications hit her, she was appalled. But before her embarrassment could take hold, he took her hand and brushed it against the corner of his mouth.

"Whatever?" he murmured. "That would be *my* choice."

III

"I'm sorry, Morgan," Gael said.

Sullivan said nothing. Love—according to a best-seller he'd once picked up and put down almost immediately—meant never having to say you were sorry. Their relationship, evidently, was different; that, he was beginning to think, consisted of nothing else.

"It's my fault," she said. "I know that. I thought I knew what I wanted, but apparently I don't. He's not dead for me yet, it seems, and so—afterwards—I felt I'd betrayed him. And what makes it worse . . ." She hesitated. "What makes it worse is that it was so good.

"It was good," she insisted. "That's why I feel so . . . uncomfortable. Can you understand that?"

Good? Technically, perhaps. Successful at the level of physical release. But just bodies, he thought; just bodies coupling, attempting to fuse in the moment of combustion, but falling back afterward empty and separate, more separate than ever for having made the attempt . . . She had turned away, lain silent beside him in the darkness. He had touched her shoulder and felt it shaking. And when he'd turned her toward him he'd found that she was crying.

"Can you understand?"

Sure, he thought. The consolation prize: "I feel guilty because it was so good. But it *was* good, Morgan, so you can leave now with your masculine pride intact." Bullshit, he thought. If it was so good, then why are you crying? And if you feel guilty, why did you do it? Guilt, he thought: the worthless currency in which the emotionally spendthrift pay their debts.

"I need time," she went on. "I need to let this sink in. To sort out how I feel. I'll call in a few days, maybe . . . Can you give me that much, Morgan? Can you? . . . Please?"

Wheedling, he thought. Using his name like a caress to comfort him. It made him angry. The whole thing made him angry. He had not pushed it, or even sought it; she had. And now she was backing away, leaving him naked and wounded, excusing herself with phrases you could hear any afternoon on the soap operas, from one to four: "I need time" . . . "I'll call you in a few days, maybe" . . . Christ, he thought savagely, at least write your own lines!

"No big deal." His voice sounded strange to him, flat, as if someone else were speaking. "We had dinner is all. And afterwards we went to bed. Maybe that was a mistake. But it's no great tragedy. No bones were broken . . . So, sure. Call if you like. I'll probably be around."

He didn't look at her. He didn't want her to see the hurt and sense the dishonesty, didn't want her to feel the ugliness gathering inside him. "We fucked is all" was what he felt like saying, "and a fuck is a fuck is a fuck." An untruth to repay an untruth. A hurt for a hurt. As if that would make him feel better.

She wouldn't call, that was obvious—it would be too uncomfortable. Much easier to let things lie. And he wouldn't call her, either; he was too vulnerable already. So they would let inertia— or cowardice—make the decision. Only they wouldn't call it that; they would call it pride.

Waste. That was what it really was. Just senseless waste. Something lost because they were too timid to reach in through the nettles to grasp it. He wanted to shout it at her, to take her by the shoulders and shake that truth into her. But it was his cowardice too, and instead he just stood there.

"I'll be going now," he said.

"Yes." She nodded, turning away so he wouldn't see the tears that were gathering again in her eyes. "I suppose that would be best."

CHAPTER 15

I

There were moments, Sullivan thought, when life was stretched so thin you could see right through it. It was like the negative of a photograph: no depth to it, no substance, nothing between you and the emptiness of heaven but a strip of celluloid, faintly marked with shadows.

On leaving Gael he had gone home, showered, shaved, fed Cooper, made coffee and drunk it, but all with a curious lack of conviction, as though habit, not choice, were controlling his actions. They were preparations, he thought, but for what? For time to be spent simply marking its own passage? For a day leading to nothing but another day like it?

He turned to his mail. The D.C. Bar Association, announcing its annual dinner, urged him to send thirty-five dollars (check or money order—no cash please) to secure his reservation. A certain P. J. Albright, from Arizona, was willing to sell him (minimal down payment, generous financing) ten acres of desert almost adjacent to Phoenix and likely to be zoned Commercial in the next convulsion of the city's growth. His brokerage house reported that the value of his portfolio had declined during the month. The market was acting uncertainly, the letter informed him, and the house recommended to its clients a defensive strategy aimed at preventing further erosion of assets.

Erosion. Was that what he had to look forward to? Was the future itself just another wasting asset, his stock declining daily and the utility of what was left diminishing as his capacity to enjoy it faltered? Bullshit. He was the same as he had been yesterday. A prospect had opened in the course of his evening with Gael and then closed—that was all. Nothing else had changed. There was no call for this adolescent self-pity . . . And yet, he thought, while that was mostly true, something *had* changed. Today was unlike yesterday in that it had brought a slight but perceptible sense of loss. In a way it was like turning forty: outwardly his circumstances were no different, but the event had altered his perceptions, reducing his sense of what was left. Time and loss, he thought, feeling old; there were days when time and loss seemed identical.

Mid-life anxiety. He despised it. He was just overreacting to a minor disappointment. And even if the disappointment was really more than minor, he was not helping it any with these maudlin ruminations. The thing to do was get busy, to go on doing what had to be done, and rely on activity to supply its own momentum. Stonemason's tale should be checked, the dead burglars should be pondered, the revised version of Theta should be put under the microscope. Go to the office, he told himself: get on with the job, and leave the future to erode by itself.

Stonemason was real, of course. Sullivan had known he would be. He'd checked only to satisfy his sense of thoroughness and from a lingering resentment at the man's self-assurance. The number, in any case, turned out to be a genuine DIA listing—a friend in the Defense Department had helped him verify that—and the DIA, when consulted, had confirmed that S 135 257 was currently active. And if Stonemason was real, so, presumably, was the bug. Sullivan had toyed with the notion of examining his phone but decided against it. Stonemason would hardly have gone to such great lengths simply to tell him a fragile and pointless lie. The bug was real enough. But what did it prove?

Beyond the obvious fact that someone was interested in his telephone conversations, it proved very little. In that respect, he thought gloomily, it was typical of the inquiry as a whole, which seemed to have turned into a particularly frustrating example of the paradox of knowledge—the more he learned, the less he understood. Each time he felt able to sort the known facts into some kind of coherent pattern, something new popped up and turned his carefully arranged sense into gibberish.

Theta was a case in point. Tyrell's revised version might very well be true. It was coherent, for one thing, and if unpleasantness was any indication of truth, it was fully nasty enough. The trouble was it seemed surrounded by inconsistencies. Somebody had killed those two burglars, for instance, and though it was possible they were not the ones who'd raided Gael's apartment, it was his gut feeling—and Brady's—that they were. But if the raid (further assumption) had been connected with Seligman's list, and if the burglars (reasonable hypothesis) had been killed to prevent him from establishing that connection, what did that tell him about the revised version of Theta? It might tell him simply that the revised version was untrue. And the bug, assuming it had been planted by the Agency, could be taken to imply the same thing. But there was another explanation, unfortunately just as plausible, that suggested rather the opposite. Perhaps the burglars had been murdered, and the bug planted, by someone at pains to throw suspicion on Roy. Perhaps someone wanted him to *think* the revised version was untrue.

That, really, was the choice. It boiled down to a question of whom he believed—Tyrell or Spearman. Either Theta was, from first to last, a misinformation exercise, or it had been twisted into something more sinister. In the first alternative the movement offstage—the raid, the murders, and the phone tap—was unconnected with Theta but designed to befog the inquiry and revive the suspicions that for so long had demoralized the Agency. Here the obvious villain was Spearman—a mole until his dismissal and now a puppet master working the strings from outside. But Spearman's suggestion also made sense. Perhaps Theta was simply a cover for an operation designed to destroy the Agency's assets and subvert it from within. If so, the movement offstage was the scuffle of the mole's assistants hurrying to obscure his tracks, and the mole was one of the principals in Theta: Brayer, Patterson, or Tyrell. And since it was his operation, the favorite was undoubtedly Tyrell.

Only when he took a sheet of paper and wrote out the alternatives, an exercise chiefly in testing the theories for coherence and making sure he hadn't left anything out, did Sullivan realize that he had, after all, made some progress. Both theories, and indeed *any* explanation that took account of all the facts, led him inexorably to the same conclusion: there *was* a mole, and whether inside the Agency or without, he was still around, still tunneling and undermining.

There remained the problem, of course, of deciding who he was.

II

"Mole rumors?" Patterson sounded puzzled. "In 1977?"

"Yes." Sullivan nodded. "Were there any?"

"There always are," Patterson said. "There have been as long as I've worked here. But I don't remember 1977 as being particularly a vintage year."

Here we go again, Sullivan thought. The usual routine—the puzzlement, the evasive generalization, the fuzzy memory, the half-truth. And the worst of it was it didn't necessarily mean anything. Evasiveness was habit with these people, a kind of *omerta* applied reflexively to all outsiders whether there was any point to it or not. In a way, he thought, you could hardly blame them: they were programmed for secrecy from the moment they entered the Agency, brainwashed into believing that indiscretion was the unforgivable sin, and overwhelmed thereafter by an avalanche of classified trivia to the point where probably they could no longer distinguish what they had learned from the files from what they had read in the newspaper. No wonder, then, that they adopted, in self-defense, a policy of undiscriminating silence.

"Eastern Europe." He tried another tack. "Didn't you lose an unusual number of agents there that year?"

"Did we?" Patterson frowned, his eyes focusing on some remote point in inner space. "Yes. Now that you come to mention it, I believe we did. But these things tend to go in cycles. I don't know that I'd attach much significance to that."

"I don't know that I do. I'm not at the stage of attaching significance yet. I'm still gathering and sorting."

"Ah." Patterson smiled. "*That* stage. That stage can go on forever if you're not careful."

Yes, Sullivan thought. And it *will* go on forever, if you guys have your way. "Tell me," he asked, "were any of the 1977 rumors from Eastern European sources?"

"Probably." Patterson shrugged. "It's such a rumor factory, Eastern Europe. And moles are their specialty. It's their way of keeping us off balance. When Spearman was still around, for instance, the merest suggestion was good for months of turmoil."

"But Spearman was gone in 1977."

"True," Patterson conceded. "He was, wasn't he. But anyway, old habits die hard."

Folklore again. The instinctive retreat from the specific into thickets of generality. Pin him down, Sullivan told himself, flush him into the open. Don't let him lose you in there.

"CSX 04," he said. "Any mole reports from there in 1977?"

"CSX . . ." Patterson mused. "Czechoslovakia, isn't it?"

Sullivan nodded.

"It's possible," Patterson agreed. "My memory's not that specific, obviously, but I could check if you like."

"I'd appreciate that." Sullivan's voice was dry. "This morning, preferably."

"Will do." Patterson got up. "I should check with Roy first, though. They're his files, after all."

"If you wish." Sullivan shrugged. "It's really not necessary. My mandate will cover you, if you're worried about protocol. I have the power to subpoena evidence and examine witnesses—under oath, if necessary. You don't really need Roy's permission. But by all means get it, if it will make you more comfortable."

He hoped Patterson's pride would prevent him from going to Roy, for Roy was more than capable of deducing from the continuing interest in the CSX 04 source that his latest account of Theta was not unquestionably accepted. And that would be another nail in the coffin of their friendship. But the friendship was dead anyway, he thought gloomily, so did it really matter? Probably not. But, on the other hand, how much would it help him to know that the CSX 04 source *had* been the author of mole rumors? It would tilt the scales against Roy, of course, but not decisively. For the destruction of that source didn't prove, necessarily, that Roy used Theta to silence threats to his position. It was also possible to argue—and Roy no doubt would, if challenged—that mole rumors from East European sources were no longer taken seriously, and that the source in question was simply one of the "assets" given up to establish Seligman. It would be business as usual, he thought. An embarrassment of suspicion without an iota of proof.

He realized then, with something approaching despair, what a morass he had been sucked into. He *had* to find proof. It was the only way out. He couldn't walk away now and leave the thing unresolved. One way or another the Agency was being destroyed, and while he disliked the institution and detested its methods, he had never questioned the need for its existence. Simple duty, therefore, demanded he finish the job. Beyond that, there was the need to satisfy himself. Unless he did, he would spend the rest of his life racked by conflicting suspicions: that, on the one hand, he had been callously duped and used, and on the other, that he had wronged his friend.

But how would he ever find proof? He could keep probing, he supposed, in the hope that something would give, that someone eventually would panic. But how long would they let him go on doing that? He was drawing on Spearman's sources of credit, and these sources, as Spearman himself had found, were rapidly exhausted. And besides, how likely was it that anyone *would* panic? Roy certainly wouldn't—if he had anything to panic about. Neither Brayer nor Patterson seemed likely to. And as for Spearman, there was no way he could think of at present to put any pressure on him at all.

The more he pondered the problem, the more Sullivan found his thoughts straying wistfully to his abandoned law practice. He longed for a world that made straightforward sense, for the law's great reassuring simplicities: guilt and innocence, fear and greed. Fuck them, he thought, fuck the whole devious, prevaricating crew!

He was to echo this sentiment, even more forcefully, later in the day, when Patterson got back to him. Unfortunately, Patterson said, it was not possible to answer his question. Earlier in the year, it seemed, the files relating to the 1977 mole rumors had been condensed and consolidated. The reports were now summarized in a single file whose sources were described simply as "Various, Eastern Europe; authenticity untested." They might have included the CSX 04 source, but then again they might not. There was no way of knowing, for the original reports had been destroyed.

Who had ordered the consolidation? Here again Patterson, blandly apologetic, couldn't say for certain. The thing had been done apparently to conserve filing space. The suggestion, therefore, had probably originated with Registry. But they were Tyrell's files, he added, so the consolidation had probably been authorized by Tyrell.

CHAPTER 16

I

It was going to rain soon, the boy thought. And not just a drizzle, a downpour. All afternoon, like floating mountains, the big thunderheads had been drifting in, until now the whole sky was heavy with them—a solid, overhanging mass of slate. The heat was oppressive. In the last minutes the wind had died, leaving the air as warm and thick as blood. It was still but not peaceful, trembling sometimes at the mutter of distant thunder, charged, it seemed, with a scarcely suppressed violence.

Not a time to be hitchhiking. And for some reason people weren't stopping this evening, just roaring by in big empty cars, accelerating as they passed, and keeping their eyes on the road. He'd gotten one ride—the short hop out to the turnoff—but since then he'd had to walk.

The storm would drench him, he knew. It would batter its way through the poncho in a matter of seconds. Yet a side of him almost welcomed it. It was one of the hazards, part of the reason hitchhiking was an adventure. He always welcomed adventure, and that was why, though his finances demanded it anyway, he always hitchhiked. It was like putting to sea: you were at the mercy, ultimately, of circumstance, and in that uncertainty there was excitement and a kind of freedom. You simply took to the road and left the rest to chance.

He walked slowly, not because he was tired, but because he had reached the long straightaway beyond the turnoff and it was here, he figured, he was most likely to get a ride. Straight bits gave people time to spot and weigh you up before they made a decision, and if they had that time they were much more likely to stop. He would stop and wait at the end of this stretch, he decided, because the road beyond it was bends for several miles.

He didn't signal every car that passed. Experience had taught him the good prospects, and he seldom bothered with the others. Women driving alone, for instance, almost never stopped; nor did semis. Among the better prospects, he'd learned, cars with one occupant were less likely to stop than those with two; young people stopped more often than old ones; pickups stopped more often than cars. Traveling salesmen, whatever they were driving, stopped most often, but you couldn't identify them at a distance, and in any case, they usually talked too much. His favorite ride was a pickup, because he could ride in the back and forget about making conversation.

Two cars and a truck went by before he reached the end of the straightaway. He flagged the cars, but without much hope. They were big, flashy models, carrying no one but the driver and going, he reckoned, a good bit more than the speed limit. As they drew level with him both drivers accelerated, zooming by as if they hadn't seen him. Why was it, he wondered, that when they didn't stop they accelerated? They felt guilty, perhaps, for not stopping and were therefore anxious to get away as quickly as possible.

He sat down on the grass by the road and waited. The thunder was closer now. A large, cold raindrop splotched onto his wrist, another onto his leg. He got the poncho out of his day pack and put it on. Should he take shelter under the trees, he wondered, or should he stay put? If he stayed he would get soaked, but if he took shelter he gave up his chance for a ride. He stayed put.

While he waited he thought some more about his cousin's wedding, which had dragged him to Baltimore. Weddings puzzled him. Why did the men look so uncomfortable and the women always cry? And had it really been necessary for him to go? He had raised the latter question, tentatively, with his mother beforehand, and the squawks of outrage were still ringing in his ears. It was unthinkable, she'd declared, not only bad manners but a mortal insult; his cousin would be hurt and his uncle deeply offended. And yet, though he'd never seriously contemplated not going, he couldn't help feeling that his absence would scarcely have been noticed. Consuela had been too busy, as usual, being the center of attention, and his uncle, most likely, had been preoccupied with the cost. Far from being deeply offended, he'd probably have been happy to have one less mouth to feed.

In any event, he thought, the whole marriage business was curious. His brothers, for instance, spoke of it as some kind of trap, yet they seemed, on the other hand, to accept without question that they too eventually would stand up at the altar in new dark suits and white shirts, with flowers in their buttonholes and that uncomfortable, self-conscious smirk on their faces. Why would they do it? It couldn't be for sex—not these days, not in this country. But why then? What did marriage offer that a man would give up his freedom for it? He had raised the matter with his parents one night over dinner, but his father had just shrugged and raised his eyes to heaven, while his mother had laughed complacently, called him her little barbarian, and promised him that someday, when he was older, he would understand.

He was so deep in this problem that he nearly missed the green Oldsmobile. In fact, he did miss it. It was almost up to him before he heard it, and fifty yards past by the time he'd jumped up to flag it down. The driver must have spotted *him,* however, because just as he was starting to curse himself for inattention, the brake lights came on and the car skidded to a halt and started to back up toward him.

II

Afterward, looking back on the events of August 12 and 13, Sullivan would see in them a mysterious, almost sinister, sequence of ifs. If the timing had been different, for example: if Stonemason had got to him earlier, if Gael had not been at the senator's party, then Brady's message might never have been left so long on the answering machine and the boy would have been left out of it. And in that case the whole outcome might have been different.

As it was, he got the message at four-thirty. Somehow, probably because the evening with Gael had driven most other things out of his mind, he had forgotten to check the machine before he left for the Agency that morning. He remembered when he returned home, but by that time the message had been on the tape for over eighteen hours. And that, he figured later, was about an hour too long.

He called Brady immediately, of course. But he wasted time by going out to a pay phone. Using his own phone meant alerting the wiretappers to his knowledge of the bug, but the danger he feared should have outweighed that completely. In any event, it made little difference to the boy, but it might have, and afterward he blamed himself for doing it.

"Where *is* the boy?"

"I don't know," Brady said. "Home, I imagine. Or on his way to Lusby. He went to Baltimore for a wedding, but he was going to leave early, he said. Procter expects him back by seven. They're going to call me when he gets there."

Things were going well for a change, Brady thought. When he got Procter's call he would drive out to the Coast Guard station and take a statement from the boy. After that he would pay a visit to the mysterious house on the inlet. With any luck the man would be there and the boy would be able to identify him. And in that case, he thought, the case might break rather quickly.

"How is he getting to Lusby?"

"Hitchhiking, I guess. It's what he usually does."

"Shit," Sullivan said.

"What's the problem?" Brady was puzzled. Sullivan was acting weird, he thought. Here they were with the prospect of a breakthrough and he started discussing transportation for the boy. Why? Sullivan wasn't normally given to irrelevance.

"My phone has been bugged. Your message has been sitting in the machine since late last night. So whoever bugged the phone must know by now that the kid can lead us to the guy who was having those meetings with Seligman."

"So you're thinking that if the guy who was meeting Seligman was connected with the people who bugged your phone . . ."

"Yes," Sullivan said. "I'm thinking about Seligman. Shot in the head and dumped in the Bay. And those two burglars down by the canal. There's someone mixed up in all this, I'm thinking, who has very few scruples about killing people. So I don't think the boy should be hitchhiking tonight."

"Shit," Brady said.

There was silence from the other end of the phone.

"I don't know where he lives," Brady said. "Neither does Procter. So how do we get in touch with him? And how does anyone else, for that matter?" He brightened at the thought. "Even if you're right and there *is* a connection, *they* won't know where to look for him either."

"The phone book," Sullivan said. "The kid's Mexican, isn't he? With an unusual name. All they'd have to do, probably, is look in the phone book."

The Obezos were Mexican, Brady thought, dialing the first number, and the kid had slept on the beach; the odds were they were poor. So they might not have a phone. At least he hoped they didn't, because there were only three Obezos in the Baltimore phone book. Of course, Sullivan's fears were not necessarily well founded, but if they were, the boy was not going to be difficult to trace. Jesus, he thought, I wish your name had been John and your parents had been called Smith.

The phone was answered on the second ring.

"Mr. Obezo?"

"Yeah."

"I'm Corporal Brady of the Maryland police department. Do you happen to have a son named Jesus?" He pronounced the name "Hayzoos," in what he hoped was an approximation of the correct accent, but the voice that answered was obviously American—pure Baltimore nasal.

"Look," it said, "let me get this straight. I do not have a son, and if I did, I wouldn't call him such a dumb-ass name as Hayzoos. And I'd be obliged if you guys would make a note of that fact so you don't keep calling me every half-hour."

"Someone's already called?"

"Damn right they have. And not just someone—you guys . . . Sergeant Barnes, or some such. Burns, maybe. I think you guys should get your act together. What did the kid do, anyway? Commit a murder?"

He didn't get the courtesy of an answer, because by the time he had finished Brady had hung up and was dialing the second number. Jesus, he was praying, don't have a phone.

But Jesus did have a phone.

He wasn't home, his mother told Brady. As she'd explained to the other officer, he'd left about an hour before to hitchhike to Lusby. He wasn't in any trouble, was he? She sounded worried. He was a good boy. She just couldn't believe he'd gotten into trouble.

III

"You want a ride?" The driver rolled down the window as Jesus ran up. "Or are you just sitting there, waiting to get wet?"

A wiseguy, Jesus thought. Salesman most likely. Computers, probably—to judge from the double-knit suit and the white shirt—or office equipment. He had an odd feeling, though, that he'd seen him somewhere before.

"Lusby," he said. "Are you headed that way?"

"Where else?" The man grinned. He reached over and opened the passenger door. "Jump in."

As Jesus did, the storm burst. There was a rattle of thunder, a sudden gust of wind, and the rain came down in a single continuous torrent, drumming against the body, washing over the windshield, dancing and leaping on the hood. It was as if the sky, unable to hold its burden any longer, had simply dumped it.

"We timed *that* right." The man let in the clutch. "Another minute and I'd never have spotted you."

"Lucky you did." Jesus settled himself in the seat, his pleasure in the storm enhanced by the prospect of being able to enjoy it in comfort. "I could have been swimming to Lusby."

"Ah well." The man grinned. "Fortune favors the lucky—to coin a proverb . . . Whereabouts in Lusby?"

"The Coast Guard station. But I'll walk from the center of town. I don't want to take you out of your way."

"No problem," the man said. "All roads lead to Rome."

"Yes." Jesus nodded. The remark made no sense to him, but it wasn't worth pursuing. He eased his feet out of the sandals. He shouldn't have worn them, he thought; they were all right for slopping about the Wharf in, but not so good for hitchhiking. But then, he'd never anticipated having to walk much.

"Mint?" the man offered. He held out a box containing small, shiny-white tablets.

Jesus hesitated.

"Go on," the man urged. "Try one. I'm a connoisseur of mints myself, and these are special. The Château Lafite of mints." He chuckled. "Robust, full-bodied. Subtle and elegant bouquet. Guaranteed no hangover. All that bullshit . . . Go on. Take one."

He didn't really want one, but there was something faintly bullying about the man's manner. A refusal, it implied, would question his taste and slight his generosity. Jesus shrugged. The man was giving him a ride, after all; the least he could do was humor him.

He took one. It had a fierce, almost fiery, peppermint flavor, beneath which was a certain suggestion of bitterness. He didn't like it much, but there was no discreet way to get rid of it. Instead, he crunched it up and swallowed it.

"You didn't chew it!" The man pretended shock. "These mints are for lingering over. For sipping, not gulping. Have another."

"Thanks." Jesus shook his head. "I don't eat much candy."

"Perhaps you're right." The man put the box away. "I eat too much myself . . . Ah well," he sighed. "One man's meat, as the saying goes."

They drove for a while in silence. It was hot in the car, Jesus noticed, but he couldn't wind down his window because of the rain. He studied the dashboard. There was air conditioning, he saw, and he wondered if he could ask to have it turned on. He decided not; it wouldn't be polite.

But it wouldn't be polite, either, to fall asleep. He was feeling decidedly drowsy now, as if he'd had too much to drink. He'd had a glass of champagne and a plate of chicken at the wedding. But that was hours ago, he thought; they shouldn't be making him feel like this.

"You live in Lusby?" He attempted to overcome sleep with conversation.

"Thereabouts." The man nodded. "You work at the Wharf, don't you?"

"Yes. How did you know?"

"Thought I'd seen you there. I used to go there quite often. Had a friend who kept his boat there."

Odd, Jesus thought. He knew most of the regulars at the Wharf—by sight, at least—but he couldn't place this man. There *was* something familiar about him, though. He was sure he'd seen him somewhere. In Lusby, maybe. Or perhaps he was just a type, one of those faces that were so common they always seemed vaguely familiar.

But when he turned to study the face, he found it an effort to move his head. His whole body was suddenly deadweight, his stomach leaden, his chest a burden pressing on his lungs. He was sweating profusely, too, though he no longer felt hot. And the man's features wouldn't come into focus. He seemed to be seeing them through a mist, all blurred, the colors leaching out of them and running into one another. Before his eyes, it seemed, the whole world was turning gray . . . He was not falling asleep—the knowledge hit him in a wave of sudden panic—he was passing out.

"Please," he managed to gasp. "Feeling sick . . . air . . . need air."

"Yes?" The man didn't seem to understand: the voice was unconcerned, the glance oddly incurious.

"Sick . . . must stop . . . must pull over." He tried to shout, but all that came out was a whisper. He felt himself going now. There was a roaring in his ears. A tide of blackness swirled around him.

"Having a dizzy spell?" The man, incomprehensibly, was making no movement to stop. "It'll pass, don't worry. Everything passes."

"You . . . don't . . . understand."

The man turned to face him. The eyes held him, and he saw that the man did indeed understand. The mint. That was it. Now everything was clear. For in that moment of lucidity he remembered, too, where he had seen the face.

But it was too late. The black tide rose up and sucked him under.

IV

Patrolman Davis stared at the windshield. A water drop, forming at the top left-hand corner, joined forces with another and took off on an erratic downward course, gaining momentum as it went. Halfway down, impeded by some invisible obstacle, it stopped. Next to it, perhaps a quarter inch away, a smaller drop edged laterally toward it.

"Go on," Davis said.

The smaller drop continued to creep sideways until it was less than a millimeter from the other. Then it too stopped.

"Go on," Davis coaxed, all his attention fixed on the infinitesimal space between the drops. Nothing happened. He reached out and tapped the windshield with his forefinger, gently at first, then more firmly.

The second tap broke the tension that kept the drops apart. The larger swallowed the smaller. Too heavy to be held back any longer, it spilled over the obstacle and ran like quicksilver to the bottom.

Released, Davis sat back.

"Christ," he said. It no longer bothered him to talk to himself on duty. "What a hell of a way to be passing the time!"

The rain had stopped, temporarily, but the clouds were still ominous. Davis hated the rain. For one thing, it would probably wash out the Orioles game, which he had looked forward to watching on TV. Palmer was to have pitched tonight, and with all those sluggers in the Cincinnati lineup it had promised to be a classic duel—precision versus power. Now, instead, he would be condemned to three hours of tepid sitcoms. His wife would be happy, but there was small consolation in that. It was years since he'd paid much attention to his wife's state of mind.

What was worse, though, was the boredom. The downpour had slowed traffic to a crawl. And what was the point of running a speed trap, he asked himself, when all the world was creeping along at forty?

It was not that he cared about giving tickets. In fact, most of the time, if he had filled his quota, he would let people off with a warning. He liked the diversion was all, the opportunity to exchange a few words with a fellow human being. He also liked to drive.

If things had been different, he sometimes thought, he might have been a race driver. He had the judgment for it, and the reflexes—they had told him that at the school—but he'd lacked the opportunity. So instead of burning up the track at Indy, he ran imaginary races against the drivers he picked up for speeding. He would give them a good head start—half a minute or so from where he'd clocked them on the radar—and take off after them, sliding his Dodge through the corners, gunning it to the limit on the straight. He'd had some near misses on occasion—a brush with a semi that had swung wide on a corner, and a couple of dinkbrains who'd changed lanes without signaling—but they were worth it. Worth it for the thrill of controlling three quarters of a ton of protesting machinery at speeds in excess of a hundred and twenty, and worth it too for the very considerable pleasure of ambling over to some quaking motorist and delivering, in the good-ole-boy drawl he reserved for the occasion, his favorite opening line: "Well now, mister, I don't see any sign around here says you can drive at seventy."

But there was none of that today. Nothing to amuse him but the forlorn activity of watching raindrops run down the windshield and listening to the laconic messages that came over the radio. And there was little of interest in them. Things were dead on the roads this evening; the rain had taken the sass out of everyone. The only thing that had caught his attention was an all-cars alert an hour or so back. Some kid was missing—run away from home, probably—and was thought to be hitchhiking in the direction of Lusby. That lay on his beat, so he'd cruised around for a while but seen nobody. It hadn't surprised him. In this weather, if the kid hadn't copped himself a ride already, he'd have taken shelter somewhere. It wasn't a good day for hitchhiking, Davis thought. There'd been enough rain to drown a duck.

He was parked off the road close to a T-junction, on the cross-bar of the T. There was a shallow bend in the left-hand approach to the junction, and cars were apt to sweep around it and spot him a little too late. From his position he could also monitor the junction in case anyone failed to observe the stop sign. That wasn't nitpicking, exactly; the junction was something of a hazard. The left-hand approach was almost blind, so a driver who ignored the sign ran a real risk of causing an accident.

The green Oldsmobile ignored the sign.

"Stand over here by the curb, please. We don't want anyone running you over."

The man looked apprehensive, Davis thought; but then, they generally did. He was also soaked. His hair was plastered down against his head, and his suit clung to him like wet laundry. He looked as if he'd just stepped out of the shower.

"You look a bit damp." Davis grinned. "Have a flat, did you?"

"Right in the middle of the storm." The man nodded. "I'd have sat it out, but I have to be somewhere."

His expression was sour. First the flat, it implied, and now *you*.

"What did I do, anyway?"

"May I see your license and registration?"

The man handed them over.

"Did you see the sign back there?" Davis asked. "The stop sign just before the junction?"

The man did not reply.

"Because if you did"—Davis's voice was calm, avuncular—"you ignored it. And if you didn't, you should have. So I'm going to give you a citation. I wouldn't normally; I'd just give you a warning. But that happens to be a very dangerous corner. Been a lot of accidents on that corner. If someone had been coming when you rolled through that sign, we wouldn't be standing here talking—I'd be scraping you up off the road."

"Oh."

The man didn't seem very interested. But then, they never did, Davis thought. They simply resented you for giving them a ticket and wondered—often out loud—why you weren't out catching criminals instead of harassing harmless motorists. Harmless indeed! In most of their hands, an automobile was a deadly weapon.

"The signs are put there for your protection." Davis tore the ticket off his pad and handed it to the man. "This here is thirty bucks' worth of reminder, if you want to look at it that way. And whichever way you look at it, it's a hell of a sight better than being dead."

"Yes," the man said.

"Have a good day." Davis smiled. "And drive carefully."

The man was getting back into his car when Davis remembered the alert. The kid had been coming from Baltimore, hadn't he, and was thought to be heading for Lusby? Maybe this guy had seen him.

"Hey, mister." He ran back to the Oldsmobile and tapped on the passenger window.

The man reached over and rolled it down.

"Did you come from Baltimore?"

The man nodded.

"You didn't happen to see a hitchhiker on the road, did you?" Davis leaned on the door frame and stuck his head in the window. "A young Mexican boy? Aged about thirteen. Five six or thereabouts. Dark hair, dark eyes. Carrying a day pack. Wearing cutoffs and sandals."

As he spoke, he happened to glance down. On the floor, half hidden by the seat, was a day pack. And sticking out from beneath the pack, the toes of what looked like a pair of Mexican sandals.

He looked back at the man. The man followed his glance, and as their eyes met, there passed between them a current of instant, intuitive communication.

Davis stepped back. His hand moved to the holster on his hip.

"Turn off the motor and get out of the car." His voice was no longer affable.

But the man did no such thing. Instead he let in the clutch, hit the accelerator. The Oldsmobile took off like a jackrabbit.

It was a pity, Davis thought, that it wouldn't be more of a contest. For one thing, the guy just didn't have the kind of wheels he had; the Olds could move, all right, but it lacked the power of the Dodge. Besides, it handled badly. The featherbed springing was fine for comfort, but it was too spongy for high-speed cornering; the body and the wheels tended to go in different directions; the rear end tended to drift.

The decisive difference, though, was in the drivers. The guy was on the edge, or very close to it. He wasn't used to this kind of speed, and it showed in the small mistakes he was making. He was using the brakes instead of the accelerator, misjudging the line through the corners, overcorrecting for the rear-end drift. He himself, on the other hand, was well within his limits. He could catch the Olds very easily, if he wanted to, but he wasn't going to try. If he got too close, the guy might panic and push himself over the edge. There were other cars on the road, and concern was owed for their safety. So instead of catching the Olds, he was content to sit behind it, harrying it toward the roadblocks, like a beater driving game toward the guns.

In two miles or so they would hit the freeway. The roadblocks would be in place by now, so if the Olds took either exit, the chase would be over in seconds. If it went straight, on the other hand, it would be trapped between him and the patrol cars up ahead. Its only real chance of avoiding capture was to make a one-eighty and cut back in the opposite direction, but to do that successfully it would have to take him by surprise. And that meant getting far enough ahead of him to complete the maneuver before he could spot what was happening. So while he didn't want to push too hard, he couldn't afford to let it get out of sight.

They'd be coming to a long straightaway soon, about six hundred yards, slightly downhill, leading to a long, sweeping right-hander that got tighter as it curved. Beyond that there was another straightaway—maybe two hundred yards—then the freeway exits. The Olds was between two and three hundred yards ahead, Davis figured, and unless he closed that gap sometime before they hit the right-hander, the Olds might have time to double back.

There was a curve before the first straightaway. He took it at eighty, swinging wide into the left-hand lane to make the arc as shallow as possible, accelerating slightly as he reached the apex, correcting just a fraction to keep the tail end in line. Then, as the straightaway opened up in front of him, he put his foot to the floor.

It was that damn storm, the man thought. If it hadn't been raining, he wouldn't have hurried. And if he hadn't been hurrying, he wouldn't have forgotten the day pack. And if . . . Excuses, he thought. What was the point in making excuses? Who would buy them? The Resident? The District Attorney? The twelve men and women who would sit on the jury? Forget it, he told himself bitterly; he didn't even buy them himself.

He'd been careless; that was the long and short of it. But how had they known? How come they'd been looking for the boy before he was even properly missing? Something had blown somewhere. The operation was in jeopardy. More to the point, so was he.

There'd be roadblocks ahead now, cops waiting at every exit. They were driving him into a bag. And when he was in it, they would draw the neck tight and sew it up. And he was helping them, running right into it. But he didn't have any choice, did he? There was nowhere else to go.

Except, maybe . . . Maybe the neck was not shut yet. There was that traffic cop behind him, so maybe it hadn't occurred to them to block the exits in the Baltimore direction. If he could cut back, perhaps, past the traffic cop, he might get out of the bag and lose them in the maze of country roads behind. He could abandon the car and take his chances in the open country. It was a faint chance, he knew, and if he made it they would have to pull him out. Drummer too, probably. And that meant the end of the operation. But the operation was shot anyway, especially if he didn't get out of the bag. He would make a deal, in that case—everything he knew in exchange for a reduction in the charges. He'd served them loyally for thirty years, but loyalty, like everything else, had its limits.

It all depended on whether he could open up enough distance between him and that cop. If he was going to cut back, he should do it soon, before the freeway. He would do it in that last stretch, he decided, when for two hundred yards or so the bend would hide him from the cop. He would hit the brakes as he came out of the bend and be halfway back before the cop had time to realize what had happened.

But when he looked in the rear-view mirror he found that the gap, far from opening, had narrowed. The Dodge was barreling down on him, gaining appreciably with every second.

He glanced at the speedometer. The needle was hovering around ninety. The Olds was shuddering as if riding on cobblestones. It wasn't built for this kind of driving, he thought, and neither was he. Nevertheless, he stepped on the accelerator. Beggars can't be choosers, he thought. Fortune favors the bold.

He was doing a hundred and fifteen when he started to brake for the bend. He started too late, anyway, and he didn't brake enough. As the curve tightened, the rear end started to go.

What happened then was that he seemed to split apart. His body went on reacting; all his reflexes worked—his foot went to the accelerator, his eyes stayed focused on the road, his heart kept on pumping blood to his brain at the rate appropriate to his predicament—but his mind detached itself, stood aloof, crossed over, perhaps, into another realm of time. He became, in a sense, a spectator of the last seconds of his own consciousness.

There was a point at which it seemed he might make it. The sliding rear end responded briefly to the thrust of acceleration. But almost as it did, he hit the bump.

It was not much of a bump. Just enough to take the weight, for a fraction of a second, off the back axle. The Olds slewed around at a right angle to the highway. He corrected . . . Too much. The car took the curb like a hurdler, cleared the ditch, ploughed through the fence. He tried to wrestle with the steering, but the Olds had become a projectile, responsive only to the laws of motion. It was still doing sixty when it hit the tree.

Davis got out of his car and approached the wreck. He did so carefully, gun at the ready. It seemed unlikely that anyone had survived, but he was taking no chances. When he got closer, however, he put the gun away.

The Oldsmobile was about three quarters its normal length. The impact had folded it up like a telescope. The front end had given way entirely. The steering column had been driven into the front seat. The tree, surprisingly, appeared unharmed.

The man was pinned to the seat by the steering column. He was spread-eagled, motionless, his head slumped forward on his chest. Davis tried the door. It was jammed. He took out his pistol and shattered the window. Then he leaned in.

As he did, the man raised his head. His face was unmarked except for a pink froth about the mouth. Arterial blood, Davis thought. Ribs had snapped, evidently, and one of them had pierced a lung.

There was a sound, a croaking gargling sound, reminiscent of speech, but inarticulate.

"Don't try to talk, fella." Davis put a hand on the man's shoulder and patted it softly. "I can't move you now, but there's an ambulance on its way. We'll have you out in a while. Hang in there," he added. "It's going to be rough, but it's going to be all right."

But the man was beyond reassurance. What he had to say evidently was important. He made another attempt, the froth bubbling at the corner of his mouth, his body trembling with effort.

"Boy . . ." he managed. ". . . Trunk."

CHAPTER 17

I

"He's losing ground," the doctor said. "Frankly, I don't hold out much hope."

"Oh."

Some comment was called for, Brady felt, but he wasn't sure what. He and Sullivan were like vultures, he thought, waiting for a chance at the carcass. Only it wasn't the bones they hoped to pick, just the brains. In any case, his role here made him uncomfortable. He believed people should be allowed to die in peace.

"How's the boy?" Sullivan asked.

"Not much the matter with him," the doctor said. "He's a mass of bruises, but there are no fractures or, as far as we can tell, any internal injuries. We're keeping him overnight, just to be on the safe side. He's objecting, of course, but not very strenuously. Apart from everything else, he's been heavily drugged. "And"—he grinned—"he has the hangover to prove it."

"That's a relief."

"Yes."

Silence.

There was something more than a little odd about all this, the doctor thought. At first they'd told him it had been an ordinary car accident. But then these two had shown up. That had made him wonder. Brady was no traffic cop, obviously. And as for the other one . . . he couldn't place him at all. So when it transpired that the boy had been drugged, he'd asked for explanations, but that hadn't gotten him very far. National security was involved, they'd said; they weren't at liberty to go beyond that. They'd cautioned him against talking to anyone about the condition of either patient and insisted that the boy's parents see them before talking to the boy. Now, though it was almost midnight, they were still hanging around, hoping, apparently, for a chance to question the man.

"Look." He frowned. "There's not much point in you two staying. I doubt he'll regain consciousness tonight. And if he does, he'll be in no state to answer questions."

More silence. Brady glanced at Sullivan.

"We'll stay," Sullivan said.

"I don't think you quite understand." The doctor began to lose patience. "The man is very probably going to die. I'm doing all I can to prevent it, and as long as there's a chance I'm going to work at it. And that means that even if he does come around, I'm not going to let you see him. So you might just as well go home. If there's any change, I'll call you in the morning."

"We *have* to see him," Sullivan said. "If he's going to die anyway, I don't see the harm."

"Possibly not." The doctor's voice was dry. "Reasons of national security are always very compelling, no doubt . . . Well, I wouldn't know about that. And right now I can't say I care. My concern is for the patient. I'm sorry if you find that annoying, but it's the way it's going to be."

Doctors, Sullivan thought: self-appointed gurus, experts on everything—including ethics—their natural lack of humility aggravated by six-figure incomes and the adulation of an ignorant public. Useless to ask this one to look beyond his oath to the lives that might be endangered if the man died without telling what he knew. Those lives were abstractions to the doctor, totally lacking the appeal of the one mutilated, futureless life that now lay in his hands. Well, he thought, he wouldn't argue the point. When the time came—if it came—he would simply go higher up the ladder.

The door opened. A nurse entered. Ignoring Sullivan and Brady, she went over to the doctor. There was a whispered consultation. The doctor took off in a hurry, the nurse right behind him.

"He's going to die," Sullivan said.

"It looks that way." Brady nodded.

"So what are we left with?"

"Not enough, so far. We have a name, an address, the skeleton of a biography, some bits of circumstantial evidence. Not enough to take us anywhere. His name was Pollock, originally Poljak, but he changed it when he emigrated here after the war. He was Serbian by birth, came here in 1946, took out citizenship in 1953. Beyond that, nothing. The FBI had a file on him for a while—nothing significant in that, though; they kept files on all immigrants from Eastern Europe in those days. In any event, they found nothing against him, and the file was closed in 1951. No police record, of course."

"I'm impressed." Sullivan raised his eyebrows. "That's a lot to dig out in three hours."

"Yeah," Brady agreed sardonically. "We're good at that sort of trivia."

"It's not entirely trivia. It sounds to me like deep cover. They sent him here after the war, probably, mixed in with all the other refugees. Told him to establish an identity and lie low until needed. They did that with hundreds of them, maybe thousands, each one a virus floating around in our bloodstream. God knows how many of them are still here."

"Could be." Brady nodded. "The other evidence supports it. He was a ham radio buff—at least, there was a lot of equipment found in his house. He kept a marine supply store, too. We haven't been able to check yet if he stocked the kind of diving belt they used on Seligman, but it doesn't much matter. It all points in the same direction: he was almost certainly Seligman's contact, and very probably his killer. But as to how and why . . ." He shrugged. "We need a confession. And we're not going to get it."

He was right. Fifteen minutes later the doctor returned. He looked tired and despondent.

"We lost him," he said. "For a while there he seemed to be gaining a little, then poof . . . he went. Ruptured aorta, probably. Maybe the spleen. That's the trouble with these internal injuries— you can't tell much from the X-rays. When the real problem shows up, it's usually too late.

"We lost him," he repeated. "Odd how we always say that . . . as if there was much we could have done. There wasn't really. There hardly ever is in cases like this. But we always expect to be miracle workers." He shrugged. "Arrogance, I suppose."

Arrogance? Sullivan, hearing the drained, exhausted voice, recalled their earlier clash. Possibly. But if so, doctors were not alone. Lawyers were just as bad, he thought, if not worse.

"So that's that." Brady got to his feet. "There goes my case. And there goes your inquiry. All that chasing around, and all for nothing . . . I feel like him." He nodded in the direction in which the doctor had departed. "I sometimes wonder why we bother."

Sullivan didn't reply. It seemed he hadn't heard. He just sat there staring at the ceiling, frowning.

"It's over," Brady said. "The man died. It's time to go home."

"He *didn't* die." Sullivan didn't move.

Brady stared at him. "Of course not." His voice was expressionless. "It just seems that way. His body went into retirement, but his soul goes marching on. And it's up there right now." He nodded toward the ceiling. "Explaining everything to You Know Who. The trouble is . . ." He paused. "You Know Who will probably neglect to fill us in."

Sullivan ignored the gibe. When he responded, finally, he seemed to be part of another conversation.

"We got on to Pollock by accident," he said. "He rolled through that stop sign, and panicked when he saw the patrolman. The boy was in the trunk by then, of course, which would tend to make anyone nervous . . . Then when he crashed he was injured—but not fatally—and the boy was discovered. So now he faces kidnapping charges, and he wants to make a deal: everything he knows in return for a reduction in the charges . . . There." He turned to Brady. "How does that sound?"

"I'm no judge of fiction." Brady shrugged. "It's got violence, I suppose. It might do OK, depending on the market. Paperback would be best. I don't see it in hardcover."

"It's all we've got." Sullivan was back to life now, his voice urgent, excited. "Look, here's what you do. You call up in the morning. Around ten. Tell me the story as I just gave it to you. Pollock has regained consciousness, realizes he's in deep shit, and is willing to testify. Say you want me to be there when he does."

"Ah." Brady began to be interested. "I think I see what you're getting at."

"They don't *know*, you see. All they know is we got on to Pollock because of the boy. Beyond that they're in the dark."

"I do see." Brady grinned. "We're shaking the tree again. Isn't that it?"

"The hell with shaking it," Sullivan growled. "I hope we're chopping it down."

II

On his way home Sullivan called Stonemason. He was tired of pay phones, he thought, and tired of people who couldn't be contacted directly. He didn't have to wait long, though; within five minutes Stonemason was back to him. Considering the hour, he seemed amazingly alert. Sullivan wondered if he ever slept.

"I'm taking you up on your offer," Sullivan told him. "I need help. Lots of help. And in a hurry."

You could say this for Stonemason, he thought later, he was a good listener. There were no interruptions until he had finished explaining, and the comments then were short and to the point.

"How much time do we have?"

"Ten hours, maybe. Brady will call around ten. If anything is going to happen then, it will happen in a hurry. You should be set, I'd say, by twelve at the latest."

"That's tight. There's a lot of exits to cover: the airports, Union Station, the port at Baltimore. And those are just the obvious ones. If he uses a private plane or small boat, I don't see how we're going to stop him. Perhaps surveillance would be safer."

"They'll be looking out for it. And if they see it, they'll send him to ground. Then we'll really have a problem. But if they haven't guessed we know about the bug—and if they have, the whole enterprise is doomed anyway—then most likely they'll just put him aboard a plane. It's speed they'll be worrying about, not secrecy."

"I guess you're right," Stonemason conceded. "It just seems rather iffy. You're assuming, for one thing, that Pollock, had he lived, would have been able to tell you a lot. But to me he sounds more like a hatchetman. I doubt he'd have had much to give."

"Possibly not. But he was crucial enough, don't forget, that they were willing to contemplate kidnapping and possibly murder to protect him. They'd hardly have done that for a hatchetman. In other respects you're right, of course. It *is* iffy. Bluffs always are. But if they call it and sit tight, we're no worse off. And if they move, at least we'll have him in the open. He may succeed in getting clear, but his useful life will be over."

And perhaps that would be best, he thought, because a trial was probably out of the question anyway. It would be one of those cases where the national interest would not be served by revealing how much the national interest had suffered. Besides, what good would it do to put anyone in prison? It wouldn't deter the others; it never did. And retribution in this case seemed more than usually beside the point.

"One of those three, then," Stonemason said. "Spearman, Tyrell, Brayer."

"Four," Sullivan corrected. "You're forgetting Patterson."

"I'm not forgetting him. I'm ruling him out. He works for me, you see. Has for years."

You and who else? Sullivan thought. But he didn't say it.

"Three, then," he said. "I don't see any other possibilities. Do you?"

"I don't see that many," Stonemason said flatly. "But then, I have certain advantages over you. If I were a gambling man, in fact, I'd have a small bet on the outcome."

So would I, Sullivan thought. And I'd be praying to lose it.

"One more thing," he said. "We should do something about the hospital. Pollock is supposed to be alive; we should go through the motions of protecting him. They may try to get to him, as they did with the boy. A goon or two at the entrance, perhaps. Just obvious enough to discourage them."

"Yes." Stonemason almost chuckled. "I thought of the FBI; they're perfect for it."

After that, there was nothing for Sullivan to do but go home to bed. Not to sleep, of course; to lie awake, wondering and waiting. Well, he thought, he was almost out of it now. He had set the trap and baited it; someone else could spring it.

He was glad of that. That, at least, was a mercy.

III

Brady was perfect. His call to Sullivan—dead on time, Sullivan noted—had exactly the right tone of cautious optimism. Pollock had recovered sufficiently to face some preliminary questioning,

Brady said; he understood the gravity of his position, and he was eager to talk about a deal. He now knew of the boy's testimony about his meetings with Seligman, and he'd hinted that if the price was right he might be willing to shed a great deal of light on the Seligman affair and on other matters of interest to the CIA. Of course, Brady conceded, it might all be bullshit—an attempt to save his skin with some hastily improvised spy fiction—and the DA's office was so far noncommittal. What he, Brady, suggested, therefore, was that Sullivan meet him at the DA's office at eleven, where they could kick around, in a preliminary way, the possible terms for a deal. They could go on from there to the hospital, where a meeting with Pollock was scheduled for twelve. Sullivan might want to bring with him, Brady added, someone from the counter-intelligence section of the Agency to help assess Pollock's story.

Restraining a chuckle at the sense of irony revealed in Brady's closing suggestion, Sullivan thanked him gravely. Yes, he said, he'd be at the DA's office at eleven. But no, he didn't think, at this point, that he wanted to involve the Agency.

Stonemason, too, revealed an unexpected flair for the theatrical. By noon the hospital, to the evident bewilderment of most of its staff, had become the setting for a drama in which atmosphere almost compensated for the nonappearance of the main character. Men in gray suits and gray hats, with newspapers and magazines they quite obviously had little interest in reading, lounged conspicuously at every entrance. An area on the second floor of one wing had been closed off, and visitors were subjected to the scrutiny of two plainclothesmen who made little effort to conceal the Police Specials they wore in holsters at their belts.

At five of twelve Sullivan arrived, together with Brady and an official from the DA's office. They were accompanied—a nice touch, Sullivan thought—by a stenographer. They proceeded solemnly upstairs to the closed-off area on the second floor, where, behind locked doors, they spent the early part of the afternoon killing time.

Sullivan and Brady played chess, perfunctory, error-filled games on a pocket set Brady had thought to bring with him. The man from the DA's office, disdainful of such frivolity, busied himself with papers from his briefcase. The stenographer smoked and uttered inanities.

At one they sent out for lunch, the hospital providing a tray for the "patient" but declining absolutely to extend its hospitality beyond that point. At three they departed, with the same grim formality that had marked their arrival. Never, Sullivan thought, had he spent a more uncomfortable few hours. The whole thing struck him as a bizarre parody of government service—hundreds of tax dollars devoted to having four people sit around for several hours doing nothing.

Whose eyes, he wondered, had been watching the charade? None, he hoped. For the illusion they'd created was too fragile to survive any but the most perfunctory inspection. There were too many people involved; too much time had gone by while the stage was being set. A couple of questions in the right quarter and anyone could establish that the man they were all supposed to be guarding and interrogating had died in Emergency late last night. And in that case, the mere existence of the charade would ensure the defeat of its purpose.

The timing, however, was in their favor. Whoever had been listening in on Brady's phone call would have had to conclude that shortly after twelve Pollock would utter the vital information. On that assumption there would be very little time to evade the consequences. Unlikely, then, that they would spend it tracing the hospital and asking around among the staff. The safest course would be to prepare for the worst and run. If that happened, the whole thing, amateur theatricals and all, would be justified by the result. If not . . . He was reminded of the thin line that separates tragedy from farce.

IV

Arthur Fordham, of the U.S. Immigration Service at Dulles Airport, liked to think of himself as being, in a modest kind of way, in public relations on behalf of his country. His job, which consisted largely of stamping passports and checking visas, was not, he was prepared to concede, terribly important, but being the last official contact for travelers leaving the United States gave him the opportunity to influence, to some degree, the impression of the country these travelers took away with them. He believed in making the most of that opportunity. "Sunshine Arthur," his colleagues called him, and he accepted the nickname as he accepted most

things—cheerfully, welcoming the positive implications and ignoring the sneer.

He'd been on duty since eight. It was one of the light-traffic mid-
week days, which he particularly enjoyed because the absence of
rush gave him the leisure to employ his talent for courtesy. Nevertheless, after five hours of smiling and stamping and issuing invitations to "come back and visit us again real soon," he was ready
for lunch.

He glanced at his watch. Five of one. Parsons would be reliev-
ing him in five minutes. He must remember, he thought, to tell
Parsons about the special directive issued that morning. Unusual
directive, that. A list of four names and passport numbers—all
U.S. citizens—who were barred from leaving the country. Should
any of them attempt to clear Immigration, his passport was to be
impounded and the airport police contacted immediately. Gang-
sters? Fordham wondered. Fugitives from the IRS? The directive
didn't explain, and he didn't waste much time on speculation. It
was dollars to pennies against them showing up.

A small knot of people drifted toward his counter. Mexicans, by
the look of them, probably booked on the one-thirty to Mexico
City. He looked around. No sign of Parsons. Late as usual, he
thought, but no matter. He always welcomed an opportunity to
practice his Spanish.

There were two families of Mexicans, each with a gaggle of
children. He lingered over them, making a minor production of the
civilities natural to their language. It made him feel a little guilty,
because behind them, last in line, was an American—businessman
type—frowning and looking at his watch. Interesting, Fordham
thought, the differences in national attitudes toward time. Five
minutes was nothing to a Latin, but to an American . . . you'd
think it was a matter of life and death. We hurry too much, he
thought, we don't take the time to smell the flowers.

Nevertheless, when the man's turn came, he apologized for keeping him waiting. He liked to be cordial with foreigners, he explained, because they were all potential friends to Uncle Sam.
These days, he added, Uncle Sam needed all the friends he could
get.

"No problem." The man smiled easily and handed Fordham his
passport. "There's half an hour before my flight leaves. I guess I
just share the national aversion to standing in line."

Afterward, Fordham would be inclined to blame the directive. The sensible thing, he argued, would have been to let the man clear and pick him up later when he boarded. In any event, his own conscience was clear; he'd followed instructions to the letter. Beyond the letter, really, because his smile had not faltered when he read the name in the passport, nor had he flicked more than the briefest of glances at the names listed in the directive on the desk in front of him. He was not willing to concede, either, that he had made a mistake in taking the passport with him when, excusing himself politely, he'd gone over to a neighboring counter to phone the airport police. The directive had instructed him to impound the passport, and that was exactly what he had done.

All he could say, really, was that the man had somehow been alerted. Because when he'd returned to the counter, about two minutes later, the man had disappeared.

CHAPTER 18

I

Sullivan was in the restaurant by the river. It didn't change. In dozens of visits it had never changed. Outside, beyond the peeling shutters and the rusty handrail, the current coiled and writhed interminably, black as an oil slick and gleaming dully under the restaurant lights. Inside, the ceiling fans described their languid, endless circles, the flowers wilted, as ever, under the suffocating heat, the waiters mopped their faces with napkins and drifted sullenly between the tables. He heard voices chattering in three languages, and in the occasional lulls there came from the Delta, in a kind of ground bass, the unwearying thump of the guns. It was Saigon, his personal Saigon. In the geography of his dreams there was no other.

But though the setting hadn't changed, the people were strangely unstable. Sometimes it was Charley who sat across from him, smiling and talking; sometimes Gael; sometimes a puzzling combination of the two. The waiter, also, took on curious disguises. At times he was himself, hostility palpable despite the Asian mask; at other times he was Spearman, the yellow eyes unfathomable, the mandarin features set in an enigmatic smile. He was also, more disconcertingly still, Roy Tyrell—a laughing, convivial Roy who spoke to them in Vietnamese and recommended dishes from the menu.

Beneath the incongruity there was still the menace. He kept waiting for something to happen. He expected at any moment to see the grenade come tumbling across the floor. He expected shrieks of panic and the sound of falling bodies, the blast, the stab of shrapnel, and the blood. Instead, from somewhere beyond the dream, faint at first but getting louder until it drowned out the dream sounds entirely with the shrill jangle of reality, there came the noise of the telephone.

He awoke sprawled in a chair in his study. He must have fallen asleep there when he returned from the charade at the hospital. Beside him, on the table, the phone continued to ring.

He picked it up.

"Morgan?" It was Gael. "Can you come over? Now. Right away."

"Is something the matter?"

"I can't explain now. I'll tell you when you get here. Just hurry. Please."

Something in her voice prohibited further discussion. In any case, it didn't seem to matter. She had called—that was the main thing. The whys and wherefores were unimportant.

"I'll be right there," he said.

The lights were on in Gael's living room, but the curtains were drawn. As he walked up the path he saw one of the curtains pulled back a few inches and let go again quickly. Looking out for me, he thought, it *must* be urgent. He was reaching for the doorbell when he heard footsteps in the hall.

The light in the hall stayed off. In some corner of his mind he registered the fact as odd, but by then the door was half open and his attention was on Gael. As she stepped back to let him in he caught a glimpse of her face in the half light from the street. She looked worried. No, more than worried: she looked panicked.

"Gael—my God! What is it?"

He started toward her, then stopped abruptly. There was someone with her. Behind her, silhouetted by the light from the living room, he saw a man.

"Come in, Morgan. Shut the door, and then switch on the light."

It was the man who spoke; the voice almost as familiar to Sullivan as his own—a pleasant voice, utterly calm, almost a drawl.

For an instant Sullivan's mind refused to function, refused to accept what he had heard. It was as if, in the moment of recognition, he wanted the world to stop turning, to stop right there and blank out the future. But it was only for an instant. Later he would remember with amazement how little time it took—no more than that skip of a heartbeat that sets the living apart from the dead. How easily, he would think . . . how easily we accommodate disaster, how quickly we adjust to the unbearable.

"Do as he says, Morgan." Gael's voice was choked and unnaturally high. "He has a gun."

"A gun?" It was as if he hadn't really been listening. "A gun . . . Yes. Of course. He would have." Then, with more energy, the words sharp with the pain of that betrayal, "But why you, Roy? Why in God's name does it have to be you?"

"This isn't, believe me, the way I wanted to do it." Tyrell addressed Sullivan, but the gun was pointed steadily at Gael. They had moved into the living room, Gael and Sullivan side by side on the couch, Tyrell across from them slouched in an armchair. "But all the other ways are closed apparently. So I shall have to ask you to help me.

"I tried the airport," he went on. "That cost me my passport. My friends can't help me either—"

"Friends?" Sullivan cut in. "Friends? Have you ever really known what the word means?"

Tyrell's eyes seemed to cloud momentarily. Then he shrugged.

"Friends . . . whatever," he replied evenly. "There's a full battalion of the FBI, at any rate, camped on their various doorsteps. So I shall need your boat, Morgan."

"Take it." Contemptuously.

"And you to run it . . ."

"And Gael?"

"And Gael . . . to ensure your good behavior. You'd risk your own life to stop me, I'd imagine, but not hers. Which was why, incidentally, she agreed to get you here. With her along as hostage, we're all much safer. Particularly you . . . She seems to value your life quite highly."

Sullivan shot a grateful look at Gael, but she was staring at Tyrell. She was breathing fast and trembling a little, but she seemed under control. In fact, he thought, she seemed less scared than angry.

"Fine." He returned to Tyrell. "But the boat won't get you far. It doesn't have the range. Three hundred miles is about its limit. So it won't get you to Cuba, if that's what you're thinking. It won't even get you to Miami."

In a way he was sorry. He wished Roy could get on the boat and just vanish. Himself, too. He didn't want to go through it all: the arrest, the trial—if there was a trial—the months, maybe years, Roy would spend in the grinder. He didn't want to have to remember Roy that way, to read, item by squalid item, the catalogue of his treachery. He didn't, in fact, want to remember him at all.

"It won't have to get me to Cuba," Tyrell said calmly. "Just twenty miles or so. Outside territorial waters. There's a freighter there, or there will be. I have the compass coordinates. My . . . allies were able to do that for me, at least."

"You won't make it out of the Bay. It's all covered now, Roy— the airports, the stations, your 'friends' and their various doorsteps. The Coast Guard will be out, too, checking everything that moves in the Bay tonight. The Navy will have a fix on your freighter. You're boxed, Roy; I want you to understand that. I don't want you doing anything that will make matters worse."

"Boxed?" Tyrell shrugged. "Possibly. But when the chances are slim or none, you choose slim, don't you?" He stood up. "In any case, we won't get anywhere by sitting here arguing.

"We'll take your car, Morgan. You and Gael in the front, me in the back. You'll take care to observe the speed limit, of course, and all the signs. I don't think there's any need to make the obvious threats, is there? You should know better than anyone, at this point, how little I have to lose."

"Yes." Sullivan nodded. "I know exactly how little. What I don't understand is why."

"Explanations." Tyrell sighed. "Will they help any?"

"Maybe not. But I think you owe me."

Tyrell considered.

"Yes," he said. "I suppose I do."

II

"Why, Roy?"

For the first several miles, until they'd reached River Road, very little had been said. Traffic was heavy on Wisconsin, rain and darkness adding to the normal hazards, so Sullivan had been occupied with the driving. Neither Gael nor Tyrell, apparently, had had any wish to talk. Once Gael—surprisingly, for he'd never known her to smoke—had asked Sullivan for a cigarette. She'd taken it from him with a tight little smile, puffed on it unconvincingly once or twice, and put it out. Thereafter she'd sat like a statue. They'd been like people driving to a funeral, ignoring, in an awkward and sullen formality, the uncomfortable purpose that brought them together.

Sullivan had been grateful, however, for the opportunity to think. He'd needed time to consider his options: how, and indeed whether, to do something about Roy. The how, he'd seen at once, was imponderable; means would have to be improvised when the opportunity arose. But it would not be here in the car, with Roy out of reach and Gael an unmissable target. As for the whether, it had not been at all clear to him that he ought to do anything. The Coast Guard or the Navy *would* intercept them, probably; and even if they didn't, would it be such a disaster, really, if Roy got away? Not such a disaster, he'd decided, that it was worth risking lives to prevent—particularly since one of the lives risked would be Gael's. But would Roy, when it came right down to it, pull the trigger? Here, for the first time, he'd felt the full weight of his loss: he didn't know. There'd been a time, he'd reflected miserably, when he could have answered the question without hesitation. But this was a different man he was dealing with. The Roy he'd known was gone, irrecoverable, replaced by a stranger he feared and disliked. He'd been left wondering if the old Roy had ever really existed outside his imagination, and he'd been impelled then to repeat the question that tormented him.

"Is it reasons you want?" Tyrell's voice was as placid as ever. "Or excuses?"

Sullivan shrugged. "There's a difference?"

"In this case, yes. I'm not in any need of excuses."

"I see. You're going to tell me, I suppose, that your reasons were ideological?" Sullivan's voice was sour with disbelief.

"You find that so hard to accept?"

"Roy Tyrell dreaming of the Workers' Paradise? Sacrificing friends and country on the altar of a higher ideal? Yes." He said it flatly. "I'm afraid I do."

"Then you don't know me very well."

"No," Sullivan said. "I don't know you at all."

"You just can't see it, can you." Tyrell was openly contemptuous. "None of you can see it. Self-interest is all you believe in. That's why you're so easy to deceive. 'Not Roy,' you tell yourselves smugly. 'He has nothing to gain from it. He has money, position, power, social status. What else could anyone want?' "

Sullivan was silent.

"After all," Tyrell mocked, "what else *is* there? Go ahead, tell me. You won't credit me with any ideals—you just said that—so it has to be something ignoble. But what? I *have* everything, don't I? I have every glittering component of the American Dream, and I always have had. So tell me, Morgan. What was it that I lacked?"

Richard Cory. The name floated like a bubble from the depths of Sullivan's memory, the echo of Gael's voice returning to him, clear and precise, as if she were speaking now. "He had too much, Paul said, so he had nothing." Was that it? Hadn't it been that way, exactly, with Roy? He'd had all the gifts except one, hadn't he? But that one was the most important—something to live for. Now Tyrell's own words joined with Gael's: "When I'm twenty-five feet above my protection and eight hundred feet off the ground, and I know that if I make a mistake or get unlucky I'm going to fall fifty to eight hundred feet and maybe all the lights will go out . . . I know, for those moments at least, that I'm alive."

"Excitement," Sullivan said. "I think what you lacked was excitement. So you turned it all into a game, the way you always do. It was too dull otherwise; you had to manufacture a risk. It was the only way you could keep yourself interested."

"Crap!" Tyrell retorted. "Amateur psychology. And vulgar to boot. If you can't accept what I tell you, Morgan, at least don't patronize."

"Who cares, anyway?" It was Gael who spoke. They had almost forgotten about her. The interruption shocked them into silence.

"Reasons." Her voice rose. "Excuses. Motives. What do they matter? People died—that's what matters. Paul Seligman, for one, and no doubt lots of others. But you two sit there, oh so very civilized, arguing about motives.

"You're wasting your breath." She turned, with sudden venom, on Tyrell. "There are only two words for you—plain, ugly words: traitor and murderer."

For a second nobody spoke. Sullivan laid a hand on her arm, but she shook it off.

"You're wrong," Tyrell said quietly. "I'm not a murderer. A traitor, possibly, if you insist on those categories, but not a murderer. I didn't kill Paul Seligman, I didn't cause him to be killed, I didn't even know it was going to happen. And I wish to God it hadn't. Because it was his death that started all this.

"They panicked, you see." He was speaking to Sullivan. "My masters panicked. They were always too quick on the trigger. So when Paul started to get suspicious about Theta, it was the first thing they thought of. I thought I'd talked them out of it. 'I can handle him,' I told them. 'He's no real danger; he's just poking around, shaking the tree; he doesn't have anything to go on.' I thought I'd convinced them. I don't understand why I didn't. It was just so fucking dumb . . ." He shook his head in disbelief.

"About Theta . . ." Sullivan was surprised to find, in the midst of everything, that he still cared. Roy would open up now, he knew; under the spur of Gael's contempt he would yield to the need to explain, to justify.

"About Theta," he repeated. "I've heard so many versions. What *is* the truth about Theta?"

"The truth?" Tyrell paused for a moment, considering. He shrugged. "Hell, where's the harm? It's history now. I might as well tell you."

"The Agency's trouble," Tyrell began, "has always been lack of proportion. They're not bad at what they do—the nuts and bolts of it, at least—but they understand less about cost and benefit than any dime-store operator. They're always desperate for product, any product, anything to justify the size of their budget, so they seldom stop to bother about price. That was what made it so easy to sell them Theta.

"You'll remember," he continued, "how I told you about the source in Moscow we used Theta to protect? Well, that was true, as far as it went. What I didn't explain was that the source was a double, like Seligman. And, like Seligman, he passed only what he was authorized to pass. He was a mirror image of Seligman, in fact, but with one important difference—the value of what he was authorized to pass.

"It was good stuff, of course, as it had to be: solid intelligence of great temporary value. But the operative word is 'temporary.' Moscow was giving up information—on troop movements, political developments, weapons specifications—that would help the U.S. in the short run, but become obsolete rather quickly. What they were getting in exchange was far more enduring—our sources, our networks, our methods of operation. To extend, for a moment, the business analogy, they were trading product for the means of production. In the short run, perhaps, the Agency looked like a winner; in the long run it was trading itself out of business."

"I see." Sullivan thought about it. "What I don't understand, in that case, is the need for Theta. They had *you,* didn't they? And you could pass them, I assume, almost everything they wanted. So why give up anything in return? Why all the elaborate machinery? Why not just go to you directly?"

"Spearman," Tyrell said. "My problem was Spearman. Originally I *was* passing it directly, but a pattern developed and Spearman spotted it. Then Zukovsky defected and my problem became acute. Spearman's suspicions focused on Plans. I was forced to lie low. He didn't have enough to prove anything, of course, and with Zukovsky he overplayed his hand. Afterwards, I suppose, we could have returned to the old direct system, but by then I'd had the idea for Theta.

"It virtually eliminated the risk," he continued. "It was a license, you see, carte blanche to pass almost anything I wanted, provided it was chickenfeed. And taken piece by piece, it was chickenfeed. It was the pattern that counted."

"And no one ever checked?" Sullivan was incredulous. "You did this right under their noses and no one questioned it?"

"Spearman would have, but he wasn't around. Brayer might have, had he taken the interest, but to him Theta was just another of Roy's little games. As for Eglinton, all he cared about were his gadgets."

"What about Everett or Patterson?"

"Everett?" Tyrell's tone was a judgment. "Strictly front office. Spent his time ass-licking the President and mending fences with the Senate. Patterson was too timid. He'd seen what happened to Spearman and wasn't about to follow his example. He wouldn't stick his neck out a millimeter, that one."

"So Paul Seligman was the only one?"

"He came the closest, apparently. He spotted the pattern in the source descriptions. But I think I could have handled him. I doubt he'd have been able to figure it all out."

"Do you?" Sullivan queried. "I'm not so sure. I was getting there, after all. Why not Seligman?"

"You had the access," Tyrell said. "He didn't. Besides, you were incredibly lucky. I don't mean to minimize your achievements, of course, but if my masters hadn't lost their heads you wouldn't have even come close."

That was true, Sullivan thought, and rather curious. But for the murder of Seligman there'd have been no inquiry. And but for the raid on Gael's apartment and the subsequent killing of the two burglars, he might have contented himself with scratching the surface. But each time it seemed that the inquiry had lost momentum, something had happened to give it a shove. It could all be explained, perhaps, as a desperate, improvised effort to protect Roy. But Roy hadn't seemed to think he needed protecting, and there'd been something oddly ham-handed about the attempts. Seligman's murder, for example: presumably they had wanted to make it look like suicide, but why the empty cartridge case in the cabin when everything else suggested the shot had been fired on deck? Why the diving belts? Why the silly mystery, deliberately created, about Seligman's identity? It was almost as if the thing had been planned to look, not like a suicide, but like a murder rather transparently disguised. It was almost as if they'd been inviting an inquiry.

"Anything else?" The quiet voice from the darkness cut in on these thoughts. "I'm afraid I've given you the runaround, one way and another. I never planned it that way, and if it makes any difference, I'm sorry. The least I can do now is help you write your report."

"Kind of you." Sullivan leaned a little longer than was necessary on the first word. Roy would be startled and not exactly flattered, he thought, to know that, in this conversation at least, he conformed almost exactly to type. He was in the expansive phase now, having arrived there by the usual route—by way of what-does-it-matter, you-won't-understand, and self-justification. In the expansive phase, generally the final stage of an interrogation or confession, the subject became almost boastfully eager to share the details of his achievement. Sullivan knew he should take advantage of the mood while it lasted, but he wasn't enthusiastic. It was painful to watch Roy getting smaller by the minute.

"Two questions," he said. "First, why did you stick around so long? Why didn't you just clear out around the time Seligman became a menace? You haven't achieved much since then, have you?"

"They wanted me to," Tyrell replied, "but I wouldn't. I thought I could hold out, you see. I believed I could survive the inquiry. I survived Spearman, after all, and in this case . . ."

"In this case"—Sullivan kept his voice perfectly expressionless
—"you counted on our friendship to protect you."

Tyrell said nothing.

"Added to which, perhaps," Sullivan pursued, "was a certain
distaste for living conditions in the Workers' Paradise?"

Still no comment.

"About the K-11." Sullivan changed tack. "The spy-satellite system. Did you succeed in penetrating it?"

Tyrell gave a long, almost theatrical sigh.

"Politicians," he said. "What a passion they have for irrelevance
—the ship is sinking and they worry about the radar . . . The truth
is, it was never a prime target. I'd have gone after it if I could have
without risk. But the real stakes were so much higher.

"We were after the whole thing, don't you see? That was why
I wouldn't let them pull me out. We were going to mine the whole
institution and blow it out of the water. Counterintelligence first—
it was virtually shot when Spearman left anyway—then Plans, then
Eglinton. That would have left Research, a processing plant without input, a bunch of busy little analysts with nothing to analyze
but newspaper cuttings. We were going for broke, don't you see?
The K-11 was just a detail."

And suddenly Sullivan did see. He saw, with a clarity Roy was
too self-absorbed to achieve, the whole elaborate pattern. Every
detail was in place now, the seeming inconsistencies all resolved.
Propaganda. That was their ultimate objective—the devastating
half-truth backed by enough evidence to make it credible. It didn't
matter much that Roy had failed, or fallen short, at least, of total
success. What mattered was that they should be able to *claim* he'd
succeeded. And for that they needed Roy. He saw Roy in Moscow,
in front of the cameras, heard the cool, amused voice explaining,
with facts and dates and names, how the CIA was wormholed from
end to end, how the whole structure was dust and one tap would
collapse it . . . They needed Roy. That was why they'd tried to
pull him out, and why, when he'd refused to leave, they'd tried to
scare him out, deliberately botching their cover-up attempts in
the hope of making his position too uncomfortable. They needed
Roy, so Roy must be stopped. For the effect of what he'd done
would be ten times worse if he got to boast about it in Moscow. In
time—perhaps quite quickly—the Agency might recover from the
practical effects of Roy's treachery; it was the psychological con-

sequences that might kill it. If Roy made his broadcast from
Moscow, the allies would back away—just as they'd backed away
from Britain after Philby; Agency employees would desert by the
thousand; the Senate Committee would go on the rampage, crippling the Agency with restrictions and procedures. And what survived, if anything, would be the empty husk of an organization,
incapable of more than a symbolic existence.

Roy would have to be stopped. Sullivan realized, with a sudden
lurch of dismay, that he couldn't leave it to chance, to the Coast
Guard or the Navy. He couldn't rely on Stonemason's having been
able to block all the exits. He would have to do it himself.

III

There was the path down to the jetty, Sullivan thought: a steep
path, rocky and narrow, crisscrossed with exposed tree roots—not
easy to negotiate in the dark. And there was the dinghy. There
would be awkward moments with the dinghy—getting into it from
the jetty and out of it into the boat. Perhaps he could manage to
capsize it somehow. Or perhaps Roy would forget that there was
a light at the jetty. Or perhaps . . . Somewhere, he thought, somewhere between the cottage and the boat, Roy would get careless
and give him his chance.

Roy, however, showed no sign of getting careless. When they
pulled up outside the cottage he made Sullivan turn off the motor
and hand him back the keys. Then he got out himself and covered
Gael when she followed. Only then did he permit Sullivan to
move.

"We'll need to go inside," Sullivan told him.

"Why?"

"To get the outboard for the dinghy. It's locked up in the cottage . . . Unless, of course, you plan to swim to the boat."

"I'd forgotten." Tyrell nodded. "You're right in any case. We'll
need to go inside—won't we?—to switch on the light for the jetty."

"A flashlight would suit your purposes better," Sullivan suggested. "Less chance of being spotted by the neighbors."

"Very thoughtful." Tyrell's voice was dry. "But I don't anticipate
a problem from that quarter. There are no lights on over there.
I noticed that as we arrived." He paused. "No doubt you did too."

Mistake, Sullivan thought. Now he'll be more on the alert.

"Look, Morgan," Tyrell said. "I dislike issuing threats, but there's something I want to make clear. I don't intend to spend the rest of my life in a federal prison. So if you're planning some last-ditch display of patriotism, forget it. I won't hesitate to shoot. If it comes to the crunch, I'll handle the boat myself."

"Shoot?" Sullivan stared at him. "I'm sure you would. But you won't have to. The thing is, Roy, you're not really worth it. Not worth the risk, I mean. You've done all your damage now, and what happens to you from here on is more or less an irrelevance. I couldn't care less, personally, whether you spend the rest of your life in a federal prison or a one-room apartment in Moscow. I wouldn't risk a sprained ankle on you at this point, much less a bullet in the gut."

"Fine." Tyrell shrugged. "Then let's get the outboard, shall we? The sooner we do it, the sooner you'll be rid of my irrelevant self."

The outboard was in the kitchen. Sullivan kept it there because the previous one, which he'd made the mistake of leaving in the dinghy, had been ripped off. It was a small, one-and-a-half-horse-power contraption, heavy in spite of its size, with a tendency to leak fuel over whoever was carrying it. He felt an odd reluctance to pick it up, to mess up the good suit he was wearing. Strange, he thought, that in the midst of crisis we retain these trivial reflexes . . . But the real cause of his reluctance, he knew, was deeper. He wanted to stall, to put off the confrontation. He was afraid—that was the truth of it—not so much for himself, physically, or for Gael, though those feelings were also present, but for the outcome, for what the confrontation would reveal about Roy and about himself.

"The light," Tyrell prompted.

Sullivan switched on the light to the jetty.

"Good," Tyrell said. "Now, back over there beside Gael."

Sullivan obeyed.

"We'll take the flashlight too. For the path," Tyrell said. "Where is it?"

"In the cupboard to your right. Second shelf, I think."

"Gael." Tyrell moved away from the cupboard. "Fetch the flashlight and bring it over here, please. Then go back and stand beside Morgan."

She did so.

"Fine," Tyrell said. "Now here's how we'll do it. You'll go first,

Morgan, with the outboard. Then Gael. I'll bring up the rear, with the flashlight . . . and the gun."

The gun again, Sullivan thought: funny how he has to keep reminding us about the gun.

"When we get to the jetty," Tyrell continued, "Gael will stay back with me and you'll put the outboard in the dinghy. You can pull the dinghy up to the beach to do that. We'll get into it from the beach, in fact—me first, then Gael, then you. We'll get our feet wet, I'm afraid, but better than than messing around on the jetty. These dinghies are notoriously unstable." He smiled at Sullivan. "I can't afford any accidents."

Got it all figured out, haven't you, Sullivan thought sourly. Not taking any chances . . . It came to him that if he waited for Roy to get careless he might wait forever. Roy was not going to get careless. He would have to make his own chance. Or rather, he would have to put Roy to the test, back his instincts about Roy's willingness to shoot. But he couldn't do that, could he? Because if Gael got hurt—or worse . . . He knew, of course, how Stonemason would make the decision, in the same circumstances. And Everett. And in the simple calculus of public welfare against private interest, he knew how the decision *should* be made. But he doubted he could make it. "Abstractions." He remembered how Gael had accused him the first time they had met. "Those great big, comfortable, justifying abstractions." How much were they worth, really, when you put them on the scale against private loyalties? Ask Roy, he told himself bitterly, it doesn't seem to give *him* any problem.

"Let's get going," Tyrell said.

Sullivan stooped down and picked up the outboard. It weighed about thirty pounds. It crossed his mind that he could maybe throw it at Roy. Tyrell, however, was not going to let him get close enough to throw anything. He backed well away from the doorway to let Sullivan pass.

"Another thing," he said. "I want you two to keep at least five paces apart on the pathway. And take your time over those tree roots, Morgan. I wouldn't want you to risk a sprained ankle."

There was no opportunity on the path. Tyrell kept the flashlight on Gael, so Sullivan had to find his way almost blind, helped only by the distant light from the jetty. He picked his way down carefully, feeling with his feet for loose rocks and tree roots, staggering a little sometimes under the weight of the outboard, listening to Gael's footsteps a few paces behind.

He wondered what was going through her mind. Since her outburst in the car she'd preserved a frozen silence, obeying Tyrell's commands mechanically, but not looking at him or Sullivan. If Tyrell's threats had alarmed her, she didn't show it. Instead she seemed almost indifferent, as if the situation didn't involve her, was just some grubby little contest between the two men, not really worth her attention.

If he could only talk to her, Sullivan thought, convey somehow what the choices were, enlist her help. If he could only be sure that when the moment arrived she would know what to do . . . But there was no way to communicate. She was behind him, and anything he said would only alert Roy. He was isolated; the decision and the action would be his and his only.

But he had no energy, no will. As the moment approached he simply felt lethargic. He wanted to wash his hands of the whole thing, to ferry Roy out to his freighter, wish him bon voyage, and go home and sleep for twenty or thirty years or however long it would take to wipe tonight from his memory.

But he made the effort anyway.

"Look, Roy." He set the outboard down on the edge of the jetty. "This isn't the way to do it. They'll be patrolling the neck of the Bay. They're bound to—it's the obvious thing. We won't get through. All that will happen is somebody will get hurt. And that won't help your cause."

"What will?" Tyrell shrugged. "Are you trying to tell me that when it comes to the trial they'll give me time off because I didn't resist arrest?"

"I don't think there has to be a trial. Not unless you kill someone, that is."

If he could get Roy's attention, he thought, if he could get the gun turned on him instead of Gael, he would take the gamble. He and Gael were about five yards apart; Roy could still watch them both while covering Gael. It would help if he could widen the gap a little. He started up the jetty toward the dinghy.

"Stop!" Tyrell barked.

Sullivan stopped.

"Move up to the right." Tyrell motioned to Gael. "Where I can keep an eye on you both. And stay in the middle of the jetty. Don't get too near to the edge."

Mistake, Sullivan thought; Roy's mistake this time. Because now Gael should be thinking of the water. Two or three paces and she could be in it and more or less safe.

He glanced at her, caught her gaze for a second, then flicked his eyes to the water.

She didn't react, didn't betray by any change in expression that she had understood. She just gazed at him dully, lips slightly parted, her breath coming in short uneven gasps. She doesn't understand, Sullivan thought. The hope that had flared in him briefly guttered and died.

"And how do you figure there won't be a trial?" Tyrell had evidently been pondering the implications of Sullivan's last remark.

"Think about it. A trial means publicity—the Agency's sorry predicament plastered all over the front pages. You think they'll want that?" Sullivan shook his head. "They'll contrive an exchange: you for two or three of their guys in Lubyanka. A few months of negotiations and you'll be home free, without any hassle."

"An exchange?" Tyrell scoffed. "Are you out of your mind? Your own logic rules it out. If they won't put me on trial for fear of the publicity, they'll hardly make a present of me to the Russian propaganda machine. Besides, I doubt that the Agency will get to decide. Thanks to our friend Pollock, the Justice Department is in on the act. By the time Pollock is through, Justice will be screaming for blood. Accessory to kidnapping, accessory to murder— you name it. Pollock will swear to anything to save his own neck."

Sullivan stared at him.

"You don't understand, do you? You really don't understand."

"Understand what?" Tyrell was growing impatient. "Look, let's get on with it, shall we? We're going on your boat, and we're going now. So get the dinghy."

"Pollock's dead." Sullivan didn't move.

"Dead?" Tyrell was suddenly quite still.

"Dead." Sullivan nodded. "He died last night in Emergency. He never regained consciousness . . . There never was a confession," he went on. "Your dash for freedom was a little premature—or it was until you made it."

"But your phone . . ." Tyrell looked blank. "The message from Corporal Brady . . ."

"That was meant for you. We discovered the bug and we turned it against you . . . Disinformation," Sullivan said. "Your own favorite weapon. Ironic, isn't it, that you yourself should fall victim to it?"

For a second there was no response. Then, amazingly, Tyrell smiled. It was a smile of complicity, admiration, perhaps even pleasure. It was as if, for Tyrell at that moment, the situation had ceased to exist and he was back in the old days, sharing a joke with his friend, not at all put out because the joke was on him.

"You bastard." His mouth twitched. "You sly bastard."

His attention was completely on Sullivan.

Now . . . Sullivan launched himself forward.

He was much too slow. As he sprang, Tyrell reacted. The gun came up, and Sullivan found himself staring into it, hurled toward it by his own momentum. He twisted sideways, knowing it was too late, waiting helplessly for the flash and the jolt of the bullet.

They never came. Roy hesitated. And in that instant of indecision Gael's flying kick caught him high in the shoulder and knocked him sideways. Almost at the same moment Sullivan barreled into him, and they went down together.

Of the moments that followed Sullivan retained only two clear impressions—the gun clattering onto the jetty and slithering out of reach across the concrete, and a blow to his groin that left him gasping and retching. After that the situation passed beyond his control.

He remembered, later, seeing Gael on the edge of the jetty. She was using both hands, the left cupped under the right to steady it, and sighting along the barrel to a point in the water where a head had just surfaced, twenty feet out from the jetty but well inside the circle of light. He remembered wanting to call out to stop her. Roy couldn't go anywhere; if he got the boat started he'd be stopped at Annapolis or before he reached the freighter. But he had no breath to shout with, and she wouldn't have listened anyway.

She fired four times: four evenly spaced shots booming out over the stillness of the water. By the third Roy was no longer swimming; he was floundering. Then he was not moving at all.

"Get a blanket."

Gael nodded, but her eyes were uncomprehending. She stood there on the edge of the jetty, anchored to the spot from which she'd fired. She was in shock, Sullivan guessed, her mind no longer in control of her reactions.

"Paul . . ." she whispered.

"Fuck Paul!" Sullivan snarled. "Get a blanket!"

She turned and started to walk slowly up the pathway. She was still holding the gun.

"Hurry!" Sullivan yelled. "Don't walk, goddammit! Run!"

Obediently, she broke into a trot.

He should have told her to call Stonemason, Sullivan thought, and an ambulance. But it wouldn't make any difference. He'd managed to get to Roy before Roy swallowed too much seawater, but two of the shots had hit him, one in the small of the back and the other higher up. Roy's back was broken, probably—he'd lost the use of his legs and all feeling below the waist—and it looked as if the other shot had punctured a lung. He was dying. Long before an ambulance could get there, Sullivan knew, he would drown in his own blood.

"Morgan . . ." The voice was a whisper.

"Don't talk." He said it gently. "There's no need."

And that was true. The anger and bitterness were gone now. All that was left was the sadness. He knelt beside Roy on the wet sand, supporting Roy's head with one arm.

"Don't talk?" A smile flickered briefly across the pallid face. "What else is there?"

Sullivan had no answer.

Presently Tyrell spoke again.

"I'm sorry, Morgan. For everything. It was a waste, wasn't it?"

"I'm sorry too." Sullivan nodded. "You should have fired, Roy. Why didn't you fire?"

The faint smile again, and the suspicion of a shrug. Sullivan, the gesture implied, should know that.

"But it's better," Tyrell whispered. "Better that it should end like this. Me . . . ?" The smile became ironic. "Me . . . in the Workers' Paradise?" The question foundered on its own implausibility.

Nothing more was said for a while. Presently Gael returned with the blanket. Sullivan took it and spread it over Tyrell. He should have put it under him, he knew, but it would have hurt Roy to move him, and the blanket was no more than a gesture anyway. That was all he could do now, make gestures. He wondered if there was ever anything else.

Roy was going now. He was shivering incessantly, his breathing shallow and labored. Occasionally, when the pain took hold of him, he would wince and screw up his eyes.

"It's bad, isn't it?" Sullivan murmured.

Tyrell smiled.

"But remember . . ." His voice was very faint. Sullivan had to lean over him to hear. "Remember the Sullivan-Tyrell revision of Descartes's proof: 'I hurt: therefore I am.' "

"Yes."

He did remember. But Roy hadn't quoted it correctly, and they both knew it. And a few moments later, all through now with proving, Roy Tyrell died.

Later—he wasn't sure how much later—Sullivan carried the body up to the house and called Stonemason. About midnight, Stonemason arrived, bringing with him neither police nor ambulance, but simply a van and two assistants, dressed in overalls, who looked like junior versions of himself. He talked briefly with Sullivan and departed, taking the body with him. There would be no problems, he said; everything would be taken care of. He would be back to them in the morning. In the meantime, he emphasized, they should talk to nobody.

Sullivan was left alone with Gael. Since he'd sent her up to the house for a blanket they hadn't spoken. She'd answered Stonemason's questions indifferently, without looking at Sullivan. Now, with an effort, she turned toward him.

"Morgan." It was a plea.

He went over and put an arm around her. She buried her face in his shoulder.

"I was thinking of Paul . . . He was all I could think of. Paul in that stinking morgue and him in the water, swimming, getting away. And there was the gun . . . And so . . ."

She broke off, her body shaking with sobs.

"I know." He stroked her head. "I understand. It's late now. Let's go home."

EPILOGUE

Stonemason, as he'd promised, arranged everything. It seemed only appropriate, therefore, that he should compose the epitaph. A boating accident was his account: a tragic accident that had deprived the Agency of a loyal and dedicated servant. It was an irony Roy Tyrell would have appreciated.

The details, unless checkable, were left obscure. Sullivan never knew which doctor was prevailed upon to sign the death certificate, or how. But one was found, and he gave the cause of death as drowning. Those who knew otherwise remained silent. Sullivan and Gael, of course, had their own reasons; the others were persuaded, one way or another.

The press, naturally, was somewhat unsatisfied. The deaths of two senior CIA officers, so close together and in such similar circumstances, struck some reporters as suspicious. For a while they poked around. Their reports, inevitably, were largely speculative, and such "facts" as they did get hold of were often wrong. One report, for example, described Roy Tyrell as the Agency's Chief of Counterintelligence. Eventually the public lost interest in the story. It died, as stories will, for lack of facts.

Tyrell's death put an end to Sullivan's part in the inquiry. Before he abandoned it, however, he was able, with Stonemason's help, to clear up the mystery of Stonemason's involvement in the affair. Stonemason, apparently, had been brought in by Spearman when Spearman realized that his own departure was imminent. Thereafter Stonemason had kept an unofficial eye on the Agency, using

Patterson as a source of information. Patterson, who disliked Spearman extremely, was never told of the connection between him and Stonemason. Sullivan was kept in the dark because, as Stonemason explained, with an irony that was probably unconscious, his friendship with Tyrell would otherwise have involved him in a painful conflict of loyalties.

After Sullivan's departure, an inquiry was conducted by Stonemason into the ramifications of Tyrell's treason. Plans, to no one's surprise, was found to be inoperative. Since it had to be assumed that the KGB was familiar with every aspect of the department's activities, any intelligence it succeeded in producing was automatically suspect. The entire department would have to be rebuilt from the ground up. The inquiry found no reason to believe that Tyrell had any accomplices in the Agency, but that, as Stonemason reminded Everett, was considerably less than a guarantee.

The report to the Senate committee came out more than a year after Tyrell's death. It dealt exclusively with Seligman; there was no mention of Tyrell in it. Nevertheless, very little of the report was made public. The parts that were fell some way short of clearing up the mystery. The corpse in the Bay was belatedly identified as Seligman's and he was correctly described as an ex–Deputy Director in the Agency's Office of Strategic Research. It was impossible to determine, the report stated, whether Seligman had been murdered or had died by his own hand. In either case, however, nothing had come to light to suggest that his death was in any way connected with his work at the Agency. Nor had anything been uncovered that would detract from his record of faithful service to his country.

It was not much, as Gael remarked later to Sullivan; but it was better than nothing.